Jess,
Surviving Normal

Jim Billman

Copyright @ 2019 Jim Billman

All rights reserved

This is a work of fiction. Any resemblance to actual persons, living or dead, or to actual events is purely coincidental. The author's website is jimbillmanauthor.com

Jess, Surviving Normal, like my other books is dedicated to my wife, Karen, whose efforts consistently and thoroughly turn my stories into books.

Jess, Surviving Normal

Foreword

My objective in writing *Jess, Surviving Normal* was to create a believable story of youth featuring three and then four outstanding individuals who are smart, wholesome, and have their priorities in order. However, I worried. Was it fantasy to portray four high-achieving teenagers like Jess, Dan-el, Jen, and Ella in today's society? Where's the drugs and alcohol, the rebellious natures, the resentment of establishment, and the acrimony toward adults? With paranormal and extra-normal books atop the best-read lists, who wants to read something about four "normal" kids who earn the successes they have?

So, I asked about the feasibility of my book, and one answer resounded. "Look at me and my high school friends. We were those things. A lot of us were." I ran with that. I think there are some good lessons between the covers of *Jess, Surviving Normal,* life lessons, sports lessons, and moral ones. As a teacher and coach, I can't stay away from getting my opinions and experiences in there; and as an altruistic individual, I express hope for a society of people that can come together for all humankind.

My hope for *Jess, Surviving Normal* is to have it read inter-generationally. There's a lot of sports play-by-play, and a lot of commentary about what helps a young person succeed to go with some pretty factual stuff. And there's a lot of situations that relate to parenting issues—open dialogue, adult leadership, and family environment things, but definitely no "how to do this or that" because there is no perfect way to be a parent. To me, *Jess, Surviving Normal* would be wildly successful whenever a mom or dad would take the book to their son or daughter and say, "I'd like you to read this paragraph, page, or chapter." Or, if a teenager would take the book to their mom or dad and say, "I'd like you to read this…whole book."

Prologue

Pass too low. Picked it up, put it on my hip, juked right, dropped it behind and went left. Got 'im--too slow, on his heels. Soft off the board for score. I put it to the dude but never got in his face.

After scoring, he turned slowly as if to lope downcourt at a leisurely, celebratory pace only to dupe his opponents. As if possessing a prescient sixth sense, he abruptly turned back just in time to intercept a lazy in-bounding bounce-pass. An old basketball move.

Put the rock on the floor once, get my feet under me. A 'Nova head and arm fake and go up for two more. Dude all over me. Love the sound, ball fallin' through the net. Stop, pop, and drop!

Four points in a matter of a few seconds...if the game clock had been running.

A whistle, "Okay, take it in. Showers!"

For Jess Jemison, it felt good to pull the Velcro straps of his Nikes and feel the texture of a basketball after several days with little physical activity. In this new setting, the universality of basketball returned the assuredness he linked with competitive sports.

Big locker room. History next if I can find the room. Gotta hurry. First period wasted getting schedule they shoulda given me when I registered. 2nd P.E. it said. Glad I brought a towel with my stuff. Place smells like pine mixed with piss and shit. Old green lockers with half the doors gone or hangin' from one hinge.

No one had gone out of their way to welcome him. It seemed reasonable to choose the first row of lockers to be near the shower room. He was the only one; everyone else somewhere deeper in the cavernous old behemoth, fucking this or fucking that.

Loser talk.

The teacher's directive to shower fell on idle ears, probably always did.

Shower? Most of them hadn't done anything to work up a sweat. Just sat on the bleachers playin' grab ass. This school's a hole.

A few days ago, when he registered, Jess was told Physical Education class was part of the state-wide mandatory program. Required or not, it was apparently acceptable for this teacher to allow students to sit on the bleachers in clearly defined groups pushing and poking at each other. Jess had been a bit confused by this behavior, but to say something? He didn't know anyone.

To add to Jess's dubious first impressions of Jefferson High, the stench of cigarette smoke wafted throughout the dank air making Jess even more skeptical of his new school. It was already mid-morning and he'd yet to attend a real class.

Not like it was back home.

Half-listening to the din, Jess reflected back to his mother's words when a younger version of himself sat at the dinner table and experimented with some vulgar words he'd brought home. "Common gutter talk by people not in possession of a proper vocabulary. You're bound to hear these words, but you also learn better ways to express yourself. Cussing is risky business." Jess often remembered things Mom told him, even now that he was nearly twice that age.

Gotta talk the talk or you get made fun of. Bullied even.

Habitually, Jess showered after sports practice—everyone did back home. Sweaty and not thinking much about it, he grabbed his towel and headed for the nearby shower room. He found out why when the hot water faucet refused to respond with what it indicated. The next one over offered only a truncated stream at room temperature after thirty seconds or so. With only one overhead bulb working, much of the grime was unseen.

There's no soap.

Actually, there was—in the soap dish attached to the water pipe a sliver floated in a milky pool.

Glancing at a huge water bug crawling from the drain grate, the barely wet Jess decided he'd forego any future attempts at showering.

Enough of this crap! I'm prob'ly dirtier now than before I showered. Hurry.

Jess, Surviving Normal

Returning to his locker, Jess couldn't believe what he saw. He'd neither been issued a padlock nor given a thought to bringing one. Not only were his clothes scattered on the floor, but someone had smeared feces on the bench in front of his locker. Later, Jess would recall that at this point, the entire room had suddenly appeared to have taken on an eerie fringe-shaded yellowish color. All extraneous noise gone, only the ping of a bent blade from an exhaust fan could be heard. Jess was alone; he was naked, wet, shivering, and suddenly, he was scared. A prickly feeling, his thoughts instinctive.

Get dressed—get out of here. Where's everybody?
The gym teacher, where is he?

He picked up his jeans and saw they too, were besmirched.

Wiping at the mess with his towel, he saw his wallet was torn apart and tossed to the back of the open locker likely without the few dollars it held. He didn't see his shoes. His breath now coming in audible gasps; tears blurring his vision. *A shadow. Too fast. An arm around my neck. An odor. A tat. Yanking me back.*

"You pretty stupid, jerk off."

Guy pushing now. Tripping on bench. Shoved, off balance, falling, Locker door.

"Don't never mess..."

Whatever else may have been said was lost as his body was slammed viciously forward, his head striking an edge of the open locker door, and going unregistered was the stick from a blade penetrating two inches into his right kidney.

Crimson...black...nothing.

Chapter 1

The announcement that rocked Jess's world had come six weeks previously and over four hundred miles removed when his father, mother, and younger sister, Julianne were having their evening meal. This was the time the Jemison's shared events of the day; the time Jess endured at the insistence of his mother. Indeed, she had informed him on no few occasions that, "A family should have time together each day."

It wasn't a wish, but an edict. End of discussion.

It'd be nice to just sit and chow down once in a while.

Jess sometimes thought his parents weren't as interested in what he had done as they were in nosing into his personal business. He wasn't naïve. He'd seen the anti-drug messages telling parents to get involved in their children's lives. God, how transparent. The worst was that lady with the whiny voice, "Do you know what your children are looking at?"

Then other times, Jess thought it was kind of nice that his parents were concerned especially when some of his classmates talked about hardly seeing their parents from one day to the next. He knew that his feelings ran hot and cold. His friends never discussed such matters, but Jess thought himself more retrospective than others. He'd often spend time reflecting on past events – about things he'd said or done that may have been done differently, better. Sure, simple things like striking out, making a bad pass in a basketball game, absent-mindedly missing an easy question on a test bothered him. But not as much as comments he unwittingly made at the expense of another, brushing one person off for another, or not bothering to be considerate of kids in his class that weren't very popular. And he knew there were limits. You can only go so far in that department, but don't make the same mistakes over and over.

"Mood changes are stimulated by overactive adolescent hormones and, although difficult, are controllable," a teacher once said as if feelings were something a person could pull out of their pocket or wear like a nametag.

Hello. Today my mood is 'Kiss my butt.' Leave me alone because I don't want to talk about it. Today I'm the color amber, better steer clear if you know what's good for you. Dad said they used to have mood rings, how about mood shirts?

Jess knew he could do better. So much of life was spontaneous, though. And the case in point was his family. Standing by his chair (Yes, they did that!) waiting until everyone was ready to be seated, Jess's mind took inventory.

His dad was Mr. Predictable at the dining room table. Light and friendly, usually playing the role of the master of ceremonies, his stories almost always ended with a little "Mm-mm" giving an unknowing person the impression that he was chuckling at himself.

What was it you put in that pipe you smoked when you were in college, Dad? Oh yeah, you didn't do that kind of stuff in your day.

And no one in their right mind could miss that at the root of each of his father's cheesy little stories there was a moral to be pondered.

Must have majored in Aesop, Pop.

Mom left no stones unturned. She could make an inquisition out of a hiccup. A crusader for truth, beauty, and justice, she was a bulldog for doing the right thing. Yet, regardless of the trauma, she was always there to support and love her family.

Gotta watch what I say 'cause, every word is accountable to the Queen of Innuendo.

All things considered; however, Jess had decided that his parent's attempts to forge a strong family relationship were the lesser of two evils. He was mostly okay with his family. Mom, regardless of the fact that she ruled with an iron fist, didn't embarrass him by trying to dress like she was his classmate. Dad wasn't always hanging out at practices trying to suck up to the coaches like a couple of the other fathers whose egos hung on the success of their sons.

Jess considered Mom and Dad to be typical. Although he did little in the way of being attentive to their problems and concerns, he'd pick up snippets of their conversations in passing, but rarely inserted himself in their topics. Some things, current events and environmental concerns, of course, couldn't be avoided. Dad was quite opinionated and Jess had laughed when his Dad mentioned that he wondered why the circus had closed after so many years. "Americans love the circus; they elected a clown to be ringmaster who surrounded himself with a bunch of monkeys. Actually, a bunch of monkeys is called a congress. Mm-mm."

Jess did love them, but his age-fifteen hormones demanded he could reciprocate only so much.

Mr. and Mrs. Jemison worked for a national window manufacturer and had done so since Dad had finished college. The about-to-be graduate met his wife-to-be at a job fair where Mom was a recruiting representative who spoke to job-seeking seniors about the company. She explained what they were looking for in their new hires, what they could expect in the way of wages and benefits, what training they might go through, and where the plants were located.

Dad, according to Mom, was struck by a thunderbolt and didn't hear a word she was saying as he stared at her like a little puppy. Evidently, he did hear her say something to the effect of, "Would you like to leave your resume?"

The rest was history. Dad had his resume reviewed, was called for an interview, had a second interview, and was offered a position. Fatefully, it was at the same plant where Mom worked. Mom said the company liked the fact that Dad was a veteran and had worked his way through college at numerous jobs to supplement his G. I. Bill.

Dad's version ended the same way; however, there was some discrepancy between their meeting and marrying. Dad claimed that he had remembered the young lady who interviewed him, but had forgotten about her until one day at work when they happened to pass in a hallway. Recalling that they had met previously and seeing that she looked so lonesome, Dad asked her to have dinner with him. Mom had fallen hopelessly in love with him during their first date, thanks to his general wisdom, winsome personality and athletic build. Dad's story got even more suspicious when he explained he got his athletic build by fighting off all the girls at college.

Jess suspected the truth to be somewhere in the middle, but skewed toward his mother's version. He enjoyed his parents' stories about the times before they were married—some funny, and some not so funny. One reason was it took the focus away from him.

Maybe I hear more about their conversations than I think I do.

Despite the depth of the mealtime interrogations and the thinly-veiled psychology, Jess usually left the table with a full belly and a not-too-negative outlook on life. No, his parents weren't ogres. They had rights, too. For example, Jess had heard the old "you're not the center of the universe" speech so many times, that his mom could've saved her breath by giving it a number. "Speech #3, Jess." During those times when he couldn't endure one more "How was school today?" he knew that it would only take once for him to answer with, "I don't know, how do you think it was?"

His sister, Julianne, *WAS* the center of the universe with her entire essence filled with third grade activities and stories. Convinced her knowledge was breakthrough information, she shared it nightly with exuberance. The way she would sometimes get her tales twisted; how one word taken out of context or a misunderstood contraction could totally change her understanding was priceless. Jess not only marveled at her imagination but welcomed the distraction she brought to the table. Annoying as she could be at times, he loved his little sister.

****

On that now-infamous evening there had been something in his mother's voice and manner that tweaked Jess's sense receptors; put him on red alert. A Tuesday, a few weeks after Daylight Savings Time, and Jess was feeling pretty good about things. Although a sophomore, he'd played enough to earn his first varsity letter. Football was steeped in tradition, and the coach had determined that players meet definite criteria to earn their letters. The team had gone 7-2 and made the play-offs where they had won their first game but later lost to the eventual Class AA state champion. Their final 8-3 record showed improvement over the previous year and prospects were excellent for the next year as only seven seniors would be graduating.

Basketball practice had begun with a strong nucleus of returning players. The head coach was also Jess's Biology teacher, a person who brought the same hard-work expectations he demanded in the classroom to basketball. Jess liked that. He also liked his opportunity to battle for the vacated spot on the team at the #2 guard position, a position for which he had practiced through the summer. There was always a pick-up game in progress at the city park, and Jess attended a basketball clinic at a nearby college that improved his defensive skills. The clinic was also memorable because he had his nose broken and reset in a 30-minute span during one of the scrimmages.

Indeed, Jess was feeling good on that fateful evening as he sat down for the "Great Inquisition," his private name for it the time when "Dad grills burgers and then Mom grills me." The meal, stuffed pork chops, mashed potatoes and gravy, peas and Hawaiian rolls held the promise of being a good one, maybe even approaching greatness. Nevertheless, Jess couldn't let go of his nagging premonition that something major was about to come down.

It was Julianne's turn to give the blessing, which she delivered in a little sing-song rhyme she made up.

God is great, God is mighty.
Thank you for our food tonighty.
Bless my Mom and bless my Dad.
Being together makes me glad.
And don't forget my brother Jess
Who I also want you to bless."

Tonighty?

She was truly a neat little girl in Jess's estimation, and even though he was seven years older, she'd rarely embarrassed him in front of his friends. Whereas Jess was a quiet, studious person who preferred working alone, Julianne thrived in social situations. From the time she began talking, she showed an astounding vocabulary gained by mimicking older people. Despite the fact that she didn't understand some of the meanings, few words escaped her memory. When classmates would diss their siblings, Jess usually remained silent.

It was apparent to others, too. Watching his sister, he remembered Aunt Martha saying that Jess was the type of big brother that would "protect" his little sister, especially when she got to the higher grades.

We'll never be in the same school unless I fail half my classes and Julianne is accelerated. She'd be like Mike Thrush, 'the nerd bird turd who's just a bit of a shit.' Also, like 'Bee Stings' Hargrove who doesn't have any boobs and wears a tight sweater."

He snapped out of his reverie when a little chuckle escaped him that passed as an acknowledgement to the quality of the meal Mom was setting on the table.

After the chorused "Amen" to the prayer, Mom added "And may God lead us down the right path during our need for guidance."

God, Mom, that sounds like we're going into battle or something.

Mom had been uncharacteristically quiet that evening and didn't have her usual bevy of questions about school. She'd kept her eyes down except for an occasional glance at her husband which had been a sure tip-off to Jess that something was awry. Nothing at all like the way she usually acted.

Julianne was her chatty self, explaining how some butterflies would fly a thousand miles all the way to Central America so they wouldn't freeze in the winter. She had developed the idea that if her class would catch as many butterflies as they could and then send them to her friend Maria's cousin in "Costa Rita" the butterflies wouldn't have to work so hard. Julianne explained that her class could place the butterflies in jars that had air holes and leaf beds and pack the jars in big boxes.

She asked Dad what butterflies ate and he deflected an answer by wondering what the butterflies might think about going south that way. "Perhaps their trip is part of the life cycle of the butterflies and they might get confused. Maybe they wouldn't be able to pass the correct information to their children like where they were going or when to turn south. Or they might not know which motel wall they were supposed to cling to that night, Mm-mm."

Jess got into the conversation by explaining what Coach Mercer said about human interference and how it often upsets the ecological cycles that are so important in maintaining a balance of nature.

Julianne still thought it would be a good idea for some of the butterflies to take a plane ride to Central America, "Just to see if it would be okay for them to go that way."

It occurred to Jess that her comment actually suggested something scientists might do in their study of the Order Lepidoptera. Research like this might actually be helpful in understanding migratory habits of certain species that has some baffling behaviors.

Right before dessert (Jess had seen some chocolate pudding in the refrigerator), Dad pushed his chair back slightly, cleared his voice, and said something like "I have some news that I want to share." The words made Jess's stomach flip; he'd been right with his premonition; this was not going to be what he wanted to hear.

"First of all, let me share the good news. I've been offered a promotion at work." No mm-mm.

Jess intuitively knew what was to follow.

"However," his dad continued, "the new position is in another town. Well actually, it's in a city that's quite distant from here."

Darkness filled Jess's periphery.

Oh no! Not now!

Time came to a standstill, and brought an expression to Jess's face that not only registered his displeasure, but sent out shock waves.

Why now, just when things were looking good for me. It happens every damn time!

His mood had changed so quickly and so drastically that he almost threw down his fork. Scraping on the floor, Jess pushed his chair back as if to leave the table, but Dad overruled that notion with a stern look void of the usual aplomb.

Nor was there a hint of jocularity in his voice. "Now wait a minute, young man." Dad's tone became the voice of authority and bore listening to as Jess had learned from past situations. "I'm not done talking and your mother and I are not sure this is what we're going to do. All I said was that I had been offered a new position, a promotion at a plant in a different city. I did not say that I had accepted it. And, why would you think that we'd do something like this and not take your feelings into account?"

He followed with the most famous parental cliché of them all, "If you want to be treated as an adult, then act like one." And next, the refrain, "After all, we're a family and everyone has a say concerning what this family does."

Jess was looking straight ahead, repeatedly clenching his jaw stifling any comment—a peculiarity of his when hearing something he didn't like. *You mean we're going to vote? Yeah, the vote will be 3-1 to move because Julianne will do whatever Mom does.*

As if she'd read Jess's mind, Julianne said "We can have a vote."

Julianne began to ask about the school in the new city, but Mr. Jemison raised his eyebrows slightly and gave her "the look" but a softer version of the one Jess received. Julianne immediately recognized it as a signal for silence.

With that done, his tone was less harsh, "Just a minute, Honey. Let me finish and then we can decide what we're going to do. Your mother and I have talked this over in some detail, and we're not convinced that this is what we should do either. A person grows roots in their community and in their organizations. Moving won't be easy; it never is. It'll be hard because this is the only home that you and Jess have ever known. Julianne, you have a lot of friends and we know it will be tough for you to leave them."

Looking at Jess, Dad continued, "Jess, it'll be even more difficult for you because you're older and involved in so many things. It's for these reasons that I've asked the people at the factory to give us, and I do mean 'us' as a family, some time to think this over. And I want you to know too, that the possibility of a new job is not something that your mother and I have known about for a long time. The offer came just recently."

Jess listened but hadn't moved or changed his expression as he continued to imagine his destroyed life. Julianne was quietly looking down at the table, and took advantage of Dad's pause. "What about Mee-maw? What will she do if we move? Where will I go every day after school? Where are the roots we grew?"

"We plan to involve her in our decision. She's a part of the family and she will have a say in the decision," Mom said.

Grandma Wilkerson, or Mee-maw as she was called ever since Jess babbled them, was Mom's mother. And like Mom, she had lived in the same place most of her life. The window factory was the town's major employer and Grandfather Wilkerson had worked there, being one of the plant's original employees. He died three years ago from a massive heart attack while working in his shop. His unexpected death was devastating to the family, particularly to Mee-maw, who suddenly found herself without her partner and proclaimed soul mate after 47 years. Jess was likewise affected and, for the first time in his life, experienced a period of extreme sadness with the unfairness of the entire situation. Going through a time of depression, his grades suffered, and he got into fist fights with several of his friends for no good reason. He behaved like a total jerk until Mee-maw coaxed him back to reality. She had been the one most affected by Granddad's death, but she had also been the one who showed the most resolve in making the adjustment without him.

Jess felt that Mee-maw would not look very favorably on their moving away so he may have an ally. Maybe things could continue the way they were. But on the other hand, she'd often mentioned that she didn't "want to interfere in young folk's lives."

Mom had risen from her chair with the pretense of being busy.

Is that a tear I see?

Dad continued, "Your mother and I feel that it would be the fairest to everyone if we didn't talk about this anymore until the end of the week. Then, on Saturday after lunch we'll each come back with our questions, discuss the matter thoroughly, and vote. Hopefully, your grandmother will be here, too. How about Saturday, each of us will get to explain how we feel and no one will interrupt or argue over what's said? After that, we'll cast our final ballots. If the vote isn't unanimous to move to the new city, we will not move. Does that seem fair enough?"

Mom's name was Rebecca. "Becky?"

"Fair enough."

Jess almost laughed when he heard his dad. There was no way he'd vote to move.

"Jess?"

"You bet!"

Julianne?

"That's fair, Daddy. I can't wait!"

"Okay. It's settled then. Mom and I won't tell you very much about the new city or my new job offer until then. And, of course, we don't know anything about the schools except that if we do vote to move, we will always try to do the best we can for both of you. Now let's dig into that chocolate pudding."

To Jess, the pudding was tasteless.

****

Supper lasted longer than usual, but without diminishing Mom's declared 'Official Study Hour' on school nights. No television, no phones, and no exceptions unless it was an occasion of great importance. School activities or 'educational' television could pre-empt this time, but otherwise Mom remained steadfast. "It's easy to break a good habit and hard to break a bad habit."

Almost ritualistic, each member helped in their own way to clear the table, stock the dishwasher, and whatever needed to be done. Once finished and weather permitting, Mom and Dad would go for a walk consisting of a lap around their neighborhood waving at passing cars and greeting acquaintances doing the same while Jess and lately, because she was 'older,' Julianne would go to their rooms to study. Actually, what he studied was arbitrary and was a time when Jess was left alone. He liked that.

Adolescence brought and continued bringing changes both physically and mentally in his attitudes and perspective, but it also provided a measure of freedom. Mom wasn't as protective as she was when Jess was younger. Dad, maybe too late, had talked to him about the "birds and the bees" to their mutual embarrassment, particularly the part about nocturnal emissions and bodily changes. That aside, Dad's primary message was for Jess to respect others, especially those of the opposite sex.

Why would I ever be disrespectful? Jeez.

There were other sources of information, too. Staid, WASP-ish schools as Jess's had sponsored programs on the subject that most adolescents laughed at, that some parents objected to before they were shelved. But not soon enough. In seventh grade Jess had watched an obviously far outdated film in a gender-segregated class and snickered 'knowingly' with his pals. However, as it forever has been, the real pipeline of sexual information for young people came from their cronies who were supposedly more knowledgeable about the ways of the world. Information that left kids like Jess confused and feeling ignorant.

But there was an even more insidious source that everyone knew of—the internet. Copping the attitude that if it was there, it was okay to look at it, Jess had seen some graphic examples that left him shocked and consciously appalled. His inaugural excursion into the world of graphic sexual exploitation happened after school with a group of cohorts who egged him into one of those double-edged sword situations. Ridiculed if he didn't look and individually ashamed after he did.

These people weren't like Mom, Julianne, Mee-maw.

Temptation was everywhere: lingering, disruptive, and chaotic in the dynamic life of teens who outwardly claim that nothing ever happens.

An idle mind...

Residents of a small city or a large town depending on how one looked at it, much of what happens revolves around school activities. Theirs was a closely-knit community steeped in the Midwestern ideal valuing family, church and work. With slightly over twelve thousand residents, New Holland grew by another thousand or so when the small college was in session. The Jemison's were part of a community low on crime and high on trust.

With only one public high school, Jess was one of its "rising" athletes enjoying a relative position of esteem. Athletes were often reminded of a responsibility to uphold the reputation of the school and community. The importance in displaying a positive attitude, as hokey as it may have seemed in some other places, was an important part of every extracurricular school program. In several ways the quaintness and ethnicity of the town was a throwback to years past; a quality that was openly held to ridicule by some of the other, "more progressive" nearby towns.

The high school that Jess attended had approximately 400 students and included grades nine through twelve. Like the town, it was not a large school and shared the number of school-aged students with a smaller K-12 Christian school. Activity-wise, the state divided the schools into four classes based on the average daily attendance and NHS was a little larger than the average. The fact that four schools could claim state championships in each school sport and activity brought more opportunity for success at both the individual and team levels.

On this particular evening, Jess found it far too difficult to concentrate and sat at his desk pondering what might be his future. Glancing at his English text, he was reminded of the time the guidance counselor had visited his English class. Mr. G, as he was known to students and faculty alike, talked about an analogy in which a funnel represented opportunity. Mr. G had asked each of them to imagine having to pass through the funnel to adulthood, but with a choice about which way they would do it. Entering the small end and coming out of the large end represented having a lot of options; whereas, coming out of the small end offered only a few possibilities. Thinking back to that time, it occurred to Jess that maybe the funnel analogy was appropriate to the possible move.

Could moving actually be an opportunity in disguise?

Jess's mind raced as the cell diagram in his biology book blurred.

What would it be like to go to a large school where you wouldn't know all the members of your class?

Images of his present classes and classmates floated past in his mind.

I know the name of everyone in my classes.

Additionally, he knew the name of every teacher in the school; they were present in so many things that comprised his life as a student. Like the principal said during orientation earlier in the year, "We're a community because we have come together for a specific purpose. Our purpose is education and all the things related to education."

Jess's mind also flashed back to some of the things in his life that he wished he would have done differently. He wished he would have asked his classmate, Courtney, to the Homecoming Dance. He stewed for three weeks only to find out via the pipeline that she wanted Jess to ask her. Then three days before the dance, she agreed to go with a senior boy that Jess didn't particularly care for. The guy was also on the football team, and once during a pile-up during a scrimmage at practice, for no particular reason other than that was the way he was, he punched Jess right in the testicles. Further, that guy's locker room references to girls were consistently vulgar. Jess stayed away from him, knowing of his bullying mannerisms that, despite the school's efforts to the contrary, still existed. Then, only two days before the dance, Courtney and the senior goon were an "item' in the hallways.

It almost sickened me to think of her with him.

Also, Jess would have liked to be more outgoing and not so "narrow" as his biology lab partner had intimated. "You're always so serious, Jemison," she'd said. "You seem as if you're some kind of robot. Are you programmed?"

Musing these issues, Jess considered that maybe a change would give him a chance for a new start. There were always things in sports, too. Bigger than striking out or dropping a pass he should have caught. Certain teammates seemed to be inventive in the things they could do and the ideas they had. Jess thought he just didn't have the imagination some of the other athletes did and envisioned himself having little flair for innovation. Not that that was all bad, but he sometimes thought he made work out of games that were supposed to be fun. The notion grew when he felt that he didn't play up to his personal expectations in a game.

Granddad said I made too big of a deal out of everything. I should relax. Trust myself.

Maybe his biology lab partner was wrong in her assessment because she wasn't exactly Miss Popularity. Always a flip side, and even though he didn't see himself as being innovative, he did get as much playing time as the more imaginative athletes on his teams.

I'm only a sophomore. Maybe when I'm a junior I'll be more relaxed.

As he shifted his thoughts back and forth, the specter of the unknown daunted him.

In a school like mine, I can play three sports and make the team in each one of them.

The larger schools in places like Des Moines and Cedar Rapids cut their teams and merely going out for the sport did not mean that a person would even get to practice with the team.

In his mind, Jess pictured an imposing, drab concrete school building that loomed Gothic-like in semi-dark setting on top of a hill. He imagined himself standing in the center of a hallway with students rushing by him in total disregard as they moved like automatons to unknown destinations. The scene was intimidating as he visualized himself entering a new classroom

Jim Billman

with forty sets of eyes following him as he trekked across the room reporting to a teacher whose face displayed scorn.

What to do? He closed his Bio book and looked around his room; the pictures of family and of his favorite professional players; the memorabilia he had collected on his dresser; his baseball glove placed just right in an empty space in his bookcase; his bed and the poster-adorned doorway to his closet. This was his domain. This was what he knew; it was his life.

How can I ever give it up?

Grandad had an answer. "You take it with you."

****

Morning brought the usual family scene to the Jemison household. Dad was of the opinion that in order to have the day start correctly, a person must get up a full two hours before the time they planned to leave the house.

What a strange man.

By following this routine, Mr. Jemison believed that everyone would have time to enjoy a leisurely breakfast and get their thoughts organized. Although Dad denied it, he was obsessive about being on time and would rather miss something altogether than be one minute late. Jess didn't openly admit it, but in this case, the seed hadn't fallen far from the tree. Mrs. Jemison adhered to the notion, but she didn't stress over it.

Mom likes the old proverbs like the early bird getting the worm. She didn't like it when I told her it's the second mouse who gets the cheese from the trap. She calls them "Yeah buts."

Unheard of in most places today and testimony to the New Holland lifestyle, Jess had a paper route from sixth grade through most of junior high school. Required to have his papers delivered by 7:00AM, he had to be up and out of the house no later than 5:30. A rush, Jess would leave home for the paper drop within fifteen minutes of getting out of bed and nearly three years of morning papers had wired his biological clock for early mornings. More times than Jess cared to count, he heard adults tell him of the character-building results from carrying a paper. He dropped his paper route thinking sports and the classes would be more intense and require more of his time. Now, still on "paper route" time he could exercise, read, or just take his time doing whatever.

Julianne, the baby of the family, enjoyed having her mother come into her room to wake her. Sometimes, she'd stay in bed waiting for Mom, which had become their little routine. This particular morning was no different and nothing was said about the possible move.

Concerning school work, Jess was surprised to find very little difference in the degree of difficulty between junior high and high school. The big change was in the expectations the coaches placed on their student-athletes.

Jess was an inch taller than he was as a freshman and nearly as tall as his father at 6' 1" and his long arms and legs made him appear to be thinner and weaker than he actually was. Broad-shouldered, his body hinted at a capability to carry more bulk. With only a few zits, his creamed coffee skin, large eyes and tightly curled dark hair blended together nicely. His thin nose sporting a little bump near its bridge from having been broken hadn't done much to hurt his looks. Happy to have his cumbersome braces replaced with a single wire, he welcomed the opportunity to breathe with his mouth closed. Mom had often tweaked his ego by telling him that he was very handsome when he was smiling, and kind of good-looking when he wasn't. Which, for the last twelve hours, wasn't very often. Jess was very conscious of the braces and disliked being teased about his dimples.

Dimples are a genetic defect.

The Jemison house was a little less than a mile from the high school, the two being in opposite parts of town. As badly as Jess had petitioned for a school permit that would allow him to drive to and from school, he had failed to convince his parents that it was a win-win situation for everyone. The "Yeah, but all the other kids..." argument didn't work very well on his father, either. Dad took him to school and after practices, Jess could usually find a ride home if he wanted, but actually enjoyed the reflective time walking gave him.

Mom had the uncanny ability to tell when something was not going his way, often saying "Things will be better in the morning," or the variation, "It'll look differently to you in the morning." Last year as a freshman, taller than most of his classmates but thin and gangly at hardly 140 pounds, Jess had been the target of a group of seniors' deriding remarks regarding his color. Mom's advice had proven valuable in bringing the harassment to an end. "Look them right in the eye and smile your best smile when you have to pass near them, but don't incite them. You don't have to say anything back to them. Just go about your business." To his relief, that wasn't a problem this year.

Today, Jess had awakened with the same opinion he formed at the supper table; no move, no way.

My mantra: Look out for myself, no one else will.

Throughout his morning ritual, Jess mulled the wisdom of Dad's approach to family voting.

Why even go through with this vote thing because surely Mom and Dad can see that I am happy right here, where we are? Well, reasonably happy anyway. They know how important sports are in my life. Maybe I should have been more vocal and outgoing in talking about school and playing up all the good things.

Jess also wondered about Mom who was pretty quiet through the conversation last night.

She works in Personnel. What would happen to her job if we move? Dad's new position can't be that great, especially if he was willing to gamble on one dissenting family vote. Maybe Dad really doesn't want to move and is looking for an excuse to say no to his bosses at the company.

True to what he thought last evening about Julianne voting like Mom, there was a possibility that no one would vote for the move.

Maybe Mom and Dad want to put the blame on me—make me the scapegoat.

None of his thoughts made a lot of sense. Yet, they kept coming.

Maybe only Dad will move and he wants me to go with him. Maybe Mom and Dad are getting a divorce. A lot of the kids I know have parents that are divorced. Maybe I could stay with Mee-maw and the rest of them move. What exactly is the job Dad's been offered? Where is this city? Dad said it was a city far from here. Maybe I can find all the plant locations on the internet and figure out where. What will happen when my friends find out we might move—Julianne will probably tell everyone she knows first thing. How cheesy is a family meeting? A vote? Worse yet, what will Coach Mercer do when he finds out?

The wheels were churning in his mind but they weren't cranking out answers.

****

Jess moved through the remainder of the week in a veritable trance. Twice he was called on in class to participate and had been embarrassed when he had to ask the teacher to repeat the question. During a practice stint with the supposed other members of the starting line-up in basketball, he had wandered around as if he were lost. Coach Mercer even asked him if he was feeling okay. "Jess, you're supposed to set a screen for the high post and then roll weak-side to the basket for a pass from the corner. C'mon man, let's get it right."

Another time, Jess was ten feet past Courtney before he became aware that she'd spoken to him in the hallway. Oh, Hey, uh," he turned and fumble-mouthed to the back of her head. The week seemed to drag and it was a restless sleep Friday.

Were the truth known, the rest of the family hadn't fared much better. Mom and Dad had tried to maintain a pretense of normalcy, but mealtime conversations were disjointed and general. How was your day? Fine. What did you do in biology? Learned about classification. How was basketball practice? 'K. It was all trite. Julianne's chatter incessant as usual, but she too, was talking just for the sake of talking.

Nothing new there.

No colossal world event kept Saturday from arriving and the meeting began on schedule, Dad would have it no other way. Grandma Wilkerson came over for lunch, Jess had a morning practice that he sleep-walked through, and clanked a couple of threes during the scrimmage. The last to join the others, the family assembled themselves around the dining room table in anticipation. Mom made sandwiches earlier and served them with some chips. Contrary to standard procedure, sodas were available for Jess and Julianne.

A real occasion.

While they were eating, Mr. Jemison explained where the new job was; in a large city named Trentsville over four hundred miles southeast.

I was right! There's a million people there. The Battle of Trentsville in the Civil War. My first guess.

Dad's new job offered him the opportunity to move from a supervisor's position to one of manager, and pending his decision, he would be in charge of the Production Department. To complement the offer, Mom could make a lateral move within the company with no loss in pay or tenure but would have to wait for an opening in Personnel. One was anticipated next June. If the Jemison's chose to move, this would allow Mom time to get the household matters settled in their new surroundings. In discussing what he called the "details," Dad related that he and Mom had agreed that both Jess and Julianne should stay with their grandmother until the end of the semester. By then everything in the new city should be taken care of. They'd have a place to live, their possessions moved, and time to get Jess and Julianne enrolled in their new schools over Christmas vacation.

Still, Jess felt as if he had been railroaded; that the decision had already been made despite what Dad had said last Tuesday.

All this planning probably convinced Mee-maw to vote yes. I don't believe this is really happening. What a snow job! This sucks big time. They think I'll vote yes?

Next, Mr. Jemison explained the "rules." Each person would be given a chance to speak their mind about moving before they voted. Julianne passed around the ballots that she had made so the voting would be "private and no one would know how anyone else voted" to which Jess skeptically replied, "Yeah, right. Like no one can figure it out. Why not give each of us a different colored crayon to vote with."

Mom's recrimination to his comment was acerbic, particularly for her. "Jess, you have been nothing but negative about this entire thing, you've skulked around the house and barked at your sister all week. Yet you have the power with your vote to lay it all to rest. We're trying to be democratic by involving you and Julianne; and for that matter, your father is doing the same thing by sharing this decision. Actually, it could have been entirely his so I think it time that you reached up, young man, and took that chip off your shoulder." Whether or not the democratic process remained or not, Mom had pulled her rank on Jess.

Julianne put in her opinion. "That's right Jess. Why don't you just vote right now and the meeting will be over?"

Dad was patient, his voice calming. "Julianne, Jess knows what his options are."

That the cloud wouldn't hang over the table, Mr. Jemison said he'd take the lead to get the ball rolling. "As you know, I am the one responsible for all of this, and I want to offer my apologies for the turmoil. The one thing I think important to say is that I did not seek this position, but it was offered to me from corporate headquarters. I like to think that it was a result of my hard work and dedication to my employer over the years. Jess, you and Julianne may not understand quite how a larger company operates, and they're not all the same. Where your mother and I work, as people retire or go elsewhere, their vacant positions are often filled by giving the qualified employees an opportunity to move up in the company. Then, people in charge of hiring, your mother being one of them, look at the people who are already employed and make suggestions to the bosses. Without going into it more deeply, there are both good and bad features related to this method, but it's the one we use. And incidentally, your mother had nothing to do with my offer; it came from the main office."

He continued, "I have been honored to have been the choice for this new position, and was told that no one else was considered nor would anyone else be considered unless I declined the offer. I was tremendously pleased to say the least. Another thing that you two probably don't quite understand is that in companies like ours a person is given a choice like mine only once. Yes, they make a person feel like there would be no hard feelings if I would say 'no,' but they would likely not offer me a promotion ever again. I don't know that for sure, of course, but it's one of the games big companies play.

"Another thing is this: a person goes to work to give their employer a 'day's work for a day's pay.' If that person does their job well, the boss notices it and that employee becomes more valuable to the company and is given opportunities to advance. Many workers want to move up the ladder and have more responsibilities as well as the higher wages that go with the responsibilities. I was hired more than seventeen years ago as a line inspector, progressed to supervisor, went to quality control and then to my present position. I did this by applying for, interviewing and when offered, accepting each promotion as it came along. So, you can see why I'm flattered to be offered this position.

"There's more to it than just that; the human aspect. There is an inner drive within each of us that goes into making us who and what we are. When I took business and psychology courses in college, the professors told the class about self-actualization. In other words, we were told that a worker not only wants a position worthy of his ability, a pay check capable of supporting his family, but he also wants to feel appreciated. Jess, you'll learn more about these things before you leave high school, but it's a lot like sports. It's not enough for most athletes to simply make the team so they can sit on the bench, but they also want to get involved and play the game. And after a while, the players like to know that they are appreciated for their contribution to the team's success. Call it whatever you'd like, but a person wants the respect of others at any age.

"You see, I have been given this opportunity but it certainly comes with strings attached to it. For you Julianne, it means that my choice is not an easy one because there are other things that I must think of. Important things like you, Jess, your mother and grandmother, not to mention my friends and the community where we live. The biggest 'string' is for you not to see me as being selfish if I cast my vote in favor of moving. No, I have not decided how to vote. I want to wait to hear what each of you has to say."

Dad ended his speech visibly affected, pushed his glasses higher and put his hand on his brow. Reaching over to Mom, he grasped her hand and gave it a little affectionate squeeze before sitting.

Mrs. Jemison scooted her chair back so she could cross her legs and promptly said, "I'll go next if no one objects." She remained seated as she spoke. "Dad and I feel the same way, so I want to start by saying what I know he was unable to say. Family comes before work, and before personal accomplishment in our eyes, and it is much more important. I know that we're told at church to put God first, and I suppose we do, but in a different way. Our family and the love we share is God's gift to us. I know it sounds corny, but our jobs and the work we do are tied in with what love is, all balled together. I feel that we put God first by respecting and loving the gifts He has given us. That's part of our faith as we understand it. Your father and I put family first because our family is God's greatest gift to us."

Pausing for a moment, Mrs. Jemison looked at Mee-maw. "Mom, I don't mean to exclude you. I'm sure you understand that you are as much a part of this family as anyone. My dad too, from his spot in heaven will no doubt influence what each of us decides today.

"I feel a queasiness in my stomach just thinking about giving up all that is here in order to move to a place where I know very little. It's scary for me, too. Change is scary to most people because we get comfortable in our lifestyle. In thinking about it, and, believe me, I've been thinking about it, the feeling I have is also one of adventure. We don't know what lies ahead of us no matter what we decide to do today. Life is full of surprises and they come without guarantees. I think that a little spirit of adventure lies in each of us, and that most of us like to explore new things. So, like your father, I'm still without a decision because I'm torn between the life we have and all the good things, familiar things that are here. Yet the adventure in building new relationships in a new place is not so much a chance to start over as it's a chance to spread out and see more; to experience more. It's a chance to live life more fully, if that makes any sense.

"Except for the times when you kids were born when I took time off for each of you, I've gone to work at the same job for nearly twenty years. I've been promoted, too, and share the same feelings as your father about the company. I've met hundreds of people both coming and going through the years and sometimes I'm embarrassed when a person sees me someplace and tells me that they remember talking to me or working at the plant, and I don't remember them. Sometimes, I think I'm ready for a change, but then that feeling of not knowing, of being scared, comes back. And too, I get bored with the same old job, same old plant day after day. Most of the time, though, I love it right here and I am completely satisfied to be where we are.

"I guess what I'm saying is that I will support whatever is decided today. At this point, I want to hear what each of us has to say first. For every positive I think of a negative; for every negative, I think of a positive. I do know this: We have each been blessed by what we have been given and as long as we're together in spirit, everything will be fine."

Jess, listening intently, had constantly been revising his speech as he heard his parent's voice their concerns.

Are they being clever or really honest in what they said?

Neither of them seemed to have given a persuasive speech as much as they were just expressing their feelings. Jess had expected long formal speeches. Dad had almost come to tears and Mom had spoken about some pretty heavy stuff.

"My turn," expressed the always exuberant Julianne. "You know, I'm not as young as you might think. I understand what you said, Dad. And Mom, you said what I thought you would say. I think Dad has a great job waiting for him and Mom will be there for all of us no matter what. Just like always. Anyway, Marcia's mom and dad just got a divorce and now she has to spend part of her time with her mom and part of her time with her dad, and she is NOT happy. She wasn't happy when they told her they were getting divorced, but no one listened to her. She told me that she didn't count for anything in their lives and hated her mom and dad for what they did to her. She wishes that she could come live with us.

"Friends mean a lot, but family means more because one day a person at school is my friend and the next day, they are with someone else giving me hateful looks. I try to be nice to everybody; well, except for the boys I don't like.

"I think it would be brave of us if we move. Like Mom said, we'd make new friends and see new places. When we come back to visit, we'd have so much to tell other people. And I see all these places on television and we study about all the places in the world. They would be fun to see in real life.

"I thought about a new room where I could choose my colors and maybe get some new furniture, too. I think it would be exciting to do all these things.

"But I don't want you to know how I will vote; I might vote no."

Julianne talked so fast that she hardly left space between her words, or "came up for a breath" as Mee-maw often said. The discussion was not taking very much time at all. After this, Dad said there would be a question-and-answer period.

"Mom, why don't you go next?" Mrs. Jemison said.

"Okay." She fidgeted a little and reached out to nervously rearrange the place mat in front of her. "Well, this old town is my home and has been ever since I got married. And I really, really appreciate the offer to move with the rest of you, if and when. I've thought about moving from my home ever since Granddad died. But for me, that would be running away from reality. I can't vote for or against your move and I thank you for making such pretty ballots, Julianne. I will keep mine in one of my scrapbooks to remind me of all the good things that are being said here today and how you have come together to make this decision.

"Rebecca, you and Craig will understand this more than the children, but the one thing no parent ever wants to be is a burden on their children. I will get older and feebler with time; and although I can fend for myself today, it won't always be that way. I don't want to become your responsibility. The time will certainly come when I will need more help, but until then…oh, it's just something old people worry about.

"Another thing is that parents never want is to stand in the way of their children. So please don't complicate it any more than it already is by letting me influence how you will vote this afternoon. Anyway, you will always need a place to stay when you come back to visit; and I know you will want to do that a lot. And too, if you do move, I will have a new place to visit.

"So that settles that; don't consider me. You're all young and the talk of new adventures, building new memories, and making new friends excites me for you. But I've done all that. My enjoyment comes in living each day at a time, sharing time with my friends, and as the Bible says, knowing that I have 'fought the good fight and run the good race.' And there's so much of Granddad that is still here I can't leave behind.

"I say that whatever you do, I support your decision and wish you well. I am so proud of each of you and even more proud of you as a family."

Julianne and Mom were crying; Dad and Jess somber. Grandma Wilkerson had touched their hearts. After a minute or so of quiet, came the inevitable. "Well son, that leaves you," Dad said.

Whatever Jess had planned now escaped him. "Yeah, it's my turn. Hey, I don't know what to say 'cause of what everybody else said. None of you, well maybe Julianne did, really come out and said that you wanted to move or tried to argue why we should go. I was all prepared to argue the other way, but now I see that what I was going to say was only from the way I saw it.

"Dad, I read a book not too long ago about how this baseball player had all the talent in the world, but couldn't go play baseball and leave his wife and children. He just walked away from ever playing again even though the local people made him a legend by telling stories about how good he was. It made me think that you have the chance to go play in the major leagues and my vote could keep you in the minors forever.

"If we don't go, we will always wonder what it would have been like. If we do go, we'll know. I listened to Julianne and thought that she was showing more courage by saying what she said than I would have shown by arguing the other way. Mee-maw, you were right, too. I will want to come back and see the town and my old friends as well as stay with you just like I used to do when I was Julianne's age. Then too, I might come back here and go to college in a few years; who knows? Mom, you made me decide that I was being selfish and that I was acting like a baby. What you said was exactly the way I really felt deep down. I don't want to be the 'chicken' of the family and say we can't move so I'm going to mark my ballot right now and not wait for any question-and-answer period. I'm going to vote 'yes' and never look back."

What have I just done?

Everyone had spoken their mind. No one spoke from a scripted speech. There were no questions from anyone toward anyone else. Mr. Jemison asked if they should take some time alone and come back in a while to vote. After a chorus of negatives, Dad asked for the ballots to be given to Mrs. Wilkerson. She would look at them and announce the outcome. It took no more than fifteen seconds for everyone to mark their ballots and pass them to Mee-maw. Even Jess, who had spoken aloud how he would vote, was eager for the outcome.

Mrs. Wilkerson announced that the results were 3 – 0 in favor of making the move with one more abstention—Mr. Jemison. No one made an effort to move away from the table. Finally, Mr. Jemison said in a quiet voice full of emotion, "I will announce my acceptance at work on Monday. We all have a lot to do in the days to come."

Jess, Surviving Normal

I guess that's what family means. Dad puts us ahead of his advancement, and we think so much of Dad that we support him. Mm-mm.

****

The differences in Julianne and Jess were quite apparent. Despite Jess's prediction, Julianne hadn't said anything to her friends and now couldn't wait to let everyone know. Jess was quite reluctant to mention it, even to his closest friends. In thinking about basketball, maybe his departure wouldn't be a great loss. He hadn't won a starting position or even a key spot off the bench. Basketball season lasted well into February and hopefully into March if the team kept winning. By the end of the first semester, they would have played less than ten games. He dreaded having to talk to Coach Mercer. Hopefully everyone would understand.

I can't think the team will be much worse.

Thoughts raced—yin and yang. Jess was world-class at over-analyzing.

Should the team not do so well, I will be missed. If the team is good, they will have forgotten that I was a part of it.

Jess didn't like to think about himself before the rest of the team. Moral upbringing, coaches' influence - whatever.

But that's the way I am.

Word did travel quickly. By third period Biology on Monday, Jess's lab partner and candid critic said she heard he was leaving at the end of the semester. "I suppose this means that I won't have anyone just sitting and watching me do all the lab work." She'd said it with a smile and tone that meant the opposite.

Who'd thought it, but I'll even miss Stephanie and her criticism. I wonder if she would have gone to Homecoming with me?

At the end of class, Coach Mercer asked Jess to stay for a minute and they walked down the hallway toward Jess's locker. Coach said that moving could be an opportunity, but what he made of it depended on him. Coach hoped Jess would continue to participate in sports, and said any coach would like to have a player of Jess's caliber and integrity on their team. Jess couldn't hold back the tears that streamed down his face as Coach put his hand on Jess's shoulder and told him that they would talk later. "I will be glad to write a letter of commendation to your new school if you'd like."

Tardy, Coach Mercer wrote a note so Jess wouldn't get a detention.

Good thing it was a four-minute passing time and everyone didn't see me bawling.

The hubbub over Jess's leaving continued. Where he was moving, would he be leaving or staying with his grandmother and what did he think about it? Some said they would miss him; some mentioned the sports teams suffering; one friend summed it up with, "Man, you got hosed."

Yeah, you don't know the half of it. I hosed myself. Fell on my sword.

Not used to the attention, he was glad when the school day was over and time for basketball practice. With two weeks before the first game, the atmosphere in the locker room was mixed with anticipation, anxiousness, and now, a little wonderment. The leaders of the team, the apparent starters, knew that Jess's absence could affect the season. And true to Jess's prediction, the rest of the players knew they now moved up one notch on the supposedly non-existent "depth-chart." Sports were prime examples of the pecking order.

"Hey Jesse James, I hear you're going pro at the end of the semester. Who drafted you, the Celtics?" one of the starting forwards said over the usual din of the locker room.

"Naw, it was some girls' team in Mississippi," said another player, trying to show a southern drawl.

"We'll miss having a girl in the shower, though," came another comment amid laughter.

It's nice to be among friends.

After the shootaround, Coach called them to center court and made the formal announcement. He told Jess that he was sure that everyone on the team wished him well and his contribution to the team would certainly be missed. With several good buddies surrounding him, the sentiments made it a little less emotional and easier for Jess than it had been that morning in the hallway.

Coach continued, "Guys, we obviously have some options but the only one that makes sense is to proceed as we are and make the most of Jess and his talents until then. We'll play together with what we have available. Jess will be with us until the Christmas break and that should motivate all of us to step up our game. Jess will have something to be proud of as well as knowing what he has been a part of. Put yourselves in Jess's position and ask what you would like to happen. Sound fair enough?"

There were mumbles of consent. "Okay. Jess plays and enjoys his status as a member of this team until he moves."

The chorus of "yeahs" and the friendly little thumps and shoves were gratifying.

The way I played last week, I'm lucky to even be on the team.

****

Mr. and Mrs. Jemison were given from the second week in December to the new year to make the overwhelming transition from New Holland to Trentsville. They realized that taking their time was the wiser choice, but the immediacy of keeping the family as a unit and 'getting it done' took precedence. In an executive position. Mr. Jemison enjoyed certain benefits such as having the window company manage the selling of their New Holland House, a moving stipend, and paid leave. The task, however much assistance was offered, remained fraught with details.

Jess and Julianne were in turmoil, too. They had to decide what were the necessary items to take to Mee-maw's and what would go with the movers when that time came. Items overlooked made for some schooldays frustration and scurrying from one house to the other. "Where's my notebook? My permission slip for the field trip? I need my snow boots. I left my game day shirt in my closet at home." Routine matters became big deals from misplacing things to being late that led to frazzled tempers. Bottom line was that Mee-maw had times when she changed her opinion on how wonderful her grandchildren were.

Another benefit for was the window company's preferred realty group that helped families like the Jemison's find a place to live. There was an initial meeting to determine parameters and from that the realtor would make a list for Mom and Dad to start looking. They looked at some new houses in new subdivisions, two newer houses in suburbs, and one older home in a stately neighborhood.

Mom liked the wide streets and was looking for a house with 'character,' and the neighborhood of the older home

Jim Billman

reminded Dad of the area in Chicago where he grew up. They both eschewed lot-sized production homes with a single tree in the front yard and were enamored to an older home, a block away from the one the realtor picked that was also for sale. "No problem, I can show you that house, too," the realtor said.

They liked the interior, too. Dad knew enough about houses to notice the way it was built, the dry basement, and the excitement his wife was exhibiting. He also knew enough about marital relationships not to mention some other things he saw thinking that they were minor and could be fixed in time. The house was barely in their price range, but the fact that the house had been on the market for over sixty days suggested they make an offer substantially below the asking price.

"We have to check out other things," Dad mentioned.

"Like, accessibility and most importantly, schools," Mom answered.

Discovering the main branch of the city library was three blocks away, that four denominational churches were within a mile, and shopping center not far away sweetened the deal. The realtor had information on the schools as well as the demographics for the state and city at her disposal. "I'll be happy to take you to the Central Office where you can talk to a representative."

The next day, Mom and Dad sat listening to a school official glossing over some numbers she claimed to be 'somewhat misleading in the big picture.' "Statistics are dated by the time they're published. We're on the rise both in the state and here, thanks to getting a higher school tax bill two years ago and new appropriations from the capital." She further explained that a person's address put them into a particular district, but each district's boundary was 'gray' depending on numbers. "You know, population densities shift, so you never know. "However, if you decide to send your children out of district there will be tuition."

As the realtor predicted, the seller countered with a price in the middle of the original asking price and the Jemison's offer. Relieved to have found a home they both loved albeit] Mom a bit more than Dad they related the news to Jess and Julianne. Jess was told of how the school districts worked and they discussed the possibility of a private school. Told of Jefferson's winning basketball and baseball programs was just fine for Jess.

Chapter 2

Jess awoke to find himself in a hospital bed. Adjusting to the brightness, he moved his arm and felt an annoying little sting from the IV attached to the top of his right hand. Next, he saw Dad leaning forward in a nearby chair, his hair tousled and an anxious expression on his face. Beyond realizing where he was, not very much was coherent for Jess.

Dad stood, broke the silence, "You've had quite an ordeal, son."

Mom was in a waiting room with Julianne. Hearing the news that Jess was awake, a nurse's aide was summoned to stay with Julianne so Mrs. Jemison could visit her son. Sobbing and emotional, Mom expressed her sorrow as Jess tried to make sense of how all this happened. He recalled the locker room but had no knowledge of going to the hospital. Half-hearing and staring at his parents, Jess felt restrained, overcome with an urge to sit up. The nurse who brought Mom to the room put a compassionate hand on his shoulder and told him to stay where he was for a while longer.

I was shoved into the locker. My head.

With the fuzziness clearing, Jess was told how a student from the next class had discovered him unconscious and half-crumpled between the bench and his locker. Nothing was said about the other circumstances.

I was naked.

He started to sob. Attacked and left helpless in a locker room, He'd been humiliated, his pride compromised, more than abused—violated. Jess's sporadic breathing created a pain in his side.

Why? I know why…but?

He reached up with his left hand and felt his head. More pain. Stitches.

Some of my hair's shaved.

Far greater was his emotional pain, his soul laid bare for the world to gaze at him—an unclothed spectacle on a granite bier.

He could imagine others standing around him, looking at him with their admonishing comments.

Ain't seen him before. Who's he think he is coming here? You see the way he was dressed? Them shoes he wore? Punk-ass preppie, you ask me.

Mom laid an assuring hand on his shoulder giving Jess his moment, her anguish boundless and mixed with self-incrimination. Dad turned to the window, equal in remorse for what he brought on. Perhaps he, better than his wife, could relate to the internal torment that young men experience in times like this; total desperation with no place to turn. Dad knew; Jess felt that he lost face.

Later, after gaining his composure, Jess was informed of his ulcerated kidney. Mom explained that was the reason for him being in the hospital, then too upset to continue, Dad described the scene as it was explained to them: two pools of blood laying below him, one larger than the other. "Head wounds bleed a lot."

Jess was told how the reddish-blue slit from the knife on his backside had alerted an incoming student to immediately search for the teacher.

The next class? No one from my class said anything?

As it was related to Dad, another student had pushed the button on the intercom speaker only to have it fall from its bracket and dangle uselessly from a single wire. Others with the consideration to cover him with his damp towel were fearful of trying to move him. All these things done to help, yet each attempt prolonged the time for medical assistance to arrive. Anyone witnessing the grisly situation could see a deliberate act of violence.

Dad, struggling to retain his own self-control, was doing his best to placate Jess. This could very well have become a homicide if a renal artery were pierced. His son didn't need to know how close a call it was just yet; he'd figure it out on his own later. "Another act of needless violence on undeserving victims. It happens all over the world every single day."

Mom, with a tissue just in case, continued the story. Help had been summoned and the First Responders, two of whom were former medics having served in the Middle East, arrived in short order. It wasn't the first time this Emergency Medical Team had been called to the school. Jess was rushed to the nearest trauma center, checked for vital signs, cleaned, and received six stitches just above his hairline for that wound. Again, Jess reached up with his free arm and felt his head, wincing at finding the tender spot. His fingers then searching to determine how much hair they'd shaved off.

Mom said the knife wound was a stab from a small knife. "A stiletto or whatever. It was serious because of concerns about infection. From the environment, too."

Jess recalled the repugnantly dirty locker room and the feces.

I was probably laying in it.

"All this added to the urgency to clean and treat your damaged kidney, Honey. After they did that, you were taken from the Emergency Room to this room. And here you are, convalescing." An expression of compassion on her face.

Mom explained that the IV was necessary to maintain necessary liquids and nutrients his body needed. She didn't mention a massive dose of antibiotics to combat the possibility of infection. The nurse could explain the morphine pump.

As Jess became more lucid, he saw that his parents looked haggard, wracked with guilt and blaming themselves for what had happened.

They probably suffered more than I have.

But now, awake, he realized he would carry the consequences.

There may have been more said that Jess missed as he closed his eyes and fell to sleep.

Later, he learned the rest of the story. Being a crime scene, the locker room was closed. His clothes and personal effects were gathered and the Resource Officer had taken pictures, for this was definitely a felonious act.

Jesus! Pictures of me? Naked? I'll be a joke. I wish I'd never seen this place!

Police investigators scoured the area and each member of the class was questioned. No one knew anything.

Hell no. They knew everything. Took pictures on their way out. Shitshitshit!

The attack made the local evening news, and a school spokesperson assured everyone 'that measures would be taken to bring charges against the perpetrator.' The 'Eye on the News' reporter ended her report by mentioning the malfunctioning intercom and having the camera pan the locker room to emphasize the obvious condition of the facility.

"Oh, look at that freak without any clothes. Let's see if we can get a close-up. maybe get a shot of his sacred member to show everybody."

Jess's physician explained that a punctured kidney was very serious and that he would spend a couple days in the hospital under close supervision. Again, there was concern that no toxins from the perforation would enter the body and infect anything else.

My brain's been infected. My reputation shattered. Even back home.

The wound was opened in the operating room and a clotting tissue had been inserted to combat this, and now, every possible precaution needed to be taken to give his kidney a chance to heal. "We want it to become as functional as can be expected, considering the damage incurred," the doctor said.

Sepsis was a word the doctor used. If all went well, Jess would go home and rest for a week or so before returning to school. Any blood in his urine should diminish as the kidney healed. "Until you leave the hospital though, you should use a pan."

I expect I'll have to talk to the police.

His thoughts shifted.

I see Mom and Dad's devastation. They blame themselves—the move to Trentsville and going to Jefferson High. This would never have happened back home. But like Dad says, you can't take back the past and you have to live with your mistakes. Anyway, it wasn't a mistake; we did what we did. Duh! Mom and Dad should move on. For me, I'll remember. You bet I will.

The anger roiling within him was an emotion different than any he'd experienced. Festering and raw, Jess would make a conscious effort to keep it within, from being noticed. There would be a time when he would look back at the road traveled and try to distinguish the one most defining event, the proverbial fork in the road from which all other decisions hinged, either in part or whole. At fifteen, though, this was far too abstract.

****

Jess, Surviving Normal

Two weeks into the new semester, Jess and his parents sat in Jefferson's Conference Room accompanied by a lawyer. Driven by the knowledge of the deep pockets common to a school's insurance carrier, legal representatives specializing in injury litigation had figuratively come out of the woodwork offering their self-serving notions disguised in words of righteousness and concern. However, the Jemison's, believing it would make a spectacle of Jess, weren't interested in suing the school or in the notoriety a lawsuit of this nature would bring. What they wanted was for Jess's case to be properly resolved and to have the assurance that stricter measures would be employed against this sort of thing happening again. Their decision to hire a lawyer was for "legal padding," as Mr. Jemison put it, and he retained a lawyer with the firm that sometimes represented the window company.

Wondering if anyone was coming, the side door finally opened and Principal Lewis, walked briskly into the room with her cheeks and hair bouncing rhythmically. She was followed by two other people whom she introduced as one of the school's attorneys and an assistant principal. Known throughout faculty circles for her hands-off approach to crisis, the diminutive principal promptly excused herself. "I have a preemptory matter that calls for my immediate attention. I'm sorry." She expressed her hope that Jess was well onto the path to a full recovery. "We're glad to have you back, Jess," she said over her shoulder on the way out of the room.

And I'm so happy to be back.

The staging was obvious, she was five months away from retirement and to be complicit in something like this could prove disastrous. The farther away from the entire ordeal she could get, the better the chances for her to not be found culpable.

The meeting was left for the assistant principal, Mr. Martin, to chair. A nice-looking man in a sports jacket with a short haircut and chiseled facial features.

Mike Trout. He's her hired goon.

As the person in charge, Mr. Martin appeared relaxed and capable. He acknowledged everyone and cordially repeated their names in an attempt to defuse any coolness the presence the two lawyers may have brought to the room. Rather than standing at the podium as Principal Lewis briefly did, Mr. Martin sat at the conference table opposite Ms. Walls, the school's lawyer.

At least we can see him.

He spoke without notes, his tone suggesting that he didn't concur with what he was supposed to do. "Mr. and Mrs. Jemison, Mrs. Lewis asked me to take a minute to tell you a little about the Trentsville Metropolitan School District." Evidently feeling a need for clarification, he asked, "So you understand our system. Is that okay?"

Receiving a silent assent, he began. "A few years ago, our district, consisting of twenty-six high schools, showed a disparity in student achievement scores. When the results went public, this differential caused a not unexpected backlash from the parents of students in the schools not scoring as highly as those from other schools. Reduced to a common denominator, the district's outlying schools had higher achievement scores than the five more centralized ones. As is often the case, interested people cited causes rooted in the demographics of the city. Foremost in this outcry was the notion the school district was failing to focus on our central-city youth. And to make the charge even more apparent, we at Thomas Jefferson High School were in the lower grouping. Compositely, we fell two percentile points below the next higher school. That's a big disparity in edu-speak."

Then close it. That's a no-brainer.

As if he read Jess's mind, "Don't get what I'm saying wrong, Jefferson is not on the country's list of lowest one thousand schools and will not be closed." Mr. Martin, his hands folded together and resting on the table, paused for effect as Mr. and Mrs. Jemison exchanged glances before continuing.

Guy looks like he could kick some butt.

"And so, the school board and administrators, rightfully concerned, first tried to reassign some of the so-called stronger teachers to the inner schools as a means to address the situation, but to no apparent avail. Those reassigned teachers protested through their union and some threatened to resign. That plan was scrapped before it started.

"Plain and simple, Trentsville had a socioeconomic problem like many other older, inner-city schools, and no matter how the situation was explained by the educational experts, where people live often says a lot about the school they attend. I'm sure you follow what I'm saying. We've all heard about issues often associated with Affirmative Action movements as they apply to schools and their product--children. Among other things, No *Child Left Behind* was a national effort to this end."

Yada, yada, yada.

"The next alternative for our schools was to look at open enrollment. This allows secondary students with parental endorsement who do not live within the boundaries of a particular school to petition the school they would like to attend. By this, the intention was to remove gerrymandered district lines and form "magnet" schools throughout the district that featured certain academic assets such as strong science or language departments. Serving as an incentive for students to pick and choose accordingly, this seemed quite reasonable on paper, but impractical for a city our size. You can imagine the chaos this would create, over fifty thousand students with the option of twenty-eight high schools further complicated by the annual transience of personnel all schools experience."

The assistant principal, glancing at those in attendance and acknowledging a subtle prompt from the lawyer across the table, said, "At this point, I will defer to Counselor Walls who is a member of the district's legal team and can certainly explain the details better than I. Ms. Walls..."

"Thank you, Vice Principal...uh... Martin," as the attractive attorney looked over her half-moon glasses at his name plate as she stood. "Our district has designated its secondary schools to be centers for open enrollment under the provisions of our state's Public Education Code, Chapter Nineteen, Section Fifteen, Amendment Two, Entitled, *'Designated Public Schools and Open Enrollment Act.'* We have chosen to be a participant subject to the provisions of the Code and participate fully in offering a choice to our students concerning where they prefer to go to school. To clarify what Mr. Martin said, our city's public schools do make school assignments from a clearly delineated specific area of the city, but we also allow certain numbers of students to petition and consequently attend schools out of their home area within our guidelines. We do this for accommodation, but we also must balance enrollment numbers. We can't involuntarily move one student to oblige another, and that's why we require open enrollment applicants to justify their reasons for open enrolling. We do all of this to better serve our diverse student population."

'Diversity is good--for others' my History teacher joked last semester.

The Jemison's lawyer spoke, "Hasn't this decision been publicly scrutinized due to general ineffectiveness? If I understand correctly, it seems that some parents voiced their concern over Amendment Two making it too difficult, to demanding to open enroll?"

Ms. Walls spoke imperiously. "As I implied, we are concerned for the greater good of all students not the few. The form is rather exacting to restrict students from merely jumping from school to school, yes. But I'm not aware of being exclusionary.

Mr. and Mrs. Jemison again exchanged querulous looks with each other. "So where are we going with this?" Mr. Jemison whispered to his wife, wishing that no one noticed him having just glanced at his watch.

It didn't take long to answer that question as the Jemison' lawyer asked, "Did Jess Jemison and his parents get apprised of the open enrollment possibility?

Ms. Walls: "I don't know. Shouldn't he have?"

Momentary silence. Ms. Walls sat down.

Lawyer: "Amendment Two clearly states that students may not open enroll at the semester. I think there's a technicality that Jess Jemison and his parents could pursue as a new student. Further, there is no mention of open enrollment in the student handbook or in any literature the family was given. Mr. Martin, could you explain the everyday situation at your school?"

Assistant Principal Martin spoke. "For the record, only three of our students have open-enrolled elsewhere. The reasons for this are speculative, but clearly open enrollment brought little or nothing in the way of change to Thomas Jefferson. Young people are intensely proud individuals, especially when they come from lower-income families. In a way, I applaud their attitude, but this pride also leads many of them to develop an indignancy that make good choices more difficult. In short, I feel that our students have a perception of being embarrassed in front of the rich, white and Asian kids were one of them to be thrust in among another

Jess, Surviving Normal

school in an outlying area. Assistant Principal Martin knew that Ms. Walls held him accountable for where the meeting had gone.

Lawyer: Does Jefferson have a youth gang presence in your estimation?

Martin: Trentsville has gangs. I would suppose if not a gang presence, there is a gang influence in spite of our efforts otherwise. We also have a high rate of faculty turnover, a lot of transient students, and many issues that can't help but affect a kid's performance at school."

You got that right, Mike Trout.

Assistant Principal Martin hadn't known how else to explain the situation other than to say what he did. He'd been at the school for over three years and was directly involved in the educational quality of his school. But it hadn't taken him long to feel trapped in the middle. Making suggestions in the operational management of the school meant putting his own position in jeopardy. The Trentsville School Board overseeing the Central Administration under the direction of the Superintendent of Schools made the rules and the individual school administrators were hired to uphold these rules, not to question them. It was not a good idea to "buck" the system or to give any indication that a person was anything but a team player; first, last and always.

Nevertheless, believing that a person must live their personal convictions, Assistant Principal Martin had had enough of the shenanigans; job or no job. He had struggled for some time trying to find a way to address a discipline problem that severely undermined the intent and purpose of education. Further, he'd thought long and hard about what happened to Jess Jemison and decided this incident was the one in which he was going to speak out; to possibly risk his career.

Rebecca Jemison asked the inevitable question, "And when are we going to stop school violence? Was what happened to my son because of a gang presence that picks on students at random?"

Ms. Walls had recognized an edge in Mr. Martin's voice as he spoke. In her mind, he had no business saying the "G" word that seemed to put the school in an unfavorable light. "Perhaps we're getting ahead of ourselves here," she inserted. "How a group of students chooses to dress and identify themselves should not in any way implicate them as hardcore gang members in the manner that an uninformed public might perceive them. We can't assume that your son was a victim of a gang, or of any orchestrated group of boys. It's a giant leap between admitting to gangs as they have been referred to, and placing guilt on a member of this group. I think what Mr. Martin means is that when young people are put in close proximity for periods of time, some of them see cause to act out against others; and sometimes, this is contrary to the rules. A very small percentage of students are this way, but this happens at any and all levels of society. Until we know exactly who is responsible, everything is hearsay. I'm sure you will respect the school's stance on this, but we know that strong words provided to the wrong news person can bring wholesale confusion and contentiousness to a situation."

Jess was getting a full dose of how adults talk in circles to the points of confusion and parried back and forth.

This is getting pretty good. They're going at it. Donner und Blitzen (German for thunder and lightning)

Lawyer: "All said, Jess Jemison was assigned to Jefferson because of where he would live and that is the way it's done." He folded his hands ad steepled his index fingers under his chin in lawyerly fashion.

Ms. Walls: "There was the private school option."

Another momentary pause.

If I have this right, Mom and Dad could raise a big stink about my attack.

Reaching for his folder, Assistant Principal Martin took a paper from it. Preparing to write, he looked at the Jemison's and said, "We need to move on. Jess, do you feel that you provoked anything that may have caused what happened to you in the locker room?"

Jess was startled that he was suddenly asked to speak. Swallowing and almost choking, he replied, his voice raspy. "No sir, we were playing basketball like the teacher told us."

"Could you be overlooking something? Anything in your demeanor? What you might have said or done?"

"I just played basketball. That was all I did."

That didn't sound very smart. Why do they think the guy playing ball has anything to do with this? I haven't said anything.

"You didn't say anything or get in anyone's face about it? You did nothing to intimidate another player; nothing to flaunt the fact that you were more athletic with your play?"

A disapproving 'Har-umph' from the lawyer intending to let Mr. Martin know he was still there.

"No sir."

"Were the baskets that you made against the same opponent?"

"I made several other baskets during the time I was playing, but I made two at the very end of the period against the same guy. Another player stayed back to help bring the ball up court for their team."

"Would you recognize either of these people if you saw them again?"

"Probably. I think I would if I saw them in PE class. In the halls, I don't think I would." Jess felt himself sweating, glad to have worn a t-shirt under his button-down.

"Jess, would you say that this person might have been upset over your "showing him up' on the basketball court?"

"I didn't see anything because the teacher told us to go to the lockers right after my last basket. I didn't know anybody else."

"Do you think that this person, the one you scored the last baskets against was the one who attacked you? What's your gut feeling?"

The lawyer for the Jemison's interrupted. "Jess, you may not want to answer that question. Mr. Martin, wouldn't it be obvious this young man would *think* there would be a connection?"

Mr. Martin: "Yes, sorry about that. What I was coming to was whether or not Jess may have heard the perpetrator say something or there may have been an emotional or angry exchange of words. The fact that Jess had his money and his shoes stolen could suggest that the attack was otherwise motivated."

Jess remained silent but he could feel his face redden as his thought returned to the moment before the attack. Shifting in his chair in expectation, he was relieved when Mr. Martin didn't ask him the question again. In looking across the table, Jess saw Mr. Martin clench his jaw and purse his lips as if sending a signal saying that he did not have to ask the question. He knew the answer.

I like this man and I like the way he takes charge. He doesn't want to embarrass me in front of these other people. I suppose I shouldn't trust him, but he seems okay.

To Jess, much of what was said in the meeting seemed to have no relevance to his going back to class; not that he was anxious to return, particularly at this school. As the meeting ground on, as the adults jockeyed back and forth, Jess was certain that the assistant principal's hands were slapped.

Gotta watch what I say in front of lawyers. If you do speak, say it so you could make it mean several things at the same time.

His dad had often reminded him to be sure to "engage your brain before your mouth" and this meeting had been a prime lesson of Dad's advice. Jess had read a few books and seen movies involving lawyers where words in court cases led to extenuating circumstances. "Without provocation" was a phrase that came to his mind.

I wasn't attacked without provocation; I know who the scum bag is, but I'm not going to tell them that.

Mrs. Jemison, ever practical, got to the crux of the meeting in asking a simple, "Now what happens?"

Assistant Principal Martin answered with aplomb, "Jess was assigned to Thomas Jefferson because our enrollment is down and he was an entering student living near our assigned boundaries, to which I previously misspoke."

Wink, wink.

"I can't comment on the process that placed him here over the neighboring school that corresponds to his home address other than they were overcrowded. I do know, that in looking over his transcript, I was pleased to see his academic accomplishments from his former school. One of his teachers has even written a letter of recommendation on Jess's behalf. Selfishly I suppose, I didn't question why Jess was assigned here or what he knew of open enrollment; we need students with his credentials and were pleased to have him. What happened to him was too unfortunate; too unfortunate to happen to any student, anywhere."

Right on. A hell of a welcome!

Pushing his chair back, Mr. Martin addressed the Jemison's, "The decision is yours, and correct me if I'm wrong, Ms. Walls, Jess can seek open enrollment."

She was in thought, her brow furrowed, and she smelled a possible lawsuit. "I will make sure that Jess can to any public high school in Trentsville, tuition free."

Dad, in turn, asked Jess what he would like to do. As all eyes fell on Jess, he spoke barely above a whisper, "I started here and I guess I'll stay." Jess had surprised himself with that reply, but he had been impressed with Mr. Martin's professionalism. He didn't want to go through the enrollment process again and lose more time. Jess would eventually learn that prior to becoming an educator, Mr. Martin was an Army Ranger, and played a year of minor league baseball.

Mr. Martin wanted to reiterate the dress code for the benefit of the Jemison's. It also came out in the discussion that dress codes had been established in the district placing restrictions on certain styles and manners of dress, and certain messages and innuendos regarding alcohol, tobacco or drug use were forbidden. Likewise, students could not wear clothing that identified with non-school organizations, specifically certain monikers or colors relating to gangs. This, as it was written, inadvertently extended to church groups and pro sports teams. For a goodly number of the students, the new rules put a crimp in their wardrobe. As is often the case, rules become double-edged swords; instituted with good intentions were often capable of being twisted around to be more beneficial to negative factions than to positive ones.

As the meeting wound down, the Jemison's were reassured that the search would continue for the person or persons responsible for Jess's attack. So far, no one had discovered anything or been given anything pertinent for the police to work with. They had suspicions and they'd questioned suspects, but not enough to hold anyone. "So, they're 99% sure and the guilty person is still out there walking around," Mom said getting no response. Her concern was for another attack on Jess, but like her husband, she deferred to Jess's wishes. It was his wish—the Jemison way.

As if to again assert her importance, Ms. Walls had another bomb to drop. Being that Jess was involved in altercations leading to physical contact mandated a three-day suspension from both school and school-related activities. Explaining that, she ended with, "Technically, you've served your suspension and can start as soon as possible."

Jess's mother virtually come out of her seat in protest when she heard this, "You're saying that my son was responsible for this vicious attack? I can't believe that you might think Jess provoked this. This will go on his record?"

Mr. Martin quickly intervened by telling Mrs. Jemison that there was no way Jess's record would reflect a suspension regardless of what the rules might say. "Not on my watch. This is an extenuating circumstance."

Whenever Jess glanced at Ms. Walls while Mr. Martin spoke, his suspicions were confirmed about the little war they waged. She sat with her lips tightly closed and with a look of disdain in the principal's direction whenever he spoke. Jess sensed an ally in Mr. Martin.

On a final note, Jess was told that he could have his schedule rearranged to place him in another PE class, and he could start all over at Jefferson High School. Of course, changing his schedule would be no guarantee that he wouldn't encounter the party or parties responsible for his injury. "Until we can identify them and bring criminal charges against them," Martin said.

Upon hearing this, something made Jess object to it. Maybe it was the comment about being brave that Julianne had made all those weeks ago, or a value instilled in him: I'll make it work. Then too, Jess did foster a measure of revenge; he had been attacked from behind without a chance to defend himself. Absolutely, he wanted a chance to square that account. "No," Jess heard himself saying, "I'd like to keep the schedule I have. I'm already two weeks behind. I don't want to run away from those who have seen me."

Seen me? Like in the locker room? I should a got out of here and gone to Tenmileaway High School. Such a martyr.

Jess would keep his present schedule. Again, his call. While the group was leaving the room, Assistant Principal Martin sidled next to Jess and quietly said, "I do not want to hear of any reprisals on your part, Jess."

"Yes, sir."

I hope you don't hear about one either, but there'll be one.

Looking at Mr. Martin he realized the assistant principal knew he hadn't been totally truthful when asked whether he would recognize the guy he played basketball against.

I'd recognize that piece of crap in a dark movie theater.

Chapter 3

First Period Homeroom/Activities: Jess didn't play an instrument other than the air guitar and didn't sing when anyone could hear him, and hadn't signed up for any of the clubs so his was a study hall. Second Period P.E./Study: P.E. met on alternate days and Study meant go to the commons, to the library's quiet rooms or go outside to the area called the Patio away from the academic area. Third Period English: A substitute teacher called the roll sans Jess's name, gave a reading assignment and stood by the door. So far Jess found where he was assigned. Fourth period Geometry: The instructor, accepting a good portion of the class's diffidence, focused his attention on the few students that were attentive. 'Do not disrupt' the one rule. Lunch was an open time where students could go outside, again use the Patio area or even leave the school grounds.

They could rob a bank and be back in time for fifth period.

Jess had a peanut butter and cheese sandwich or three in his backpack and found a lunch table in the Commons that looked harmless enough. Glad that he'd decided to bring a lunch rather than stumble through the cafeteria line, the group already at his table paid him no heed.

World History followed and he reported to the teacher as directed—this time a few minutes late having difficulty finding the room Jess was the point of interest standing in the front of the room. Pointing to a desk in the front row, the walrus-mustached teacher asked Jess how it felt to be Jesse James' son loud enough for the class to hear.

Jess had heard that at least a hundred times in his life. His face flushing by being singled out, "It's Jemison with the 'e' sound, not an 'a.'" With the class hushed, Jess's reply was also heard.

Trying to be funny at my expense.

Jess was correct.

"Whoa! you hear that Mama Cassie? This dude's a 'e' and not a 'a,' a student sitting close by chirped to a girl three rows of desks away, distinguished by her flowery muumuu and huge hoop earrings, apparently not distracting enough to violate the dress code standard.

"Whatever," came back from the girl amid a few chuckles.

Now disinterested, the teacher finished his exaggerated bookkeeping chores as the class bantered back and forth about anything and everything except history. Jess sat seething, thinking how much he disliked this school and this balding clown of a teacher.

Jess had a quality of altruism; he trusted people. Trouble was, he expected it from others and was easily hurt. He knew he could have laughed along with the teacher who probably wasn't trying to be hurtful as much as merely funny, maybe even friendly. Additionally, Jess's analytic nature made him appear gullible, 'slow on the uptake' when he accepted what he was told at face value. Things that many other teens would question.

"Collegiate skepticism" his mother called it. "Be grateful that you don't question everything, that you don't ridicule, or make fun of other people's speech and appearance. It's a special person who doesn't look for flaws and try to show everyone how clever you are because most of the time, it's done to defray their own shortcomings."

As he cooled down, thinking that all eyes behind him were watching, something his Dad said came to mind, too. "You'll find many people who believe they've seen the worst of human nature and they use that as an excuse to doubt, to be unaccepting." One of Jess's birthday gifts when he was thirteen was *The Seven Habits of Highly Effective Teens* by Steven Covey.

The glass half full or half empty, stuff. Sure, question things because it's healthy, but seek understanding."

Once finished, the teacher began a canned lecture that increased the cacophony and droned on for the remainder of the class time. Jess noticed that as the class continued, the buzz from the students lessened as several fell asleep or languished at their too-small desks. Jess had taken out his notebook and started to take some notes until he noticed a couple of students looking at him as if he were a peculiarity.

That's me.

Jess, Surviving Normal

Next, Sixth and Seventh Period were a combined block to facilitate those courses that had laboratory sessions; for Jess, it was General Biology.

I've gone this far into the day without saying one word to another student.

Making it before the bell, he recognized a few faces from Geometry class. With only minutes gone in the period, an announcement came over the room's intercom (this one worked) requesting Jess Jemison to report to Assistant Principal Martin's Office. "If it is all right with you, Mr. Hoffman." Amid the typical chorus of ooh's and ah's accompanying him as he left, Jess was once again embarrassed as he gathered his belongings and left the room. Fortunately, he knew where the office was.

Now what?

Mom was there. "Come in, Jess, and close the door, I want to talk with you and your mother," Mr. Martin said, ushering him into a tiny office.

Mr. Martin held a paper as if he were going to read from it. "Jess, I mentioned before that we received a letter from your former biology teacher and basketball coach that says you're a pretty good kid. In fact, I've had it for a while and had every intention of talking to you before now, but circumstances kind of got in the way."

Ha-ha.

"In addition to being an excellent student, you're quite an athlete, particularly in the sport he coached you in. Not many students transfer in here with letters of commendation."

Coach Mercer. He said he'd do it.

"Thank you, sir."

Mr. Martin continued, "I had to bite my tongue this morning when I was quizzing you about what might have led to your being attacked. I knew very well that you put a move on someone who was humiliated because you took them 'downtown.' But enough of that. I want you and your parents to understand that my main concern at this school is for the success of the students. From success in school to success in life."

Mr. G's funnel.

"After reading Mr. Mercer's letter and what I saw in you earlier today showed me that you are a focused young man who tries to succeed within the system. Already, you may have noticed that a large number of our students merely tolerate the rules. They put in their time and play the game. Do you follow what I'm saying?"

Jess was caught a little off-guard. He'd never considered himself one thing or another. "Uh, I guess so. I saw the lady giving you some looks."

"Yeah, me too," Martin chuckled. "And it didn't make me feel very comfortable. But I made up my mind that I was done kowtowing to the status quo at the expense of good students and their futures. I am also aware of the concerns of parents, and I can't sit quietly drawing a paycheck and let this plague of apathy go on."

Nodding to Mrs. Jemison. "There've been too many students cheated out of an education at Jefferson because of other students, lackadaisical teachers, poor parenting, and rules that get manipulated. For example, high schools are measured in large part by two sets of numbers that pretty well echo each other: One, the percentage of student drop-outs that should be low, and two, the percentage of students graduating that should be high. There are other numbers, but none quite so defining as these. Sure, we're concerned about homelessness, fighting, sports championships, merit scholars that are too few and too far apart, and daily attendance numbers; but those first two, drop outs and graduations are the big items."

His small corner office on the second floor was crowded with only Jess and his mom facing Mr. Martin. A few official-looking certificates adorned the wall, a picture of a lady and a young child on his desk, and a stuffed bookcase with sagging shelves made the room emit "principal." Placed behind an adjoining cubbyhole where his secretary had a desk and a few chairs along the wall, the two rooms were side-by-side closets years ago. With no windows and the closeness, it was no wonder that Mr. Martin was often outside, prowling the hallways.

His jacket removed and tie loosened, he continued. "Mrs. Jemison, you and your husband have every right to be disappointed in this school and in me as an administrator, and I want to make every effort I can to change that opinion."

Mom said, "We knew there would be a big upheaval in our lives and we understood that there'd be obstacles. Our biggest concern in moving was for our children. Our former home offered a good school in a somewhat insulated community away from much that is going on in the world today. When Craig was offered his new position, he and I saw, along with everything else, that a change like this would offer our children an opportunity to see the world more the way it is, rather than through the rose-colored glasses our former residence offered. That's not to say we didn't encounter problems back home, though."

Mom looked at Jess to see if her comment had caused a reaction. A stoic Jess stared at the wall.

She returned to Mr. Martin, "Yes, we were very disappointed when Jess was attacked and learned that he could have died in an unsupervised locker room with a broken surveillance camera. In fact, it went beyond disappointment, Mr. Martin, way beyond. This was *our* son; one half of the two most precious possessions in our lives. How could we justify our good intentions with our son unconscious and unattended with a knife stuck in him?"

Rebecca Jemison had tears streaming down her face. Mr. Martin offered a box of tissues, and Jess fidgeted, not knowing if he was embarrassed for his mom or appreciative of the way she expressed her feelings.

"My husband and I want this to work for our children. And yes, we know that something else just as serious could've happened if we hadn't moved. He could have been in a car accident or been run over crossing a street. There are bullies in every school and there were incidents at our school before, but the fact is it happened here. And we feel Jess's attack could have been prevented."

With defiance in her voice, "Craig and I also wondered why the 'unofficial rules' weren't explained to Jess or to us when we came in earlier to register him for school. The main office downstairs gave us a school handbook, yes, but it didn't tell us a thing about the way it really was. No one took the time to sit down and talk to us about anything; it was just 'here's your schedule, take it to room whatever and pick up your textbooks.'

"And the presumptuousness of that lady lawyer to suggest that Jess may have instigated the attack was infuriating. How was he to know that he shouldn't play a game of basketball in a Physical Education class to win? How was he to know that you didn't shower after playing basketball for fear of having your possessions stolen? To have some miscreant defecate on his towel and steal from him? How could he have known to be on the lookout lest you get your head slammed into a locker and stabbed with a weapon that has no place in any school?"

Tears flowing, but her voice steady, "I know, Mr. Martin, you get it from all sides. We watched as that school lawyer nearly choked on the word 'gangs' this morning. It would seem they can't be wished away by not mentioning them as your fellow employee insinuated. My husband said that your bosses probably have a "gag rule" that doesn't let you call a horse a horse. On that aspect, we applaud your taking a stand, and we support your efforts to make things better. I hope you succeed."

Mr. Martin listened intently. "I appreciate your comments, Mrs. Jemison. I know they're from the heart and I sense the love you have for your children. My wife and I were married for fifteen years and had a son." Gesturing toward the picture on his desk, "That's the three of us. There's nothing worse than losing a child. I don't say that to let you know how miserable my life was with my losses, but a person never knows what may befall them and no amount of trite condolences can right a wrong. It was a drunk driver that took my family when I was deployed in Iraq. A strange twist of fate. Believe me, I'm truly sorry for what happened to Jess. I can't make it up to you, but I will try to make it not happen to someone else."

Looking at the picture of the smiling trio, Jess was saddened to hear of Mr. Martin's loss.

Trying to lift the somberness of the moment, Mr. Martin said, "I want to tell you something else; I called Coach Mercer wanting to return the courtesy and let him know that I appreciated what he had done on Jess's behalf. We had a nice long talk, one educator to another. I felt something special for him, probably much the same as you do, Jess. He was quite adamant about wanting me to talk to our basketball coach and giving you a chance to try out for the team as an in-season walk-on."

Jess already lost basketball time while in the hospital and convalescing. He still felt a twinge of pain when he moved a certain way. And now, the basketball season was winding down and it would soon be tournament time when one loss ended the season. Mr. Martin thought perhaps he could find a spot on the taxi squad and at least get a chance to play against the varsity. To make the varsity squad at a school this large was quite an accomplishment in itself as the level of basketball in this city is quite high. "Basketball and baseball are Jefferson's redeeming virtues."

Mr. Martin went on. "I want to say one more thing and then we can bring this to a close. I've been working on an idea for a period of time and it all came together last week after talking to John Mercer. I'm putting together a loosely-defined organization of selected students, both boys and girls, and I'd like you to consider becoming one of its charter members. I'm hoping that this little "club" can address some of the problems we have at Jefferson. Like your mom said, if you'd had a mentor or guide assigned to you for the first day or so, we'd avoided your being attacked. Anyway, it'll be soon."

Mr. Martin ended. "That's all I have, but we'll be in touch. I am happy to have this time with you, Mrs. Jemison, and I will look forward to the next time. Please give Mr. Jemison my regards. Go ahead and go home with your Mom, Jess. I'll tell Mr. Hoffman that you'll be in class tomorrow for sure." Jess didn't know how to feel, he'd never been taken into the confidence of a principal before.

What did the guy mean; a club? Charter member?

Leaving the school, Jess felt good for the first time in several weeks despite the recurring jab of pain when he unthinkingly stretched his right side too far. Otherwise, he was optimistic, no different than most young people passing through the teen years to the who-knew-what next dimension of adulthood. At some point in the future, he would understand the old adage, "Youth doesn't know self," but now his perspective on life changed like the weather. He could swing from onerous to righteous as quickly as an idea could flash into his consciousness. Aware of physical changes and apprised of hormonal ones, he nevertheless, struggled for consistency without recognizing that the only thing consistent in life was change. Jess inherently knew right from wrong, but often could discern only black and white. Gray was a diffusive fringe. Some adolescents had little problem transitioning through this stage knowing they would grow out of it while others never would.

He was at a crossroad in this new place. Would he be just one of the numbers or stand as a number? Assistant Principal

Martin believed he was the latter. Jess would soon meet a girl who excelled in the present because of her vision for the future and a boy who already passed through the portal. Two refreshing digressions from the norm.

I had trouble sleeping after Mr. Martin's meeting. Worrying about going back to school and plotting how I would get retribution. Yesterday, I stood like an idiot trying to figure out where the History Room was. Everyone else knew where they were going and I stood there in the way. I got bumped several times. Once again, I was a spectacle walking into class after the bell. Tomorrow will be my third try to make it through a school day without an interruption. Hope for the best and brace myself for more of the worst. I'll definitely have butterflies.

****

Jess had yet to learn there were several entrances to Jefferson High. The school yard was rimmed with a six-foot high wire mesh fence rife with gaps, some large enough to walk through. Three adjoining buildings comprised the complex: the academic building, the gymnasium, and the physical plant were centered in a big square area, larger than a city block. The foreboding dark red bricks bespeaking hardness were accompanied by pairs of dulled white lintels and sills defining the windows, all symmetrically similar and massive in height.

The facility was surrounded by a grid of streets and set atop a small hill; Jess's first thought was to think of Batman's Gotham City. Oddly, the structures, complete with a huge smokestack, looked much like he imagined they would. The corners of the building were topped by a concrete thing that he would be told was a depiction of a maple bud. The architecture was completed with three protruding entrances each with pair of white spires at their corners. Driving by it with their parents, Julianne called it creepy. Jess gaped at it with a sense of Déjà vu.

Gothic.

Inside, the cylindrical hallway lights hung from black chains attached to a high ceiling that was barely visible. The doors to the classrooms were dark wood, the finish worn thin where years of young hands rubbed against them. For Jess, the numbering scheme for the rooms was beyond comprehension. Classrooms ringed three-sided around the offices, stairways and restrooms in the inner parts of each of the two floors, the third different with an auditorium occupying its center. The fourth side of the school abutted the gymnasium.

The school was finished in 1928, almost a year to the day before the stock market crash of '29.

Contrary to Jess's expectation, the start of the day brought a nice surprise when the Jefferson High School basketball coach summoned him out of Homeroom for a quick introduction. Coach Cottison told Jess he had talked to Assistant Principal Martin, read the letter from Coach Mercer, and now wanted to "meet such an outstanding young man." Of course, he knew about Jess's injury and understood that Jess wouldn't be ready to go full speed for a while.

"Perhaps you'd like to start by hanging out at practice and just doing whatever feels comfortable. Get to see how we do it. You know that once tournament time starts next week, one loss and our season is finished."

Coach also felt this might help Jess get acquainted with some other people and help him make some friends. He explained that in a school with almost two thousand students, give or take a hundred or so a day, that it was very difficult to play varsity basketball. "In fact," the coach said "it's probably harder for a player to make the Jefferson High School team than it would be to make many college teams. There's lots of fierce competition for every position, and basketball is the sport of choice in Trentsville."

Coach Cottison thought it would be best if Jess started by working with the sophomore team and Coach McGrew. Then next year he would be given a try-out and a fair assessment by each of his coaches regarding his chances of making the team. "You'll have to work hard between the seasons on your own. There's always a game somewhere, there're camps and AAU leagues. But be careful what you do so you don't lose your eligibility. Don't ever play for money or bet on a game."

Jess had had never experienced having to try out for a team or the admonishment of playing against opponents in a play-for-pay game or one with side bets taking place. "If there's any kind of money knowingly transferred based on the outcome of a game, you can be declared ineligible. And speaking of eligibility,

I want to check to see if we can't get you another semester because of your injury."

Redshirt me? Why would I stay in high school more than four years?

****

As in New Holland, Jess was given a seat in Biology class next to a girl. Sharing a small table-desk with her, he had inquired about which days they would do lab work, and with a little laugh was informed that the teacher had decided they "weren't capable" as students to handle scalpels or use Bunsen burners. Without laboratory exercises during the last part of the block, the students were instructed to work on biology or "whatever else" needed to be done.

The girl said, "Sometimes the class goes to the computer lab and we do virtual experiments which is kind of interesting. Normally though, this part of the day amounts to little more than a free period for us to do whatever school work needs to be done—as if we have any school work."

That's half the school day I have to study.

Having taken a half-glance at her, Jess had no difficulty in recognizing his table-mate's attractiveness. Blonde and trim with a single braid, she wore a short-sleeved gray sweater. Her slim left wrist resting on a zippered notebook sported a Minnie Mouse watch. A thick, dog-eared paperback with a picture of a cathedral on its cover lay on the desk in front of her.

Sensing that he should say something back to her, Jess lightly commented, "Yeah, I understand why they don't want to put scalpels and dissecting tools in the hands of some people around here."

The girl, Jennifer Steffen, replied, "You're probably right after what happened a few weeks ago." She seemed pretty nice and looked Jess in the eyes when she spoke rather than giving him the no-look mumble typical of so many. She picked up on this new kid's dialect and was curious about him—light bronze color, pretty big, intelligent eyes, spoke in full sentences.

Jess recognized an opportunity to find out what the gossip might be about his attack. Sounding nonchalant, "There's probably a lot of stories going around."

Pictures?

Jess, Surviving Normal

"This dude..." she looked at him again, "Oh God, you're him! You're that guy." Despite the extraneous din, she spoke loudly enough to attract some attention from other, nearby tables. Jess flushed with embarrassment being the type of person who would have been embarrassed if she had merely said, "Oh, you're a new student," loudly enough to cause others to look at him.

From a neighboring table came, "You're sittin' next to a Jefferson celebrity, Jen girl." The person noisily scooted his chair across the grain of the old pine floor over to Jess's and the girl's table as he spoke. "Story is, your new non-lab partner here put it to one of the boys in the High Aces on the hardwood. Hey man, you must've given him the red ass to make him go after you like that. Didn't anyone bother to tell you half that class is future High Aces and that we's s'posed to respect them?" Respect said sarcastically.

Jess was the center of attention. Even the teacher perked up to hear what was being said.

From the back of the room, where two boys sat huddled around at their table, came a reproving "Nuff," said in a voice with a finality followed by a fist pounding forcefully on the top of their table. Jess glanced back at them; maybe they were members of the gang this kid was talking about.

He knows who stabbed me!

The teacher immediately tried to defuse what could have become a volatile situation by telling the class to hold it down; it was okay to talk to those near you during the second hour, but don't start with across the room stuff. "Anyway, there's an exam coming up pretty soon and I want to spend this hour reviewing. Which, by the way you would be wise to be studying for in the second hour."

While the teacher riffled through a stack of assignments and was calling student's names to claim them, Jen's voice was more hushed. "Was it one of those two?"

Sitting with his head down while his embarrassment subsided, Jess mumbled out of the corner of his mouth, "I didn't see who attacked me. I never looked at their faces."

I'm lying. If I forget that guy's face, I'll remember other things. His smell.

Again, the new member of the table spoke but a bit lower, "No one saw who did it. And nobody ever will though half the school suspects who it was. Jefferson High keeps its secrets."

"They're afraid. It's silly, that mafioso code of silence," Jen stated.

"Honor among thieves." Jess had heard someone say that before.

"No one wants to be a snitch. It's the end of their social life," she said.

The new guy said, "And an invitation to get bullied." Still speaking in a subdued tone,

Mr. Hoffman gave his review, asking a few questions throughout. A portion of the students took some notes; others sat wearing their best 'entertain me' faces. The 50-minute 'hour' up, the bell rang and students had five minutes until the next bell. Being a two-period class, most students stayed in their seats and talked. The kid that scooted his chair over previously, returned.

"Hey, I'm Dan-el White, the next black President despite my antithetical last name and you're Jess…uh, Jemison. I'm in Ge-om with you, too. And this beautiful lady you have the good fortune to sit next to is my truly best friend and confidante, Jen Steffen. Known to basketball aficionados as the 'Swish Miss,' kind of an oxymoron—should be' Swish Made.' Get it? Made-maid? Being that she's the point guard on our basketball team. She probably didn't introduce herself…"

"Because you so rudely interrupted, I didn't have a chance."

Dan-el rolled his eyes at Jen and smiled as he continued, not missing a beat, "And I'm probably the next one to get pushed down the stairway. I forgot that those gorillas haunting the back of the room put in a rare appearance today. Must be too cold out on the street. They think they own the school and all the toys in the box. Always together in a pack, they are. If my constitution allowed it, I'd fight both of them mano a mano anytime, but they won't let that happen."

Dan-el's rancor toward gang members obvious, Jess recalled Dan-el as the guy who participated in Geometry class a couple times. He also was asked to put a two-column proof for a pair of congruent triangles on the board.

I got the impression it was a class between the teacher and Dan-el.

Dan-el wore glasses with heavy black rims, and his patterned V-neck sleeveless sweater over a print shirt with a white collar gave him the appearance of a geek or a throwback to the last century. "I'm sorry that the reception committee here at Jefferson treated you so poorly and because of that, I'm going to take the job of bein' your mentor; free of charge." Gesturing toward the back of the room, "Not all of us are like those guys; there's a few of us who would like to get an education around here. Right, Jen?"

"Right, Dan-el, do you know any of them?"

Dan-el smiled, "You're pretty witty for a girl, especially a blond one." Jess could see that they were good friends by the way they smiled when trading barbs.

"Anyway Jess, my man, I'm here to save the day for you and to offer you my services so next week you don't find yourself flying out of a third-floor window without the benefit of a cape. Just be careful whose precious feelings you might hurt; the High Aces have a one-hundred percent virtual presence around here and they think their defecations don't stink. They're definitely the alpha dogs that haunt our hallowed halls, just ask one of them."

Jess had not said a word since Dan-el began talking.

"First lesson, hang in pairs or threes like us. Jen counts 'cause she can whup half of them herself. And it's best to not pee at school; hold it until you get home. Anyhow, just stay aware and in no time, you'll know who and what to avoid. There're some other guys, and gals who aren't High Aces that're pretty bad, too; mostly they think pre-Civil War thoughts. Jen can tell you about the High Queens, she's their president."

"Oh C'mon, Dan-el. You're so full of it."

Dan-el abruptly raised his hand and got the teacher's attention. "Mr. Hoffman, when are you going to tell us about coyotes and polecats?" The two in the back of the room either didn't hear Dan-el's rhetorical question or didn't connect his reference to them by it. Mr. Hoffman caught it and didn't bother to answer looking at Dan-el doing the one-eyebrow-lift thing.

Man, this dude is wired. Never comes up for air.

Jess actually managed to get a few words in edgewise and they continued the conversation for the rest of the school day. Jess asked questions and learned as much as he could about the subculture of students at this strange new school. Dan-el and Jen wanted to hear about Jess's school and what it was like to live in the 'Tall Corn State.'

A city school, Jefferson was situated in a struggling neighborhood and reflected the demographics consistent with the times: a scarce job market and families living in tenements at or near the poverty level. Trentsville's city administrators claimed that urban renewal was a high-priority item but it took time to attract committed investors. Several old buildings no longer suited to modern manufacturing stood idle and darkened the horizon not very far from the school—structurally strong and too costly to tear down. The window plant that employed Mr. Jemison once considered renovating a former textile building but opted to build a new plant in the newer, industrial areas of the city. Roads and infrastructure were the primary reasons that made it more cost effective. Another problem was, although many of the people were willing to work, they neither had the technical expertise nor the education required for the positions offered. And, in times of robotic machinery and computerized systems, there was a smaller demand for workers, who thirty years ago, had no trouble finding work. It's easy to say that there were too many people for the available jobs, but the more insidious culprit was greedy management policies outsourcing jobs to places of cheap labor. As Jess's dad had explained, "Business equations often don't include the human factor."

"Jefferson High School is racially mixed, a typical old worn-out building half full of shit-upon kids who are victims of their surroundings," was how Dan-el put it. When Jess asked, he spurned open enrollment. "You can find what you look for at any school, and there's more opportunity here than in some stuffy school somewhere out in the 'burbs. Stick with Jen and me—you'll see."

Jen pointed out that Dan-el was on the Jefferson Academic Team. "He doesn't need glasses, but wears them for effect."

In a more serious vein, Dan-el told Jess that he was a member of a gym downtown and was in the boxing club, which clarified his earlier remark, "If my constitution allowed it…" Boxing club members didn't fight on the street unless it was to defend themselves or in a situation allowing no recourse.

As for the feminine half of his new acquaintances, when Jess looked into her striking violet eyes, he got a dizzy sensation. Her effect on him escaped logic; he couldn't talk coherently while looking at her. She seemed relaxed, at ease with the five W's. She wasn't trying to impress others; it wasn't important to her and likely never would be.

Jess perked up on Dan-el again mentioning that Jen played basketball, and looking sidelong was about to ask about it. Dan-el kept talking, now somewhere between irony and truth, "Jen is the token white girl on the starting lineup."

He learned she was a sophomore, and she lived less than a mile from the school with her mother and two younger twin brothers. In time Jess would be told that her father and mother had divorced and he had moved out. "No big deal, their iciness toward each other affected all of us kids," she would say.

In conversations like this one, Jess would hear that Jen Steffen was interested in becoming an architectural engineer and was taking all the elective courses appropriate to engineering that she could. One of them was a CAD/design course in which students designed their own houses or similar structures and then built scale models of them from balsa-wood components. There was talk of 3-D printers being available at the outlying high schools.

As he gained confidence during their time Jess told the other two more about himself. It seemed that his life had been so dull and boring. Portraying himself as just another kid, it prompted Dan-el to tell him, "Don't be so hard on yourself, man; you sound like you got a lot going. Three-sport athletes are unheard of 'round here."

****

Inevitably the Physical Education class brought mixed feelings. Not knowing what might await, Jess wanted to show that he could 'take it,' but was fearful of more of the same. It helped that other adjustments were made when he noticed that the P.E. teacher was waiting just inside the locker room as the students filed by. Changing clothes, Jess overheard the teacher ask a few of the other students where the kid was that got hurt.

He doesn't remember what I look like.

Once identified, he approached Jess with an exaggerated display of concern. "Jess Jemison. Glad to have you back, son. Hope you're feeling better. I see here on this note that you're on the medical excuse list. Don't bother to dress out. Come sit with me in the bleachers and. I'll let you mark attendance."

I guess that's what years of teaching does to you.

It didn't dawn on Jess that the teacher could have, should have lost his job over what happened. His indifference exposed; he would have been terminated at most schools. In fact, he was in his twentieth year at Jefferson, met minimum standards and showed up on a regular basis—all distinguishing credentials, considering. He approached school matters with a 'no harm, no foul' attitude and could appeal a dismissal with legal representation provided.

But with Jess, there was a foul this time. The teacher had been grilled, but not incessantly, asked only the perfunctory questions:

"Where were you when this boy was attacked?"

"I was helping another student who needed attention."

"Do you understand your responsibility to be present at all times?

"I was present; I can't see everyone all the time. I have over forty kids in every class. That's beyond the maximum in our contracts. That's something we should discuss."

"Do you know that the school could very well be sued for negligence and you for dereliction of duty?"

"I have union protection. I think they'd be interested in a lot of things that go on here."

There were more back-and-forth questions that went nowhere toward finding who stabbed Jess. In the end, the teacher was given a verbal reprimand. He'd sat through interrogations from the police as well.

Truth was, the inordinate number of 'gang bangers' in this particular class made the teacher apprehensive to interact on more occasions than this one. He stayed out of the locker room if possible, doing little more than sticking his head through the door and hollering for them to hurry. There'd been incidents before when he called the resource officers, himself preferring to stay back. Only the severity of Jess's attack made this incident different.

Despite its common wall with the main building, the gymnasium housed the P.E. program and the shop classes that separated them from the so-called academic area and was rarely visited by the resource officers. The prevailing thought was that the teachers were former "jocks" and lumberjack types who could take care of trouble by themselves—an unfair assumption.

Relieved that it played out the way it did, the class began with Jess sitting in the bleachers beside the teacher watching the mayhem. The attendance book was never presented and when Jess asked, he was told that. "It's all right. I'll take care of it later."

The teacher didn't take roll. he doesn't know our names. He just sits there chewing on something and looking at his phone.

Like all curricular courses, PE classes had standards and achievements but in this particular situation, the teacher occupied a position few wanted, and those who would take the job weren't certified even though they could have done a better job. PE was definitely a class designed for bullies as Jess watched the balls become flying missiles thrown about the gym in dodge ball fashion—head-hunting version. This lasted for ten minutes or so until the teacher put down his phone and blew his whistle, shouting, "Basketball!" It was much easier to throw out a couple balls and let the rest of the class sit around the gym poking at each other.

Per usual, one of the students took it upon himself to form the teams. No one questioned his authority when he chose four cronies and pointed to five other boys sitting in the bleachers. In the process, the self-appointed leader pointed at Jess and said, "You wanna play, Oreo, or does your back hurt too much?"

Jess, remembering Dan-el's advice, nevertheless couldn't keep from glaring at the guy and mouthing "asshole." Seeing this, the student answered with a smirk and a hand motion prompting Jess to come down. The teacher once again blew his whistle, stood up and told the offending student to knock off the crap or he'd send for an in-school cop to take him to the Office.

"Yeah, yeah." He'd heard it all before.

Jess could feel the knife injury as he sat idly.

I don't care; I'm not going cower to these jerks. If they jump me after class, I'll get in a few shots of my own.

Sitting next to the teacher, he did not see his alleged attacker.

Probably for good reason.

Watching the rag-tag scrimmage, Jess recognized none of the players he had previously played against the day of his knifing. He remembered the guy he scored on to be thick in the torso, having heavy arms and legs more like an older-than-high-school type. Throughout the period, recollections of that day haunted him.

Thwarting the possibility of another confrontation, the teacher dismissed Jess early while the rest of the class went to the lockers. Jess knew that in being singled out inadvertently by the teacher and confrontationally by the basketball player, everyone else got a good look at him. But this time, the anger in Jess overcame the fear. Protecting himself was his only recourse.

Dan-el can help me.

****

In addition to being the last period of the day, Jess looked forward to Biology for the time he could spend with his new friends. As the first weeks passed, Dan-el had been kind enough to include Jess in his circle of friends that hung together before school, and Jess soon grew accustomed to the daily routines of Jefferson. Further, basketball practice helped Jess get acquainted with a few of the other players and to become more familiar in his surroundings. No mention was made of photos of the stabbing in his presence.

I might be lucky. No one looks at me like that.

All things considered except the setting; Jefferson High was really not much different than other schools. Jess's incident was extraordinary; unfortunate that he got caught in the underbelly which rightfully distorted his perception of the whole place. Again, like everywhere, most students simply wanted to blend in without making too much of an impression--favorably or otherwise. If the proportion of detractors at Jefferson was out of whack, only a part of the wrongness could be blamed on the gang presence. Jess discovered that most of the teachers were willing to help if they knew the student was willing to learn. The bulk of the blame for many of the shortcomings was due to the snowball effect. Like any school, once it begins to slip academically it brings an avalanche. Large staff turnovers created changes that were not always pleasant and rarely consistent, and a 'me versus them' attitude often developed between teachers and students as well as between teachers and administrators. Installing more and more rules only made it worse for everyone.

Once a manufacturing hub of the Mid-south, Trentsville was caught in the fallout from the rust belt. A downturn in the textile, coal and aluminum industries trickled down to the neighborhood schools and hit the cities right in the gut, especially the inner-city. Funds were cut everywhere, but they had a greater effect on older schools with aging boilers to repair rather than schools with weight rooms to build.

Dad explained that schools are socioeconomic mirrors. The trick was to address the object and not the image.

Jefferson suffered not because of its product--the kids, but by being measured by the wrong yardstick. Jefferson suffered because too many people looked at it from the outside and without an energetic representation from the inside. Sadly, Jefferson was stereotyped and too few leaders recognized that when it comes to human beings, there should be no discrimination. Hence, the snowball effect.

****

Jen, of course, was a study in progress. In Iowa, Jess was attracted to Courtney and he enjoyed trading barbs, some flirtatious, with his caustic Biology class lab partner. So far, he'd never had a relationship with anyone he could call a girlfriend. He'd been on dates and "met up" with a couple girls that had resulted in some situations that he might have described as "getting to second base," but nothing serious. His ever-conspicuous braces made him think that no one would want to kiss him in the first place, and secondly, how would he approach kissing a girl without hurting her with his mouthful of hardware. Everyone in the teen world had heard the story about two kids whose braces got locked together.

Whether shy or stigmatized, Jess was caught in a trap of his own design. He worried that being forward would meet with a girl's disapproval. Knowing that rebuke didn't bother some of boys his age, it would bother him and kept him in the background when it came to the opposite sex. But despite constraints, the urges were present, particularly as he got older, and his few experiences were memorable. His mind often raced with fantasies until his conscience laid a guilt-trip on him.

And too, there was the crassly explicit internet that gave many adolescent boys some erroneous notions about the submissiveness of girls. Jess's fear of exploring such nether places and being found out barely overcame his curiosity. Having been taught respect and morality both at home and at church was a powerful deterrent, too. A friend told a story about how his screen froze at the same time his mom walked into his room and he lost his privileges for a month. "Little things became big concerns when it comes to sex, pun intended," another friend had intoned.

At first, it was natural that his mind's eye saw his relationship with Jen to be platonic. Placing her on the proverbial pedestal, he thought her to be above kissing and certainly above his clumsy pawing. Being lithe and athletic in her movement she exuded an unpretentiousness that drew Jess to her, but again, in a collegial way more than a sexual way. Sure, he could imagine making out with her; in fact, it was difficult not to think it, but right now it was more important to get to know her than to want to ravish her.

Ha.

Jen didn't adorn herself with blushes and shadows. Her clothes were fashionable but modestly fitting rather than clinging. All together, these qualities blended together to make her the most fantastic creature Jess had ever encountered. Consequently, it was into the second month before he managed to overcome his initial difficulty in speaking coherently and looking at her simultaneously. But even then, he still thought he came off as being pretty stupid most of the time when they were together.

Once I mentioned that I liked to read rather than watch a lot of TV. I said I was a bibliophobe.

Each day Dan-el would scoot his chair over to their table during the second hour, and the three of them would just hang out. Usually at a loss for words when it was only Jen, Jess was grateful when Dan-el joined them during the second hour. They'd talk sports and school and gossip about common things they shared, including e-mail addresses and social media handles.

One Friday afternoon, they were summoned from Biology to the school's Assembly Room. Jess had no idea there was such a place so he followed Jen and Dan-el's lead, although he did have an inkling why they were called. Upon reporting, a teacher's aide ushered them into the first few rows of seats with others already seated. More students came until about forty rather speculative young people filled the designated spots; all of them wondering what they had done.

Mr. Martin entered through a side door that adjoined the room, walked over to the podium and extended his arms for attention. Dressed in khakis, a white short-sleeved shirt and the characteristically loosened blue tie, he placed his hands on both sides of the podium.

Smiling in acknowledgement he began, "I want to share some thoughts with you today. And no, you're not in trouble, so relax." He paused for the murmurs and exaggerated expressions of relief. "As you look around, you won't see that you have much in common. However, there is a common denominator. In your own way, by grades, by extracurricular performance, or by my 'eye in the sky' each of you has shown a degree of conscientiousness and maturity. Today, I want to appeal to those qualities. I might add that you are the third such group that I talked to."

He paused for what teachers call the 'significant second' while watching some of the more demonstrative students. Then, smiling again, "I'm sure I made some mistakes, though."

He continued, "With as many students as we have in Jefferson, I've selected around one-hundred of you to consider what I have to say and then let you decide for yourselves what you'd like to do. Presently, I am in the process of trying to put together a team of student ambassadors that are willing to help make some positive changes here at Jefferson."

Mostly everybody immediately recognized that Mr. Martin was speaking of sedition; that he wanted them to snitch, to be an Uncle Tom. Their reactions said as much.

Raising his arms for the murmuring to subside, he said, "I can guess what you're thinking. That I'm asking you to spy and then squeal to the administration. That you're violating your fellow students. I know this could be dangerous and socially harmful for you, but hear me out. Please!

"I want to improve the academic standard of this school. I observe an attitude that many students do not recognize the importance of school in their lives, and it's not just here but in high schools in many places. They have no purpose because they don't relate. You all know that many of your classmates are doing very little beyond the bare minimum, just getting by. And most of you know Jefferson's student achievement numbers are in a tailspin that suggests the school is not serving its students' needs. The situation is worsened when students don't recognize that education is vital in order to become capable of making their own way in the world. There must be a major paradigm shift in the way academics are approached in the U.S. and at Jefferson." He paused, shook his head negatively and ran his fingers through his hair. "Sorry, I'm getting carried away with edu-speak.

What's in it for us?

"Each of you in this room has experienced how one disruptive student can render a class totally unproductive. Teachers react in different ways to these disruptions, but in general, they have been taught to deal with it themselves because removing a student from class is a sign of a weak teacher. And no teacher can escape scrutiny if they toss every student who looks cross-eyed at them. Teachers, like students, feel handcuffed by a set of double standards. In many cases, my hands are tied, too. You see, the expectations of public education assume cooperation. And you know what happens when you assume something."

He didn't finish explaining what happens, but most had heard the saying and knew the implication,

"According to the experts on education, success is measured in the percentage of students who graduate." Listening, Jess remembered this was much the same as Mr. Martin said a few weeks past when he'd talked to Mom. "Driven by these numbers, it's easy to figure out what has happened. Schools have lowered standards, adjusted grades and accommodated a student's pathway to graduation by watering down their courses and teaching to the tests. The by-product to this is that it handcuffs student achievement and denies the teacher her individuality. Worst of all, it teaches students how to beat the system—in a way, to cheat."

Doesn't everyone cheat one way or another?

Pausing for effect, he again looked at his charges, moving his eyes from left to right and then back, "I didn't call this group together to make you feel good about yourselves just because you put up a few good numbers on standardized tests or you caught a touchdown pass. I called you to make you realize that you're not competing against others at Jefferson High School but against the rest of the world. Compare your numbers against theirs and you'll understand what I'm saying.

"It follows that you will need every advantage you can muster to live and succeed in the world when you leave Jefferson. In the vast majority of cases, student pathways to success in life follows their achievement in training. Oh sure, there are exceptions, but the odds are stacked that you're not going to make it with a guitar or a basketball.

"A giant step can be made by demanding accountability in the classroom. When someone is acting up, don't be complacent but use your influence to get the class back on track. I've taken adult education classes where students are vocal toward another student detracting the teacher or the rest of the class. They say things like 'I'm paying to listen to the teacher, not you.' When students are held strictly accountable, whether in a school like ours or in a private school like Catnap Academy, achievement levels on the part of the students rises significantly.

"In many ways, choices high school students make are far more important than those at later stages because what you learn now will determine what you can do later on. Not only do I think that raising standards is beneficial for all of us, but you could avoid paying college tuition prices to take remedial courses that teach you what should have learned in high school."

Heard it all before, man.

His voice reaching a crescendo, a vein showing on his neck, "The biggest travesty in society today is found right here in public education. Yet few of you have stood up and said 'I want this to stop.' You are the victims. You are being robbed of your right to an education, and when you let it go on, you condone it! But I'm not here today to tell you what you already know; I'm here to tell you that you can do something about it. Think it over. Accept the challenge to bring about change"

Some students nodded assent, some squirmed, some glanced at their cohorts and some took on defiant looks. Their reactions were a mixed bag. Mr. Martin's tone said as much as his words. Many weren't accustomed to being talked to in this manner.

Mr. Martin continued; his voice lower. "Okay, I'll get off my soapbox. Now let me talk about bullying. This morning, I broke up a group of boys who had formed a circle around a girl and wouldn't let her pass. In tears and shaking, she told me that every time she tried to walk between two of them, they would poke their fingers at her chest and shove her back into the center of the ring. Her books were strewn over the floor and she was frantic when I came around the corner and saw this.

"We also had an incident in the restroom yesterday where two boys threatened to put another boy's head in the toilet if he didn't give them money.

A swirly. A head tornado.

We have physical encounters of violence and sexual abuses almost daily."

Please don't mention me. Please, please.

Shifting from lecturing to appealing, Mr. Martin was visibly upset in recounting these incidents. His face was flushed and his knuckles white as he grasped the sides of the lectern. "We have rules against this and penalties attached to them, but we can't be everywhere. This school has three assistant principals, three resource officers and teachers who are supposedly vigilant at all times. But it isn't enough. A teacher in the hallway between classes can't monitor his or her classroom as it fills up for the next class. Many students are afraid to go to the bathroom; some won't enter the lunchroom for fear of being accosted in one way or another. I have teachers who are afraid of certain students, and for good reasons. What I'd like to know is this: Where is your sense of responsibility when you know this kind of thing is going on? Can you content yourselves with the fact that no one has bothered you or you've figured out how to avoid certain situations? Again, can you look at yourselves in the mirror when you stood by and laughed at the misfortune of someone else being harassed? Schadenfreude is a precise German word describing that kind of behavior."

I know that word. Make fun of someone else to save yourself.

His voice rising as before, "Some of you have been victims yourself, some of you have been perpetrators, and some of you are playing out some distorted notions that you have a right to seek 'payback.' C'mon, wake up and get your heads out of the sand! Take the circle of boys that I just mentioned, that's criminal abuse. If two senior boys with a "J" on their letter jackets come up to a group like this and say something or step into the middle of the circle, they can stop the abuse right there."

I don't know about that from what I've seen. They might divert it to themselves.

"A sophomore girl can too by using sensible intervention tactics so don't get the idea that I'm suggesting a strong-arm approach. Further, if a few Ambassadors would keep an eye on a restroom just by hanging out within sight, you would know who's in there, and simply by your presence, affect that situation. You can help make a difference by supporting what this school stands for and what this school has to offer you. And has it ever occurred to you that omission is a form of bullying, too?"

Again, Mr. Martin stopped and swept his eyes slowly around the room scrutinizing those he saw. After a moment, or an hour as it may have seemed, he raised one arm.

A papal dispensation?

"I want to mention one more thing today and that's the prison yard mentality that pervades teenage thinking. I'm talking about 'Don't be a snitch.' Perhaps you can explain to me the wisdom behind this dishonorable, despicable practice when students sit in silence allowing the person next to them to do something wrong. Or when you know something wrong has happened.

"The power of change rests in this room. *You* can initiate a change in our school. And *you* will bring about change not only for yourself, but for the person next to you and for every student in this school. We will meet again next week at this same time. If your name is called and you don't want any part of becoming an Ambassador, then don't come. I won't ask you twice."

****

"The man made some sense," Dan-el said to Jen and Jess. Then to Jess, "I live in an apartment operated by the Housing Authority and I see shite every day that speaks volumes for what Martin said. So many people livin' down there've given up hope. There're no prospects for honest jobs; just hustling one way or another is all there is. You ought to come and see me some weekend; hell, Mr. Martin oughta' come, too. My mother put it pretty well a few weeks ago when she said that our part of town has 90 percent of the crime, fifteen percent of the people and not one percent of the wealth.

To which Jen quickly said, "And ninety percent of the fifteen percent are trying to cheat the remaining ten percent of the fifteen percent out of what little they have."

Jen sounds like a story problem in math.

"Aren't there some industries and factories for people to get jobs?" Jess asked. Not commenting on Jen's statement.

"Dude, this is America. America doesn't do jobs like they used to. Where's your old man's plant; probably outside the city in some antiseptic industrial park?"

"So?"

"So, my fine-feathered friend, how are people from where I live going to get to places like your dad's plant when the city buses don't go out there? The city buses don't even come into my neighborhood after 6:00 p.m."

"Can't they drive?" Jess asked.

Dan-el scoffed, "Yeah, they hop an Uber or Lyft or borrow some drug dealer's wheels."

Jess asked about area and neighborhood businesses and if there weren't jobs for people at those places. "I know they don't pay much, but it's work."

Dan-el said, "There you go. 'Helps you to see what Mr. Martin's got his shorts in a bunch about. What do you need an education for if you're going to stand behind some counter sacking burgers or selling cigarettes and lottery tickets for businesses that won't be there a year later? That's if you be lookin' for an honest living.

"A sandwich shop opened about two months ago, and last Saturday I saw it was closed, gone out of business. Know why? Because it attracted people who just hung around the premises and scared away folks who really wanted some food. Other times, people would come in, order a sandwich and not pay for it. Or they'd eat half of it and then complain that something was wrong with it and want their money back. You can't be in business when your clientele treats you like that."

Dan-el was just getting started. "Next, on top of everything else, some low-life extortionist comes in and wants money for protection. Or on the other end of this, some high and mighty rich non-extortionist won't support a venture down here without higher interest rates. An' you can talk all you want to about color and stereotype; free speech and amendments; but we're all people. That's Economics 101 the way it is down there."

Jen commented, "Isn't all big business extorting its employees?"

"Maybe not so much. Where would most people be without businesses that hire them?" Jess asked.

Dan-el continued, regarding Jess's question as a comment. He and Jen had had discussions like this on several occasions, and he knew that her sense of fairness had her leaning toward democratic socialism. "People react to their environment. I don't know what really happened to close the sandwich joint, but things like I said sure have happened in other places. And here's a piece of truth. My uncle wanted to open a consignment store and if he'd paid all the hands stickin' out, he woulda been thousands of dollars in the crapper just to get a permit. Where Martin's only half right is when he said kids today aren't being responsible; the way I see it, responsibility takes a back seat to what it is and where you is--kid or adult. And what he didn't say is that a lot of them don't know the meaning of the word because they don't know any real-life stories about it. Responsibility to a lot of kids in this school is the same thing as self-gratification."

"Except what they get from the teachers at school," Jess said.

"And they can't relate to the suburban and exurban attitudes taught in the classroom and they see in the textbooks. It's not like life on the streets that they do know. They're trapped in their environment. Of all the science that gets thrown at them, Darwinian theory is the one that makes sense to them when he wrote about the survival of the fittest."

Jess found Dan-el's knowledge of matters like this impressive. "What you're saying is the gangs like the High Aces become what they are because they don't have a choice?"

"They have a choice, man. I had a choice. I'm no 'banger. My brother had a choice, and is—was. Who knows? He's doing a nickel out on the 'farm,' right now for borrowin' a car that he was gonna take in for a make-over." Dan-el often spoke in the vernacular. "If you guys look ahead a little in that twenty-pound biology book or watch the Discovery Channel, you'll see the difference between hyenas and lions. That was my choice; to be a lion." Dan-el did his best lion imitation seen at the beginning of many movies, "You pagans know the story 'bout Dan-el and the lion from the Bible?"

"Hold it down back there Dan-el," Mr. Hoffman said.

Chapter 4

At home, Mrs. Jemison reinstated her "study time" mandate, saying there was no reason to alter the procedures from before. Jess protested on the basis that he really didn't have any studies because students at Jefferson had ample time each day that could be used to study alone or go to the Commons and study in small groups. Mostly though, "study in small groups" was synonymous with "socialize in small groups." Further, the Biology teacher was rarely able to secure the outdated computer lab for the second part of the Biology class block so this was also a time when Jess could get his homework done – with Jen and Dan-el. In Geometry, the teacher would explain the work for the day, put a few examples on the board and the rest of the time was spent allowing the students to seek individual help or work on their assignments. This was the method that worked to keep problems at a minimum for teachers. Except for the History teacher, none of his teachers seemed to spend much time in the front of the class engaged in lecturing.

"Mom, there's so much free time at this school that I get everything done there. Hardly anybody ever takes a book home." He immediately realized his mistake.

No sooner than the words left his mouth, his mother had countered with, "If that's the case, I'll assign some extracurricular work for you. The study hour should be two hours if you're not getting it at school."

Thusly, Jemison children continued the practice of evening study time. If Jess didn't have school work, his mother had a ready supply of "classics" to go with an inexhaustible list of suggestions. Jess actually enjoyed most of them, particularly *The Last of the Mohicans*, *Moby Dick*, and *Huck Finn*.

Jim Billman

I loved Hawkeye. Like a white horse, a white whale would be ostracized by his own. I bet Mom would hardly find him an ideal son.

A book by Charles Dickens was on her current list and Jess had been given *David Copperfield* as punishment in Jess's opinion. "This will take me forever," he complained.

"But you have ample time," Mom returned. "You said so yourself. Anyway, you'll enjoy it. Dickens tells about the lifestyle in England in the nineteenth century and describes social issues. There's some moral lessons typical to young men of any time."

Jess wasn't so opposed to reading these books other than it was one more instance of being told what to do.

It fed my compulsory need to sulk.

Julianne, into the routine of her school, reported that her teacher was a "man." At first, she didn't know whether she was going to like him or not, but changed her mind after he extended his personal welcome to her. She really liked when he read out loud and would designate different students to be the characters in the stories. Another thing he did was to ask the students to pretend to be a character in the story and tell the rest of the class about what it was like in his or her world. "We really have to use our imaginations and think about things. And you have to pay attention all the time."

Mr. Jemison was initially given some time to get familiar with his position and interact with key people. His new job involved a lot of responsibility being in charge of many of the employees, and his early impression was favorable but there was room for improvement. He told others that his biggest concern was moving into his new position with the least amount of disruption possible. "People often say they don't mind change, but they really do mind it if the change takes them out of their comfort zone." At the present time, Dad was spending some very long hours at work. Of course, his wife let him know of his obligation to be home in time for their evening meal.

Rebecca Jemison had fallen in love with their nice family home in an established neighborhood along a street lined with oak and maple trees. She decided that a two-story brick colonial built about forty-five years ago with a very traditional floor plan fit their needs. Somewhat pretentious but in line with other houses in the area, theirs had a nice two and one-half car unattached garage and two Bradford Pear trees that shaded the back yard. The deck with a pergola over it was an obvious add-on. Julianne claimed the bedroom facing the street, which gave Jess the one facing the back yard, the one he would have chosen in the first place. Mom called it a solarium because of its two rows of windows. Jess liked the flat concrete driveway seeing the potential for a basketball hoop, and envisioned the basement with its fairly high ceilings as a future recreation room. Amid the rush of suggestions each person had, Dad held up his hands and said, "Whoa, we can only afford so much at a time."

Situated on a quiet street devoid of truck traffic and within ten minutes of an aging, mid-sized mall, the location was quaint in the fact that in the next block from their house there was a small, stucco gray grocery store that had been owned by the same family for over seventy-five years, Bob's Market stood adjoined to Hanrahan's Butcher Shop.

Mrs. Jemison kept busy getting the rooms arranged, repainting what "absolutely needed to be done," and tending to Jess during his convalescence. She voiced mixed emotions concerning going back to work. "I could get used to being a stay-at-home mom."

The Jemison's first impressions of their neighbors was good enough. Most of the residents in the area seemed to have jobs that kept them too busy to socialize on a daily basis, typical of what America had become. There were a few suggestions of "getting together" from some of the new acquaintances, but no one actually named a time. Mom remarked that, "People often say things like that to be friendly" when Julianne asked. "They know we need some time to get familiar with the city and our work." One of their new neighbors told Mom that friends were often made through folks going to the same church, a thinly-veiled message to keep to yourselves.

I was settling in. No longer intimidated by the size of the city and all the traffic. Aside from those changes, we live in a little circle just like always.

There were feelings of reservation as news of Jess's stabbing rippled through the neighborhood. Some people wondered how such an event could have happened without some provocation on Jess's part. "Why is he going downtown to

Jefferson when Westfield is closer?" one older neighbor not familiar with the districting asked another.

True to form, there were undercurrents stoked by the fact that Mrs. Jemison was Caucasian and Mr. Jemison a person of color. Even in Iowa, mixed marriages, as some people still called them, bothered more than a few folks. "Who do they hang around with, whites or blacks?" was another point of confusion with those who thought the color of one's skin made a difference. Although it was never been a dinner table topic, Mrs. Jemison could sense there was always a little hint of unacceptance in her neighbors, but nothing like the condescending remarks she heard in lily-white Iowa when she and Craig married over sixteen years ago.

Mr. Jemison confided that he felt some racial tension at work, too. "Several hundred miles north or south makes a big difference in the way people treat each other. A lot of folks are friendly, but they just don't have the time to become friends. Then too, we're the newcomers and we have to prove ourselves," he said.

For Jess, he'd endured disparaging slurs in "trash talking" during sports events and had heard whispers about his color at his old school. Again, his freshman year had been particularly difficult because of the senior boys who used him as a target. Julianne was totally comfortable with who she was and wasn't affected by 'names that would never hurt her.' She'd handled taunts with challenges such as, "Would you like to race me? Let's see if you can do more chin-ups than me." Julianne had no difficulty looking at people dead-on and asking why they felt they had to say what they did.

However, south of the 230-mile Mason-Dixon Line, racial prejudice was slower to die out, if it ever would. Although none of the Jemison's knew, one neighbor had vowed to build a fence around his yard and remarked that, "This is just the beginning. Pretty soon they'll be parking their cars in the yard." His counterpart, another retiree after directing a string of obscenities at the real estate agent that sold the house to the Jemison's, undertook to list his house with the same agency.

The Jemison's found other problems, too. They liked their new home, but it needed some basic updates. For example, woe be upon anyone in the shower whenever someone flushed a toilet; hence, replacing the water valves to protect against getting burned

Jess, Surviving Normal

became a high priority. In truth, a diligent home inspector should have discovered this before the sale was finalized and it would have been the seller's responsibility. In searching for the source of a mildew smell, Mrs. Jemison discovered that some window sills on the west side of the house had started to rot because rainwater didn't properly drain. "It's nice that I can get a discount on windows, Mm-mm," Mr. Jemison said.

And of course, there were new sounds and squeaks to get used to as wood, concrete, and metal went through seasonal and diurnal expansions and contractions. Julianne had learned the locations of all the squeaks in the floor so she could "sneak" around the house without being detected, getting incessant pleasure from "popping up" when no one expected her. On one particularly warm week in February, the Jemison's declared war against an infusion of ants that showed up--in a trail making a mass migration.

As if skin color made him something less, Mr. Jemison picked up some subtle hints from a few workers who treated him distantly. Not often, but occasionally, there were references that made him wonder. Having grown up in the Chicago area, he was aware of caste prejudices as much as racial prejudices and had been the target of deriding remarks when he and Rebecca were dating. Nothing overt, though. He knew of Emmet Till's murder in the 1950's and the Chicago race riots of 1919, but those were a long time ago. Since moving to Trenstville and going to work, he saw bumper stickers and license plate frames in the parking lot that suggested a more prejudiced society than Iowa's. Being one of only two African-Americans in management at the plant, he was fairly sure that representative numbers of people working at the plant didn't match the ratio in the Trentsville metropolitan area.

Mrs. Jemison's start date for her job came and went; the person she was to replace decided at the last moment not to retire for another year. And now, amid a periodic economic downturn in the building industry, a freeze had been put on new hires. Her husband, as a plant executive, could have probably pulled some strings, but again, that wasn't how the Jemison's did things. Mom was torn about work, but knowing she needed to do something, started to look elsewhere for employment, at least on a temporary basis.

Despite the initial flowery reports, it turned out that Julianne hadn't fared much better than Jess. A boy ran past her and purposely knocked her down in the hallway that resulted in a severely sprained wrist that required an immobilizing wrap. And once again, Mom and Dad were involved with another school incident that shouldn't have happened. Julianne told them that she was on the floor while students walked by her giggling and acting like nothing happened. An older kid had purposely stepped on her hand and still, no one offered to help. She said a boy call her a "dumb itch"

Rebecca and Craig Jemison were openly upset toward the officials at Julianne's school, and Mrs. Jemison asked to be put on the agenda at the next school board meeting. Instead, she was told of the school's Site-based Council, a committee composed of students, parents and teachers that discussed current issues and heard grievances. The school's principal informed them, "With over 60,000 students in our system, we cannot put every parent with a grievance in front of the school board. These are professional and business people that have very important issues they have to discuss."

Mrs. Jemison exploded, "Doesn't that alone suggest that something is seriously wrong? You have people that know nothing about managing a school system in charge of running the schools."

"Ma'am, I don't have a say in policy. Our Site-based Council meets every third Wednesday. You might attend one of their meetings and let them know how you feel. You can call Mrs. Sanchez to be put on the agenda." She took a business card from her desk and offered it to Mr. Jemison.

"And they'll listen to me and tell me they are aware of such happenings. Then they'll wag their heads and shrug their shoulders in acquiescence and let me know that they're doing all they can but they are limited. They're limited all right!" Dad placed his hand on Mom's shoulder as a calming gesture.

"Ma'am, the minutes go to our school's Governing Board and they make the rules for each individual school. I can give you a copy of the rules and regulations for our school."

Mrs. Jemison said, "We have a copy. One was given to us when we enrolled our daughter. It clearly states that bullying and fighting will not be tolerated, but it still happens on a daily basis."

Jess, Surviving Normal

"We try to do our best, but our teachers and supervisors can't be everywhere."

Mrs. Jemison was clearly distraught. "That's right. You can't be everywhere so you just keep things as they are. My son had a knife stuck in his back at Jefferson High School that could have killed him, and my daughter who won't step on a bug gets shoved down and stomped on while you are busy doing your best! Perhaps that's true, but things need to be changed so you can really do your best. From what I've seen, no one in the system has the courage to speak up to the almighty School Board composed of "business and professional" people. Has anyone ever suggested expelling kids who break the rules? Damn it, lady!"

Mr. Jemison had been quiet. Although he totally agreed with his wife, she really was getting too volatile. "Becky, Mrs. Quinn's suggestion to attend the meeting of the Council is our best opportunity to be heard. I'm sure that she will do all that she can in Julianne's behalf."

****

Jess, of course, followed his old basketball team back home and dearly missed being a part of their success. He spent many nights in his room thinking about his past life. Yes, he missed it, but was getting a bit more accustomed to his new one, thanks to people like Jen and Dan-el. At fifteen, and 185-pounds he wore a size twelve shoe. He was shaving a couple times a week and spent too much time looking at himself in a mirror. He kept his tightly-wound hair short, slightly longer than a military buzz-cut.

I would look good with a moustache.

His conditioning program helped him to regain the strength lost during his convalescence, but it didn't come quickly. Having spent time with the sophomore team running drills and watching the other sophomores scrimmage the varsity, he was disappointed that none of the coaches said much to him or had given him a chance to play in the scrimmages. The basketball season ended when the varsity lost in the third round of the District Tournament to their arch rival, City High.

If not basketball, baseball was Jess's other sports love, and he reported with several of the basketball players for try-outs, hoping that he could earn a place on the roster. Like basketball, competition promised to be fierce and practice had already been going on for several weeks for those athletes not in basketball or wrestling. After the first three try-out sessions, Jess was convinced he'd not done well. Thinking himself completely healed, he discovered otherwise by moving stiffly and not responding fluidly as he should. Basketball helped him recover his athleticism, but baseball was a different sport.

Jess pitched through his years in Little League, Babe Ruth and at his old school, and was the number three starting pitcher as a freshman. This time he decided to forego that position and report as a first baseman, and was pleased when he survived the first cut. The way it was explained, a third of those remaining would eventually be placed on the junior varsity team and another five or six players would oscillate between the JV and varsity. Another cut in the squad was imminent before the actual season started.

School, as Jess had indicated earlier to his mother, was considerably easier in terms of the classwork and homework. Mom suggested that Jess sign up for some Advanced Placement classes his junior year and for him to look seriously at one or two of the more global offerings as part of the International Baccalaureate Program. He'd nodded understanding at her suggestion, but had already developed his own schedule to hopefully include taking as many classes as he could with Jen; and if not with Jen, then with Dan-el.

As the weeks passed, Jess and his preoccupation with the High Aces waned somewhat. Because he was a member of the baseball squad, he was not required to take Physical Education meaning there'd be no more confrontations on that front. Occasionally he would notice some guys he suspicioned to be High Aces in the hallway, and of course, there were the boys from Biology Class in the "High Ace Training Academy" as Dan-el had called it. Nothing took place that could be termed confrontational, and it was seldom in Biology when the two were in attendance.

Noticing that Dan-el was right when he said you knew the weather was bad when the two came to class, Jess commented, "From what I see, those two have no possibility of passing the course so why do they even came to school?"

"None besides bad weather, lunch and a chance to out-source some product?" Jen answered.

Dan-el enlightened him. "Let me offer still another edification to your ed-ju-ca-tion, Jess. First of all, those clowns are nothin' but wannabes; call them Low Aces. Secondly, they will pass the class, no teacher in his right mind would want to see those punks back in his class next year which is the way it's often done around here. Both of them will get a "D minus" for a grade and no one will say anything, and they'll graduate with a general diploma if they stick around or live that long. If they come back next year, they will be a year older and two years nastier than they are now. Keep failing them and they'll be doing the same thing when they're eighteen years old. Guys here are lower echelon dealers, they're eyes and ears for what's happening. Third, the real High Aces have very little presence at school, but don't ever underestimate their intelligence or their organizational skills."

Dan-el's words sent a chill down Jess's spine. "If you're on their list, and you are, they know way more about you than you can imagine. You think they don't have all three of us under the glass? Think again. Among other things, those two in the back of the room have been keeping their eyes on us as part of their to-do list, another reason to sometimes come to this class."

Dan-el explained that the High Aces had a complex hierarchy. "Mostly, the ones that go to school are fulfilling a set of requirements to determine their worthiness. "The Low Aces, my name for them, serve as look-outs to determine who among potential buyers are legitimate and who might be in cahoots with the cops. If you search the ones at school, they won't have any product on them and nothing's in their lockers. You, Jen, or I couldn't score from them mainly 'cause we couldn't get a reference from wherever or whoever.

"Being in the gang doesn't mean you're rolling in money, but it pays better than just holding up a wall down in the projects, or waiting for some D-1 recruiter to discover you on the playground. And like we've all heard, membership is definitely earned by doing 'Dirty Deeds' whether it be sellin' business insurance, teaching respect as was done in your case, or to sell products ranging from weed to whips with no plates. Oh, they'll pull an occasional mugging or grab a melon if they can get away with it, but most of that's done by the older crack heads that roam the area. And, of course, there's the mandatory fights with other organizations in their never-ending quest to control their territory."

By now Jess was comfortable in speaking his mind with his friends; a mind that had evolved considerably in the past eight weeks. "I think a lot about getting even with the ones who gave me static. I rehearse in my mind what I would do if I met the one who stabbed me. I know from playing basketball with him that I'm faster, and if you'd teach me how to box, I'd kick his butt good."

Jen hadn't heard this kind of bravado from Jess before and registered a slight smile. She'd spent time thinking about him since they'd met, too. He was naïve but not backward; a study in progress that she found intriguing. She sensed a gentle, caring nature and noticed early-on his work ethic--all good qualities to her way of thinking. Jen couldn't help but notice that he was pretty much ill-at-ease in talking to her, and she was having fun watching and listening to his gaffes. Plus, he was pleasant to look at. Lately he seemed to open up a little bit, and now, here he was professing that he was going to beat up some High Ace.

"Be careful on that front, Dude," Dan-el said. "I act like I know all about them, and I do know they run pretty deep into guerilla-type tactics. Like I said, they're organized; you're not going to meet one just strolling down the street in front of your house lickin' on a Dairy Queen. You remember my comment about the hyenas? Where there's one there's two and where there's two, there's a pack. You catch one alone, another one is watchin' out for him. Even if what you say might happen, you think you're going to whup him 'cause you can box? You meet one of them on the street and if he doesn't recognize exactly who you are, that means you are a threat and he's got his hand on a weapon or he's got a plan for how he'll take you out. No, bro, give that idea up. Say you got the dude spotted and want to jump out of an alley or a doorway to blindside him. High Aces are on to those things. They don't walk close to walls where they can be ambushed. They're ever vigilant to what's comin' down the street at them and what's behind them. They're always with a plan and they all got phones. They don't even play basketball without posting guards around the playground. If you want retribution Jess, you better be patient until you're fully equipped for every contingency."

Jess, Surviving Normal

Now Jen spoke. "Jess, you said your sister was bullied not too long ago. Dan-el, could that have anything to do with Jess?"

"Don't know, girl. Like I said, Jess would be surprised learning what they know about him."

Jess interjected, "Okay, we have our meeting with Mr. Martin coming up in a few minutes. You think that the High Aces know what Mr. Martin is doing?"

Dan-el answered, "Most assuredly. That's the other reason you're a person of interest to them. So do the CG's and the Phalanxes who have their spies."

Jen, having lived in Trentsville her entire life, found his words unsettling to think she might be on their list. "Wow, I knew they were organized, but never this much. I know they're here and go with the flow from one class to the other to stay in the crowd. I've never given it much thought.

"You're on the basketball team and good for the neighborhood," Dan-el said, "That's why the Queens never bothered you, but rest assured that you're on their radar."

Taking a moment to reply, "I have a cousin going to Washington that had her money and phone taken last year. She was in the restroom with a pass during class time when three girls came in and grabbed her purse. One of them dumped it on the floor and kicked the contents all over while another one pushed her into a stall and advised her that 'she didn't see anything, or else.' My cousin lost her phone, too. Then a few weeks later she saw one of her attackers and clocked her from behind. She said that she hit that girl in the back of the head as hard as she could with a book and knocked her flat on her face. My cousin hasn't had any trouble since then."

Jess gave Dan-el a smug 'See' smile and nod.

"Good for her. She sounds bad enough for me to want to meet her."

"That could be arranged. I have no doubt she could tame Dan-el, the lion. Then too, why would I introduce her to some guy that wears sleeveless V-neck sweaters with a diamond pattern of attending students?"

****

The Ambassadors, as Mr. Martin called his student assemblage, were hearing how they could change both student decorum and the general attitude at Jefferson. This would be their third meeting, and the number of students attending had winnowed considerably. Of the original group, approximately 50 students remained agreeable to what they heard. Word spread that Mr. Martin was forming a group of enforcers to clean up the school which was not the case but fed the rumor mill and provoked the possibility of forthcoming confrontations. Jess felt like a poster child of sorts for the program so he felt obligated to attend, Jen had never questioned her participation despite Dan-el's caveats, and Dan-el was interested in the direction the program might take.

Mr. Martin informed them the remaining school year would be spent in organization and that was why he'd excluded seniors. Understandably, freshman couldn't participate being new to the school. Accordingly, Mr. Martin envisioned that a member's seniority would carry weight concerning how the student body would perceive the participants; high schools being prime examples of pecking orders. He'd expected some backlash, but not as much as there was if for no other reason than the student body thinking the program to be confrontational. Already, the Ambassadors-to-be were referred to as policemen, Nazis, and squealers to cite a few descriptors. It divided some friendships, created jealousy among some of those excluded and spurred rumors from the ridiculous to the sublime. Mr. Martin had worked hard to dispel that idea, but it wasn't going all that well for him. He knew the numbers of Ambassadors would have to be larger than those assembled in front of him to be effective. However, most of the students remaining were convinced that the program could work in spite of the naysaying.

"We can become an exemplary school, and we can prove it despite what anyone thinks. But like everything, it starts small and takes time. Sure, you will move on, maybe be gone before the Ambassadors do much of anything, but you will have started something. You have an opportunity to leave a legacy that speaks to others."

Stated simply, the group would function as a service fraternity dedicated to helping others in whatever need they might have. He didn't want them to be considered as police officers in the sense of enforcing school rules as much as having the Ambassadors reinforce rules by their presence. More than

Jess, Surviving Normal

anything, he wanted them to be outwardly helpful to others. Mr. Martin talked about students who may be handicapped or temporarily infirmed who needed assistance in getting to their lockers or issuing elevator passes that were normally off-limits to students. He had thought about Ambassador-administered tutoring. He would have pairs of Ambassadors walk the halls before and after school helping merely by their presence. Certain Ambassadors, probably the upper classmen, would have radios to communicate with the Central Office in case of a problem that might call for a school official or a resource officer. Ambassadors would have regular meetings, officers, faculty sponsorship, and would wear identifying armbands. They would receive a commendation for community service to their school that would become part of their transcript. As emissaries, they'd make the school a focused and safer place. The end product for Mr. Martin was for the student body to harmoniously absorb the Ambassadors.

As with any school organization, the Ambassadors would have to get an okay by convincing officials of their adherence to policy—whatever that was. A presentation involving Mr. Martin and two representatives from each grade was scheduled to make a presentation at an upcoming meeting of the Jefferson High School Governing Board. Dan-el was selected to be one of the sophomore representatives along with a girl that Jess didn't know. They practiced on questions such as: Would members of the Ambassadors appear as an elitist group with preferential treatment? How would the Ambassadors keep their intentions pure and not become a strong-armed contingent of bullies themselves? How could the Ambassadors not be seen as a challenge to other school functions, official and non-official?

Dan-el was skeptical. "We don't have snowball's chance in Hell of being sanctioned. They wouldn't allow the Boy Scouts to meet when I was a freshman; said they were sexist even though they allow girls. And here we're gonna wear armbands like Hitler's Youth? No way."

Still, they went ahead in preparing a plan complete with an objective, a rationale, a plan of action and how they would evaluate the effort. If all went well, they would present their charter one week before the next Governing Board meeting and get on the agenda.

"There is much that is good in this school," Mr. Martin said at one of their meetings. "We need to accentuate the fact that schools exist for several reasons, not all of which are comprised of learning facts, but also learning form and function. Learning of all types, from each other, and from failures and successes. A good example can impress another person. It's a fact that people treat others the same way they get treated. Whether in a classroom situation or in peer groups, we can be examples for others."

Abruptly stepping to the side of the lectern, Mr. Martin did a quick pivot on one foot, came to a stop and extended his arms. Breaking into a rap, he chanted and swayed, "Adduction and abduction are how we move, subjunction gets us in the mood. Now that's the function that defines the form and which rhymes with norm. Ambassadors normal without being formal and if we do well, our school will excel." Exaggerating the motion, Mr. Martin made like he was dusting off a shoulder, straightened up and returned to the lectern. Mocking an academic he cleared his throat and struck a stern pose, waiting. The reaction of the group was mixed, not knowing quite what to think.

He's not always so serious.

Dan-el whispered, "What a cornball! He from Iowa, too?"

Jen looked at Jess and rolled her eyes as Mr. Martin smiled, saying, "Sorry about that, Sometimes I just can't help myself."

Then continuing, "We have students at this school who represent a diversity unparalleled at any previous time in the history of the human race. There are students at this school with talents that make them capable of unimagined accomplishments. There are electronic geniuses in our midst; students who can direct a flow of electromagnetic waves to change the world. There are students with great mechanical ability who can improve on anything that has moving parts. And we have people who can put these two skills together and build robotic devices unimaginable to the geniuses of only a generation ago who sat in the same seats as you. We all know of those among us with athletic skills, and we enjoy the performances of the gifted musicians that we share space with as they command their instruments at will. We have dreamers; those abstract thinkers among us who need to be encouraged to act on their ideas. We have leaders; benevolent individuals who will step up and take responsibility for the benefit

Jess, Surviving Normal

of all people as they put the common good beyond their own egos. And we have a plethora of just everyday good people whose understanding and compassion make the world a better place. All they need to flourish are an opportunity to achieve in a safe place and a channel for their ideas. Have I left anyone in this room out? Have I left anyone in this school out?"

A girl in the back of the room started to clap her hands in approval. A few more followed until fifty-five attendees applauded for Mr. Martin as they stood in support.

I'm impressed. Mom should've heard that.

The undercurrent came from other sources, and the rumors encircling the Ambassadors also reached the administration. The Assistant Superintendent in charge of student affairs made a visit to Jefferson the very next day, and Mr. Martin was chastised for acting on his own without first submitting his plan to his superiors. He was told that he was wrong in the manner in which he implemented the Ambassadors and for jumping the chain of command. He had no right to go directly to either the school's Governing Board or the district's School Board.

Mr. Martin had indeed talked to the Principal prior to his meetings with students, but now, she said that she only "remembered a vague, rambling, *in situ* conversation that really hadn't made much sense." Mr. Martin's memory of that conversation was totally different.

****

The following Monday, students saw a new face, stern and with arms folded across his chest standing in the assistant principal's doorway watching students pass. When asked, knowing staff personnel were evasive and most of teachers were as surprised as the students. For the Ambassadors, they knew without being told that there would never be another meeting.

Dan-el's "Status quo" comment needed no explaining. "If you're looking for fairness, it ain't gonna happen 'round here."

Jen said, "I'm more disappointed over Mr. Martin than the Ambassadors never having a chance."

Jess brought the news home and Mom predictably spoke out in criticism of the system. As if it mattered, Dad explained that as a salaried employee, a person serves at the whim of those above him, commonly a board of individuals who give the organization the auspices of being open to ideas. But, in reality, boards were often puppets for powerful individuals within the organization. School boards fit this mold, but without tenure, employees could be present one day and gone the next. Teachers were a group of employees who could be terminated for a certain list of infractions, many of them good in their intent, but sometimes vindictive. The employees could appeal and ask their union to represent them, but administrators weren't teacher's union members.

"After all," Mr. Jemison said, "big business, like schools will often tell an employee that they have more lawyers on their side than the victim has on his or her side. Further, it is the right of an employer to dismiss an employee. Matter of fact, in some States an employer doesn't even need a reason to fire an employee. Mm-mm."

"Autonomously democratic," Jess said. "Once the people elect you, you get to do what you want in the position." Autonomous, another word he had picked up from Dan-el.

"Especially when they're using OPM, other people's money," Dad said.

Jess knew that coaches were fired for not winning and the administrators always mentioned something other than a losing record for the coach's release in trying to put a positive spin on everything. They'd say it wasn't a good fit or they wanted to go in a new direction when it was really the powerful individuals who made the decisions with their checkbook. It was an ugly part of sports that besmirched the very reason for athletic competition. For every winner, there were far more losers. Referring to the great John Wooden Jess could remember Coach Mercer lecturing how teams and players could be losers even though they won the game or achieved high individual acclaim. Accordingly, that was Mr. Martin's fate.

Rebecca Jemison vowed that she was going to get to the bottom of this "blatant, unjustified firing" if it took her all year. I'm going to find out and I'm going to go straight to the Central Office and demand to know as soon as they open their doors tomorrow morning."

"You go girl," Julianne said, bringing a bit of levity to the rest of the meal.

By doing so, Mrs. Jemison learned that Mr. Martin was dismissed from his position as a violation of the Trentsville Teacher's Contractual Agreement, Section three: Reasons for Employee Dismissal, Article Nine: Ongoing insubordination not consistent with the mission of the school district, and Article Eleven: Failure to utilize the chain of command to accomplish personal objectives not in the common interest of the District."

"So much bullshit," she said to her husband later. "Yes, he may have been a little over zealous in his desire to make the school a better place, but everything he did was for the good of the students. I can't accept the fact that he tried to make himself look good at the expense of someone else."

"You're right," Mr. Jemison said. "He was overly anxious to change something that was going downhill. There's that old army saying 'hurry up and wait' that carries over to education and even in corporate business. Change doesn't come overnight. Mr. Martin was wrong by wanting to do right. On the way to school this morning Jess was telling me why Coach Mercer wouldn't make a successful big-time college coach. Jess thought the two of them were a lot alike. I tried to point out that there *are* successful people in university coaching jobs who *are* very moral and up-front in everything they do. Anyway, we had a good discussion; I don't want Jess to draw some bad conclusions from all this."

Becky Jemison was somewhat reflective and admitted that her reaction was a little over the top, but consistent with who she was and what she stood for. "It just seems to me that Mr. Martin deserved better than he got. Craig, I've seen you maligned to your face, and it just made me so mad to watch you act like nothing happened; like nobody had insulted you or your race. I saw all those disparaging looks when we were dating, and I had to listen to face to-face lectures about the trouble we would have down the road as well as the injustice we would be doing to our children. You can defuse things better than I can. My blood just boils sometimes."

"That doesn't make you wrong, Becky. You and I have different perspectives; we approach things differently. You aren't afraid of a good fight. At times, I would like to fight, but learned that as a black person living in a white man's environment, I couldn't win. I made my fight an internal one because I could win that one. I had to hold my feelings in order to advance later.

Because of those times when race was a more volatile issue than it is today, we reacted differently.

"I told you what I'm seeing at the plant. The Mid-south is 25 years behind the northern states as far as racial issues go, but again, the demographics make each area what it is and what it has become. No, never feel badly about being a reactionary. You've made me the happiest person in the world every day since you first asked me for a date."

"Was that how it was? I must have had an off night and thought by saying yes to your pathetic ministrations; it would be good for a few laughs."

"And we're still laughing and loving each other 'real good,' And by the way, where did Julianne get her 'You go, girl' from?"

Chapter 5

Jess welcomed an earlier spring than he was accustomed to. It didn't take long for him to realize the brand of baseball was better than he expected and was pleasantly surprised when he was chosen as one of the sophomores that would oscillate between the JV and the varsity. If he didn't play in the varsity game, he would play in the JV game that followed. Impressed with Jess's control on the mound, the coach wanted him to pitch at the JV level and play first base for the varsity when the regular first baseman, also the ace of the staff, was pitching. Like basketball, the size of the school enlarged the talent pool; everyone in the lineup was solid at their position and exhibited a good understanding of the game. Consequently, Jess regarded himself fortunate to be in the starting lineup for the opening game, batting sixth.

Jefferson's baseball field was named for a former student, Archibald (Moonlight) Wright, who had gone on to play in the major leagues, albeit only one game. The field was enclosed within a concrete block structure built in the 1950's that players affectionately called "the Prison" because of its high walls. Once the home for a minor-league team, it featured a covered grandstand held up with exposed I-beams and easily the best field Jess had ever played on. Time had taken its toll on the structure itself, but the field was immaculately kept by a trio of volunteer groundskeepers who'd followed Jefferson baseball for over thirty years. To the crowd's delight, they led the crowd during the fifth inning stretch in singing, "Take Me Out to the Ballgame."

Concessions were sponsored by the Jefferson Letter Club, and with its nominal admission charge, there were few empty seats for many of the games. Making the experience complete for the fans, the public address system featured a polished announcer and plenty of between-inning music to ramp up the excitement. Jess's first game came on gorgeous spring day, and a raucous roar erupted from the crowd when the Jefferson team took the field to open the season. The contrast between Jefferson as an institution of learning and its sports teams was extraordinary.

Jess's pregame butterflies amounted to a couple hundred migrating monarchs fluttering around inside him. Jen and Dan-el were in the stands as well as Mom, Dad, and Julianne. He was glad that all his teammates were lined up between home and third and couldn't see his face during the National Anthem when a swell of pride caused his eyes to moisten. Life was good; his new school not so bad.

I wish Coach Mercer and some of the guys were here.

As the game started, for one of the few times in his life Jess hoped that the ball wouldn't come his way until he felt more comfortable. He could feel some muscles in his chest quivering rapidly as the pitcher went into his windup and delivered the first pitch of the season. "Strr-iiike," echoed through the venerable old stadium.

Working the count full, the lead-off hitter took a high pitch for ball four. Jess was tutored at practice in the fine art of holding a runner; the footwork, when to break away from the bag, and so on. Baseball was complicated with all its situational occurrences, and this one would likely call for the batter to bunt. Jess held the runner, positioning himself so he was an easy target in case of a pick-off attempt and obscuring himself from the runner. The pitcher went into his hesitation, looked at the batter who had shortened up on his bat, showing bunt. Jefferson's pitcher threw high and a little inside putting the ball in a difficult place to bunt. The batter pulled his bat back and took the pitch, ball one. Jess broke in on the pitch so he would be in a position to field the ball, and by leaving his base the second baseman ran over to cover first. Everyone on the infield moved in unison. On the second pitch, rather than bunting, the batter once again pulled the bat back and this time, took a little slap-swing hitting a slow roller past the charging, twisting Jess and just beyond the reach of the lefty pitcher whose follow-through took him toward third base. As the ball slowed, the second baseman ran over and scooped it up unable to make a play, putting runners on first and second with nobody out. Had Jess not been so quick to charge in, he could have possibly made a play on the grounder and started a double play. All possible because Jess was also a lefty and throwing to second was a much more natural move than it would have been for a right-hander. Returning to his position, the second baseman said, "That's okay, we'll get them next time." Jess felt mortified, but the butterflies were gone--on their way to "Costa Rita."

The next batter hit a medium fly ball to left field and the runners were unable to advance. The fourth man up cracked a sharp single to right that the fielder had to run down making it easy for the runner to score from second. It was 1-0 with one out and runners on first and third. The next batter hit a hard one-bouncer to the shortstop who threw to the second baseman for a force out. Going away from first, the second baseman had to make a snap throw to first in hopes of a double play. Jess was in position and as the ball came, he stretched and reached as far as he could just in time to nip the runner by a half-step for the third out. Jess's stretch had made the double play possible.

Jefferson High failed to score in the first and their defense held in the top of the second inning, the pitcher retiring the side with only eleven pitches. Jess was the second batter in the bottom of the second, coming to the plate with a situation much like the one his team faced in the first. The first batter of the inning singled and Jess was asked to lay down a sacrifice bunt to advance the runner. In a way, getting the bunt sign was a relief as the butterflies returned for an encore while he was in the on-deck circle. As he stepped into the batter's box, Jess knew several hundred fans were focused on him. The first pitch was low and away and reaching for it, Jess missed the ball completely.

Baseball has thousands of catch phrases such as "today's hero is tomorrow's goat" and naturally, reversible. So far Jess's mental error of rushing in too quickly on the bunt was compensated by his good play at first to complete the double play. Now, he shouldn't have tried to bunt a ball he couldn't have reached with baseball's proverbial ten-foot pole. Jess had a strike and everyone in the park knew he was up there to bunt; opposing fielders acting accordingly. Being a rather tense moment, the fans were pretty quiet as the pitcher readied for his next pitch when a resounding "C'mon Jess, whack it!" cut through the air from the stands that could have come from only one person, Dan-el White.

Jim Billman

Jess got the bat on the ball, but not quite as well as he wanted and the ball dribbled out in front of the plate about three feet, not far enough to give the runner much of a chance to make it to second without a play being made on him. However, as the catcher scooped up the ball and threw it beyond the reach of the shortstop, out into right-center. The Jefferson runner on first kept running and made it to third and Jess was safe at first. Runners on the corners, nobody out. The next batter worked the count to 3-1 and Jess saw the third base coach flash the hit-and-run sign. Jess would break for second base on the pitch and the batter would make every effort possible to put the ball in play. Not only did the batter put the ball in play as the pitch came right down the center of the plate, he singled to the gap between the outfielders, the ball sailing over the head of the shortstop. Seeing the ball in front of him, Jess rounded second and sprinted toward third. Approaching third, he saw the coach waving him on. Unable to turn on short notice made Jess's path to the plate longer, and in racing toward the plate he could see there would be a play. The catcher was in front of home and because of a new rule, wasn't allowed to block the advance of the runner. Jess veered to his right as the catcher caught the ball and began to pivot all in one motion. As this was happening, Jess purposely slid behind the plate so his body was out of reach of the catcher, but not so far that he couldn't touch home plate with his left hand. "Safe." The crowd roared.

The game ended with Jefferson winning 7-6. In his other at bats, Jess had struck out swinging and had tomahawked a low liner between the third baseman and the bag; not a pretty hit for a lefty batter, but still a double that would look as good as a line drive in the box score. Feeling a part of the team, Jess was pleased with his happenstance contributions to the victory. He would sit for the following junior varsity game unless there was an emergency.

Entering the Biology room the Monday following the game, Jess was greeted by Dan-el and Jen quietly chanting "MVP, MVP!" He was grateful for such good friends who'd reached out to accept him when he came to Jefferson. Both were smart and fun to be with at the end of each school day. Dan-el, the outspoken genius and natural leader, and Jen, a talented athlete and supportive friend in every sense of the word. After his rocky start, these friends made Jess's acclimation much easier. More comfortable now, earlier feelings of inadequacy were mostly left behind and thoughts of his past were less frequent. If anything, Jess wanted to be worthy of his friends.

The russet-haired Dan-el was living proof that a person could rise above strife. With broad shoulders atop a slim waist and standing 5' 9", he cut an imposing figure as he moved with a cat-like quickness and grace through the halls of Jefferson. His dark-framed "Clark Kent" glasses and high cheek bones hinted at the intelligence that rested within. Outspoken and funny in addition, Dan-el's natural magnetism drew people to him as a leader. He and Jen were fast friends ever since they met as first-day freshmen, meshing together as brother and sister.

Jen, as a member of the girls' basketball team also had her circle of friends and throughout grade school, she'd shown more interest in the rough and tumble games during recess. Her mother was a nurse and with two younger twin brothers, Jen lived in one of the many older, characteristic, two-story red brick row houses noted for being solidly built but boringly consistent in design. Jen's neighborhood was predominantly white, working class Scandinavian and Baltic families that clung to their heritage. In a way, her neighborhood was reminiscent of Jess's home town with its annual celebrations and activities. Also coincidental was the fact that Jen's father worked as a line supervisor at the same window plant as Dad and they knew each other.

Jen gave the impression that she "fit" whether in the classroom or on the basketball court. She wasn't flashy as she was steady; not as outgoing as she was nice to be near. Exuding that type of aura, her wholesomeness needed little cosmetic enhancement. Tall at 5'10", she generally kept her blond hair in a single braid that extended several inches below the nape of her neck. Her widely-set blue eyes and a small smattering of freckles around the bridge of her nose still caused a hypnotic effect on Jess. She didn't try to be glamorous in the way so many high school girls and as he got to know her, all thoughts of Courtney were laid to rest. Listening to her and watching her break into a smile always sent near-electric sensations through Jess's body.

Like Dan-el, she was a product of her surroundings and recognized obstacles were mere hurdles to be attacked along the way. Both of the mindset that to accomplish their career goals, scholarships would ease the pathway. Jess, conversely, had never considered things like this--college was just something he would do. Recognizing this, Dan-el had good-naturedly chided Jess, "You're just a victim of affluency."

Perhaps it was the consistency that Jess brought every day that attracted Dan-el and Jen to him. Growing more comfortable with his surroundings didn't persuade Jess to demonstrate a swag that many teen-age boys think important. He was a sensitive, thoughtful person who rarely made thoughtless remarks--troubling to him because he thought it made him a non-entity. But these traits were what endeared Jess to his friends. Dan-el and Jen liked him just like he was. Yes, he lacked self-confidence but that was just his newness. In a way, his addition made the triangle equilateral. Dan-el intuited this shortly after they met, and Jen, inhibited by the boy-girl thing, liked his courteous demeanor.

Jess didn't get to see Jen play basketball, but sports often served as the catalyst for something to talk about. She said that she enjoyed baseball and softball but worked at a neighborhood bakery/delicatessen during the week-ends and summer made evident when she brought day-olds to school. The owners, a long-time presence in Jen's neighborhood, were very supportive of her school activities yet she didn't want to ask too much of them. Plus, as she said, "I need the money."

Among school events, blatant gossiping, and sometimes even subject matter, the trio discovered quite by accident that biology was a vast, fascinating subject. The teacher, Mr. Hoffman, proved to be a wellspring of knowledge when engaged. Disenchanted with the apathy so many students showed, he sometimes spent the second hour of the block with one of the small, loosely-named study groups. One time he had mentioned to Jess, Jen and Dan-el that, "Biology should be a senior year course. It would be much more meaningful to the students if they had the basics of chemistry and physics before they took Biology, even General Biology like this class. For example, for blood to clot from a simple cut, it takes over a hundred chemical reactions in a matter of minutes to work to completion."

"Where can I get a look at them? You have a book I can see?" Dan-el asked.

"The majority of them involve organic chain reactions made possible by enzymes supplied by the body. One incomplete reaction because the enzyme isn't there or couldn't be manufactured can lead to the person becoming a hemophiliac—a bleeder. I have a medical journal of physiology that I'll bring for you to look at. It's pretty heavy stuff."

Dan-el, ever ready with a thoughtful response, commented. "That's great, Mr. Hoffman. You know, maybe school oughta be that way. Kids just shootin' the breeze 'bout what's goin' down and teachers come around like you're doing. That way, we'd learn about things that interest us. Teachers would fill in the blanks and tell us what we want to know, not what some 'suit' thinks we need."

Jen shared her opinion on the educational process, "The Information Age is over. I can find anything I want to know without being told or force-fed and then being measured with an exam. Give students a chance to ask about their dreams and have teachers there to help dreams become reality."

Hearing this, Mr. Hoffman's expression showed that he was amenable to what was being said. "One's education should be a period of enlightenment that allows questioning and fostering insight." Looking at Jess, "And what are your thoughts on the subject, Mr. Jemison?"

To be put at the center of the circle even among his closest friends, was intimidating but also escalating. Here was an opportunity for the quiet newbie to show his confidence in this new setting, to show that he did have opinions and that he could express his ideas. "'Teachers as facilitators' was something I heard my mom talk about that made a lot of sense. To me, teachers that outwardly try to impress students with how much they know are really telling us how much they don't know by stifling our time to think and to question outside of the box. I agree with what's being said, school should be a period of mutual discovery via experiment and sharing. Sure, being shown the right way is okay and often necessary, but students need time to fail on their own because you learn a lot more when you fail, just as long as you don't give up. Teachers as facilitators means that they guide, inspire, and make their knowledge available. Learning is communicating, and communicating is a two-way street. Teachers should listen to their student's needs as much as preaching about what they think the students need to know to be able to take a test. Yeah, it's important for us to be measured by test scores, but it's more important for the school because our test scores compositely make it look good or bad.

"Wow, the oracle has spoken," Dan-el said.

No one realized how prophetic Jess's words would become in their lives.

****

Friends during school, the three of them had yet to hang out. Friday afternoon punctuated with 'see you Monday,' which prompted Jess to wonder what his new friends did on Friday nights, Saturdays and their free times. In Iowa, school activities dominated, and it wasn't uncommon for students to spend fifty hours a week at school when classes, practices and activities were added together. Especially in the time since Title IX, schools had changed to become activity centers as classes and activities overlapped. Jess had been with the same group of kids since kindergarten and it was natural to spend weekends with the same pals as you went to school with.

Differences at Jefferson were not only the numbers of students, but cultural, societal, and even spatial. Whereas in Iowa, there was less of a problem with racial problems because the minority groups were so minor, they were welcomed. The predominantly white population 'felt good' to include others. Biracial, Jess had been around so long that he was just another kid—mostly. He learned in elementary school that if he made a big deal about his color, he could alienate himself pretty quickly.

Proximity in Iowa worked both ways; pettiness and jealousy often led to vindictiveness on one hand, and knitted tighter relationships on the other. If Jess wanted to do something with a friend in Iowa, he could walk or ride his bicycle. In Trentsville, he had yet to learn how friends navigated the city—he had little idea where Dan-el or Jen lived. The only thing Jess could figure out was that kids living in an area probably meant who they chose to be friends with.

All this troubled Jess as he sat at home watching television or playing a video game during the weekends. In New Holland, he was always with someone whether at a school or church function. Iowa was communal around those two visible institutions plus a third, which Jess was just starting to get involved with, the party life.

Jess, Surviving Normal

He decided to seek answers from his new friends. He also wanted to show them he wasn't as 'out of it' as he thought Dan-el and Jen found him. "What do you guys do on weekends."

Jen looked at him as to say, "What do you mean, what do we do?"

Nether Jen nor Dan-el responded. Jess felt pinned. "I don't know. Like we always did stuff in Iowa."

"You mean stuff like drugs, drinking, and copulating like a congress of monkeys?" Dan-el asked. "I read some statistics about you Hawkeyes, Party City."

"No, well kinda, I guess." Jess, thinking he wasn't going to back out, now. He'd started it and wanted to know. He noticed a little wince from Jen at Dan-el's comment.

"Dude, I live in the Projects. A couple thousand people with a disproportionate number of people under twenty-five packed into a group of buildings give me a choice like no other. I want to get stoned, drunk or laid, I don't have to work too hard at it."

Jess picked up on Dan-el's tone, thinking that his friend was playing 'the poor me' card as Dad called it. He still had a lot to learn about his friend.

"Life starts early. Did for me anyway." Dan-el said. "I was puking drunk when I was eight, pleasantly abused by an eighteen-year-old girl when I was twelve, and have yet to toke snort, or shoot. But I don't put that on where I live or how I live—it's just that there's a lot of choice for a dumb kid who hangs out with the wrong crowd."

Had Jess thought about it, what Dan-el said was fairly obvious.

"Sometimes I go over to St Sebastian's and spend time. Dance, eat their snacks and joke around. Always someone to talk with, something to poke fun at. You know how gregarious I am.

I guess I do.

It was Jen's turn, who'd sat quietly so far. "Dan-el's right about choices coming early in life. A girl I work with is thirty-three and already a grandmother. When I was in first grade, I asked Mom if I could use her lipstick because other girls were coming to school wearing makeup. The environment everywhere sends mixed messages to make young girls look desirable, sexy.

Then too, are the TV shows for kids where every adult is portrayed as stupid. We get conditioned to that way of thinking."

Jen wasn't finished, "What do I do? I snuck around, mostly in junior high—told lies about where I was going. I was too concerned about how to kiss when I was thirteen. My reputation was hurt by some mean girls saying that I hung around boys when all I really did was play sports. This year, I've been called a dyke because I'm a basketball player. To answer you, when I go out, I usually go with my cousin to the mall and/or to a movie. I've been on dates since high school, but not many."

Jess didn't particularly care to hear her say that.

"How about you, man? You a party hog?" Dan-el asked.

The tables had turned. It was Jess's turn. "I was just asking because Trentsville seems so remote even though it's a big city. Yeah, I know what beer tastes like, actually like it. Been buzzed, but never falling down drunk. It's hard to avoid and be popular. Guys on teams go out and celebrate. I was just getting into that when we moved."

Dan-el again, "So's you're looking to go out and hammer a few some weekend? We can do that."

"My mom has talked long and hard, even too long, about living in the day. Act your age, but she doesn't know what my age acts like. When my dad lived with us, we had wine a lot at our big meals. I was given a glass like the adults, no one ever said much about drinking it and getting drunk. I was told to sip, not drink it like a soda," Jen said.

I wasn't sure whether my question was answered or not.

****

Dan-el and Jess usually ate together at lunch following Geometry. Their lunch table was often full and Jess was able to meet more people that way. Other times, if one of the smaller, four-chair little square tables was vacant they would sit there and have more private conversations. Occasionally, Jen would join them. During one of the days of the last week of school, Jess mentioned the fact that he thought that Jen was a "pretty girl" and he wondered if she had a boyfriend. "She probably has a lot of guys chasing after her."

Jess, Surviving Normal

Dan-el laughed at 'pretty girl.' "Is that what you call them in Iowa? Jen is hot, man; she's like a holy vision. I was wondering when you'd bring up the subject of Jen's pulchritude."

Jess wasn't sure what the word meant, but was fairly sure there was more to come on the subject of Jen.

Dan-el looked at his friend and chuckled, "Sorry, I didn't mean to embarrass you. It's just that the chemistry between you two is apparent but you're both too bashful to make a move. Jen was askin' about you just a few days ago usin' the same 'by the way' tactics. Jeez, all the stuff I got on my plate, now I gotta play matchmaker, too."

"No shit? What did she say?"

"What did who say?" Jen had approached from behind just after Jess asked the question and set her tray on the table. Dan-el, of course, had seen her coming.

Dan-el kept his smile and shook his head like he couldn't believe what was happening, "Hey Jen, perfect timing. Ol' Jess here was just telling me about this chick he knows that's really getting to him. Said he's havin' erotic dreams and even sits in class with a stiffy just thinkin' about her. Now he's askin' me to talk to her cause he's such a weirdo."

"That's not true!" Jess moaned and buried his head in hands.

Jen remained standing with her tray and closed her eyes for a second before she caught on. "Really, and what did this chick say when you told her this?"

Dan-el asked, "What *DID* she say, Jen?" Dan-el had killed two birds with one stone in a way that only he could have done.

Dan-el passed the ball to Jess, "I love you man, but this moo-cowing between you two has gone on long enough. You gotta **say** somethin' to each other."

I'm sorry Jen, I didn't say those things Dan-el said, but...well...you know. And there's no girl like he said. Well, there is, but not like Skunk Breath said." Actually, Dan-el did him a favor, and about all he could do without sounding more foolish was to look at her with a sheepish grin.

Jen, wanting this little melodrama to end, "I don't know that I want to be a part of some of the things you said Dan-el, especially the part about causing Jess any physical discomfort. I guess I'll just sit down and eat my lunch."

The bell for fifth period was about to ring, making Jen eat quickly. Dan-el spoke up, "Another thingy. As you know, the first round of the Golden Gloves is Saturday down at the old Armory Building. I'd be honored to have my two favorite fans there to watch me get my heinie kicked. It starts at 7:00 with the lighter weights."

****

Much to Jess's chagrin, Mom and Dad made a major production out of his "date." He knew there'd be a thousand questions, and really hadn't expected his parents to be so supportive when he told them what they were planning. Mom sorted through his closet suggesting clothes he would look nice in. "Mom, chill. Dan-el said it's a dirty old gym." She settled on his newer pair of jeans, a conservative blue and white button-down and his Chuck Taylors. His protest had two syllables, "Mo-om."

"And wear socks." Dad thought Jess should take a small bouquet of flowers. "You only get one chance to make a first impression, Mm-mm."

The man has to be joking. Maybe I should borrow one of his old pocket protectors for my pencils. Socks? Hell, yes."

Jen met him at her door. She'd chosen a pair of grey shorts with a pale red tank. She had a small cross-body purse and looked resplendent in her gray-soled navy sneakers, sans socks. The weather was warm and Dan-el had warned them that the gym would be sweltering so there was no need for a jacket. He noticed that Jen had done something to make her eyes even more stunning than usual and her hair was no longer in the braid. She'd undergone a transformation from her from a demure beauty to a radiant beauty.

Don't stare! Sodom and Gomorrah. Lot's wife. I'll turn to a pillar of stone.! Jeez.

As statues, they stood in the doorway looking at each other. Stepping back to get a better appraisal, Gentleman Jess took Jen's hand and with a little half-bow said, "You look very nice like always." Unfortunately, what actually came out came out was, "You ready?" spoken by a Neanderthal with his knuckles dragging on the ground.

Jen, with a smile, stood in her glow looking back at her date and answered, "Why, thank you Mr. Jemison. You're very charming to say that." But like Jess, her response sounded more like, "Sure, let's go."

Both of them knew this 'date' arrangement would call for some adjustments from the way they were in school, but neither of them knows quite how to go about making the adjustment. Whereas Jess tended to worry himself into a stupor and go comatose, Jen would wait and see what developed and then react accordingly.

The gymnasium was the only building still standing from the time when the Armory had been a weapons and munitions storage facility. Still owned by the government, today it served as the headquarters for a National Guard unit as well as a last-choice community center for civic functions. No showpiece for the city, it set on a jutting piece of land extending out into a bend in the river protected by a U-shaped flood wall giving it a fort-like appearance.

The Police Athletic League of Greater Trentsville sponsored the Golden Gloves competition each spring. Dan-el had been in the PAL program since he was fourteen, and this would be the first time he could compete. A fighter's safety was paramount, requiring: parental permission for those under eighteen, a physician's approval, and protective headgear. Larger gloves were mandatory, too. Knockouts were very rare and refs quickly stopped a one-sided bout.

Participants came from clubs and gyms throughout the city and the surrounding areas. All told, over 200 young men and women, divided by weights, age and gender were scheduled to test their skills that evening and following afternoon. The Gloves were strictly an amateur event, but with the young aspirants having watched prize fights and the hoopla surrounding them, there was always a bit of posturing prior to the opening bell. The vast majority of the competitors entered with some knowledge of boxing; however, many of the matches rapidly turned into slugfests with the pugilists flaying at each other throwing roundhouses and overheads as long as they could endure. Often, bouts ended with both fighters bent over from exhaustion with their gloves resting on their knees unable to lift their arms. Two-minute rounds could seem like an eternity.

Jen and Jess waited on one of the rows of planks surrounding the ring that Dan-el would fight in. This was the first time Jess had been alone with a girl in something other than a school function—that he had told his parents about. They sat stiffly in the second row, Jess fully aware that his hip was touching Jen's despite the sparse crowd, ecstatic that she was the one that scooted over. He wanted to appear natural, which in reality he was, because he couldn't think of anything to say--his brain frozen inside the warm gym. As he often did when he was nervous or apprehensive, he rubbed the back of his head. "Excuse me" was the extent of his conversation when he bumped Jen's shoulder, reaching back. Feeling a drop of perspiration run down the inside of his arm made him even more distressed.

I wish this would get started. C'mon think. I've already said it was hot in here three times. Basketball. School. Cat videos. Politics. Not weather.

The best Jess could do was ask things like, (And he wasn't sure he'd actually done it or just imagined it.) "Do you ride the bus very often?" (Dad dropped him off at Jen's and the two of them had taken the city transit downtown.) "Did you think the Biology final was tough?" (The teacher had read the test to them the day before to help them get ready.) "I sure hope Dan-el wins." (Duh!)

Jen, looking around at the old building, carried the conversation. Looking at the exposed underside of the roof she saw that it was held up with barrel trusses made of iron and wondered if building codes needed an engineer's seal when they were made, probably in the forties.

"They look pretty flimsy to me," Jess said.

"They are until they're perpendicular with their primary stress."

"You know a lot about buildings," Jess almost said, 'for a girl,' but caught the fatal stereotype and mumbled something else complimentary about her knowledge of buildings. Then, "Barrel trusses, I can see where that name came from."

He was interested in this kind of stuff, too, and they sat on their plank-seats looking upward, at last engrossed in a lively conversation involving truss configuration, wood strengths vs. steel strengths, and spans.

I knew she liked all this. I could study engineering. Yeah.

. "They had plywood back when the building was built but didn't trust the glues because of the humidity differentials between the inside and the outside. That's why they used wooden tongue and groove boards that also fit the curvature better." Jen was a book of knowledge.

"And the tongues and grooves add lateral strength between the trusses and counter warping. Dad told me that you can be sure of two things in construction; wood will move and concrete will crack."

"Not bad for a boy." When Jen said it, it was funny. Their eyes met. Jess was in love.

Jen gave him a little nudge with her shoulder. "Sometime we might talk about concrete, the air-entrained kind. You'd never guess that I want to be an architect."

Time passed quickly and Jess was slightly disappointed when Dan-el's and his opponent's names were placed on the placard and Dan-el climbed into the ring.

This was a new experience for Jess—he'd talked with a girl without being confrontational. It was a breakthrough time, a conversation that required more than quips and grunts.

Their focus shifted. Dan-el had worked up a sweat before entering the ring, and anxiously kept moving his hands and feet awaiting the call to the center of the ring. "Fighters, remember to defend yourself at all times...blah, blah," Jess had asked Dan-el what the ref said to the fighters. "He tells us what he had for breakfast for all I hear."

Dan-el's weight division was from 147 to 155 pounds and being a novice meant the fighters had less than ten fights. Oddly, local and state rules for the Golden Gloves differed slightly until they were unified at the regional level. Dan-el's bout was the first one in his weight division, and having watched fighters at the lighter weights whose knees were bigger around than their thighs and whose boxing gloves looked like giant beehives at the end of broomsticks, Dan-el looked like a gladiator in comparison. With defined deltoids and developed pectorals glistening in the overhead lights, he looked every bit an experienced boxer. Waiting for the bell, he was hopping on both feet in anticipation with his eyes, chin and cheek bones hooded within his headgear. His mother and grandmother were also present, and having no problem finding his friends among the twenty or so spectators, he gave them a mock salute right after the bell rang and the two boxers met in the middle of the ring.

Dan-el was a student of boxing. He'd adopted former heavyweight champion Floyd Patterson's 'peek-a-boo' stance by holding both hands high to protect his head and by keeping his elbows down and in to guard his ribs. This stance took away one's power punches but allowed for numerous short, quick, wrist-twisting jabs that could quickly recover back to the defensive position. Moving in a complex choreograph, Dan-el danced and feinted as he'd step in to throw some jabs and quickly back out. He'd studied Mohamed Ali and Sugar Ray Leonard, watching only their feet as much as the old videos allowed. His conditioning was readily apparent as Jen and Jess watched him completely dismantle his opponent and take a unanimous 3-0 decision.

After congratulating their friend and still early in the evening, Jen suggested they walk along the River Park walkway, a part of downtown Trentsville's renovation project. As they walked, they heard a band playing and decided to sit on one of the benches and listen for a while. "Do you like to dance?" Jen asked, watching another couple.

"I'm not very good. I feel like everybody's watching me and then I lose the beat. I kinda' think I dance like one of those big long things that blow in the wind at used car lots."

With no pavilion, people just danced where they were while others walked by paying little attention. "Well, no one's watching you now. Let me show you how I learned. Rather than standing and facing me, get behind me and copy my moves until you pick up the rhythm. Dancing is just moving to the music. Put your hands on my hips"

Doing as Jen suggested, Jess was able to follow her movements and slowly released his inhibitions knowing that Jen wasn't watching him directly. After the song, Jen turned around and they danced facing each other with Jess a half-step behind. Ending their set with an oldie by Elvis, *Can't Help Falling in Love with You*, Jess was more experienced and holding Jen in his arms brought out a rush of new feelings. His body autonomically responding as well.

Back away.

Sitting on a bench awaiting the band, Jess was more relaxed and talked about his family and some of his Iowa adventures; his paper route and going to the State Fair. He was thoughtful enough to ask whether she would like a soda from the nearby concession stand. "Yes, whatever you get is fine. I'll stay here and keep our space."

The evening went from a slow start, to splendid, and then got better. They danced, laughed and thoroughly enjoyed each other. Later, walking to catch the transit back to Jen's drop-off, Jess called upon his new-found confidence and took Jen's hand in his.

I wish the evening would never end.

****

Dad arranged to pick Jess up at 10:30 at Jen's front stoop, the same way he dropped his son off earlier in the evening. Ahead of schedule as usual, Mr. Jemison had about fifteen minutes to waste. Thinking that he didn't want to be waiting for them he spotted a convenience store a block ahead rather than turning at the intersection that took him to Jen's. Trentsville's zoning ordinances allowed neighborhood businesses that made it rather unique. Like Bob's Market, this little store wasn't more than two blocks from Jen's. *I'll give Jen and Jess a few minutes alone to say good-night. I'm thirsty anyway. I don't want to appear over-protective.*

Meanwhile, Jen and Jess were past sharing their observations of Dan-el's impressive skill in the ring and were talking freely about whatever came to mind—equally contributing. Arriving in front of Jen's house, Jess thanked Jen for going with him and Jen thanked Jess for taking her. And now, the moment he both dreaded and anticipated was upon them, "Dad must be a little late. He'll be here soon." Again, they agreed they both had a great time and with neither having anything else to say, the moment became even more awkward. After a pause, Jess mustered the courage to do what he had wanted to do all evening—he leaned closer and kissed her tenderly, tentatively. Afterward, they looked at each other, Jen smiled and they kissed again, this time Jen leaning into Jess and the kiss lasted for a longer time.

I wish Dad has a flat tire.

Remembering that thought, the "I wish" would never pass from Jess's lips again as long as he lived.

As Mr. Jemison stood in front of the coolers deciding what to buy, several rows of ceiling lights darkened and he heard the clerk call out, "Closing time, everybody out."

Kind of a bossy tone for a business serving the public Mr. Jemison thought to himself.

He was the last person in line when he paid for his drink and exited the building. Stepping away from the door, he saw several cross-shaped, bright white flashes coming from an open window of a speeding car. Neither could he react nor did he register the sound of the two of the eight raking rounds from the bump-stock modified AR-15 traveling at over 700 feet per second that struck him, one in his left hand holding his caffeine-free soda and the other in the center of his chest.

****

Jen and Jess, lost in their world, watched and heard the ambulance as it raced through the same intersection less than five minutes later. The nearness of the noise to the Steffen's home brought Mrs. Steffen to the window where she saw her daughter and Jess standing on the front stoop watching the flashes of light from the ambulance bouncing off the houses and street. Close, it was apparent to her that it was at the convenience store. Random, indistinguishable sounds echoed from the commotion as they stood in wonderment. Jen, concern in her voice, asked her mom, "Do you suppose that crackling noise was gunfire?"

She hadn't heard. "Gunfire!?"

First one and then another police car, sirens blaring rushed down the thoroughfare.

Mrs. Steffen ushered Jen and Jess into the house saying, "Jess why don't you wait for your Dad inside, I'm going to put on a housecoat and go see if there is anything I can do to help. Jen, keep your brothers in the house if they come downstairs. I don't like the feel of this."

Stay inside!

Waiting ten minutes or so, both Jen and Jess tense but not saying much and still holding hands, the twins now downstairs groggy from being awakened amid the drone of yet another siren, Jess realized Dad should have arrived. Questioning. "Jen, Dad should be here by now." Now past 10:30. Always punctual. Senses alerted, Jess with a terrible thought.

Jess, Surviving Normal

A silent scream. "Dad!"

He immediately grabbed his phone and called Mom letting the phone ring, hoping she would answer before going to message. After five rings, her voice drowsy, "Jess, hasn't your Dad picked you up yet?"

"Mom!" All he could say. He knew! The feeling powerful, sucking away his breath.

No time to explain. Panic-struck, Jess hurriedly gave his phone to Jen. As the phone was being transferred between them, it fell on the terrazzo floor of the foyer disconnecting the call. Jess was already through the doorway and down the steps.

No!

Later, when recalling the sequence of events, Jess would not remember running toward the lights of the police vehicles gathered at the convenience store. Nor seeing his mother and Julianne arrive.

Mr. Jemison was pronounced dead by the EMT's soon after they arrived at the scene; efforts at resuscitation failing. An innocent victim of a drive-by shooting. When Mom got there, her husband's corpse rested on a gurney in the rear of the ambulance. Seeing him, she screamed and collapsed to her knees on the concrete, keening. Julianne, crying loudly and hugging her mom's shoulder, her feet alternately up and down in place. Devastated beyond reproach. Jess, in shock, sat on the curb in front of the store with head down, his hands over his face, sobbing uncontrollably.

A police sergeant would later describe the incident, telling the three that this street of the city was "managed" and in all probability the store refused to pay for services. "Or it could have been from a group from another place in town. We'll keep looking, ma'am. This should never have happened."

Never. Should. Have. Happened.

Still not fully composed, Rebecca Jemison screamed at the police officer as she looked at her husband's blanketed body in the ambulance. "Can't you do anything to stop this type of thing before it happens? MY HUSBAND IS DEAD! And you stand there and prattle! What good will catching someone do for my husband, my kids, me? Ruthless, lawless gangs run the streets extorting businesses and murdering innocent people. "STOP IT,

STOP IT!" she repeatedly struck the heels of her hands on his chest, out of control.

With his regrets and attempting to calm her continuing, she realized what she was doing and leaned, crying into the embrace the officer. In his right hand, he held a bedroom slipper that Craig Jemison had worn on his way to pick up his son.

Why?

The next two weeks were a blur. Outbursts of anger, disbelief, and questioning accompanied the crying, heartbreak, and sorrow. Mr. Jemison's remains were taken back to Iowa for his funeral service and interment. His mother, brother and his wife, and his sister came from Chicago, and another sister and her husband from Denver. Iowa was his home—where he'd married for life and where his children were born.

Information scant beyond his obituary, stories swirled throughout the area. Iowa had murders and people died violently, but random killings were virtually remote in the minds of the local people. Here was a kind, compassionate man ripped in life from his family for no understandable reason other than another person's act of violence. One person supreme over another because of an instrument—a weapon of human destruction.

Tongues wagged.

"Such a nice family. Was it because he was, uh, black?"

"Probably drug related." "I told Craig that he shouldn't move."

"Those cities are a war zone. Worse than Afghanistan."

"I don't know what the world is coming to."

"End times."

Most of them not realizing that the per capita murder rate in the entire State of Iowa was very close to Trentsville's. A clergywoman told her congregation, "This could happen anywhere; this is everywhere. Jesus's message of love and compassion toward others is on the wrong side of the tipping point with rampant stubbornness and selfishness justifiable in so many minds."

Helpless to know what to say or do, friends and acquaintances turned out to support the grief-stricken family. The empathy helped relieve Jess's sorrow as his family slogged through the process of saying good-bye to their husband and father.

"We're so sorry."

"If I can do anything, let me know."

"He was a good man."

"He will be missed."

Others, their grief apparent, had no words; aren't any.

The condolences helped, yet they kept the Jemison's in the moment.

Following the funeral Mass, the cemetery rites, and the meal in the church basement put on by the good ladies of the Altar and Rosary Society, the family went to Mee-maw's house. Later, as the front door closed behind the last mourner it was just them—Mee-maw, Mom, Julianne, and Jess. The feeling of finality struck. Dad was gone. It wasn't a bad dream. There wasn't another dimension to jump into. Jess was left with a feeling of total helplessness. He rushed from the house to the backyard, leaned against the big old oak tree still supporting an old tire dangling from a rope, and cried inconsolably.

It is often said that no parent should suffer the loss of a child, but however horrid losing a child might be, it is equally catastrophic for children left without a parent. For Jess, it would have been easier for him to have never had a father in his life than to lose one as loving and attentive as the one he had. Children and young adults have little experience in coming to grips with the loss of loved ones.

Taught fairness, Jess and Julianne's father's death abruptly and callously usurped any further belief in that expectation. Stripped of Dad's unconditional love, their belief system, sense of security, and level of comfort was shattered in an instant, ultimately and forever gone. Now only a memory. Awash with no justifiable causality for a young mind to grasp, with no understanding praise to the Almighty for what had been given, and with no sense of going forward—the lack of fairness becomes the issue most troublesome.

Any sense of fairness abandoned me when Dad was killed. Why? Why? That was all my mind allowed, the single unanswerable question that stayed with me. People offered sympathy, so many tried to console us—all of them meaning well, but no one being able to address "why." Some mentioned God's will and several times I heard "God's ways being different from man's ways" but nothing helped. I was mad not only for how I was affected, but for all of us. What will we do without Dad? He and Mom tried so hard to do the right thing. I cursed to myself, to God, and at God. I sulked around the sympathizers and sought solitude whenever possible. Nothing helped. Why? Why?

Julianne and Jess would, over time, come to accept their father's death but they would always remember it from their perspective. For now, the only thing they knew was that their lives were minus a force. For Jess, at a crossroad of life, this was the single most defining event he would ever experience. And he knew it, would carry it with him, define him.

One person, a close friend of Mom and Dad's said something that stuck with me. He put his hands on my shoulders and looked at me straight on and said, "Jess, there will be better days." It didn't help much at the time; actually, what he said sounded pretty lame. But as I thought about it, "There will be better days" got more and more profound. Even to become a driving force in my life. If there were to be better days, I'd have to be the one to make it that way.

Shock of their loss was greatest in Julianne who hardly remembered her grandfather's passing. But she would recover the quickest. Jess became surly and played the tough guy outwardly, but cried himself to sleep every night in the solitude of his bedroom. His conscience would never let go of the blame he felt. Rebecca Jemison knew she had to remain strong for her children's sake, and so, she must carry her pain internally. Given the life she and her husband had forged, hers was the worst grief of all. Jess would never forget the vacuous look in his mom's eyes when she wasn't trying to hold everyone else together.

It occurred after standing around the hole in the cemetery that I made so much of the entire ordeal about me. What would happen to me? What would I have to do? This changes everything. Sure, those thoughts included Mom and Julianne, but were mostly about the unknown adjustments that I'd have to make.

And my guilt was always there. It was Dad whose life had been snuffed out. If I would have arranged to call Dad when we got to Jen's ... One second one way or another. My thoughts all over the place—my fault, all mine.

I chastised myself for being selfish. What did I really know about Dad, his thoughts and what he experienced when away from me? What did he think and do when he was my age? All I had really bothered about was how his guidance and parenting played into my life, always well intentioned, yet not received that way. In Biology class I talked about communicating, and I hadn't even made the effort to communicate with my own father. It was pure selfishness on my part. When did I ever ask for his ideas and thoughts? I was too self-centered to recognize what I was not doing. And now it was too late!

I dwelled on what I didn't do more than anything. That could never be repaired. No more chances. When did I ever thank him or look at him and say 'I love you?' Julianne did it all the time. Oh no, that would be too sappy for me.

****

There were decisions to be made—many of them. As they sat at Mee-maw's kitchen table the morning following Dad's burial, the ever-present box of tissues setting between them Mrs. Wilkerson asked her daughter whether she had given any thought to what she would do. "Rebecca, you're welcome to move back to Iowa and move in with me. You know that."

Mom said, "Yes. Thanks. I have to go back and settle Craig's dealings before I can give much thought to staying in Trentsville or moving back here. It'll take time."

Setting her cup of coffee on its saucer, Mee-maw said, "Whatever you decide, I can stay with you for a while, too."

Raising her head to look at her mother, "That might be good for the kids to have you around as they go through the transition. You know Jess is on the baseball team, and he's head over heels in love with a girl from school."

They were quiet for a moment until Mee-maw said, "I know how hard it was for him to leave here, and he's had such a tough time at school down there. Poor Jess. He gets so deeply involved in whatever he does."

They heard the noise from the other room as someone was coming down the stairs. "We'll talk about all this a little later," Mrs. Jemison said. A few seconds later, Jess walked into the kitchen. "Hello sleepy-head, I'm surprised that you stayed in bed so late."

Jim Billman

Chapter 6

Again, Jess had a sport disrupted, and by the time the family returned to Trentsville, Jess had missed five games. He couldn't expect the coach to reserve his spot any more than he could expect his game to be unaffected by the layoff. The most telling factor, however, was that Jess's heart wasn't into baseball and it showed during practices. The coach, a believer that fundamentals were the most important aspect baseball, wisely knew they paled in comparison to the fundamentals of humanity, and suggested that Jess stay with the junior varsity until he felt more like playing baseball. The guys on the team knew about Jess's misfortunes, first the knife attack and now the drive-by killing of his father, and offered their condolences variously: words, fist bumps, and pats on the shoulder. It was true that Jess had been accepted by the other players, but not into their inner circles--still the "new kid." As the season wound down, Jess's performance on the junior varsity was okay, but not spectacular. He sat on the bench as the varsity played their tournament games.

Both Jen and Dan-el held summer jobs yet remained steadfast in support of their friend. Jen wasn't sure where her relationship with Jess stood after their brief time as boyfriend-girlfriend. She felt blame, too; trickle-down blame, and with Jess back in Trentsville, she puzzled how he might regard her. She asked Dan-el to come with her the first time she planned to visit Jess only to hear Dan-el remark that he was just about to give her a call and suggest the same thing. Both expected him to be subdued but beyond that it was a guess.

Sprawling on the lawn furniture on the Jemison's deck while talking about anything that would keep Jess's mind off the tragedy, Dan-el told his friends about his job. He'd been hired as part of a grant program at the local university. He was on a crew that culled trees and pared scrub brush from wooded areas in order for the remaining trees to grow unencumbered by competition. "It also helps against fires." His specific duty was to clear the fallen trees and load the debris onto trucks that hauled it to a paper mill.

He mentioned the occasional snake they would discover and how someone would yell "Snake in the grass" and everybody would jump around like "cannibals around a boiling missionary." Dan-el's arms were scratched from the brambles and harsh grasses that were part of the undergrowth. "We're supposed to wear long sleeves, but it just gets too hot to wear heavy clothes all day." Considering the exhaustive work and the long days that left him very tired, Dan-el's presence proved that he was indeed a good friend.

Jen kept regular hours at the Deli where prepping the vegetables, cutting the fresh bread just right and stocking the condiment table kept her pretty busy. Another girl took care of the trash and bussing the tables, but when it got hectic, everyone did everything and Jen would be called to be the relief cashier. Although she loved the owners, the job was always hurry, hurry. When her shift was finished, she went home and took care of her brothers who were watched by an elderly neighbor lady they called Aunt Oley. Her brothers were too young and too ornery to be left alone. With all this, Jen had plenty of stories to share.

Jen's mother was helpful in picking up and returning Dan-el on the nights they visited. Expressing to her daughter that she wanted to offer her condolences to Jess's mom led to them becoming acquainted. The third time this happened, Mrs. Jemison suggested that she just stay rather than come back and forth. The twins, a year younger than Julianne, played school (Julianne the teacher), hide-and seek, and tormented anyone older than them. Mom was grateful for the diversion and the opportunity to learn more about Trentsville. Mrs. Steffen was the first person that Mom really got to know and could converse with since the move.

In this difficult time, there was a life lesson learned. Dad's loss created an irreplaceable void that had be filled one way or another; a precarious situation. Dan-el and Jen, unaware of what they were doing or the psychology within it, laid the foundation that would help fill the void for Jess. They couldn't replace what was lost, but they could lend their support through patience, presence, and that multi-faceted word, love. That's the prescription for grief.: be there, be patient, and share the aura we understand to be love. In acknowledging that things will never be the same for the aggrieved, it fell on Dan-el and Jen to guide Jess, not lead him, to acceptance. And they did exactly that.

Jess, Surviving Normal

Life's problems often create chasms and obscures the path ahead. In Jess's terms, it could be described as batting against a good pitcher—you never know what pitch he's going to throw. You can turn away from the pitch or step up. He accepted his friends' good intentions on his behalf, and his friendship with Dan-el and Jen grew over the summer vacation. Rocks that he could lean on.

I could describe my feelings better with emoticons than with words. I'd heard people say that they married their best friend. Not Mom and Dad, though. I think they became best friends after they got married. Makes more sense. Whatever, Jen and Dan-el were a good diversion for my sadness.

Thusly, Jess began the last part of the grieving process, acceptance. It doesn't diminish the loss, but rather, brings a person to the reality of coping with it.

****

To this point, Jen saw Jess as a nice guy, one who was polite and unassuming. And she'd been watching closely. Worthy of noting, he was conscientious from the clothes he wore to the respect he showed others. He lacked the skepticism and the 'so what' attitude of many of the guys she'd seen in her rough and tumble schoolyard games. Jess seemed different to her; an interesting challenge, but not in terms of making him a subordinate. She'd found that she could relax with Jess and that was something she'd never done with a date. Unlike Dan-el, she knew there would be strings attached with Jess—boyfriend-girlfriend strings. She entered the relationship with eyes wide open, and now, she had to contend with a not unexpected "What else can go wrong" attitude, hoping it was temporary. Since meeting him, Jess seemed to surround himself in antagonistic energies.

Jess was on a perpetual roller-coaster ride with his emotions. Sometimes he'd feel guilty and disrespectful to the memory of his father when he was enjoying time with her. Other times he was on a cloud with Jen. Of course, he couldn't help but wonder if Jen didn't agree to go out with him out of sympathy.

Why else would she go out with someone as boring and unexciting as me? I don't even know how to kiss.

Alone, on dates, they would often go to an early movie and then come back to Jen's house to watch some TV. Jen insisted that they would take turns paying for the evening, but the one paying got to choose the movie. "Chick-flicks one week and holocausts the next," Dan-el teased when he heard.

Without asking for her children's input, Mrs. Jemison decided the family would stay where they were. Her husband's supplemental life insurance policy from the window company was part of the employee benefit package and she applied its premium to their home loan. This would lower their payments each month to a much more manageable expenditure. "The other policy, your father's life insurance, will go into a trust fund for yours and Julianne's college. I've kept some out to help us until I can find work, but things are going to be pretty tight for a while, maybe longer." She didn't say, but she knew the trust fund wouldn't begin to cover the expense of one college education, let alone two.

"Whatever thoughts you had about getting your own car are going to have to go on hold." As if to add one more ill-timed occurrence, Jess had 'celebrated' his sixteenth birthday during the time they were back in Iowa for Dad's funeral.

With summer passing into July, the baseball season ended and the trio's conversations turned to the approaching school year. "Dude, football practice starts in two weeks, you gonna' try out for that too?" Dan-el asked. Jumping out of his lawn chair, striking the Heisman pose, "I played in middle school."

Jess answered, "I don't know, man. I like football, but there's so much competition for any of the teams at Jefferson. There's no way you can do three sports and be good in all of them. The other thing is the players at the varsity level pretty much begin the year knowing who is going to play what. Teams are already decided based on the last year. Even if I was Dallas Clark, I would take somebody else's position and have to go through all of that stuff again."

Jen said, "Even if I <u>were</u> Dallas Clark," not able to help herself.

"Who's Dallas Clark?" Dan-el asked.

Looking at Jen with a little twinkle, "He were an all-American tight end from Iowa that played for the Colts as a pro."

Jess, Surviving Normal

"Oh, that Dallas Clark. I must have lost my mind for a while." Jen snickered at Dan-el as he slapped himself on the forehead to jostle his memory.

Jen spoke up. "After what your friend did, Dan-el couldn't go out for football if he wanted. I'll bet he never told you this story, Jess. Dan-el was the quarterback on the middle school team and during one game, they were on the two-yard line, fourth down and our team behind 17-13. The coach called a time out and gave the play to Dan-el and the teams lined up ready to go. Well, Dan-el didn't like something he saw with the defense so he called an audible. Call it again Dan-el so Jess can hear what you said."

"I shouted out something like, Change of plans! We're going to McDonald's on three!"

"Go on Dan-el. Tell Jess what happened next."

"Hut one, Hut two, Hut two and half, Hut three. I got the ball and threw a pass to a wide receiver on the bounce before he crossed the line of scrimmage. If you throw a football straight at a person with a spiral the ball bounces like a basketball. Our wide receiver, Jamal, you know him, caught it on the bounce and acted like the ball was dead 'cause it hit the ground. The defense thought the same thing, but the ball wasn't dead at all. So, with everyone standing there, Jamal just waltzed nonchalantly across the goal acting like he was going to toss the ball to the ref. We won the game. 'Course I had to tell the ref that we were going to do a trick play beforehand so he wouldn't blow the ball dead."

"You really did that?" Jess asked.

"Yeah, but my coach wasn't very happy about it. Said I had a bad attitude. He didn't let me play in any more of the games. 'There was only one game left."

'Whoa? You won the game!"

Dan-el replied that he didn't know why, for sure. "I think I was supposed to run the play Coach called, and my audible made a mockery of the game or something like that. Jamal and I practiced that play over and over on our own just for a time like this. I guess I decided that football was too serious for me if you couldn't have fun playing it."

As Jess laughed, a memory crossed his mind, *"There will be better days."*

Jess voiced another reason for not going out for football. "You guys both work. I'm thinking I could get a job and help

Mom out. Plus, I feel like a slacker 'cause you always come to see me like I'm stricken or something. Guys, I'm okay now. I can deal with it," his throat constricting as he said it.

Dan-el, always ready with a suggestion, had an idea. "Jess, it's time you had a new experience. Why don't you hop the bus downtown, get off at 14th and Broad and meet me next Friday about five. I'll introduce you to my neighborhood and show you how the 'other half' lives. My Mom and Gramma have been wanting to see what a kid with corn silk stickin' out from under his hat looks like and this'll be a good time. Wear something so we can shoot a few hoops, too. You'll be safe, dude, remember I'm in a protective cloud. Plan to stay the night."

Jess said, "My Mom might not think it's a good idea." He immediately wished it hadn't come out like it did.

"Work on her. Tell her that I live there, for God's sake. We have inside plumbing and refrigerators and ranges and..."

"Okay, okay, I didn't mean it that way. My bad."

****

That Friday, Dan-el was waiting as Jess got off the City Transit. Dan-el hadn't been to his apartment yet, having just returned from his job. His jeans muddied from the previous night's rain, his long-sleeved shirt slung over his shoulder and the neck of his t-shirt distended from sweat. With a sweeping bow to his friend, Dan-el said, "Excusez moi, Monsieur, I lacked for the time to become my usual splendid self. Dan-el White at your service."

The Whites lived in a complex of five identical three-story buildings, each of which sported wings radiating in 120-degree directions from a centrally located commons area. Built in the late eighties, the forty-acre project had playgrounds and grassy areas permeated with a network of sidewalks. The buildings showed signs of wear, and the parking lots that ringed each triadic building in a semicircle hosted some clearly inoperative vehicles. Some old, tenements rife with graffiti were standing nearby, their ground-floor store fronts clearly absent of any recent commercial activity.

On the Wood's Park side of the street, there was activity everywhere. Kids running and old people hobbling. Not knowing what to expect, Jess got the impression that among the chaos there was order within the complex for the 2500 residents that called it home. He'd been leery about visiting, even a little scared from the way Dan-el painted the picture, but now the hodgepodge of people seemed crowded.

Sensing that, Dan-el said, "Relax yourself. We're people, like everybody else, "And to think, Mom, Gramma, and me are some of the few White people in the whole place."

Jess found the White's apartment to be meticulously tended and tastefully decorated although the public accesses in Dan-el's building were otherwise. The walls of the corridors were scuffed and the carpeting in the commons area showed wear. Had Jess taken the back stairway, he would have seen an area somewhat neglected with occasional holes punched through the drywall.

Just people, like everyone else.

Being later in the day, the commons of Dan-el's building was another hubbub of activity. A few groups, mostly teens, congregated together in spirited conversation. One such group greeted Dan-el and he led Jess to them. Jess recognized some of them from school and the others that he didn't know seemed pleased to meet him. A girl told him how handsome he was. "If you get tired of hangin' with Dan-el, I'll keep you company tonight." Amid the laughter that followed, Jess, as usual, felt his cheeks grow hot with a rush of embarrassment.

After a few minutes of teenage conviviality, Dan-el said he had to get going. "You know my Gramma and what she thinks about being late for supper." As they passed another group of men in their late teens and early twenties, Jess heard someone mumble, "White chocolate, I'm gonna' git me some."

"Don't pay them any attention, Jess," Dan-el said.

Dan-el explained, "The unwritten rules around here are pretty much like at school. Go where you're going and don't go gawking around 'less you catch the eye of someone who's offended. Not many people will take offense if you look at them and most of them would stop and talk if you wanted, but there's a faction that has a hard-on for everyone else, white or black. You won't see many Hispanics until you get to the other end of Broad."

"What about me? Is there a club for us Mulattos?"

"Yeah, it's called 'earth' and you have every right to be as proud of what you are as any person on it so don't go usin' that term around me. You're better than that, man."

Jim Billman

The White's apartment was on the third floor. A three-bedroom, bath and a half on the middle wing based on the layout of the main entrance. Constructed with train-style corridors, each unit was rectangular in shape, virtually as deep as they were long. Dan-el explained theirs was one of the larger apartments, and they may have to move once the Housing Authority realizes that Dan-el's brother no longer lived there. "But for now, each one of us has our own bedroom. Actually, Mom's been looking at moving into our own place if she can find a decent house at the right price—two things that don't go together."

Dan-el's mother was employed as a counselor for the Health Services Department of Trentsville and much of her time was spent with indigent single-parent families. She advised her clients of available assistance programs, helped them find jobs and daycare facilities doing whatever she could to help. Dan-el had described his mother as an ardent supporter for both equal and civil rights, and in meeting her, Jess could tell that she was a strong woman who was used to being in control.

Like Mom.

Dan-el's live-in grandmother tended the apartment and prepared most of the meals. Known as "The Guardian" for her vigilant patrol of the building and grounds, she was always reminding the residents to be responsible. "Pick up after yourself. Uh-uh, that's not the way to talk around here. Are you watching that child of yours? Hey kids, there's no screaming inside the building." Some saw her as a busybody.

Dan-el always minimized any questions concerning his father with a "don't know" or "can't say." Jess had heard Dan-el refer to his Gramma as Gramma White, but had never dwelled on his friend's lineage.

Dan-el would shower before eating, and Jess sat in the living room talking to Mrs. White. Gramma remained in the kitchen, a pleasant smell wafting through the apartment, "Hope you like pulled pork, baked beans and potato salad, young man," she said from the kitchen. "Understand I'm making two sandwiches for you, so you can't be bashful. No one goes away hungry from my table."

The evening news was on, barely loud enough to hear. At the commercial break, Mrs. White muted it and expressed her sadness over Dad then immediately apologized. "Oh, Honey, I'm sorry. I didn't mean to bring up something so sad. I want you to enjoy your time here. Dan-el thinks so much of your friendship; he's always going on about you."

"That's okay, Mrs. White." Jess felt his lower lip stiffen and his chin begin to quiver. "There's so much violence everywhere." He looked down at his lap, hoping that Mrs. White wouldn't notice his reaction.

Shifting the conversation without abandoning the subject, "Yes, the violence in the world today is out of control. Legislators pass laws that almost encourage people to carry guns. Why people need automatic weapons is beyond me. Second Amendment rights written in the Eighteenth Century don't apply to the Twenty-first Century. People stretch and twist their rights to fit their own selves."

The umpteen commercials over, she left the sound off and kept talking. "And speaking of rights, what about the right to work? Washington brags about low unemployment but here in Wood's Park we have high unemployment, over 100 working-age people that can't find jobs. And some aren't even counted as unemployed because they've been without work so long. They've given up hope. And to make it more difficult, many have no training, not even a good high school education. Then, like a job solves all the problems, getting paid peanuts is an insult to people who want to work. So, you have to wonder who they expect to come along and hire them. Dan-el's brother was one of them. He's incarcerated as Dan-el has probably told you."

"I'm sorry," Jess said, his facial tremor under control.

"He brought it on himself. Mom and I love him and do everything we can for him, but we don't love what he was. I suppose you can say John Terrill, Jon-el they call him, was coerced into the gang life, and you could argue that he was doing it to support his family, but he knew he was wrong all along. I can't buy into the 'can't see the forest for the trees excuse.'"

Jess didn't know what to say other than to sit on the couch and wag his head empathetically.

Again, "Honey, I didn't mean to start telling you this kind of thing. I just get carried away. I really wanted to tell you how welcome you are in our home and how much Dan-el thinks of you. You and the Steffen girl are his best friends."

"He's been a great friend to me, too, ma'am." Jess stammered, stroking the back of his head subconsciously.

Dan-el entered the room wiping his hair and stuck his head into the kitchen, "Supper ready?"

"Soon as you pick up that pile of dirty clothes that I know you left on the floor and make yourself presentable, we'll eat," Grandma said.

****

The following morning after breakfast, Jess thanked Mrs. White and her mom for their hospitality and gathered yesterday's clothes into his backpack. He and Dan-el had decided to shoot some hoops before Jess would take the city bus home. Just outside the building, they noticed a receptacle for cigarettes surrounded by discarded butts carelessly thrown down beside a trash can lying on its side with the top fallen away. "The animals must have been restless last night," Dan-el remarked, sounding apologetic.

The basketball playground featured four courts packed together in a cross-like shape with one end of each court near the end of the other three. Water fountains served each court at the conjoining ends and a single, small set of three-tiered bleachers complimented a single side of each court. The backboards were made of heavy Lucite and the rims were of the breakaway type that could withstand hard dunks. The rims were extremely rigid and balls were more prone to bounce awry than to allow players to "get the roll." Dan-el found a couple balls along the fence amid several empty cans of Red Bull and started to shoot at one of the far ends of a court where the players were engaged in a half-court game; three on three. Playing on the same court signified a challenge to play the winners of the current game.

Jess noticed that Dan-el had a slinging type of motion to his shot, but despite the style, his arching shots fell through the hoop with a fair consistency. Also, Dan-el's ambidexterity was apparent as he shot close shots with either hand. "The way this works is the loser of the game gets off and we play the winner…if they do it the way they're supposed to. Sometimes the losers don't leave and sometimes the winners decide to quit. We'll ask one of the guys on the losing team to play with us unless someone else comes along and wants to be with us."

Jess was a little nervous as they continued to shoot while they waited. Dan-el explained the Wood's Park half court street rules. "Half court is really more popular because it doesn't favor the faster players who can run away from the big butts. Half court play keeps the ball in the scoring team's possession. Fouls are supposed to be called by the offender but that depends on a lot of other stuff so expect it to be rough. A foul gives the ball to the offended team meaning that in a close game no one wants to give up the ball. The 'No fighting' signs on the fences means that there are fights, but mostly it's just shoving and bullshitting. Each basket counts as one and a team has to win by two. Fifteen baskets are the usual game. Questions?"

Jess was pretty familiar with street ball and knew that each rec court had its own house rules.

"You guys need a third player for your challenge?" a voice came from behind them. Jess turned to see no one else but Jen approaching, a baseball cap on her head and dressed in light sweats against the cool of the morning.

"I was wondering if you'd make it, girl," Dan-el said, a wide smile stretching across his face. "Surprise, Jess!"

"I switched shifts, and got the morning off. Didn't want to miss playing with you two."

Jen picked up a loose ball and spent a moment with some ball exercises to loosen up before she went over to the basket and proceeded to do a put-back drill. She stood a few feet to the right and in front of the basket and shot a bank shot with her right hand, grabbed the ball as it fell through the net and did the same with her left hand moving to the other side of the basket. Working her hips and body she repetitively completed several cycles of the right-left drill. As Dan-el and Jess continued to watch, Jen went about ten feet away from the basket and shot little jumpers from close in. She'd shoot, get her rebound, shoot and continue with the close-in shots. She didn't miss very often. "Don't you two want to get ready for our game or do you expect me to carry the load?"

Although Jen could hardly be mistaken for a boy, her hat, worn in the style covered most of her hair, her face was without any make-up, and the loose sweat suit hid her figure. There was nothing but gracefulness in her movements as she aligned her legs and body at a right angle to her shoulders that smoothly coordinated her body with each shot. Her slightly aquiline nose,

Jim Billman

the nose that made her face distinctly beautiful to Jess, distracted considerably from her appearing as just another guy basketball player. Jess couldn't help but notice how Jen got her body under the ball when she shot rather than the way a lot of girls did, their bodies more behind the ball as they pushed the ball.

"Next," the three of them heard a call from the other end of the court.

Dan-el knew the players on the team they were about to play. "What'cha got for us Dan-el, a couple recruits from uptown? Ain't seen you two afore."

"Friends from school," Dan-el said as he picked up the ball. "Challengers get first out. Game on."

"Hey, at least let us get a drink before we kick your butts.'"

A few minutes later, Dan-el passed the ball inbounds to Jen, she took a couple dribbles as Jess positioned himself on the other side of the backcourt and Dan-el headed to the low post, off-side. Jen passed to Jess coming to the ball and headed to the base line corner to set a screen. Dan-el instinctively came toward the ball and Jess fed an overhead pass to him in the high post. Taking the pass, Dan-el pivoted to face the basket, made a jab step to back the defender up and skipped a bounce pass to Jen, now waiting in the opposite corner after her pick. With a little bend of her knees to get the proper spring, she knocked down a fifteen-footer. According to the playground rules, the ball stayed with Dan-el's team who passed it in this time. Jess inbounded to Dan-el to Jen and in to Jess on the elbow. Not bothering to protect the ball as he brought it up from his waist, one of the opponents stripped the ball away and passed it back out front. After the other team scored three goals, Jess grabbed a rebound and the ball stayed with them for five baskets before Dan-el bounced the ball off Jen's foot with an errant pass. The teams see-sawed back and forth and with the score 14-11, Jess intercepted a pass, went back on top of the key to Dan-el who scored for the win—a hilarious bankshot from 21 feet.

"Played it that way."

Another threesome had the challenge and was waiting while Dan-el, Jen and Jess went to get some water. After getting rid of the jitters, Jess had found his groove and was playing comfortably doing something he thoroughly enjoyed. As a player,

Jess, Surviving Normal

Jen was a pleasant surprise, showing both athleticism and grit against the supposedly stronger and faster males. If she had shown any weakness in her game, it would have been her unfamiliarity with the slightly larger ball. Dan-el, although raw, did a nice job orchestrating the team as a passer. Jess couldn't help but notice that every player on the court dribbled like the ball was an extension of their body—much more so than kids in Iowa. After a quick drink of water and congratulating each other, they saw that their next opponents were older and more formidable than their first one. This team featured two players who were taller than Jess and seemed to have brought a contingency.

"Oh-oh, that one guy is on scholarship to a D-1 school and the other tall guy played on the city championship 3 v 3 team last year. They're good," Dan-el informed Jen and Jess.

"Who's the third? You know him?" Jess asked.

"You don't want to know him. He's a High Ace. Big shot. I'll guard him."

In looking at the High Ace, Jess felt himself take in a sharp breath, almost freezing in place. *That's him! He's the one from gym class.* Not knowing what to do, Jess walked off to the side of the court and knelt down as if to re-tie his shoelaces in order to think. A rush of adrenaline surging through his body and his mind racing back to the dressing room, Jess began to hyperventilate and his vision occluding exactly like last January. Dan-el noticed Jess's behavior and rushed over to see what was wrong with his friend. Jen followed.

The dissonant moment passing, Jess remembered disavowing knowing who attacked him from the time he was in the hospital through the meetings with school officials and detectives. Even now, he was only moderately sure that the High Ace, no more than thirty feet away, was the same person that stabbed him; the guy was certainly the same one who was playing against him in gym class. But. in reality, Jess had not seen his attacker. He only heard a few words and briefly sensed his smell. *And the tattoo!* The squiggly tat Jess had seen in the instant before blacking out.

He'd kept the information about his attacker to himself and absolutely didn't want to be recognized by the High Ace or any of his cronies. Oddly enough, as these thoughts peaked, Jess discovered that he was more angry than afraid, more fearful for

125

Dan-el and Jen than for himself. In fact, he had been waiting for both confirmation and confrontation with this person—now was ideal for the former, the latter, the confrontation, would be later.

"You look like you saw a ghost," Dan-el said.

Jen, too, saw his pallor.

"Guys, I didn't know these a-holes were going to ruin our game by showin' up."

"Well, if we don't play, it'll look like we're afraid of them," Jess heard himself say.

"Which we are," Jen said. "It's not the ones playing us, but the ones with them.

"But we won't show it so let's do it," Jess again.

As they walked out on the court, the High Ace player taunted them with: What's it you call your team? One of you is chocolate, one is caramel and one is white chocolate. Must be the Hershey Bars cause you gonna be so easy to lick." This was followed with hoots of laughter and more jeers by those others in attendance.

Able to play above Dan-el, Jen and Jess, the challengers reeled off eight straight baskets before Jess grabbed a deep carom from a missed long-ball. The game was much rougher this time with a lot of pushing without any acknowledgement of fouls. The High Ace player stiff-armed Dan-el on one play to get him out of the way then lost the ball to a Jen takeaway. After the exchange, the High Ace guarded Jen and flagrantly moved into her path as she was driving toward the basket and knocked her backward, off her feet. "Charging," he called out and grabbed the ball. As Jen fell, she scuffed the heel of her left palm on the green acrylic-coated asphalt.

Finding how light she was led the High Ace to see Jen was a girl. Hey white girl, you got no biz'ness in this game. Shit, this here's for mens who can play. Bin wonderin' why you dressed that way, you tryin' to hide yo goods. Get your tail offa my court. Fact is, none of you's worth fuckin' with."

"Yeah, right. A real pleasure," Dan-el said sarcastically. "You can have the court."

There was no other trio challenging for the court and no one was shooting at the other basket. "Now you can play with yourselves."

Hearing Dan-el's tone more than his innuendo, the seven or so spectators the challengers brought with them stood up in support as if they might be needed. Dan-el had shown his courage to the High Ace, but the last thing he wanted was to get into a fight with Jen and Jess involved. Now, it might be difficult to avoid.

Still, the High Ace felt a need to show his superiority. "You Jon-el's little brother, and we let you be out of respect fo' him. But don't go pushin' it. Accidents happens all the time." He kept looking at Dan-el. "Hear you a boxer, too. That give you a license to bring these two onto my turf to show them how you so bad? You bad all right, bad in the head." He gave Dan-el a two-handed push that backed Dan-el away, the second time he'd shoved Dan-el.

Jess watched with his head lowered throughout trying unsuccessfully to control the shivering from the adrenaline coursing through his body. It had only taken a second for the situation to go south. Glancing over at Jen, Jess saw that she had torn the knee out of her polyester sweat pants and a lock of hair had worked itself out from under her hat. Her hand had apparently been scuffed badly enough to bleed. As the summer sun rose higher, she wanted nothing more than to walk away from this scene.

The High Ace wasn't finished with his lesson. "First mistake, you bring this Oreo and this cracker thinkin' it'll be cool. Second, you assume somethin' you don't know nothin' about. Take your circus act off this court and go over and sit on the kiddie toys. Jesus!"

Obviously, the voice of the group was careful despite all the bravado he was showing. Although shoving Dan-el was chancy, he'd been careful not to get too close or provoke Dan-el to the point that he would strike out in self-defense. Dan-el was an unknown quantity and, although it could cost him his life if he were to hit the High Ace, it would also be humiliating to his leadership to be threatened by a sixteen-year-old boy, boxing talent or not.

Dan-el took the opportunity to get away without endangering his friends and made no further remark in leaving the court. Walking to the bus stop, Jess asked, "Who was the guy giving you grief?

"That was Apex, the grand and glorious pontiff of the High Aces. It was nice that you two got to make his acquaintance," Dan-el said, his teeth clenched

"He goes to Jefferson?" Jess asked, wiping away sweat and acting nonchalantly with his question.

"Maybe five years or so ago. Why?"

Jess couldn't keep what he knew from his friends any longer. "He was the one who stabbed me in the locker room, the guy I played against in the Phys Ed class." His disclosure causing an immediate reaction with both Dan-el and Jen.

"You said you didn't know who did it," Jen said. "He looks like he's a lot older, how could he have been in school?"

Dan-el knew the answer. "He doesn't go to school, but that doesn't mean he couldn't get in the school and dress out for P.E. The teacher probably didn't notice or didn't want to notice, and Apex could a had someone open a door for him. It happens. I see High Aces inside the school every so often."

Jess sounded credulous, "But like that, in a class?"

"You're the one who saw him. Apex fashions himself as quite a street player. I should have made up some story to get you guys away from there. Shoulda' picked up on your reaction, too. My bad."

"No wonder that gang terrorizes the school."

"Anyway, Jess, how're you so sure that it was Apex? And why didn't you blow the whistle on the rat way back when?

"We played basketball, I remembered how he moved. I looked at him. And I smelled him and saw his tattoo"

"Smelled him? Was he that rank?" Now away from the basketball area, Dan-el was smiling.

"Right before I was knifed, I caught the smell of some kind of cologne or something. I forgot all about it until I smelled it a few minutes ago. That, and I saw his tattoo in the shower room when he grabbed me from behind."

Jen: "Wow, do you think he recognized you?"

Dan-el broke in, "Whether he did or not, he's not going to admit it in front of us. They're like I've been telling you-all—smart and together. High Aces know what went down in the locker room 'cause there would have been several of them there at the time. What happened was as far as it went. You insulted Apex, he paid you back. Simple as that. Event forgotten; you know what I'm saying?"

They'd reached the bus stop. Seeing the approaching bus, Jess remarked, "He might think we're even, but I don't." Understanding Jess, Dan-el said, "So, you said that you didn't recognize Apex 'cause you want to exact revenge, your way."

"Jess, you can't win against them. Give it up," Jen advised.

"Yeah, at least for now; plus, I've been working on this long-time Jess." Then giving Jess and Jen quick hugs, Dan-el said, "Thanks man, for coming down to my domain. You too, Jen. And when're you going to bring that cousin of yours around?

Getting on the bus with Jen made me think of Dad.

Jess learned two things from the encounter. The first was that he was totally overmatched in the basketball game. The player Dan-el said was a potential D-1 recruit was not only taller, but was also quicker and more fluid than anyone Jess had ever played against. The second guy on their team was equally fast as well as having the ability to play above the rim although not much taller than Jess. To see how effortlessly those two played was a humbling experience for Jess. The second thing Jess learned was who assaulted him—who was accountable.

****

With Mom's self-induced positivity the driving force, the Jemison's carried on as best they could without their patriarch. Mom's message was simple, "We have to." Mee-maw had stayed throughout much of the summer and recently returned to her home. Mom was grateful for her help but could tell that Mee-maw missed her friends and her home. It was time to move on, and both recognized that her presence was a reminder of Dad.

Julianne spent some time with a children's counselor that helped children handle major trauma and was working through her grief. Jess was fine when he was with his friends, but at home he had times when he was wrapped in a shell, still without closure. Blaming himself for what happened, the solitary Jess second-guessed himself thinking that if he hadn't done this or that, Dad would still be alive. Guilt-ridden, he carried a sullenness not unlike the one he had when Granddad had died. His refusal of grievance therapy only made it worse.

How can God let this happen if he loves us so much?
He knew that without his Dad to help, life would be much more difficult, and he often carried on imaginative conversations with his Dad. Although Mom was the alpha dog in his and Julianne's life, Dad was the enabler that made it all happen. Slowly, the ensuing weeks brought a recognition to Jess that matters weren't going to reverse, and with that acceptance came the final awakening. The way he felt was self-induced; he had to get out of his funk and be 'himself.' Mom and Julianne needed him. Recognizing that the wound would never fully close, Jess came to the realization that despair was like quitting so he must go forward.

My thoughts were jumbled. I justified myself by thinking what I did was right. I didn't realize how shallow, how incomplete I really was. I thought I was having a conversation with God when I was really talking with the devil.

Other things, too. I often thought about avenging myself with Apex, but I had no plan how to accomplish it. I could imagine beating him to a pulp, but in reality, he was probably more capable as a fighter. And, even if I did retaliate, then what?

A few years ago, when I had my paper route I would walk along with the bundle of papers under my arm and visualize myself from above as if I were two people discussing what they saw. It wasn't out-of-body as much as being a kind of game. I thought it was just kid stuff and I stopped having the feeling when I started high school. I was more in control of myself as a kid than as a teen--definitely.

After Mee-maw left and the countless matters concerning her husband's death were slowly getting settled, Mrs. Jemison decided that it was time to return to her job at the window company. She hoped a job would ease her mind about her children's mental health, and her own thoughts of justice. Her circumstances weren't much different than her son's except that she sought a lawful conviction, and Jess wanted a street reprisal.

Unfortunately, returning to work brought another setback. With global posturing and trade agreements in disarray, the country was cast in the throes of a building and remodeling downturn which effected a hiring freeze at the window company. Consequently, Mom's promised position was pigeon-holed and put on hold. Not being able to wait for 'who knows how long,' she sought employment elsewhere. Her years of experience in human resources and her Business Management degree, assets she hoped would speak positively for a position, worked oppositely. Most available jobs were of the entry level, lower paying variety. The one job she was offered would make it impossible for her to manage the household with any modicum of consistency or predictability—the exact thing she couldn't let happen.

Discouraged, she was at a loss. She could manage the family needs for a while, telling herself that no matter what, she would not touch her kids' college funds. She decided that she needed a job that would let her work from home, but there always seemed to be a catch from copywriting to online sales. She registered with an employment company as a temporary employee and was hired interviewing job applicants for a help desk organization. It was right up her alley and paid okay. It lasted for three weeks.

Counseling helped Julianne understand her father's death. She was taught that although the pain was great in her heart, a person must accept the fact that things will not be like they were before Dad's death. The counselor asked her to use her memories of good times with Dad, and to try to live her life knowing that Dad was proud of her. Also, that Mom and Jess needed her to help them, and accept this new responsibility to make the world a better place. Doing this, Julianne matured emotionally beyond her years; beyond her brother during his darkest times.

****

Football was not on Jess or Dan-el's radar. By winning his division at the Golden Gloves Dan-el was eligible to move up to amateur boxing's next rung, the Open Class. Boxing was his passion and Dan-el spent several evenings each week at the Armory under the tutelage of a detective on the Trentsville Police Department, a former All-Navy champion. For Jess, stories about the 'win at all costs' attitude of the football coach soured his desire.

"I just don't believe in this in your face stuff," he told Jen right before he remembered that acting that way was probably why he got stabbed.

I really didn't get in his face, but I didn't have to take advantage of him the way I did.

Additionally, his comment about finding a part time job was made in all seriousness, but. trying to match a job to his schedule with or without football proved difficult. For every possibility he came up with, there was a reason why it wouldn't work. Knowing that Jen had a part time job haunted him.

Sharing this one evening, Mom suggested that he write a nice letter of introduction and distribute copies of them to residents of his neighborhood. "Offer services for odd jobs. You never know what might come of it. If it goes well, you can make it fit your schedule. You're conscientious, and we have all the tools you'll need in the garage."

"But, what can I do? I don't know anything."

"You might be surprised what you can do; what you can figure out as you go."

Julianne wasn't going to be denied her proverbial two cents worth of advice. "Google it and watch YouTube. Duh!" Her comment was rewarded with two reproving looks.

"Well, he hasn't been very nice to me. He just goes into his room and shuts his door ever since..." She didn't say, "Dad died."

After a moment, a moment with everyone remembering the man who should still be in the chair at the other end of the table, Julianne sobbed, "I'm sorry."

"That's okay, dear. Dad's with us in spirit now. I'm sure that he's happy to know we all took a minute to think of him and how much we love him."

Later, in his room during study time Jess thought Mom's idea was sound. *Mom can help me write a letter and we can put it in an envelope making it look official. I'll walk around and put it in the newspaper hole or someplace where people can find it. If people want me to do something I don't know how to do, I'll just tell them. And Julianne might be right about Googling DIY's. I remember Dad looking at how to change a taillight bulb on the car and telling us how much money he saved.*

Much to his surprise, it worked. His first job was cleaning out a garage which led to constructing some shelves and learning as he worked. He looked at the shelves in his own garage and how they were put together, made a materials list for the owner and rounded up Dad's battery-powered drill and circular saw. He remembered what he'd seen Dad do and watched You Tube.

Forgetting to add screws on his list, Jess had to scour through Dad's stuff and luckily found a half-box of deck screws that worked just fine.

Before attacking the job, he asked Mom to come outside and supervise him with the saw. She didn't know much more than he did, but together, they figured out how to make it work and he practiced on old pieces of wood around the garage until he felt comfortable with it. "I didn't want to cut off a finger. Safety first is my motto," he bragged, holding up has hand and counting.

"Right. Don't shoot your eye out, Ralphie."

Mom sure says some strange things.

The plan worked even better because the Jemison's lived in a neighborhood consisting mostly of middle-aged and retired people. Knowing of his father's death and recognizing that Jess was trying to help his family played on their empathies, and several times, he was hired to work with a homeowner. The fact that Jess was polite, respectful, and steady meant a lot as word spread.

When the jobs were finished, Jess was honest. "It took me longer than it should have. I'm not very experienced, Mrs. Schwartz. A couple dollars would be fine." By accident, he learned that by asking for a figure way below what he'd really like to be paid, he was often offered a sum notably above his expectations. Lesson number two also came quite by chance. When Jess gently refused to accept the lofty amount and gave some of it back, he assured that he would have future work at the Schwartz's. He learned a lot in those few weeks.

By the time school started, Jess was quite busy cleaning out garages and basements, making simple repairs to houses, and so on. People would call him, tell him what they needed, and Jess would give them a time when he would be there. Autumn meant a lot of yard work and whatever notion the Jemison's previously had concerning snooty neighbors seemed to have disappeared, whether out of sympathy or because word spread that Jess's work was first-rate. Slowly, even the skeptics were won over and accepted the Jemison's presence. "Family is a lot more important than skin color," the man who only weeks ago vowed to sell his house when he first saw the Jemison family moving in.

"Yep, even an old coot like you can change his mind," his friend replied over the fence.

Jim Billman

****

Whereas Jess had been quite naïve last year when he walked into Jefferson High School and felt its vastness; it's exuding indifference, the events since that time had changed him. He now found it almost dutiful to work himself to exhaustion with the neighborhood jobs. And, to add to that. he'd stepped up his physical conditioning program. Things he formerly cared for had waned; for example, he barely missed football that had been a staple in his life only a year ago.

On the Friday afternoon before school started, the "Hersheys" (they actually liked the name) met in front of the school to pick up their books and get their locker assignments, a process designed to avoid the confusion of doing it on Monday. Sports physicals were also offered at this time. As Dan-el said, "They look at your vital signs. It's only vital to them that you're alive. nothing more. Just blink and you're good to go."

"I wish it was that way for girls, Jen said. Some of them are real letches the way they look at us and paw around."

During the summer vacation, vandals had thrown red paint on the worn limestone stair steps that led to one of the main entrances of the school. Much of it still remained having soaked into the porous rock, casting a desultory mood on the three of them. Dan-el, paraphrasing Dante's *The Inferno*, said "Abandon all hope ye who enter this portal."

Same old school; welcome to noir headquarters. What's a few more wounds?

The three Juniors-to-be, each encouraged by a concerned mother, had opted to take as many Advanced Placement courses as possible. Their schedules showed them together in Chemistry, English Literature and Western Civilization. "Two white people courses" Dan-el jokingly said. "Maybe I'll learn why the world is so screwed up."

"There won't be much time to hang out unless we're studying," Jen said.

"But we'll be together," Jess added right before he wished he wouldn't have said it.

What an idiot.

Passing through the portico that led to the dark corridors of the school, Jess was an inch taller, he now stood six feet two and was ten pounds heavier than the last time he was in the school.

Not only had he grown physically, but he had acclimated to who, what, when and where he was. He had done other unique things in the transition, too. For one, he'd watched numerous tutorials on the art of self-defense since his most recent encounter with the leader of the High Aces. Keeping his vows to make reparation for being attacked by Apex and finding the shooter of his father drove him forward because both of these perpetrators had a price to pay. But he was still without any kind of plan, he was without the 'how' to get it done.

When he once again asked about boxing, Dan-el immediately understood Jess's motive. "Dude, we've been down this road. Don't get any ideas about doing what I think you're thinking. Even if you know how to box, that's not going to help very much. Apex knows things that you don't; things like where he's got his gun. Don't fool yourself 'cause you'll be endin' up on a slab down at the morgue. I mean it; don't go there."

I knew that Dan-el's advice was sound. I also knew that seeking revenge went against what I was taught. But regardless of what I knew, it just wasn't right to know that this stuff went on. Gangs and bullying were wrong and it occupied my thoughts when I was alone. Anyway, it's easier to ask for forgiveness than to ask for permission. I ought to try that with Jen. Big talk. When I asked Dan-el about boxing, it was to be able to stand up for myself as much as for getting revenge. Yeah right! Tell yourself that. Dad's killing was something that never should have happened—not just to him, but to anyone, anywhere. My mind was a jumble without a clear pathway.

Another of Jess's concerns was Jen. Their relationship had progressed through the summer. By now, she knew Jess's mom, Mee-maw and Julianne. Jen had accepted Jess's grieving, his anger and retreat without trying to mend the tear in his heart. She too, had gone through emotional distress when her parents divorced and, in this way, could relate to Jess.

Seeing Dan-el and Jen this summer made me realize the quality of friends I had. I already was in love with Jen, but her presence changed my feelings into a different, unexplainably deeper love. I felt something come over me like a rush of air, like I was open from within and the feeling wrapped around me. A hunger inside, but not like being hungry. This was a new kind of love to me, not family love. Yet the joy also brought back the feeling of loss for Dad. When I introduced Dan-el and Jen to Mom and Mee-maw, I felt so much pride that I wanted to say that Jen was going to be my wife and Dan-el would be with me forever.

Jess's and Jen's relationship had grown physically through the summer, too. Good-night kisses and holding hands had progressed as they became more familiar in each other's company. All of which led to exploratory touching that kindled desires to go farther. Jen was worldlier in her experiences with boys than Jess was with girls, but both of them had questions about the affection they felt—what came next? They knew that what came naturally may not be in their best interest at this time in their lives, and they spent much of their private conversations to that end. They argued, not so much for and against anything as they tried to define such things as commitment and resolution that sometimes led to separating for the evening in a huff. Then later, when they made up, the desires were even greater than before. For Jess, his original infatuation with Jen had mushroomed to a familiarity that he never knew could exist between two people. All this, plus the awareness of each other's sexual proclivities had carried them beyond innocent goodnight kisses.

Being sixteen and possessing probationary driver's licenses opened new vistas for their wishes to be together, too. Trentsville's state allowed sixteen-year-olds to drive to and from a job or a school activity. Other restrictions also existed for new drivers to qualify; grades, attendance records, number of passengers, etc. It was pretty difficult for the law to be enforced except for the number of passengers which was obvious, and it created more problems than it solved. Dan-el was in no hurry to drive on his own, which Jess couldn't understand because a driver's license was a rite of passage in Iowa.

"What do I need a car for? Busses, taxis, trains and my feet take me wherever I want to go. I'm a member of the next great generation and you wait and see how many cars are around in thirty years," Dan-el scolded.

Jen's father had taught her how to drive, but the Steffen's only car was needed by Mrs. Steffen. She took it in stride; sure, she wanted to be able to get a license, but she didn't stress over it. Jen had always walked to Jefferson due to its proximity, and because Jess lived farther away, he'd been driven to school by his father. Jess was the one who could really benefit most with this type of permit. Fortunately, the suggestion that he could ride the school bus never came up.

Much to Jess's surprise, one evening Mom told him that she had decided rather than selling Dad's pickup truck, Jess could have it. Of course, that had come with a boatload of its own conditions, the main one being fiduciary. For one thing, the limited parking permits available for students at Jefferson were expensive, and along with operating costs, they were going to be Jess's responsibility. Of course, Mom let Jess know how much their insurance would go up with Jess driving. When Mrs. Steffen offered space in their small driveway on school days, Jess thought his fortunes to really be on the upswing. He could leave the truck there and make the eight-or-so block walk to school with Jen. A win-win if there'd ever been one.

The first day of school traditionally featured a school-wide awards assembly. Dan-el and Jen had Homeroom together and Jess's Homeroom was down the hall nearer the auditorium. It was strange that Dan-el was not at their usual meeting place before school. "Busses must be running late. First day, so a lot more riders getting on," Jen offered.

Dan-el was going to receive a citation for being a member of the Academic Debate Team, Jen would be recognized as a member of the girls' basketball team, and Jess would stand when the baseball team was mentioned. The program moved pretty quickly with the administration cognizant of the attention span of assembled students. Jefferson had not had a pep rally or whole-school programs for several years because a few rowdies consistently ruined it for the rest of the students. When everyone was called for the assembly, Jess waited outside the Homeroom door for Jen and Dan-el so the three of them could sit together.

With his friends' approaching, Jess saw that Dan-el had a bandage above his left eye and a white wrap was visible below his elbow. Dan-el was walking with a limp and helped along by Jen was having a difficult time keeping up with the flow of passing students. He greeted Jess with a grimaced smile through a split lower lip with his usual 'Hey, man.'

"Some of my 'pals' caught me off guard Saturday night and introduced me to their Uncle Knuckles. They didn't play by the Marquees of Queensbury's rules. Said I needed an attitude adjustment, among other things. Don't worry, I'm okay." Having sustained numerous contusions and a greenstick fracture to his ulna, it would take a few weeks before Dan-el was healed.

There has to be something I can do. Next, it'll be Jen.

He stewed to himself through most of the assembly. By now, Jess was accustomed to Jefferson and was just another of the multitude of students racing from class to class, from room to room with his agenda. New classes and new teachers quickly became ritualistic and hum-drum. Tripe heard in the hallways was quick to discern and criticize the changes in staff—which new teachers were 'hot,' which ones wouldn't last the semester, and on and on. Teacher turnover was large each year at Jefferson, and students were quick to notice the security force returned from last year plus one. Paradoxically, despite the changes, everything was still the same.

One evening after raking leaves in Mrs. Lewis's yard, Jess headed for the kitchen to get a drink of water when he heard Mom talking on her phone with Mee-maw. Rather than coming into the room upon hearing her say, "being at a crossroad," he stayed on the other side of the doorway and listened, thinking he might be hearing something about himself. He was right, and it was upsetting to hear that Mom presumed to know what he was going through. Mom spoke of "big decisions" that faced him. He listened further.

He heard Mom say "I worry whether he will continue to see me as the authority figure without Craig's support. I don't want to become a nagging thorn in his side." Mee-maw said something Jess couldn't hear. Then Mom said both the kids have been exceptional and that she couldn't ask for anything more, but losing their dad could change a person without their knowing it. Then he heard something like, 'little by little.' Followed by, "Jess has sullen moods and is pretty headstrong, as you know."

Deciding that eavesdropping wasn't his way, Jess made his presence known with a fake cough and by walking through the doorway. Mom was turned away and Jess watched as she dabbed a tissue to her cheek listening to Mee-maw. It always was sad to hear her speak of Dad in the past.

Still not noticing Jess, Mom said, "If I asked, he would tell me that he will continue as before, and in his mind, that's what he believes. None of us know over the long run how we'll be affected consciously or subconsciously. It worries me because all

Jess, Surviving Normal

this turmoil has come at such a mixed-up time. Physically he's a grown man, but emotionally he is in a state of flux, not understanding. He runs hot and cold, rarely a mix."

Jess retreated back into the next room, Mee-maw said something back. "That's what I mean, Mom. It's hard to tell whether he's being strong or being defiant? It's natural to cry. He and Craig were so close."

Hearing Julianne coming from down the hall, Jess walked farther into the kitchen and Mom turned to see him this time. Appearing as suddenly as he did, Mom had a look of wonderment when Jess opened the refrigerator door and rummaged through it, looking for nothing in particular.

I thought a long time about their conversation. It made me think of men that I admired. Dad, of course, was always there to lend support and encouragement. Coach Mercer was hard but fair, always challenging me to do better. I liked Mr. Martin and how he was trying to make school a better place, but I really never got to know him. Granddad Wilkerson always talked to me as an adult; he told me that he did it on purpose. Always with a ton of questions that made me think. And now, none of them are here.

When I was eight years old, Granddad often asked things like, "Are you listening? Jess, do you understand what I'm saying?" I'd always say yes, but I didn't always understand. Kids learn to say what grown-ups want to hear. I still hear Granddad, especially in dreams and times when I'm wondering about things. Granddad told me several times to take things slow and let them come to me. He'd tell me stuff and then say "think about it." Now I realize there're problems that I can solve and problems that I can't. That's true because there's always other things happening; other things to consider.

My first basketball game in seventh grade was terrible. Bad passes and just playing so poorly the coach took me out in the second quarter. Later, I asked Granddad how athletes have time to think in a game like basketball, and he said that time wasn't always a factor when a choice had to be made. In times of extreme danger, and in falling in love decisions are made beforehand. Sports are like that. The good ballplayers know what to do before they do it and that's why they're good. And after they have success in their sport, it becomes intuitive. He told me that soldiers train for the same reason so they'll know how to act in times of life-

threatening danger. "I loved your grandmother before I ever saw her, and when I finally met her, I knew that she was the one for me." I didn't really believe him, maybe because I didn't understand the point he was making. He told me that things don't always go your way, but planning pays dividends far more than just letting things come to you and then reacting to them. He told me about the five P's: Prior planning prevents piss poor performance.

"That's six "P's," Granddad.
"You listened, Pea-nut," he punned.
I heard it said that if you have no plan, you'll flounder through life. I've floundered so far. Sure, I thought I knew what I wanted, but I had no plan how to achieve it. And now, my guilt notwithstanding, my stabbing and Dad's killing were growing more remote in my memory.

****

School work demanded a lot of time during Jess's junior year. Advanced Placement classes offered both credit toward high school graduation and college credit, but the latter depended on whether a student could pass the standardized final exam. Some students opted out of the collegiate exams, preferring to simply earn the high school's credit and have a head start on the courses as future college students. Others, in the time-honored teen tradition, took an AP course because their friends did. Jess was skeptical, but with the Dan-el and Jen who wanted the college credit, it was only logical to take the final tests.

I thought of Coach Mercer's advice, first and foremost we compete against ourselves to do better. it isn't a matter of trying to beat an opponent into submission. That kind of logic made it necessary to take the final, and if I didn't get a high-enough score, at least I tried. Dad would have said, "Nothing ventured, nothing accomplished, mm-mm." Maybe two or three more clichés after that.

Reading assignments were extensive and time-consuming making their three-way group discussions invaluable. Jen was the catalyst and kept them on task. Everything seemed to come so easy to Dan-el that he sometimes got distracted. Success in AP classes depended a lot on meeting the benchmarks along the way and regrettably, the devotion and energy of the teacher. A

Jess, Surviving Normal

timesaving measure that helped with the reading assignments was to decide who matched the best with the assignment, and that person actually read the book or did the work. That same person would then share his or her copy of notes and present it to the other two. Jen and Dan-el both were very analytical and mathematically-oriented and helped Jess tremendously in Chemistry. His strong suit was Western Civilization and thanks to Mom's urgings, he'd already read some of the extraneous assignments; classics that came with the course.

During the first few weeks of the semester, I don't know how I would have found time for football had I decided to participate.

The summer had proven to be a difficult one for Jess to work on basketball skills. He'd managed to maintain his conditioning regimen through it all, and the physical exertion helped find a release for his anger. Baseball also helped, and sometimes those playing both JV and varsity would get together and play some street basketball. Coach had 'Open Gyms' scheduled on certain nights and players could come in and play pick-up games, but Jess missed more of them than he attended. So much of the time after Dad's death was now just a blur to him and basketball was like baseball—mechanical, reactive.

As basketball season approached, the positive thing was that I was more comfortable with school and work. I was anxious for the season to start.

Jen and Dan-el nicknamed him "the thinker" because he was naturally quiet and gave the impression of being studious. "Introverts need love, too," Jess reminded them.

Mom was correct, in many ways Jess was an adult and a kid. Mom may not have realized it, but Jess worked at not being as temperamental as he once was. Rather than reacting to a something, he tried to put it in context. To not find fault or take offense.

Dad once tossed me a German conundrum by asking whether people got "old too soon or smart too late?"

Jess knew that much of the advice people gave him was solid. Mrs. White was funny; she said, "I give you pearls of wisdom to rattle around in your cathedral of a cranium and what you do with them is up to you." The Hersheys found each of their moms agreed, the Junior year would be a most significant time;

one they would remember forever. Surprisingly, because he thought his friends to be so grounded, Jess discovered times when Dan-el and Jen struggled for a belief system, too. Often, mindless that they were doing so, they cooperatively melded their life issues with the help of each other without realizing how beneficial their closeness was. They were of one opinion on things like social justice and moral consciousness, and respectfully opposed on political resolution. More than once, they mentioned their moms to be much the same and that each was without a father in their home, yet each thrived because of the other two. The Hershey's: Chocolate, Vanilla, and Oreo.

I knew Oreos weren't made by Hershey, but so what? I liked it.

Jen did what Dan-el asked and introduced him to her cousin that sparked a fast-growing relationship. Now, away from school, they'd become a foursome, double-dating and enjoying fun times as a balanced group. Also, the 'safety in numbers' thing took away some of the pressure that Jen and Jess were feeling about sex. Because Jess's driver's permit was restricted until he was seventeen, they went places via the transit system or one of their parents would transport them to place where they'd meet.

Although Jen's cousin, Ella, and Dan-el hit it off from the start, her parents' archaic notions weren't very approving of the racial difference they represented. The most nervous Jess ever saw his friend was when he went to Ella's house planning to have a sit-down talk with her parents concerning both his lineage and intentions. Asked what he was going to say, "Whatever comes to mind at the time. I can't go in with a prepared speech, that's for sure."

Dan-el was the smartest, most charismatic individual I had ever met. If it would ever come to something like marriage, Ella's parents couldn't have a better son-in-law, but that was my opinion and too far in the future.

Chapter 7

As basketball season approached, Jen dropped a coolly-phrased "let's just be friends" bomb on a Thursday afternoon walking back to her house two days before Jefferson's Homecoming dance. Jess couldn't believe his ears when she said a senior guy that was in another of her classes asked her, and it got her thinking "about things." Jess didn't know him and was devastated for words, for what to do. Silent, he looked straight ahead not yet recognizing the severity in taking Jen for granted by not specifically asking her to the dance. "Anyway, we didn't have any plans and I thought it would be fun," she explained coyly.

She'll like this dick-head. She'll kiss him and find out how bad I am at everything. Damnit!

Too late. Jess learned a lesson especially since the girl's name was Jen Steffen. Sure, the four of them had talked about the dance. Dan-el and Ella were going and Jess assumed that they would double-date as usual. He and Dan-el had even talked about getting corsages for their dates in the tradition from years past.

This was a new hurt for Jess. He loved Jen and thought she returned that love. He'd hinted but never said the three little words thinking in some subverted way that she should be the one to say it--the dominant male syndrome passed on from the days of the cave man and perpetuated throughout history. Jess felt badly enough to consider going out to the garage and killing himself. He was crushed; life had no meaning.

Loser!

Mom saw it immediately and didn't need an explanation—a textbook case of the 'wounded male ego.' She listened and provided the proverbial shoulder Jess needed to lean on. She knew the answer, could give him advice but would let Jess figure it out by himself. "Things always look better in the morning," Mom said.

"Yeah, I might go from being the world's biggest loser to being the second biggest loser."

Jess didn't go to school the next day. Dan-el's texts went unanswered. Saturday morning after the dance, he didn't come down for breakfast and went straight to work cleaning out a basement and rearranging a garage packed so full that a person couldn't walk from the front to the back of it without moving things. Home for lunch, he made life miserable for Mom and Julianne. Mom left him alone, but Julianne took offense at his surliness and it wasn't long until they had declared war on each other. Jess didn't go to church that Sunday with Mom and Julianne.

Alone with his thoughts, he gradually recognized his oversight in not actually, verbally asking Jen to the dance. And the tennis match in his mind was on: he should have been more sensitive, but Jen was way too sensitive. How was he supposed to know what to do—she was his first girlfriend and Jen probably had thousands of dates with thousands of boys. The tennis ball made a bad bounce with that thought. He didn't even think about other girls while Jen was probably sneaking around with other boys. He was true; she was fickle. He was sad; she was dancing.

Jess was deep in his funk when Granddad Wilkerson visited his thoughts, "Why so glum, chum? Blindsided, were you? Taken by surprise because you didn't prepare. Think ahead. On the baseball field of life, you struck out looking—not looking in your case. So, you have no reaction except to mope around and feel sorry for yourself. The game isn't over; you'll get another at bat unless you take yourself out of the game."

I knew better than to think Granddad was controlling my thoughts but there they were.

"What's next? Are you going to add Jen to your list of people you're going to exact revenge on? Let me see, the list is growing. First, there's Apex who stabbed you and all those High Aces that make life tough. Next, you have to find out who shot your father so you can avenge for his death. Don't forget to put the guy who asked Jen to the dance on your list. You're going to be pretty busy getting all this done. Trouble is though, once you've done all that, no one will be proud of you. Will you be proud of yourself?"

I heard Jen's voice, "Jess," plain as if she were in the room. I knew it couldn't possibly be real, but then I really wasn't talking with Granddad either. But he kept it up.

"You've made yourself the center of the universe despite what your Mom and Dad taught you. And you've thought about hanging yourself out in the garage; that's about the most selfish thing you could do. Weren't you listening all those times when I was trying to teach you something about life; to prepare you for the inevitable misfortunes everyone goes through? That's really too bad but don't worry yourself over letting anyone else down. Just think about yourself. Would it help if you'd tear up your room? Throw something through the window? Maybe burn the house down? You could have a good blaze going by the time your Mom and sister got home from church."

I subconsciously had picked up the lamp from my desk.

"Did you think that Mom and Mee-maw were conspiring about you when you eavesdropped on them? Give them some credit, boy! They were trying to set you on the right track, but like Will Rogers said, sitting idle on the right track isn't much help when the train comes."

I'd never heard that saying or of the guy.

"Step up to the plate and let the cream rise to the top while you make lemonade out of the sour grapes while the sun shines."

The jumble of idioms made me smile for the first time in three days. Anyway, I knew that I would never have been able to commit suicide no matter how much I thought about it. Well, if I were surrounded by Saturnian aliens' intent on de-boning me while I was alive and I had a choice, I might swallow a cyanide pill from my space pack.

During lunch that day Julianne told Jess about the homily at church, "Do you know about Job? God tested him. He took Job's farm and his family and killed all his animals. Then…"

Mom interrupted, "Jess knows about Job, Julianne. Let's finish our lunch and then make some brownies before it gets too late in the day."

****

What would "just friends" bring to our relationship?

Because Jess parked his truck at Jen's every morning, they walked to school together. Now, the ritual would be tenuous. Jess dreaded facing her and hardly slept Sunday night. After the "discussion" with Granddad, Jess's anger subsided a bit, and he realized that it was his ego that was injured as much as anything being the 'dumpee' and not the 'dumper.'

That morning, Jess considered looking for another parking space and taking a chance that he wouldn't get a ticket for leaving his truck more than the allotted two hours for street-side parking. Thinking it through, he decided to continue doing the same thing as before; he would have to see Jen sooner or later, anyway.

I decided that if I could apologize without groveling, I would. I surely didn't want to break up entirely, and however difficult it is to admit, I was a jerk about the whole thing.

Jen, seemingly aware of his feelings, tried to carry the conversation as before. They'd never professed love, but did hold hands about every day. Jess muttered responses occasionally to things she said, neither of them mentioning the dance. Jess kept his eyes averted, recalling that less than nine months ago he got dizzy looking into her eyes. And now, he thought he'd actually cry if he tried to make amends.

I'll play it out. Make her come to me.

Crossing the street onto the school ground Jen asked, "Did you get the Chem Lab report finished?"

"No."

"It's due today, you know."

"So?"

They walked in silence.

"You're mad at me, aren't you?"

"I'm not happy."

She was trying to be nice so I decided to be a prick.

They were standing at the foot of the stairs to the school among the hubbub of the morning rush. Oher students sensing tension, their eye askance in passing. "Jess, we're sixteen and boyfriend-girlfriend is a little heavy at this time in my life. My mom thinks so, too."

Her mom? She likes me!

"We've got a lot of things ahead of us that make a serious relationship not only difficult, but burdensome."

So, now I'm a burden?

"I have friends that I want to hang out with, girls and boys. Before you moved here, I had a life, and it included going out with other boys. Jess, I like you very much and I enjoy being with you.

Jess, Surviving Normal

Always. It's just that being serious is confining to both of us. And, even though I could be with you only, falling in love isn't something I think should happen right now. Shouldn't love come about as the result of some comparison? Otherwise, how will I know for sure when I tell you that I love you?"

Hurt, Jess heard nothing positive. He was losing something that he thought was his, unable to let go of "let's be friends."

Impossible. After all we've done together?

He had no answer for her questions. Words misconstrued. His voice thick, "I don't need to compare you with someone to know that I love you." Saying that, he turned away to hide the tears.

I said it. I. Love. You.

"We'll talk again, Jess. The last thing I ever want to do is hurt you. Please?"

Jen decided it wise to not study together that day. She wanted to avoid further confrontation and would ask the Western Civilization teacher to write a pass for her to go the library for the second hour that week.

Jess didn't go to his last class that day. The lab report wasn't handed in. Basketball practice was starting for the girl's team and the routine where the three of them usually hung around by the lockers for a few minutes was ended because Jen had to get to practice right away. Jess went home and lifted weights with a vengeance; anger now displacing the pain. Jen sent several texts that he ignored. Monday night he was exhausted and slept until the alarm signaled another dreary day.

He parked his truck in Mrs. Steffen's driveway the next morning and started to walk to school without waiting for Jen. She caught up with him before he'd gone very far. Seeing the fire from her eyes, he knew there'd been another bad choice.

"Okay Jess, I'm sorry. I must have been crazy for the way I acted. God, how could I ever not recognize how much I love you! I can't eat. I can't sleep. I can't live another day without you. I need you at my side forever. Oh, darling Jess, beat me into submission! Lock me in a closet." Provocative, she turned her body against his side, touching. "Ravish me! Tell me what to do." She turned away and walked as if nothing had been said.

147

Jess could tell that she was somewhere between sarcasm and trying to be funny. He didn't attempt a rebuttal, knowing whatever he might say wouldn't be what he wanted to say or wouldn't come out like he wanted.

Fucking confusing.

Neither spoke as they walked.

Passing the deli where she worked, she abruptly turned to go inside, "You go ahead, Jess. I'll see you around."

Alone, Jess realized what she did cleared his head and showed him how he was acting. Not sure whether Granddad guided his thoughts, but the next few blocks along the way brought a measure of clarity. "Listen to what Jen is saying. You're young, enjoy the moment, and have fun the way juniors in high school are supposed to. You're not adults so quit with the pretending. Maybe, just maybe, you would enjoy a few dates with other girls yourself. And most of all, maybe you could try to be a little more fun to be with. Did you ever consider that you're about as interesting as a lamppost?"

Lamppost, whoever heard of a lamppost? Yes, Granddad was in my head again.

Again, it dawned on Jess that he was the cause of his own grief. Recalling how much he enjoyed the time they spent together last year in Biology helped him to realize the fallacy of his thinking.

I don't own Jen. That was all she was saying. Maybe we could have fun together without a binding commitment. Jen never said that she didn't want to be near me; not even when she was mad at me. She didn't say she wouldn't date me. Suck it up! Grow up! Play to win instead of playing to not lose—there's a difference.

Jess felt better throughout the day. If nothing else, he was being rational—thinking. It helped that Jen wasn't stand-offish or icy toward him when they worked on their AP courses during Study Period. He turned in a late paper and took a hit in Chem Lab.

Dan-el knew what happened; he even knew before, thanks to Ella. He'd noticed his friend acting a bit possessive toward Jen and sensed her irritation. He also knew that he would have to carry the ball in smoothing things out with them. There wasn't any guesswork for him to know how Jess would react and Jen was totally right in her conviction.

Basketball was always a good topic for a lull in the action. "So, Swish Miss, how's the team shaping up this year?"

Jen was ready and willing to talk about the team. "You know there's a Bosnian community in Trentsville, right? Well, a family with twin girls that are 6' 2" moved into the district this summer. They've played club ball and once they get used to our rules, they're going to help the team a lot," Jen reported. "Right now, they foul a lot and aren't real fast, but when they get positioned, they control the boards. Coach is trying to get them cleared so they'll be eligible."

Wednesday morning on the way to school Jen and Jess came to a consensus. "Oh, by the way," she smiled, "I declined my invitation to the Homecoming Dance last Friday. Thanks for asking whether I had a good time or not. Perhaps you and I could do something together, sometime."

I'll never understand women. I'll just take it one lesson at a time.

Dan-el and Ella had gone to the Homecoming Dance, a "maybe" Jefferson High tradition held the Saturday night after the last home football game. Known for what goes wrong rather what goes right, the dance had a nefarious past. The sometimes-on and sometimes-cancelled dance depended on the behavior from the most recent one making it an opportunity for the seniors to leave a legacy; affect an event they weren't going to be a part of the next year.

From what Dan-el related to Jess, the times when the dance was cancelled always took a virtual act of congress to get re-instituted. Accordingly, only RSVP students and their dates could attend, which made it not as much of a traditional Homecoming Dance as just a school function. There was no such thing for Jefferson as "just" a school dance as a couple scowling off-duty cops with breathalyzers complimented the strict supervision. Dan-el, as president of the Junior Class, felt he had an obligation to attend. "Can't let my adoring public down," he joked.

****

Basketball started for the non-football players on October 15 which meant that two or three guys on the football team would try out a week or so later. Despite the fact that Jess was taller and a bit more bulked up over the summer, he felt a little clumsy as he went through the initial drills. Concerned with the winnowing process and vying for the few open spots was a new experience for Jess knowing there wouldn't be a second chance if he didn't do well from the start. Although the coaches promised the hopefuls there would be no preference to players from last year, they were the guys more relaxed going through the drills. They were told this, but everyone competing for a spot knew that no more than five uniforms were up for grabs. Of course, if a former team member came back out of shape or grossly over-weight, there was no guaranteed spot on the team for him. It was easy to see the guys that were on the team last year by watching their swagger.

Attitude.

Because of baseball and his brief experience last year, Jess wasn't a total stranger to the other athletes. He didn't feel as conspicuous as last year. Coach was a 300-game winner and had been at the school as long as indoor plumbing one of kids said. Coach Cottison, each loss a wrinkle on his face, perched stoically on a portable seat during practice, his three assistants running the sessions. They worked with groups, impatiently teaching Jefferson's Motion Offense and screaming about playing defense.

Intense.

Jess was familiar with most of the drills, but got shouted at a few times when he didn't set a pick or understand where to go in the offensive scheme. He didn't feel too badly because a lot of the other kids also got yelled at. Like Coach Mercer often said way back in Iowa, "You get reprimanded because you're worth the effort. If we don't correct you when you make a mistake, that's when you should worry."

On the fourth day of practice there was a list on the bulletin board. The coaching staff had prepared four lists with six names on each list. A player that Jess had gotten to know from the sophomore team explained this what they did every year. "We play a round robin for the next two days to determine who makes the final cut. Right now, if your name isn't on one of the four teams, you're cut."

Jess couldn't find his name until he looked at the fourth list. "Hey Snail, how many make the team from the posting?"

Jess's ally was named Gary, nicknamed "Snail" from SpongeBob SquarePants. "Varsity dresses twelve, but a few of the guys here are sophomores and maybe even a freshman by invitation. Just depends. Football's over this week and they save a spot or two."

"Who coaches these games, the assistants?" Jess asked.

"Yeah, and they rotate so each assistant will work with each team at least once. Then they all get together and another list will be posted Monday before practice."

"I guess that's hard, but fair."

"Huh? It's friggin' crazy, man."

Fairness? Not much fair so far in my life,

The notion of "what's fair" conjured memories for Jess. In this case, did they base their decision on how many points a person scores, their assists, rebounds, blocks, stops, how you run the floor—what's important?

Gary was in tune as he and Jess walked toward the locker room. "What's fair is just a way for them to hide their preconceptions. They'll see what they want in who they want."

Jess agreed. "Other stuff measures a player's contribution, too. If you guard a weaker player, you can look good on defense. On offense two or three guys can show up another player or ignore him."

"It's the way they do it, man.

Jess was prophetic, "Yep, we beat the hell out of each other to get a suit, and then do the same to get playing time while the coaches yell about team. No 'I' in team they say."

There were three "games" on both Thursday and Friday. Jess was surprised to see that two referees sporting patches of certification on their shirts were present. Someone mentioned that refs had to get ready for the season, too. Before the first game, the assistant varsity coach spoke, confirming the player's hopes for being fairly judged. "Play team ball and don't leave anything out there on the floor!"

Jess's team, #4, was to play Team #1, and the teams not playing would go to the surrounding side baskets and work on skills. It was bedlam with all the activity, the coaches shouting instructions, the noise from the countless balls striking the floor, and the refs' whistle. As Jess waited at the circle for the jump ball, he noticed that the scorer's bench was occupied by three people, two with pencils at the ready. Teams would play three eight-minute quarters, with the clock stopping as it would in a real game. There would be no time-outs called.

Jess was chosen to play at the small forward or shooting guard position, which in a motion offense depended on whatever the coach wanted to call it—a "wing position." Jess was a guard and considered himself one, but having grown since that time, he decided he was probably suited for where they lined him up. His ball-handling ability in practice had been adequate, but nothing to set him apart. He was in awe of the guys who were point guards taking that position out of consideration. Standing at center court, the usual rush of pre-game adrenaline made Jess's hands quake and his body feel chilly, but as soon as the game started, that went away. This was as close to a real game as it could get.

As a team, none of them ran the offense smoothly, and in a motion offense there were a lot of options to keep it flowing—if the players worked it properly. The only way to make it go would be to practice long and hard together, and because both teams ran the same offense, the defense was aware of picks and could anticipate what was coming in certain instances. All of which favored players that were on the team the previous year. Coach Cottison was a believer in the running game so players were encouraged to get the ball down the court quickly in hopes of beating the defensive set. That too, was anticipated in the transition. All in all, these factors made for sloppy play on both sides of the ball, and the experienced players showed their knowledge of the system as much as their skill. They moved with a purpose.

Jess played well, scoring nine points on three field goals, one being a three-ball, and a pair of free throws. He thought that he could've been given the ball several times when in a position to score; however, it really wasn't team basketball that they were playing despite their instructions. Every aspiring player knew that he was competing against everyone else, whether a teammate or otherwise. Jess had a couple assists and once set a hard pick that floored one of the opponents and the ref called a foul on him. Noticing the coach of his team shaking his head after the collision—Jess hoped that it was in disagreement of the call.

Everything said, Jess also had pulled down several defensive rebounds and was fairly pleased with his performance. His group would play two games Friday, and the football contingency would report Monday to further scramble the procedure.

Sitting at his desk with his Chemistry book in front of him that evening, he thought of the old adage, "the more things change the more they stay the same." Jess packed each day full, but found that he could focus on making the team because his studies, originally overwhelming, had become more controllable. The lesson he'd learned with Jen helped his time-management skills; he no longer let their relationship monopolize so much of his life and discovered nothing really changed between them. They neither had gone 'steady' or whatever they called it at Jefferson, nor had they 'hooked up' in the way the term had evolved.

I had my fantasies, though.

Lately, they'd laughed a lot on the way to school and found other subjects to talk about. It also occurred to Jess that he owed Dan-el an apology for the way he'd been treating him lately. If Jen was offended, he'd likely done the same with Dan-el.

Put myself first.

He played Friday's games pretty much as on Thursday. Slashing to the basket resulted in two easy lay-ups and moving to the elbow off screens gave him a few ducks. On defense, he got faked out of his shorts once and left his feet on a ball fake, things that weren't good. He hit a floater on a fast break right before the half when he should have passed to another player who had a lay-up.

Payback. That guy never passes to me.

Floaters are low percentage shots, but Jess felt good about it at the time, He didn't start in their third game, but when he played, he easily got into the flow. Understanding the motion offense provided a lot of options from a minimum number of rules. "You get the offense to become second nature, then you can spend more time on defense. Offense is a known, defense is the unknown," one of the assistants said.

Makes sense.

Saturday, he and Jen went to a movie. When Jess broached the commitment issue, getting into 'what ifs' too deeply, Jen said. "Greg's a nice guy. Maybe he'll ask me again." If the new, "accepting Jess" was bothered by her remark, he took her comment as intended. He was determined not to show it. "Carpe Diem!" he commented as a reminder to himself.

The smile on Jen's face showed her approval.

"Yes, that would be nice," he hammed. "Greg is a hell of a fellow."

Yep, I am one clever dude.

Life's complications never ending, there's always something to worry about and you don't just sit down to solve them like a math worksheet. Now it was the basketball cut. Jess was satisfied with his performance and could assess the good and bad aspects, but he knew what he saw of himself wasn't what a coach saw. He tried to block it out, knowing the decision was out of his hands, and couldn't concentrate on the movie. Jen noticed and would have been the ideal person to offer council, but the one clever dude he thought he was before the movie kept it bottled within.

Anyway, she plays girls' basketball. It's different.

There was more to his haunt. He was fighting for a position on the team, whereas in Iowa he would have been one of the main players as a junior. He was human, selfish. It wouldn't satisfy him to merely make the team to warm the bench and play mop-up. It was also possible that, even on the team as a starter, he could be a role player because the motion offense was controlled by the point. The bottom line was that he could make the team and not meet his individual aspirations.

I wasn't very flashy in those games.

Monday, Jess Jemison was not on the list.

Hurt and unable to hide it Dan-el and Jen did their best to pull him out of his funk by leaving him alone. They knew Jess well and waited for him to bring it up.

"I really thought that I was one of the better players. I scored, rebounded and ran the court. I played hard on defense. I thought that I would not only make the team, but would challenge for a top-seven spot."

There. I opened up. Said what I felt.

Dan-el and Jen listened. their eyes compassionate, minds searching for consoling words. Here was their friend, again beaten down, victimized in an environment he was yet to understand.

"I was cheated. I went through a tryout and looked at the other players, and I kept a mental score in my head. Sure, you

Jess, Surviving Normal

could tell who had it made, but I was with them in the games and drills—just didn't act like I was hot stuff with the high fives and chest bumps." In the cafeteria area, Jess pounded the table top with his fist hard enough to rattle the plates and attract attention from others. Embarrassed, his voice lowered. "I did well; I just don't understand. I love basketball and this is the first time in my miserable life that I've been cut from a team."

I'm telling the truth.

"I should've taken last years' experience and seen the writing on the stupid wall."

Dan-el offered his condolences, "Sorry 'bout that, man. I suppose you were an unknown quantity and didn't figure into their plans for this year. The chemistry thingy might have been a factor to the coaches. From what I've seen, they all act like a bunch of narcissistic assholes. Tell you what: I go to a game and kinda hope they get beat."

Jess let out a little snort and smiled conspiratorially. "Humph."

Jen was more philosophical, "It hurts deep down inside, in your heart, and it becomes more than just basketball. To know that you've worked hard only but fall short is the biggest hurt. You were judged; you were on trial. It doesn't make you a lesser person or player. We know you left it all out there on the floor."

"Yeah man," Dan-el chimed in, "I hear you. All you wanted was a fair shake. You can't quantify what was subjective. That's what I hate about boxing."

"When Mom and Dad divorced, no matter how hard I tried, I couldn't do anything about it. I made it my failure; I was hurt and put the burden on myself. Ella's mom helped me get over the pain I felt by encouraging me to look ahead and to take out my anguish by being positive. She said to look at everything from above, not from within."

Jess heard them. Retorting, "Yeah right, except it's been that way ever since I came here. One damn thing after another," He wanted to hurt back, looking at Jen, "Even you wanted to dump my sorry ass." He got up and walked out of the cafeteria and left Dan-el and Jen alone.

Maybe I'll go hang out in the rest room and look for a fight.

The next day, the news went around the building that Coach Cottison had suffered a mild stroke and would not be coaching the team that season.

Dan-el said what Jess thought. "Coach had nothing to do with the decision. That team needed a couple guys like you to anchor it."

I thought of Snail. He was on the list.

Jess finally accepted the disappointment in time realizing there was no alternative other than making things worse. He didn't want to alienate Jen or Dan-el and apologized the next time they were together. "I'm sorry you guys. I don't know why I act that way."

****

With the weather colder and Christmas approaching, Jess and Dan-el attended Jen's home games. They agreed that she was superb A phenom on the court that played with a quickness that clearly set her apart. The Bosnian twins that transferred into the district were great additions to the team, and when Jen drove into the paint, the triple-option it created was very difficult to stop. Jen led the team in assists and her scoring could have easily been higher had she not so willingly passed to her teammates for them to shoot. Her team was undefeated through the first eight games heading into the holiday vacation.

"The girl not only plays with verve but with unorthodoxy," Dan-el said as he elbowed Jess in the arm.

"Yeah. Whatever that means," elbowing his friend back

The day before the break, Jen had a coach from a D-1 college visit her.

I was working on growing my social skills. Her success helped me forget my failure in the sport. Well...kind of.

Dan-el tried to help by getting Jess to think as an optimist—the old glass half-full or half-empty thing. What made the difference Jess kept asking him. "What was so difficult with understanding half of something? It's simple math."

Just kidding with him. I was on the uptick again.

Because Jen's team sometimes traveled to away games for varsity double-headers, she bemoaned the experience. "Jess, you wouldn't want to be a part of that team anyway." They're crude; they play selfishly. They're nothing like they were last year. I think Coach Cottison saw it coming even though he was old, this isn't the way it was last year."

And Jess ultimately let it go. convinced by both friends that he wouldn't have liked being a part of the cliquish nature of Jefferson boys' basketball. Selfishly, it also helped to *know* the boys' team was wallowing with a 1-5 record. Jess couldn't help thinking the team would be doing better if he were on it, but heeding Jen's advice and watching from 'above,' he probably wouldn't want to be a part of what he saw.

Jess smiled, taking a jibe at himself that got him another elbow, this time in the ribs from Jen, "And I wasn't good enough to make a poor team."

Without being out for a sport, Jess had to give up a free period for a return to P. E., that hadn't proved to be a problem, at least so far. His new teacher for P. E. held the class to task. Jess learned the teacher from last year was released from his contract at the end of the school year. It helped, too, that an additional Resource Officer was assigned to the school. With electronic locks and cameras having been installed, it made it difficult to simply walk in and out of the school whenever.

By now, Jess was familiar enough with the way things were around Jefferson High that he could negotiate without fear. He still heard some snide remarks from time to time, derogatory stuff about whether he was white or black, but never directly to his face—thanks to his fairly formidable size. It made him feel good when a couple football players asked him to consider coming out for the team next year.

Comfortable elsewhere, too, Jess sometimes went down to Dan-el's over the weekends to shoot hoops and play street ball. Being considerably south of Iowa, the winters were milder and allowed more outdoor activity so there was no difficulty in finding a game. The Wood's Park Recreational Director had organized a U-18 tournament for all the kids that lived there, and Dan-el somehow pulled some strings so Jess could participate. They played full court and the games were equally as important as any other game he'd ever played in. Their team ended with the second-best record in the round-robin tournament and Jess proudly showed the little plastic trophy to Mom and Julianne.

A lot of bumping and fouls went uncalled, and I didn't tell Mom about the trash-talking. For the first time in a long time, I found that I could have fun playing a game that was invented for precisely that purpose. The only statistic kept was which team won.

The High Aces and other gangs were still prominent. There were High Ace wannabe's that played in the tournament, and some High Aces showed up at the games but there was no trouble. Leery, Jess queried Dan-el about them and was told the High Aces and gangs like them were all about presence, street cred, extortion and 'bizness.' Not that that wasn't bad enough, but he didn't think they were into prostitution, weapons trade, or murder-for-hire 'very much.'

Dan-el explained, "In a weird sort of way, The High Aces are a protective phalanx for places like Wood's Park. They're not so much a bunch that writes on the walls and tears up the common areas. Some folks will say they do more than the police around here. I figure that time with Apex when we were playing ball was bluster mostly for his cronies' sake."

Dan-el joked that even cyber-crime was becoming popular with some gangs, but probably not with High Aces. "They're old school, Man. They went to Jefferson. Their fights with other gangs are mostly proprietary. However, the primary reason to avoid them is because they're members of a pack. And you don't want to show one up or act too big for your britches as you and I found out."

Jess took something else from the tourney that concerned him. He figured out what Granddad Wilkerson meant when he explained the differences between a good athlete and a great athlete. He learned to play with imagination on the Wood's Park court. Taking a lesson from watching Jen contribute to her team helped him tie together in his mind things that he'd not yet understood. He discovered that playing with imagination meant you played with heightened senses; your mind left your body and led it as you lost awareness of anything else. A person's entire being was tuned on a grand scale as he became one with the game, no longer merely one in a game with others. With a virtual sense of prescience, he learned to react to things as they happened. As if that weren't enough, he became the game and the game became him as his focus elevated to a previously unattained level.

Jess later tried to explain those feelings to Dan-el and Jen, both of whom looked at him like it was about time he caught on.

Jess, Surviving Normal

Dan-el's passion for boxing was his entire universe when he was in the ring. Jen agreed; she shared similar experiences and described it as being able to let go of inhibitions and self-consciousness in favor of total absorption. Watching either of them perform in their sports, even in their schoolwork made so much of it come together for Jess.

To bolster Jess's thoughts, Jen had remarked, "Mindset is what sets a person apart. It doesn't make you special or necessarily better than your opponents, but it makes **you** better, emphasis on you."

"You're constrained by your body, but it's in a zone. It knows what to do; it follows the imagination."

"Like self-hypnosis," Jess offered.

"Self-hypnosis on caffeine," Jen said

Dan-el raised his hands as a maestro, "Like the old saying, 'There ain't a horse that can't be rode…'"

"And a cowboy that can't be throwed," the Hershey's said together.

Dan-el had signaled that it was time for a round of clichés. "Leave it all on the field, or in the ring,"

Jen: "Just do it. There's no 'I' in team."

Jess: "Can't never did anything."

Serious again, Dan-el said, "You can't go beyond your talent, but you have to work like hell to reach your talent. It's like running through the wall when you're totally exhausted and then find that you can go forever.

Jess said, "Like breaking the sound barrier. You've got to want the ball when it's crunch time. Not because you think you're so good but because you trust yourself to make the play. You don't think of it as being a hero or see yourself being carried off the field on your teammate's shoulders; you see it as a team victory."

Jen came back with, "You might want the ball, but you've also got to be able to give it up. Like if the coach designs a special play, you have to play team ball and execute your part of it to perfection. You live inside the team; you aren't the team. The team is the organism at that time"

Jess, thinking of his experience, said, "I watch college and professional games and see the benchwarmers celebrate great plays their teammates make and they seem just as happy as if they were playing. Those guys know that their contribution is during practice and their efforts make the guys on the court better."

Dan-el again, "Absolutely. You have to buy into the program and accept that your contribution made the whole team better. It's hard to do because you're accepting your limitations and acknowledging others who have more talent, especially when you're a young player."

"Warming the bench hurts your ego," Jess said.

"And your butt, but it saves on shoe wear," Dan-el said, smiling.

"If you can't be a good player from the bench, you won't be a good player when you're in the game," Jen said.

"Young players often play for their parents," Jess said, "but we're into something totally different. His mind dwelling on what they said regarding not fitting into Jefferson boys' basketball.

****

The end of January brought a close to the first semester, another thing different than it had been in Iowa where the Christmas vacation coincided with the end of the semester. Their AP courses were year-longs, but participants still received a semester grade and earned high school credits. Jess's other courses were required and were pretty easy, consistent with the Jefferson tradition. If anything, Jess got to know other kids from English and Sociology classes.

The dark, old building replete with its blend of pine-scent and almost a century of students had become common-place. Its creaks and groans went unheard. The slamming of the old army-green iron lockers and the squawk of the ancient PA system were part of the daily routine. Even the clocks that made a faint click with each passing minute and let out a buzz when the minute hand reached the '12,' were all a part of life at Jefferson High. Jess found little idiosyncrasies like this were already forgotten from his days in Iowa.

At times I cried at night thinking of Dad as I lay in bed. On top of that, some dreams were so real that I awoke with the feeling that Dad was still alive and I expected to hear his voice downstairs. The reality was always a cruel slap in the face. My inability to completely "let go" lingered in my mind. I couldn't let

Jess, Surviving Normal

myself fully enjoy a good time without thinking that my dad had died for no reason. Guilt still haunted me. My moods were sometimes pretty dark and I felt destructive; like wanting to damage stuff or hurt myself. I remained unable to understand why Dad had to die.

I could only imagine Mom's grief. One morning after a particularly vivid dream, I went to her and gave her a hug and told her I loved her. She hugged me back and we both began to sob. As we embraced, Julianne came into the kitchen and the three of us were together as one in tribute to our father and husband. As we stood together, Julianne said, "Let's back up a little and let Dad in."

Mrs. Jemison was finally called to work at the window company and was once again part of the Personnel Department. Her position fortunately gave the family medical and dental benefits, but unfortunately for Jess, he was told that it wouldn't be too long before he should have his wisdom teeth out. His latest braces, barely visible, called for monthly visits, but they weren't the pain in the butt some other kids had to go through. Julianne also needed work on her teeth. Her upper cuspids were crowded forward which called for more extensive work.

Jess heard himself saying "It's always something" to Jen one morning.

Surely saying things like that are a sign of becoming an adult.

Mrs. Jemison remained on the warpath with the schools being ever-present at council and parent-teacher meetings. It helped everyone when Mee-maw came at Thanksgiving and stayed until the new year often remarking about the warmer winters. Jess could tell that Mee-maw was awfully tired at the end of the day regardless of what she said to the contrary. She washed clothes, cleaned the house, cooked the evening meal, and then insisted that her daughter needed some free time. Mee-maw thought that Mom should partake of the Personnel Department's social hour every Friday after work. "Stay until the last dog dies," she told Mom. That, of course, brought a boat load of questions from Julianne.

Mom's vendetta concerning the Police Department's inability to find Dad's killer was ongoing, too. Hardly a week passed that she didn't talk to the detectives that were handling

Dad's case, and after six months, all they had done was recover some shell casings and two slugs that lodged in the building—all sent to the lab. They told Mom that they were closing in on the illegal sources for military weapons. Also, they questioned the few witnesses at the scene as well as talking to people who had knowledge of gang cultures. So far, they were fairly sure of which gang was involved and were narrowing the possibilities of which members of the gang could be placed at the scene. All of which was filled with uncertainty. "The weapon used is surely out there. They aren't going to throw away something that's worth over a thousand dollars. It's only a matter of time until it shows up." Mom was told.

But as Mom was told, having a weapon like this spoke to a gang and of the three gangs that were likely to procure an automatic weapon such as this one, the Anarchists, a white supremacy group fit the so-called modus operandi for Dad's murder. Confounded as Mom was, she remained adamant in telling Jess to not worry about it. "I absolutely forbid you to get involved with this. You hear me, Jess? Let the police do their job. If you don't, I'll quit telling you any news I get on the matter."

Still, I had my own agenda and my own theories. Well, hypotheses to be scientifically correct.

Early December brought a similar occurrence to Mr. Jemison's from another part of town when an older lady was shot inside a bakery; killed in a spray of bullets flying through the front window. Like Dad, the conclusion was that she was a random victim in the wrong place at the wrong time. "For no other reason," the evening newscaster said, "than to satisfy a contorted requirement for gang membership." As public outcry escalated, both Dad's and the lady's pictures were shown frequently on the local news along with reward information. The mayor renewed his promise for justice and told the public that the perpetrators would be prosecuted to the full extent of the law.

Dan-el was optimistic, "There're people not in the gang that know who did the shootings. They'll come forward, Jess."

None of it made me feel any better. In fact, I had a perverse sense of fulfillment knowing that other people had the same thing happen in their family.

Jess started going to the Armory on the week-ends with Dan-el. No longer interested in becoming a boxer, but watching

Jess, Surviving Normal

Dan-el and the others train taught him a lot. Dan-el pointed out that to box, Jess would have to lose some weight to maneuver in the ring effectively. He kept telling his bigger friend of the uselessness of being "too muscled" for the ring. "Big arms get pretty heavy after a couple rounds," he chided.

Because the training room was crowded with boxers and reeked equally with the one at school, Jess often wandered off and went to the old gymnasium and shot baskets. The gym had a running track that circled above the basketball floor; something he'd never seen before, and it didn't take long to discover there were some "dead" spots in the gym floor.

I pretended to be a one-man team and created all kinds of situational events such as last second shots and "here's the Bulls' great shooting guard...as the deafening crowd roared." I was always world famous. The sting of not making the basketball team at Jefferson was no longer so present—I just loved to play the game one way or another.

One day during the winter break Jess was down there with Dan-el and noticed a signup sheet for a men's winter basketball league. Since Jess was shaving twice a week, He figured he looked old enough. He signed his name to the list that had room for forty-two names. Number 32. At the time, Jess had no inkling of how fatefully it would affect him and others.

What could they do other than tell me I can't play? What's one more disappointment to the world-famous baller?

Games would be played on Wednesday nights and Sunday afternoons starting the Sunday after the Super Bowl. Players for each team would be chosen from a pool and posted the following Monday and each team would be given two Wednesday practices prior to the first games. Excited over not being excluded so far, Jess told Dan-el what he had done.

Dan-el was encouraging, but warned, "You'll be playing mostly with a bunch of National Guardsmen 'cause they're the ones that use this place. Cops play, too. Some of them aren't much older than you and some are old enough to be your daddy. Oh shit, I'm sorry.... I didn't..."

"It's okay, man." Jess knew Dan-el would never say something to be hurtful that way.

He was so anxious that he got to Dan-el's apartment way too early the next Monday and had to suffer through one of grandma's delicious breakfasts. "I don't cook this food to throw it away." Two eggs and three pancakes later on top of Mee-maw's cinnamon oatmeal and toast, Jess waddled into the Armory with Dan-el.

"They be callin' you lard-ass you keep eatin' two breakfasts."

As promised, the teams were chosen and the sign-up sheet still hung on the bulletin board with numbers in front of each signee's name. Teams were chosen one through six with seven players on a team. Since Jess was number 32, the sequence worked out he was on team #4. Teams #5 and #6 had six players on their teams as only 40 people had signed up to play. Their first practice was Wednesday at 6:30 to 7:30, on the north half of the gym.

I hadn't been challenged; I wouldn't shave so I'd look older by Wednesday night. Ha!

With almost a year in Trentsville, Jess didn't know a soul in the entire city outside of school, his neighborhood and recognizing some people he'd seen in church because everyone sat in the same place. Dad said after their first few times at the church, "They shake your hand in church and will run over you in the parking lot if you're in the way when it's over."

Another thing that took some time to get used to was simple directions like north and south. So easy in Iowa because roads and communities were originally laid out directionally, it was confounding in Trentsville. Again, Dad had the answer why," River towns in hill areas of the Colonies grew up along the rivers and roads to the cities followed old pathways that went around obstacles rather than over them. Congress's Grid Land Ordinance around 1800 changed all that and the Western States platted their lands in directional fashion."

Dad was so smart. I hardly paid any attention to him.

It still made Jess ask when he walked into the gym which end of the gym was north. The guy he asked took one look and immediately asked his own question. "How old are you?"

"Nineteen."

"Uh-huh. And I'm Lebron James, Mr. Nineteen."

Screw him. I'm not going to take his crap.

"No, I'm Mr. 32 on Team #4. At least I don't have to shave with a chain saw like some people."

Jess, Surviving Normal

The guy didn't take offense with what I said; maybe I said it too softly for him to hear. "You're the other end," he nodded directionally.

Jess found a ball and started shooting with two others now there, both wearing gray shirts with "ARMY" in big black letters on the front. Having arranged by design to not be the first one there to mask his eagerness, Jess fumbled with his shoes and did some stretching until some of the other players filtered in amid the banter of familiarity. One guy said 'Hey,' but that was it. As 6:30 came and went according to the big old wall clock with its glass face encased in a metal grid like a catcher's mask, Jess was getting a little bored just shooting and figured someone would show up and take charge pretty soon since they only had an hour. The other team on the south had begun shooting lay-ups.

Looking around, Jess counted twelve caged overhead lights that lit the gym. He remembered a dead spot on his end of the gym that pretty much killed a person's dribble, and he had never seen a score board with clock hands rather than lights for timing. The best he could figure, numbers placed on a wheel inside the scoreboard turned to keep score.

I had a fleeting thought of Granddad telling me that his first basketball had real laces on it and a bladder inside.

Jess almost jumped when he heard someone say, "Jess Jemison." Instantly thinking that he'd be told to get off the court, he turned to see who had said his name and saw a face that was familiar but couldn't put a name. "How are you Jess? Mike Martin. Remember? I was the assistant principal at Jefferson last year for a while."

He walked over and extended his hand for a fist bump and then clapped Jess on the shoulder with the other. There was no questioning the wonderment on Jess's face. No more than a minute later, the shooting stopped and everyone on the team gathered around Mr. Martin who'd raised his right arm and made a little circling motion with his hand. "I suppose you guys think I'm your coach, being the old man on the team."

"Yes sir," three or four of them echoed, "Hoo-yah!" Dan-el was correct when he said most of the teams would be made up of men in the National Guard.

165

"Okay, then. Prepare to lose every game." Mr. Martin, whom Jess would soon learn was Captain Martin in the military, said as he winked.

I stood there, mouth open, still surprised.

Never having seen Mr. Martin in gym trunks and a T-shirt was different, and set Jess back for a moment. Awed they were going to be teammates, Jen and Dan-el wouldn't believe this. Seemingly a towering man when he was Assistant Principal Martin, he was actually a little shorter than Jess, but was a solid body. Jess worked the weights and was in pretty good shape, but beside Mr. Martin, he felt puffy—the difference between bulked and chiseled. His hair was still in a crew cut as last year.

That's understandable—Army. Do I call him Mr. or Captain Martin?

Nervous and glad at the same time, Jess was reminded how he commanded the student's attention without forcing himself on them.

Small world. Dad said a lot of high school principals were former physical education teachers and jocks so I wasn't shocked to see Mr. Martin athleticism.

As they went through some drills, Jess could tell that two of the other guys on the team had played before, too. Not that everyone was all that fluid, but four of them, Jess included, had more experience than the other three who moved with bounces and shot with jerks. In shooting drills, it was pretty easy to see some rust as the ball clunked off the rim and metal backboard.

Hearing the word "Ringer" when Jess was making more baskets than the other guys, Jess pulled some shots not wanting to stand out. Of course, Mr. Martin was aware that he was still in school, but Jess felt good and that he had an ally. All in all, they had a good practice, ending with ten minutes or so of half-court scrimmage.

When their time was up, Mr. Martin came over and walked off the court with Jess. "How's everything going for you this year, Jess?"

"'I'm taking some AP courses and I didn't make the basketball squad."

"I wondered about that when I saw you here tonight. From the game you brought, I don't know how they could keep you off the team. Anyway, how'd you ever come to sign up at a place like this?"

Mr. Martin motioned for them to sit on a row of benches rather than keep walking out of the gym and into the locker area. "Last summer, I came to watch the Golden Gloves 'cause my friend was boxing. Sometimes I come down here with him to work out."

"Dan-el, right? I remember him well. Brilliant mind. So, you're still tight with him?"

"Yes."

"And Jen Steffen?"

Jess could feel his face grow hot. "Yes."

Giving Jess a little push and a knowing smile, "You chose your friends wisely, Jess. And it's the other way around in their case, too. I try to keep up with what's going on at Jefferson since my dismissal so I kinda' knew you weren't on the basketball team. Losing Coach Cottison was a downer. I missed your name in football, too. You look like a candidate for a tight end position at a D1, man. Having been involved with the students and their activities made it hard to just walk out of the door and forget." He grew silent for a moment.

"Jess, I know about your father and I am deeply sorry for you and your family. From the one time I met him, it was easy to see his devotion to his family and his concern for his kids. I'm sorry that I couldn't have been there to offer my condolences at the time." Another pause. "Our battalion was on a six-month deployment to Afghanistan. We returned at Thanksgiving minus three good men."

Jess couldn't help tearing up. Mr. Martin brushed the top of his head with his hand and said, "We'll talk more later. We're going to kick some butt in this league. Say 'hi' to your mom for me. See ya."

Later that evening, Jess told Mom about seeing Mr. Martin and she was pleased. "You'll have someone to look out for you down there."

Still her little boy. She'd barely given me permission to play in the first place, and it was only when I explained about the 42 places on the sign-up sheet that she relented. She didn't buy into my telling her that one team wouldn't have enough players if I had to scratch my name.

"You remember that he sent a card when your father died," she said. "I knew it came from a military base somewhere outside the country when I saw the 'free' printed where the stamp goes. He's such a nice man and whoever fired him made a big mistake. I could tell how much he cared."

I had no memory of Mom ever telling me of a card from Mr. Martin.

****

The second semester brought a few new classes while the AP courses continued. The school became more a tinder box following the beat-down and mugging of a teacher in the faculty parking lot one night after school. The media pounced on the story mentioning gangs and the police department vowed even more surveillance. Per the norm, no one knew anything. The president of the teacher's union wrote a letter to the newspaper pleading for public schools to expel the chronic trouble makers. "Those types act out in rebellion to school rules and restrictions and are not in school for any good reason. They are society's problem," he wrote.

"That's assumption," Dan-el said to his friends. "Those knuckle draggers weren't students. Transients, my bet."

Although ambiguous, there was truth in the newspaper article. While the majority of kids were probably willing to work, they were forever being distracted by those with no interest in learning. Jess sat in Intro to Business one day and watched two kids sitting in class acting like they were smoking weed with their pencils as they obliviously chatted away to the distraction of everyone.

Another time, he was in English when the teacher asked a group that was talking to please be quiet and pay attention when one of them stood up and said, "Why don't you be quiet, bitch, you interruptin' me! An' anyway, you can stick all this fancy English talk up yo' white ass." The teacher, with tears instantly appearing, silently picked up her stuff and walked out the door. Jess had a new teacher for the rest of the year who didn't ever do any teaching.

When Jess told his mom about it, she asked about what did he did on the teacher's behalf. "What would you have done as one of Mr. Martin's ambassadors if the program had been instituted? Don't think I'm trying to put you down, Jess, because I don't know the answer to what I would have done. Or if I were the teacher."

"I don't know, I'd probably just sit there like I did. "It happened so fast. If it'd gone physical, I think I would have got involved. Like Dad would say, teachers spend 90% of their time on 10% of their students."

Mom smiled, got up from her chair and came over and gave Jess a hug. "He'll always be with us. You're so much like him."

****

Dan-el was fully healed from the beating he sustained right before the school year began. Ella, Jen's cousin, completed their group whenever it was possible, and going to another school barely hindered the way she and Dan-el got along as their relationship grew. Ella was fun to be around, and her quick wit was often a match for Dan-el.

The "Twin Towers" proved to be a great asset for girls' basketball. The team had taken a trip to play in a tournament in Florida over winter break and came home with the first-place trophy. Jefferson easily won the All-city sectionals and headed into the sub-state game with a 23-2 record when their bubble burst. "I think we were over-confident. One of those games when every bounce went their way," Jen explained.

Jess and Dan-el went to the game. "You had two girls playing a deny defense on you and a triangle zone in the paint. They did their homework getting ready for you," Jess told her.

"That's what Coach said. She takes the blame for the loss."

For the season, Jen's scoring was down from last year for good reason as she led the team in assists, free throws made, free throw percentage, and steals. Owning several school records, it meant very little to her personally. She garnered several post-season honors, the most prestigious being named to the all-city team. As a Junior, the letters and inquiries were piling up from colleges inviting her to spend a week-end on the campus at places like the University of Louisville and Vanderbilt. Jen remained consistent despite her accolades as she went about her day-to-day life.

"Not bad for a white girl," Dan-el teased.

Jess watched and learned. Jen's basketball presence was only a little short of an art form. She wasn't flashy or controlling, but there was no doubt that she was the floor leader with or without the ball. Making precise passes that threaded the proverbial needle along with her ability to create options when she had the ball were two aspects of her game that college scouts noticed. She played opportunistically, doing what was needed to affect the best possible outcome for the team. There were games when she didn't score in double figures and other games when she'd have over twenty points—quietly. Sometimes Jess would have difficulty remembering where all the baskets came from. But the remarkable thing to Jess was that when her games were over, she didn't revel in the win or rue the loss. Jen truly left it on the floor.

Nor did she say much about basketball or what schools contacted her. She'd tell Jess, but only when he asked. "Tennessee invited me to visit. I said okay and will go next week-end. Hate to miss work though. And you," she looked at him affectionately.

Scouts.com had listed her between three and four stars as a D-1 prospect. Jess, thinking of their relationship, often wondered about his impact on Jen's success--the old back-and forth.

Am I helping or hurting?

In assessment, Jess decided that he'd learned more about Jen by keeping things casual than if they were an item. He worried that she would outgrow him, but in talking about it with Dan-el, he came to accept it for what it was.

"Don't worry about it, man. Be yourself, well maybe not. Be a little more like me." Dan-el jibed good-naturedly. "Jen is steady, don't think too far ahead on this girl. Carpe Diem, you know what I mean? Just don't play the "needy" card with that girl."

I think I understood. Don't worry about what might happen; control it by taking what does happen in stride. Seven Habits, Dummy.

****

One evening, Mom announced that she didn't like her job as much at the Trentsville Plant as at the Iowa one. "It's the same job, but everyone here is so uptight," she told Jen and Julianne.

Jess, Surviving Normal

"The people in the office dress like they're in a fashion show. It's all 'company procedure', what to do and when. All the line-item, robotic way management dictates how everything should be done makes me tense. Like I'm walking on eggshells all the time. Even Friday night happy hours are stilted. In Iowa, we did our work without so much interference and it was fun."

I mostly knew what Mom was saying, but Julianne needed explanations.

"I'd look for work someplace else, but the benefits are too good," she said which called for more explanations to Julianne.

Julianne was now in fifth grade and undergoing some changes implemented by peer pressure matched by the fact that she was growing up. She had her own worries, from grade competition to physical maturation. Her classmates mostly represented families like hers, ethnically Christian and part of the shrinking, shifting demographic known as the middle-class. Some things were similar to her school in Iowa but others took time. For Julianne, it would be a few years before she would be thrust into the maelstrom of public education as it was at Jefferson, but for certain, she would be more acclimated than Jess was. But now, she was at an age when her steady-state world was in just starting to reach into one of daily flux.

Mom discovered that a video game Julianne played included a person named, 'Mr. Rogers.' Julianne was warned not to do that kind of thing, but in her defense, she told Mom that Mr. Rogers was a man that she and several of her friends knew from the playground. "He's there after school like a lot of parents and plays kick-ball and everything. The teachers know him."

Julianne typically stayed for the After-School Program made available for working parents unable to pick up their children when school let out. It was structured so that after fifteen minutes or so for the students to get rid of some energy they'd come back into the school and do homework or work at any number of educationally-related activities. Occasionally, After School scheduled local volunteers to share their skills and interests with participating kids. Music, art and sewing were a few of the mini-classes offered from time-to-time.

Mom asked, "Does this Mr. Rogers have kids at school?"
"I don't know. Why would he be there if he didn't?"
"That's why I'm asking," Mom said.

Listening, Jess could see exactly where this was going. Mother Hen had raised a flag, and rightly so this time.

"How'd he come to be on your computer game?"

Julianne said, "He asked me. He said Stacy, Andi, and Colette were his friends and we could all play together. We have our own passwords" Jess could tell by the way Julianne changed her expression that she suddenly understood why Mom was concerned.

"Julianne, did you ever wonder why a grown man would want to play a computer game with ten- and eleven-year-old girls?"

"No. Is he a bad man?"

"Maybe not, but I don't want you taking a chance. What is his real name?"

"I don't know, just Mr. Rogers. He sometimes helps in After School."

"Is your computer on right now? Let me have a look." Julianne and Jess shared a desktop computer in the den.

I knew that hackers could watch other people through the camera lens on computer monitors.

Mom returned after five minutes or so. "Julianne, I do not want you to play that game or whatever it is anymore, understood?" Julianne started to sniffle, thinking she was being punished.

"Honey, I know you didn't mean to do anything wrong, but there are people who take advantage of others who don't see any danger in things like this. That's why I tell you to sometimes do things that you don't understand. They could lead to something harmful. I'm going to find out about this Mr. Rogers if I can. Until I do, I want you to stay away from this man."

"What about my friends who play with him too?"

"You just take care of yourself for right now like I'm asking."

Convinced that she would lose her friends, Julianne wasn't happy. Mom left her alone to pout knowing that nothing she said would help her daughter.

About a week later, Mom told Jess and Julianne the man whose computer name was Mr. Rogers was a live-in companion with one of the teachers at Julianne's school. In speaking with the school's principal, Mom said she got the same old run-around as always and was made to feel as if she was over-reacting.

Mom was getting pretty well-known with some of the administrators. She was a burr under their saddle as she put it.

"They just don't want to have anything upset their lives. Just sit on their hands and do nothing until it's too late. Then they wag their heads and tell me they're doing all they can to insure every child's welfare. The only thing I got was the man's name, and I had to threaten going to the police to get that. My department at work runs background checks on all of our applicants. It's snooping, but not illegal. Anyway, I ran a complete check on this Mr. Rogers and found that he once worked as a counselor at a YMCA but left after six months. I also found that he has a degree in computer logistics that he completed after his time with the Y. Next, I looked for a possible criminal record and didn't find anything. Anyway, tell me more about the games you play with him."

It came out that Julianne and her friends would do things in front of their computers. Bending and twisting positions children would think innocuous, but also some that could be construed to be suggestive. Julianne also told of playing a game they called "glamour." Where the young girls would imitate a movie or rock star's poses. All of which was done under the auspices of all the participants voting for the best.

Julianne understood. With both hands against the side of her head, she was alternately stomping her feet on the floor, "Oh Mommy, Mommy, why would he do that? Why?"

Little girls?

Mom explained, "Some people have dirty minds and make the excuse that they can't help themselves. Maybe that's true, but they're addicted to what they do. People sell these pictures to other people like them. In a lot of cases, it's just another form of bullying. I really don't know why anyone could stoop so low, Sweetheart."

Mom continued, now looking at Jess as tears rolled down Julianne's cheeks. "You both know that once computers take pictures, they are public to the world. Cameras can be used in so many ways, both good and bad and it seems to me that right now the bad ways outnumber the good.

Mom kept her eyes on Jess. "Jess, I'm sure you're aware of the pornography that is available on the internet. I suspect most teenagers have taken a look."

I seemed to make a living out of blushing, lately.

"The thing to understand is that it is debasing to women because the great majority of people are not like that—women and men. When stolen, it's a crime." You both know movies and computer games show characters that are designed to stimulate sexual interest way beyond subliminal suggestion. It's not the way caring people act."

Now she's talking to me. I didn't do anything. Sure, I had looked at some of the sites, knowing their names from hearing kids at school.

Recalling that Jen told him a former member of her team wanted to take pictures in the locker room. Jess knew sexual innuendo was everywhere and had a firm foothold in adolescent minds. It sent a mixed message starting in the grade-school years.

I struggled with my conscience after the times I looked. That should count for something.

Dad's book that he'd given Jess that objectively explained what going through adolescence involved and what to expect. It viewed masturbation as being a natural act in direct contrast to religious teachings calling it self-abuse and harmful like people who cut themselves or were anorexic. Jess always felt guilty, dirty, embarrassed—ashamed. But temptation could be overwhelming, and Jess could rationalize that it was more of an abuse not to give in.

I was relieved that Mom hadn't gone deeper into her lecture and let me slither off the hook.

Retuning her focus to Julianne, Mom said she and two other parents would soon meet a school counselor and a detective from the police department. "We'll get to the bottom of this."

Julianne was scared even more, concerned the man would get her and kill her. "I wish Daddy was here to help."

"I know, baby, I do too," Mom said.

****

Jess's basketball team did well. Despite being an ancient forty-something, Mr. Martin could run the floor with the younger guys. Games were played with the clock running that stopped only for free throws and were over in an hour. Comparatively taller in this setting than in high school games, Jess often played in the unfamiliar post positions and got pushed around at first. They had a single ref that stayed pretty much at mid court allowing half of the fouls to go uncalled. More than once, Jess was shoved out of the way while in the air going for a rebound. Moving screens flattened more than one player every game. Not so much as they were playing dirty, this group of players thrived on the roughness.

Mr. Martin told Jess to get in there and play your game; don't be malicious or headhunt, just go with the flow. No one will take offense as long as you're not flagrant. Mr. Martin and a few of the other players, being officers or ranking NCO's, certainly took their share of bumps, too. For Jess, it really wasn't much different than playing at Wood's Park with Dan-el.

The coming spring meant the Golden Gloves tournament. For Dan-el, no longer having to compete as a novice, this presented his first opportunity to compete on a larger stage. His trainer/coach, a detective on the police force, advised his fighters to be comfortable with their weight and let their bodies grow to maturity meaning Dan-el would move up a weight class from last year, and as insignificant as few pounds might seem, adjustments were necessary. Whereas the lighter boxers were faster, heavier boxers hit harder; one good punch could be devastating. Reasoning that weight gain was normal, Dan-el's emphasis was on maintaining speed, improving his footwork, and rethinking defense postures.

'Eat healthy and get plenty of sleep,' he was advised—a prescription Dan-el said he liked. His trainer had cited studies where athletes constricting themselves with weight classifications picked up bad eating habits that precipitated gastric disorders later in life. "Who could cut weight by starving with my Grandma White in the apartment?" Dan-el asked.

Jen concurred, using the equation for kinetic energy. "Mass times velocity squared tells you that speed is more important in delivering energy to your punches."

"Thank you, Madam Einstein. I'll take the concept into the ring."

As if she were waiting to share her latest finding, Jen said, "Did I ever tell you about Einstein's first wife, Mitza Maric? A truly remarkable woman. She did the math Albert couldn't figure out and then he took the credit for it. Albert got the glory because physics was a man's world. Plus, the great Einstein dumped her for another woman."

Jess, in defense of his gender, said, "Like the Curies, huh? Marie got the credit, Pierre hardly ever mentioned."

Jen countered, "They were contemporaries, but never met. Maric was as much a pioneer as Madame Curie, but forgotten in history. Sad."

And so it went, as did many of their weird, yet characteristic conversations.

Three athletes, each successful but three different approaches to success. Jess generally got so nervous that he worked himself into an emotional frenzy before a game, sometimes calling for frequent trips to the bathroom on the day of a game. Then once the game started, he was fine.

Jen was 'just do it,' acutely aware and focused, she approached a game in a business-like fashion—emotion hidden by concentration. Whatever she held within, you couldn't tell the difference whether she was going to work at the deli or playing in the sub-state. But once the game started, she was non-stop energy. Dan-el was surgeon-like. Watching him compete, spar, and train prompted Jess to give him a nick name that he mimicked as an announcer, "Dan-el 'Slice and Dice' Whiiiite." Having seen Dan-el fight only in last year's tourney, there were several times when Jess watched him spar or go a round or two at the Armory. His footwork patterned, but too complex to follow, and his punch sequences designed to score points but to also save energy. Slicing in and out, bobbing and weaving, and dicing his opponent's attempts in a ju-jitsu fashion.

Dan-el described himself as a student of the game. "I plan. I fight each fight over and over in my mind beforehand; I call it mental rehearsing. Then, I develop a kind of flow chart in my mind during fights. You know, I play out if-then situations so I always have an alternative. Most really good fighters do that and lots of times a guy loses a fight because he didn't have a contingency—especially if he gets disrupted. Ali letting Frazier exhaust himself in the 'Thrilla in Manilla' is the classic. It's important to decide whether you let the fight come to you or you take the fight to the other guy. Plus, it's hard to think when you get your bell rung and you only have a second to clear the cobwebs."

The dose of reality is finding your opponent to also have a game plan. The more you play, the higher the level of competition you reach, the more elusive the goal becomes. Jess's grandfather spoke prophetically when Jess was in little league: "You play the game until you know that you've reached your limit. And if you reach it to the top, know that it won't last. Enjoy the trip because that's what life is about—the journey." Jess had written those words on the inside cover of his sports scrapbook.

On several occasions, they thought it ironic that none of them had a father that was a significant part in their lives. Jen's dad had remarried and his new wife brought three children into their marriage that left him with little time for his own children. Dan-el's father and mother never married. She became pregnant while in college and they stayed together until she graduated; the plan being for her to go to work while he pursued a doctorate. A year after Jon-el was born, Dan-el's mom became pregnant with him. With mounting pressure, his father left. Dan-el described it as a strange relationship because his father would occasionally send a letter to his mom with an enclosed check. (Jess always wondered about the "Mrs." but didn't ask.) Dan-el ambiguously mentioned that his dad, whom he never met, was a professor of "something" at Cambridge University in the United Kingdom. Both Dan-el and Jen accepted their family outcomes and were resigned to it. "I don't wish for a stepdad, but I wouldn't object if Mom wanted to marry someone," Jen said.

March brought the start to the baseball season. Mostly by default Jess decided that baseball would be his sport—he knew that would always be the game he loved the most. To prepare, most of the guys spent a couple hours each week in the cage during the second semester. For Jess, however, the basketball league continued into the first part of April making him scurry around to get everything done, especially with the school load. All he could do was give up a couple hours of sleep. Staying up later made his morning work-outs tortuous, and he found himself dozing off in school at times. "You're a narcoleptic," Dan-el told him one time when he nodded off and, after a huge spasmodic twitch, awoke with the entire English Lit class watching. Never one to sleep late, now he could have slept until noon on Saturdays had it not been for early spring yard work in the neighborhood.

Mom wanted to watch him play basketball and asked if many people came to the Armory games. With only three rows of bleachers on the sides of the court, the gym was never intended for many spectators plus Jess found it a little embarrassing to think of Mom coming. A few of the wives or girlfriends came to the games, but moms?

I didn't want to hurt her feelings, but I did want to defuse her interest.

"It's not a place for women, Mom."

"Who is it for, then?" she asked. "You mean like a stodgy old men's club or is it a place that's too good for women?"

"No, well, yes. I don't know."

She was playing me.

"Which is it? Or is it that your "Mom" would embarrass her sixteen-year-old son in front of all those macho men?"

"Actually, Mom, you might be embarrassed. There's a lot of talking, you know what I mean." He added hastily, "And the place stinks."

"You mean these brutes are cussing and smelling up the gym in front of my only son? Polluting my baby's ears and souring his mind? Why, I'm coming down there and put a stop to this stuff for sure." She was smiling.

"Oh Mom," Jess said. This was the first time since Dad was killed that he saw her old self; the inquisitor who commanded respect, but whose sense of humor could lighten the darkest situation. Feeling a rush of love for her, Jess leaned over to where she was sitting and gave her a kiss on her cheek. "No, I want you to come."

She was there the following Sunday, one of the few leaning on the rail up in the balcony rather than in the bleachers with Julianne in tow. To Jess's relief, there were others watching the game scattered throughout the gym—really more than he expected. In fact, his casual girlfriend, his best friend and Dan-el's girlfriend, Ella, rounded out the crowd. This was the game for the championship so there was a raised involvement for the players to go with the spectator noise. Usually, the gym was usually pretty quiet beyond the ball thudding on the floor, the players chatter, and the squeak of shoes.

Like old times.

Teammates were the luck of the draw, but the other team was featured a guy who had played for the University of Alabama who was six-seven and another former college player from Slippery Rock University. The teams had split the two games during the regular season, but the one they won was when the Slippery Rock player wasn't there.

Our biggest guy was slightly taller than me.

"We have a pretty sizeable task ahead of us," Mr. Martin punned in the pre-game huddle.

They lost by fifteen. Mr. Martin's team had been winning games by making that one extra pass or being patient to create open shots. Defenses mostly were of the zone variety, and crisp passes isolated the shooter or overloaded a zone for a pick and roll.

By the end of the season we weren't too bad.

Against the player that could flat-out shoot the ball and the big body who made his living getting rebounds, they were overwhelmed; their passes often tipped and sometimes even intercepted. With the other three guys mostly serving as fillers on offense, the two college players remained a step ahead, the smaller court of the Armory playing to their advantage. Like last summer at Dan-el's, Jess re-learned what it was like to play against a really good player.

My focus is baseball.

His 'entourage' was waiting when Jess and Mr. Martin walked out of the dressing room. Losing in this type of league carried little emotion, but Jess was appreciative of the "good games and the "too bads" they offered. Julianne's "You'll get them next time" was funny. Jen and Dan-el were excited to see Mr. Martin again as they exchanged pleasantries, and of course, Mom got in the mix with Mr. Martin. Always smooth and composed, Jess could see that Mr. Martin was genuinely happy to see them, too. Jess hadn't thought about it, but it pleased him to know that his part in all of this brought the group together again. They stood in the hallway, their voices echoing off the concrete walls, until the custodian told them it was time to lock up.

"We'll have to get together again," Mr. Martin said.

****

The Jefferson baseball team traditionally scheduled a round-robin tournament in Northern Mississippi on the Ole Miss campus. Coinciding with Jefferson's spring break, each team was promised four games and it was a big deal for the players. To go to a tournament with schools coming from all over went without saying that every team would be good. There were always bake sales, car washes and plenty of old-fashioned, blatant begging to raise the money for the trip.

Jess started the season at first base, it was his position to lose according to the coach. With everyone pumped for these games and eager for the season to begin, excitement was electric. Jess was slated to be the third pitcher in the rotation and would play exclusively on the varsity squad this year. As a pitcher, his curve broke too quickly to fool a good hitter, but he threw pretty hard and relied on a heater that topped out in the mid-eighties. His coach had him working on developing a change-up and elevating his release to more of an over-the-top with his first two fingers and thumb on the seams—more a slider. In practice, Jess was hitting the ball a lot more crisply this year evidenced by the sheer sound of his bat meeting the ball.

Life still wasn't coming up roses, though. His dad's death, the AP courses, working for people in the neighborhood, and even his abbreviated time with Jen all distracted Jess from baseball since last year. Although taller and stronger, Jess knew that he had to work harder to make up for the timing and poise necessary for this sport. Truly serious players would have spent more time in batting cages, joined travel leagues, watched tapes and watched more televised games. Baseball was a skill game. Nothing was more difficult than swinging a stick at a moving missile and trying to place the ball where no one could catch it.

Jefferson went two and two at Oxford; losing their first and third games. The coaches were pretty satisfied because all the games were close enough and they saw some good things in each game. "Remember, this is our spring training. Our building times." With a lot of walks from the pitchers and strikeouts from the hitters to go with too many errors for each team, Coach's words were apparent. Things like substituting without regard to the situation or the score kept the convivial atmosphere that would disappear with the regular season. "Think about your mental errors. What you could have done better: moving to back up throws; hitting the cut-off man; woulda, shoulda, coulda things." Aside from the thrill of being on a D-1 college campus and getting caught up in collegiate activity, Jess and the rest of his team didn't think the field they played on was any better than their own.

Our 'friendly confines.' Thought I'd never say that about something at Jefferson.

Jess batted in three games and went 4-10 with a pair of doubles and a two RBI.

I struck out three times. I thought about not wanting to put that in my stats scrapbook, but I have to put the bad with the good to keep it honest.

He felt awkward in striking out; one of them a swing at ball four. DH'd for in the game he pitched, he struck out four and allowed two runs on three hits and two walks in the four innings he pitched. That someone seemed to always be on base forced Jess to work from the stretch, which he didn't like. In comparison, he pitched as well as any of the other pitchers Jefferson had. Back home on Tuesday, the team would have the rest of spring break without games, but once school started again, they'd play three to four games every week.

Busy, but what else was new?

With basketball over, Jen was being hounded by coaches and their assistants trying to get her to express verbal interest in the school they represented. Phone calls, letters and brochures came daily. With her interest in architecture, Jen shared that Iowa State, not a current women's basketball powerhouse but with a solid team, and a school renowned for its engineering department, was one that contacted her. Jess was excited to learn that she was seriously considering making one of her allotted visits to Ames. "I know the campus. I could show you around."

It always tugged on his heartstrings to think that they would most likely be going to different colleges and would be separated not too far into the future, but Iowa State connected a few dots that could keep him in the picture. Jess could manage something like Iowa State himself, being only fifty miles or so from Mee-maws. Trouble was, Iowa State had dropped their baseball program several years ago, and presently fielded only a "club" team.

That might be the level of my expertise, who knows? But I should aim higher

Speaking of rules and eligibilities, it had come to mind that the Armory basketball league may have made Jess ineligible to participate in high school basketball in his state; a possibility gave Jess a funny feeling. Jess thought that surely, Mr. Martin would have told him before the games ever started if he were doing something that would hurt his eligibility.

Oh well. Too late now. I'm not going to put myself through that hassle again, anyway.

For Dan-el The Golden Gloves tournament was ever rapidly approaching, and this year he'd be fighting at 160-lbs. According to the pre-tourney seeding and the possibility for Dan-el winning through, he would likely face the fighter who won that division last year. Knowing the Gloves provided a channel for a boxer to advance from state to national prominence, even to get an Olympic trial further increased his excitement.

"Gotta be 17 to compete in the Olympics," Dan-el informed his friends. "And far beyond my skill set."

****

In times of repose, Jess would often marvel at the chain of events that brought him to know two people like Jen and Dan-el whom he loved equally but differently. "Talking" with Granddad was often a form of praying, and reminding himself that his family had provided the tools that made it possible to build the relationships he enjoyed with Dan-el and Jen. To change it would be devastating. Jess was also gratified that lately, another person was showing up for his conversations with Granddad, "Mm'mm."

I realized Granddad and now Dad were figments of my imagination, yet this was my way of examining my conscience; to consider the possibilities. I could make myself feel guilty without religion, and questioning personalized God for me. I tried to understand the whole thing more from my experiences than to simply accept a religious teaching, and it was a while after Dad died before I reconciled with God. Jen and I had some really great conversations about this. She called it the shroud and the cloud— the shroud held us down and the cloud was where our uninhibited minds took us.

Consistent with her analytical thought process, Jen explained her belief system. "There are three persons in one, the Holy Trinity. God the Father reigns over all things, God the Son is the intercessor between God the Father and the people, and God the Holy Spirit lives in each of us. I mostly think the Trinity was a human creation to help us understand the whole thing better, like a little kid understands Santa Claus. When I pray, I ask not that God would hear my prayers, but that I hear God's wishes for me." She smiled knowingly when she told Jess, "That ties everything together in my mind. The Holy Spirit makes God directly accessible to each person, and free will lets us choose our own path whether it's good works, religion, stewardship of the earth, or simply by doing no harm. Jen joked that you got points on the scoreboard of life in this manner, and yes, you lost points for things, too. "That makes it understandable for me, Jess."

Jim Billman

Chapter 8

Watching Jess put away his second plateful of tuna casserole, Mom said, 'To celebrate the end of the school year, why not have your friends over for a barbeque? We could invite their families, too."
Nothing wrong with that idea.
"Sounds good. Ella's mom and dad would never come, though."
Don't ask why. Ella uses Jen as an excuse to see Dan-el.
Seeing Jess's expression and now into solving everyone's problems Julianne said, "Don't worry so much Jess. Lighten up, Dude."
"Then another time, you can have a sleep-over with your best friends, Julianne."
"If she had any," Jess uttered.
"Jess! Be nice to your sister."
"Ten-four." Jess pushed his chair back to leave the table and bent down to kiss Julianne on the top of her head. "See ya. Gotta get over to Mr. Bingham's."
Whew. She didn't make me explain about Ella's mom and dad.

****

It was gratifying that Jess, Dan-el, and Jen each picked up an almost unbelievable twelve hours of college credit from their AP courses. They put in a lot of time, forever studying. They'd hear other kids talk about new phones and TV shows that they barely knew existed. Jess was a near-casualty by barely scraping by in Chemistry receiving a '3' and making his credit 'iffy' depending on the college. For certain, they all agreed their little cooperative plan of attack worked.

Thanks to the mandatory nation-wide testing date, AP classes were finished a week before school was out for the year which freed the Hersheys for much of the school day. Pleased with their accomplishments, they'd hang out in the Commons area sipping government-supplied fruit drinks. As they'd been told, Jefferson High School was what they made of it. You can find what you want.

On a morning early in the week, it was easy to see that Dan-el had a problem when he walked over to their table—a serious one. Right away Jen asked what was up.

At first, Dan-el was reticent, "I don't know. It just seems that every step forward turns out to be two steps backward." A comment completely out of character for him.

"Tell us, man. We're your BFF's. We're here for you."

Prodded to explain, Dan-el was anything but talkative.

It took a while before he answered, thinking about how to say it. "Cheesy as it is, you have to swear secrecy." After waiting for their nods, he continued, "I had a visit last night from Apex and two of his lieutenants. Right away, I knew that something other than giving me another beat-down was up 'cause they're too high on the totem pole to be whuppin' up on me. Whatever, I knew they weren't bringing me good news. I was right, too. One of them told me they were interested in the Golden Gloves, and in me. Jeez, I'm a friggin' seventeen-year-old kid in an amateur fight listenin' to this crap."

His face showing an ironic smile, Dan-el kept his voice low, all of them huddled forward. "Seems that my weight division will be one of the two or three marquee fights of the night, assuming we, really me, gets that far." Dan-el was referring to the fighter who won last year and the possibility they would meet him in the finals. "I guess it's some kind of compliment to think I could even get to the finals, let alone be able to beat the guy who won at that weight last year. The short version is they want me to lose."

Jess asked the obvious, "They bet on fights?

"Can't call it betting. They take the suckers' money who do bet."

Jess remained naïve, "But you could fight your hardest and still lose."

"That's what I'm sayin', man. High Aces don't bet unless it's a sure thing."

Jess understood, but not fully. "So even though you aren't expected to win…"

Dan-el finished the sentence. "They want to make sure I don't win."

Jen asked, "What if you didn't fight at all? You got sick or something like that?"

"If I were to feign sickness, they'd see right through it."

"And...?"

"Bets are off, retribution to follow."

"So, what happens if you fight and win?" Jess persisted.

Dan-el answered, "They mentioned Jon-el. Asked me how he was doing. Said that my Grandma will sure be glad to see him get out. He was talkin' smack and threatenin' me without doing it outwardly. They know how to get to people. And my brother's vulnerable."

"You said he was a High Ace?" Jen remarked.

"All the easier to get to him." Dan-el said. "It's like I've told you before, this gang stuff is organized and far-reaching. It's impressive. Especially when you're in the upper echelon.

Jess was thinking. Rubbing the back of his head as he often did. "Why you of all the fighters?"

"I live in the neighborhood for one thing. The guys betting know that and I'm probably a sentimental choice. The local Rocky Balboa."

Jen voiced another possible solution, "Could you talk to the other fighter beforehand and explain what's happening? This is obviously illegal in the first place and he wouldn't want to get caught if he knew."

Dan-el said, "That wouldn't be fair to that other guy and why would he believe me anyway? I don't know him and I go up and say, hey man I'm gonna let you win, what's he think? He's thinkin' I'm trickin' him. And, yes, if it ever got out that I threw a fight, I'd be banned from the Gloves and anything that might ever come after that."

"That's why it has to go to the authorities before the fight," Jess said. "Maybe I've watched too many cop shows where everything gets wrapped up in 42 minutes, but if we, you, go to the authorities you've solved one part of the problem."

Dan-el, sitting up straight, his demeanor echoing his feelings, "Then retribution becomes the problem. They might go after Mom and Grandma."

"Or you."

"Or me."

Dan-el's predicament deeply affected both his friends. Not knowing what to say, they would talk about it later after having time to think. The only things for sure were wishing that it wouldn't have happened, and knowing that Dan-el's personal constitution would never include losing a match on purpose. Plus, Jen or Jess had never known Dan-el to be stumped for a solution or seen Dan-el so dejected.

I thought a lot about what we could do. Somewhere in the back of my head a plan was hatching. It would break my promise, but I had to talk to Mom. I couldn't believe that I'd share something like this with her, but she was a part of this hazy idea that was taking shape.

The Armory was used jointly by the National Guard and the Police Department, two organizations dedicated to serve the people as Jess learned in eighth grade. Although contrary instances always made the news, a person assumes that both these groups are on the side of law and order and they serve the public for the 'greater good.' To think the High Aces could set up a gambling racket right under the noses of the police spoke to their boldness and to the depth of their entrenchment. Dan-el's trainer was a cop and knowing of the man's dedication to guys like Dan-el, Jess couldn't help but think that this would be another person to talk to.

After listening to her son, Mom questioned how Dan-el could get involved in something like a gambling scheme. Next, came the danger to Jess if he got involved followed by her responsibility as a parent. Jess knew this would take time and gave her time to vent her concerns.

Twenty questions.

After exhausting her contradictions, Mom's curiosity surfaced when she asked what Jess intended to do to help Dan-el.

"Mom, could you locate Mr. Martin and invite him to our barbeque?"

She suppressed a little smile, "I already did. I was going to surprise you."

"And...?"

"He's delighted. But what's Mr. Martin got to do with all of this?"

Jess, Surviving Normal

Jess explained Mr. Martin was the Executive Officer of the National Guard unit. "I don't know much about the relationships between officers and enlisted soldiers, but from what I saw, they seemed to be a pretty tight group. Pretty tough, too. I thought with Mr. Martin's help, he could organize a type of surveillance team during the Golden Gloves tournament."

Mom started to say something, but Jess continued. "Just to watch and observe, inconspicuously. The National Guard guys might see something and hone in. Surely the betting and exchanges take place near the Armory. The Billiard Parlor on Sixth Street is one place where a lot of people make bets on games and stuff."

Immediately. "How do you know? Have you been going there?

"Dan-el said."

A justifiable lie.

"Uh huh, sure."

"I don't think the average guy making a bet is very secretive. And if they were, no one would know where to go to bet on stuff."

Mom picked up on what Jess was saying. "I doubt that you're going to see money exchanged out in the open in the Armory. I suppose a trained observer can learn a lot especially if it's done together."

Mom was hooked! I knew she would help. Mom was smart; she didn't plant her potatoes above the ground.

"Then what?" she asked.

"We've got to bring Dan-el's trainer who's a detective into it. We could go to him in the first place, but from what Dan-el says about the High Aces, they would sniff it out because they study the cops and how they do things." Jess paused, thinking, and continued, "So, if Mr. Martin's guys take what they've learned to the police, who probably have a pretty good idea about what's going on, they could work together and catch the High Aces in the act."

Mom, skeptical again, said, "And five or six of these hoodlums get nabbed for gambling? Does that mean they're going to incriminate the whole gang? And how long will a gambling charge put them in jail, overnight?"

Mom must have been watching a lot of cop shows, too.

"Well, um," Jess had to think. "They sit on it, and keep watching."

"Who keeps watching? And what good will that do? There's still the fights."

"They all do. They watch and add all the things the High Aces do, from jay walking on up, until they add up and they have enough to arrest the leaders." Jess was winging it; he had no plan beyond getting Mr. Martin and the detective involved and to let them take it from there. Mom would be the adult link.

Mom knew I was flying from the seat of my pants, one of Granddad's sayings.

"I think that the more authorities we tell about Dan-el's being threatened, the better it will be for him. Protecting him and his family is the most important thing. I just think letting the police in on the whole scheme is best. They're trained; that's what they do."

The question of retribution from the High Aces went undiscussed. Jess wrongly thought that the police would have contingencies like Witness Protection Programs to take care of that problem. Further, he didn't want to push his mother whose first priority was to remove her son from being directly involved.

When Jess told Jen and Dan-el of his plan the next morning, they both showed disappointment that Jess broke their promise. He was ready for them, "We can't solve this without help. We need adult help that can be heard. Our moms are to be trusted, right?"

His point taken, they made Jess go through all the 'what if's' again and agreed that it was the right thing to do—the only thing to do despite the potential risk. Dan-el wanted to first talk to his mom before telling his trainer, and Jen, a not-totally-innocent bystander in it, would share the situation with her mom. Once they understood, they couldn't turn away.

"Be patient with them," Jess cautioned.

****

The Golden Gloves were set to begin on a Saturday that conflicted with an away game for Jess making him miss Dan-el's first two bouts. The semi-finals and final would be the following Saturday, and so far, that was an open date for baseball. But a rainout or a re-schedule could change everything just as an early defeat would end Dan-el's participation.

I tried to avoid thinking that an early loss would solve his problem.

It wasn't within Dan-el to lose a fight on purpose yet winning a bout was never a given no matter how hard a person practiced and trained. A surprise punch to the right spot, a slip on a wet canvas, or falling for a feint could turn a fight around in an instant. Through the week, it was gratifying to see their friend's self-assuredness slowly return after deciding to go ahead. Just by agreeing that they were doing the right thing was uplifting for each of them.

The barbeque party presented problems, too. Dan-el's mom knew the others only through her son, and it would take time to get acquainted. It'd also take time to build a relationship that would allow them to move on to something as serious as this. And Mr. Martin knew little, if anything, about Dan-el's situation and hadn't met Dan-el's or Jen's mothers. It was a guess how he might react.

When Jess finally got home, the party was getting started and it was good to hear some laughter coming from the backyard. He had to know all about Dan-el's bouts and tell about his game. He soon learned that Dan-el won two unanimous decisions in the ring, getting the play by play from both Jen and Ella. Dan-el 'Slice and dice' White was superb.

Jess, on the other hand, didn't volunteer that he played a pretty mindless baseball game earlier that day that prompted Coach to ask where he'd left his head after a mental mistake that let a runner advance. When asked about his game, though, he did tell them about his dinger, downplaying it to sound as a vicinity swing that happened to put the sweet spot of the bat where the ball was.

Mom had prepped Jess to realize that if the party was going to succeed, he would have to get everyone to mingle. "You can't go off in a corner so figure something out. It's really your party." After swapping their news and without a word from Jess, Jen and Ella decided to lend a hand by bringing Julianne, her friend, and Jen's brothers to a semblance of order. As Dan-el was speculating about his upcoming summer job to Jess, Mr. Martin came around the corner of the house carrying two big sacks of chips and a smile on his face. "Is this, by chance, the Jemison party?" he joked. Things were progressing smoothly, for now.

Mr. Martin was fashionably late as he told everyone. The honored guest, the teens drifted over to join the others, anxious to hear what was said; as far as anyone knew, he was yet to learn of Dan-el's threat. Jess's concern that Mr. Martin might feel uncomfortable in the group was immediately dispelled. Once pleasantries were exchanged, he fit right in and it wasn't long until Mr. Martin was absorbed in the give-and-take chatter.

The man is always comfortable. Admirable.

As the conversation went from the weather, to family, and to the Jemison's house, Mrs. White asked why he didn't bring a guest. Mr. Martin told the story how he had lost his wife and child to a drunk driver. As soon as he finished, Mrs. White said she felt terribly sorry for asking. "It's okay. Life goes on and I'm grateful for the time we had." Mr. Martin was fine. He grinned efficaciously and said, "I date, so each of you ladies be careful or I'll be asking about your availability."

If there was ever an awkward moment that evening it was past. Mom announced that the burgers and brats were ready, and would the other moms help her bring the food from the kitchen. "Adults first, otherwise there might not be anything left after Jess goes through the line."

Not funny.

While everybody was eating, the conversation turned to Mr. Martin's deployment prompting questions about when and where. His recent one was his second and he said he would soon be ending his time with the National Guard. "I'm too old," he offered.

Julianne made the comment that she liked eating outdoors in Trentsville better than outdoors in Iowa because there weren't as many flies. Jess, the biologist, couldn't help himself, "The common housefly, Musca Domestica, is the state insect of Iowa,"

"Thank you, Doctor Linnaeus," Dan-el chirped. Jess put his hands together in mock prayer and bowed his head reverently.

"Mucho Pesticus," Jen quipped.

After Jess's contribution to the group for the evening, Jen's mom asked Mr. Martin, "So if I'm possibly going to be going on a date with you, I'd like to know a little about your present livelihood. Can you keep me in the manner in which I'm accustomed?"

Mr. Martin was working toward a Ph.D., "A little more than part-time and a little less than full time, depending on my mood regarding education. I might seek an Ed. D. to avoid writing a dissertation." He went on to say that he had several ideas he was considering for his next career move, but none of them included public education unless it would be in a quaint rural setting." One like Iowa." By now, all of the moms and teens knew that he'd been dismissed from his position at Jefferson and Jess, for one, was hoping he'd say more about it.

He didn't entirely disappoint a few minutes later saying, "I overstepped my bounds knowing fully the traditions of public education in school districts across the nation and their strict hierarchies. In short, you don't buck the system or take something on by yourself to bring about change. You have to instill your ideas gently."

Remaining the focal point, Mr. Martin said, "Like any old organization that doesn't police itself, public education is top-heavy. There are too many cooks spoiling the soup and the end result is exactly the opposite of when each cook sticks to what he or she does best—like this delicious meal. No one stood over you as you prepared your dish and the outcome was magnificent. Mrs. Steffen didn't have Mrs. White and Mrs. Jemison telling her how to make potato salad. And better yet, each of you enjoyed preparing your dish just as teachers once enjoyed thinking that her classroom was her students' recipe to success." He reached over to a bag of chips and said, "Just think of the pleasure I had in preparing these chips as my contribution to the success of this meal. If I had brought nothing, you'd never invite me again."

"An apt allegory," Mom said. "But in your case, I think we'd invite you even without your chips."

"It's the same in social work. Once the too-little allocations trickle down to the people who need help, there's little more than nothing left to meet the intentions of the institution in the first place," Mrs. White said. "There's always a six-figure income at the top of the organization."

"And the constant fear that you'll do something that isn't to protocol or precedence rather than just going in there and doing what you know is best," Jen's mom said.

Jess spoke up; usually he'd be intimidated by the adult presence, but felt comfortable in this setting and his fly comment had made everyone laugh. "But the buck has to stop somewhere. Someone has to be accountable in every organization."

"But to what end?" Dan-el asked. "You have to take the bad with the good and those at the top have to watch out for themselves so they delegate their responsibilities to insure there is more good than bad under their watch."

The adults were enjoying the Hershey's getting into the discussion and were silent.

"Presumably, Jess said. "And eventually, the beast eats itself."

"Until we realize that the answer is in a social democracy, like Norway's," Jen said.

They continued, gradually solving the problems of the organizational world, from education to big box retail stores. As they did this, Mom, Mesdames White and Steffen quietly, "covered the extra food Jess and Dan-el hadn't devoured and cleared the picnic table. Returning from the house, Mrs. Jemison asked if they could change the subject to a more pressing problem. Jess noticed Dan-el's mom in the semi-darkness and saw her take a deep breath and wipe at the bridge of her nose as if to say, "Here we go." The teens scooted their chairs in closer and the conference began amid background noise from Julianne and her group, watching a movie in the family room.

Mom started. As the hostess she felt it was her place to get the discussion going. Explaining to Mr. Martin, Mike by this time to the moms, that one of the reasons for inviting him was the group's respect for him as a leader. "Although we thoroughly enjoy your winsome personality," she deadpanned, "we have a serious problem that came up just this week."

Mr. Martin, sensing a shift in the group, took on a puzzled expression as he looked at the group.

Mom, not wanting to mislead him, said, "And please, don't think for a minute that is the reason for your presence tonight. I invited you before I knew anything about this problem, this situation we share—all of us. Dan-el, would you please start by telling Mr. Martin how it all began?"

Minutes later, Dan-el finished detailing his dilemma and the group's consensus desire to do the right thing. "But it's the 'how' to achieve the right thing that we need help with. So far, we've decided that going to my trainer is the first step. Tomorrow, I'll tell him. You know him, Detective Kinkade."

Mr. Martin understood. "And you'd like me to be there, too. To lend some credibility as an adult? No problem. I don't know Detective Kinkade personally. I do know he spends a lot of time at the Armory volunteering his time and knowledge."

"Thank you so much," Dan-el said.

This was where my plan fell flat. Now what? My plan was to get Mr. Martin involved and hope.

Mr. Martin, didn't, however, offer a spur-of-the-moment solution making Jess even more anxious. The ensuing discussion was a mishmash of occasional comments punctuated with periods of thought. One question that was asked was obvious: Could the police establish surveillance teams to protect us against retribution?

"Probably not," Mrs. White said, "it would go beyond what the police have the capability to do. Trentsville is too large a city and they have a lot of ongoing demands."

Mrs. Steffen said, "What if rather than slinking around and trying to hide we turn the tables on these… High Aces? All gangs in fact. They operate illegally and they hide from the law so what's the one thing they don't want? It's exposure. We could launch a crusade to flush them out into the open. We might go to the TV stations where the news people are forever looking for good causes to support. We could email a letter to the newspapers to begin. Just do a number of things that they aren't expecting in an effort to get them to lay low, maybe shut down their betting operation for a while."

Mom and Mrs. White were so much alike.

This got the ball rolling. Mom said that she would gladly go on television and speak about Dad's murder. Mrs. White said she would likewise speak about her son being threatened. Yet, both were fully aware and agreed that doing the right thing carried risks.

"But if we're in the public eye we have people watching out for us. If it doesn't work, at least we tried. We protect our own regardless of the risk," Mrs. White said.

Dan-el asked, "Is one-week enough time to get all of this done/"

"And if it backfires, we've made them madder and more determined to seek retribution," Jen said.

No one had answers to those questions.

Mr. Martin, pensive to this point, spoke, "I have an idea that might get us someplace. The National Guard is controlled by the states designed to give them a degree of sovereignty. Each one has its governor serving as commander-in-chief. That's our mission, to serve however the governor sees fit in the case of domestic emergencies. Riots, floods, tornadoes and civil unrest all fall within our stateside mission. We also have a commitment to serve at the federal level in places like Afghanistan and Iraq."

With crickets chirping, a siren in the distance, and Cruella De Vil screaming about catching Dalmatians drifting from the house, everyone gathered around the picnic table was intent on Mr. Martin. "My point is this; The Guard does other things too. We're not always fighting disaster or unrest, but we have agricultural development teams and can, in certain cases, be called to duty under the act of *Posse Comitatus*. And like it sounds, we can act as a posse setting out to catch bad guys just like in the old-time Westerns. I'm sure you follow where I'm taking this."

There were some murmurs and nods; they liked what Mr. Martin was saying, where this was going. Jess and Dan-el were of the same mind exchanging glances visualizing a cavalry charge.

Pausing to consider his next thought, Mr. Martin continued. "Following the idea of going public, maybe, just maybe, our local contingent of Guardsmen could receive permission to act at the behest of the governor. Ideally, we could make enough noise to get the entire National Guard of the state to go after the illegal activities of gangs. But let's not get too hopeful; I don't have any influence with the governor nor do I know anyone who does. And the cost of such an action becomes the burden of the state."

Jess's idea sprouted new wings. "Undercover Guardsmen and women could watch and take pictures of illegal things."

Jen added, "CCTV could follow them, and with eavesdropping equipment we could hear them."

In no time, they had contrived a network of bugs, tracking devices, hidden cameras and an army of allies. No one mentioned drones—yet.

"Whoa, slow down; we have a week and we can do all this?" Dan-el again was looking at the logistics.

Mr. Martin spoke, "It doesn't necessarily need to be done in a week. The first priority is to provide protection from reprisal for all three of your families. Mainly, we keep Dan-el safe. And if the High Aces want Dan-el's full cooperation, Ella becomes someone they can leverage against him. But it's the Whites who are at the most risk. If nothing else I think I could enlist enough guys to put together a little *ad hoc* group to ensure your safety for a while. In the meantime, we can go through channels to see if our plan could gain support."

What's ad hoc? It doesn't matter. I know what Mr. Martin's saying. We have a plan; our 'How' is getting clearer.

The next step was to organize. They needed to delegate who would do what, who might have an acquaintance working at the newspaper, at the television stations and so on. After a few minutes, Mr. Martin raised his hands for quiet. "In my opinion, we need stealth and surprise rather than a frontal attack. I don't think it's in Dan-el's best interest to broadcast what's going on. The rest of us will lay our so-called mines covertly and then make a concerted assault from more directions than the gang can react to when that time comes. If we do nothing outward until Dan-el's fight is over, the Aces suspect nothing and its business as usual for them.

"I'm on active status right now as Executive Officer of the company and the Armory can be our operational base. I will be there during the week, and I think our surveillance squad could use some practice exercises. Like Jen said, cameras, listening devices, and security. We have the equipment." He smiled, "Your tax dollars at work."

He had more. "If Detective Kinkade is at the Armory tomorrow afternoon, which I suspect he will be, Dane-el and I will talk to him to see what he says or what he might offer. You'll be there training so Detective Kinkade will be there, too. Right Dan-el?"

"Yes sir, he usually comes in around one when all of us are getting ready." Dan-el nodded.

"Will there be any other trainers or adults?" Mr. Martin asked.

"There's always a couple other cops that come to work out and help."

"Good. Then we can get his attention, and once we tell him what's happening to you, I'm sure we'll have his undivided attention."

"One more thing. If it's all right with you, Rebecca, would you let Jess stay with Dan-el this week just for the safety in numbers thing, and that way, I will know they're together? I'll take responsibility for them."

I could tell that Mom was skeptical for all the obvious reasons. She doesn't know Mr. Martin well enough. Being with Dan-el puts me more in harm's way. Another possible tragedy in a year of them.

"Our bond to our children is equal and separate. They are our most precious possession from birth to the day that we release them to their own devices, but we only know a mother's love by looking out of our own windows. We write our lives in those terms."

She spoke far differently than the way I imagined.

Jess hoped Mom wasn't going to say something that would alienate herself, or equally as concerning, embarrass him. He glanced at everyone in the diminished light, and looking at Ella, whose parents weren't here and may not have come had they been asked. Ella had her own problems; and now she was entwined in this one. He knew the movie the children were watching was about over from the music. He experienced a momentary feeling of empowerment.

Everyone either seated at or around the picnic table as random satellites waited. Mom fidgeted with her empty glass and continued. "As a mother, I know that we moms hold our children as precious as I hold mine. As to our bond with Mr. Martin, that comes from our children who know him as an educator, and also as a trusted ally. So, what brings us together isn't based on familiarity but on trust and feeling and impression. Because those things are present, I fully support whatever Mr. Martin can do on the behalf of protecting Dan-el and doing the right thing."

Mrs. White, removing her glasses and patting a napkin under her eyes, thanked Mom for her support.

Jess was proud of Mom. That she always spoke to him as an adult in a matter-of-fact voice offering no excuses, particularly with her objective approach to problem-solving that was gratifying.

The group talked some more about plans, and there were more questions for Mr. Martin. Some indecision, adult stuff, semantics, and the need to cover all the bases got a little boring to the teens. It seemed that there was always something more than Granddad Wilkerson's simplistic "see the ball, hit the ball" approach to doing things.

With everyone in accord, it was pretty late when the party broke up. Mr. Martin would spearhead the threat to Dan-el and everyone else would carry on as usual. Ella, who lived 20 minutes away if the stoplights were favorable had to hurry to beat her curfew. Sunday would determine a lot—depending on Mr. Martin and Detective Kinkade. They would meet again on Monday. The watchwords: be patient, wait.

****

After Monday's practice, Jess planned to meet Jen and Dan-el at the deli. Anxious to the point of distraction, almost walked out of the locker room without his baseball gear. With two donuts looking at him like cartoon eyes begging to be eaten and Jen continuing to work, he fiddled with his phone—nothing from Dan-el. Each time the little bell above the door announced the coming or going of a customer, his head would jerk in anticipation.

The donuts mere appetizers, they'd eat lunch and then go to Dan-el's and stay at Wood's Park. With baseball games scheduled for Tuesday and Friday and the last day of school on Wednesday, Mom expected him to come home each day to report the happenings. Jess's truck proving essential as it beat a path up and down Roosevelt Avenue to and from Wood's Park.

Shortly, after an eternity, Dan-el arrived. Sweating from the high humidity and the hot city transit ride, Dan-el was Dan-el. "City's got air-conditioned busses. Trouble is, people always getting on and off."

They got their 'usual' to eat and Jen joined them, resplendent in her hairnet. Although taking her lunch break, she felt obligated to work the register if everyone else was busy. Taking what she'd said as a warning, they didn't waste any time attacking their sandwiches, Dan-el relating what had happened with Detective Kinkade between bites.

"Mr. Martin came to the gym about twenty minutes after I started. I pointed him to the office area where Detective Kinkade was. The door shut and I could see them through the window but couldn't hear anything. So, I kept doing what I always do. After finishing on the speed bag, Detective Kinkade opened his door and motioned me into the room."

"You sure you didn't stop for a drink of water? C'mon man, what'd they say?

Jen had to run over to the register to let a customer pay. When she left, Jess told Dan-el that he came straight from practice and probably smelled like a dancing circus bear to repeat one of Granddad's metaphors.

"Just an everyday occurrence that my olfactory receptors have grown accustomed to when you're around," Dan-el replied.

Jen returned and Dan-el continued, "Anyway, both of them gave me the twenty questions about what was said, who said what and all the stuff that went on between the High Aces and me. I know Detective Kinkade better than Mr. Martin, but either one or the other would ask me something and then they'd discuss it awhile and then one of them would ask another question."

"Did you feel intimidated?" Jen asked.

"No. Like I always say, I'm pretty comfortable with human beings and expected it would be this way. They asked a lot about what I knew of the Aces gambling and betting operation. I was surprised when Kinkade asked about Jon-el and how much time he had yet. Really just letting me know that he knew."

Jen saw another customer ready to leave and got up while Dan-el was talking. "How long?" she asked.

"He got 50 months max," watching Jen. Then said, "He's about two years and change in now." They ate some more; 'scarfed' being a more accurate descriptor in Jen's temporary absence. The deli made the best sandwiches ever.

Jen, not satisfied asked, "So what do you think your brother might have to do with this?"

"Don't know, didn't make a lot of sense. Probly nothing."

Jen came back and asked, "Maybe what Jon-el knows could help the police?"

"And get a plea bargain deal," Dan-el said. "Yeah, but at what price for Jon-el? Witness protection? His main worry'd be retribution."

"Not if they're shut down." Jess said.

"That's a hell of a lot easier said than done," Dan-el answered sounding a little perturbed. "Anyhow, to make a long story shorter, after I told them what I knew, Detective Kinkade pointed to the obvious. Fact that I had a tough fight in the semis and an even tougher one in the finals. And he's right, I could lose tryin' my best to win. The odds would say I'm an underdog."

The wheels were turning in Jess's head. "Then why wouldn't the High Aces get to your opponent and make more money by betting you to win?"

"They're smart, Jess. They still make money if I lose and it's more conservative. Plus, betting, actually seeding the favorite early on drives up the odds, and bettors are dreamers, they like big odds. Jeez, this is just an amateur fight and it's being treated like a world's championship.

"So, the way yesterday ended was pretty much like it was Saturday night. We go on just like nothing happened, and I try to avoid the High Aces. You and I hang out like Mr. Martin suggested and Detective Kinkade will let me know of new developments. The last I was told was I'd better get back to my workout, to shut the door. The two of them stayed in the coach's room."

"That's all?"

"That's all. You going to the game tomorrow, Jen?"

"As soon as I can get there after work. Save a seat for me, Dan-el."

They said their good-byes to Jen and left the deli. Jess wishing he'd been able to give Jen a kiss.

Concerned about the safety of his truck in the Wood's parking lot, Dan-el explained that as bad as the High Aces may be, there were residual benefits. "It's their way of paying back the folks around here," he joked. It's their turf, man, and screwed up as it may be, they feel some community ownership. They'll go out in the 'burbs and steal a car or come to your house and jack your truck, but our parking lot stays pretty safe. Emphasis on 'pretty safe' in case something happens,"

Jim Billman

Jess gathered his clothes while Dan-el waited in the living room with his phone, *I thought of Dad. He'd been dead for almost a year. And now, a few months from being seventeen, his truck belonged to me and I would be getting an unrestricted driver's license. I knew that I would never have a birthday no matter how long I lived without the sadness his memory brought. I often wondered how things would be different had all this not happened; the old WWJD changed to 'what would Dad do?'*

****

Driving to the ballpark for Tuesday's game, Jess was thinking more about Dan-el and the umpteen ways things could play out for him. Although scheduled to be the starting pitcher, it wasn't until he walked through the gate and got into the locker room that his thoughts shifted to baseball. Coach kept their three-man rotation in place during the season regardless of the team they were facing, and today's game featured a kid, a senior, from out in the exurbs that was projected as a third or fourth round draftee. To go that high and be in rounds that offered signing bonuses was really something. Jess remembered him from last year as one of those guys you love to hate. It didn't seem like enough for him to let his playing speak for him, his big mouth and swag made him unbearable. Most of the Jefferson players thought the same.

Game time was set for 1:05, which allowed ample time for the varsity game and then the JV one that followed before it got dark. Day games saved on utilities but were an unpopular choice for the fans. In Iowa, games were almost always played in the evening and Jess preferred night games, thinking that it was to his advantage as a pitcher.

Much had changed in baseball in the Technological Age, too. Thanks to the availability of games on the sports channels, the many how-to videos on mechanics, and the instructional camps, entire high school line-ups featured batters whose stance, swing and follow-through were similar. Granddad Wilkerson told Jess that when he was a kid, you could go to a Minor League game and predict the future major league players by the way they carried themselves at the plate and in the field; there was no need for names on their uniforms. "We knew the major league stars by their unique stance." More than once Granddad struck a pose and said

'Stan, the man, Musial'; then shifting to a right-handed hitter, 'Willie, Say hey, Mays.' He could mimic five or six more of his all-time favorites. After Granddad died, Jess wrote his name on the back of his glove, and this year he had written Dad's in the inseam of his cap.

I liked to think both of them were watching. If they were in heaven with all the great things that place has to offer, I don't suppose they'd have much interest in watching anything on earth, especially a screw-up like me. Old pessimistic Pete.

Warming up was another of the coach's by-the-book procedures, and Jess was grateful for the fact that baseball at Jefferson was played at a higher level than back in Iowa. Trentsville boasted of one major leaguer at the present time, a 23rd-round draftee that spent six years in the minors who finally stuck with the Cardinals as a utility player. Today's player, the superstar the Jefferson players referred to as "Lurch" was comparatively that much better—a highly-sought baseball player.

Jess started by throwing soft-toss for several minutes, and then backed up and focused on his wind-up and hesitation movements using full extension. Next, he went to the bullpen mound and started throwing harder and ended by going through a five-pitch set of each of his three game pitches. Jess relied on his fastball and threw his slider and 'experimental' change-up off that pitch.

So much was different between New Holland and Jefferson. Jess played at several fields in Iowa where pitchers warmed up in the outfield. Here, fields had bullpens with mounds. An assistant coach watched to make sure he did everything the way he should. As Jess reached the final stages of his preparation, the team's long reliever came out and started to loosen up for his role, just in case. All in all, Jess threw enough tosses, half and three-quarter speed pitches to equal what he would throw in the game. Last year, stamina was a major focus, but now his arm was more conditioned from these upgraded procedures. Another point the coach stressed was learning the difference between pitching and throwing. Jess thought he would've thrown harder back home, but he already had better accuracy here. Location, location, location.

High schools and colleges have long since adopted the Designated Hitter format, but the option to have the pitcher hit remains. Disappointing to Jess, his coach used the DH meaning Jess would not bat today. Whether that hurt or helped the team, Jess's numbers spoke for themselves: a .410-.667-1.120 triple-slash line that put him among the top three in each statistic. Regardless of the contribution his bat made, no one questioned their revered coach's decisions—ever.

On the way to the mound to start the game, Jess spotted Dan-el with Ella and Jen to her right sitting where they usually parked themselves under the shade of the pavilion. And behind them were Mom, Julianne and Mr. Martin. Jess's butterflies made a mass movement while he walked to the mound—all the way to Large Colon, Panama.

His first pitch was a fastball right down the center of the plate followed by Dan-el turning around to Mr. Martin and saying, "Well, there goes the no-hitter." A liner into centerfield. Seven pitches and one out later Jess's hopes for a shut-out were also gone when Lurch yanked a belt-high fastball over the inner part of the plate ten feet over the left field wall, 320 feet away. His bat flip so in-your-face it brought a warning from the umpire. After walking the next batter on four pitches, Jess regrouped and struck out the next two guys, leaving the top half of the first inning two runs down and not pleased with himself.

Look forward, you can't get back what has been done. A Coach Mercer fav.

The High School Athletic Union had rules stating how many pitches a pitcher could throw in a game and in a week given that they were not on consecutive days. Relief pitchers had their own set of rules. Games were seven innings and pitchers were allowed no more than eighty-five pitches counting foul balls, meaning that any live game ball thrown from the mound counted as one of the eighty-five. A pitcher could pitch the entire game, but it was pretty rare. Enacted for parity and to get more players into a game, the rule actually worked against strikeout pitchers. Jess left the first inning having thrown thirty-one pitches.

After the disaster of the first inning, Jess settled down and pitched well, allowing two hits, two walks and no more runs. To the delight of most of the fans, Jess struck out Lurch twice to give him the impressive total of nine strikeouts in five and one-third innings when he reached his limit. Jefferson had scored five runs and Jess stood to be the winning pitcher when leaving the field, hearing the applause of the fans for a job well done.

After wrapping his pitching arm in a towel and finding a seat on the bench, he watched his replacement allow just one hit and otherwise shut down their opponent to preserve the 5-2 win. After the game, Jess would ice his arm before showering and join the rest of the team to watch the JV game. Per Coach's orders, players had to sit as a group and act accordingly.

Despite no longer just raring back and throwing as hard as he could, Jess knew that his velocity was up this year and that allowed him to have some success with the hard curve and change-up. Over all, he was pretty satisfied with his performance. A big victory, Coach gave the team the next day off and said they'd have a light practice Thursday before the away game on Friday.

As Jess and a couple other players were leaving the ball park for the day, they noticed Lurch sitting in the bleachers talking to a guy wearing a Panama hat. "I bet that's a big-league scout," one of them said. Rather than continue walking, they stopped and took in the scene, each lost in his own dream.

****

Staying with Dan-el that week meant that I didn't have time to be with Jen. That was okay depending on how you looked at it because we had some issues of our own design. I was always looking ahead trying to design our future and Jen was more into a wait-and-see after we were out of college. Both literally and proverbially, we had become much closer to each other starting about half-way through the last semester. It was kind of funny that our relationship moved forward after we, she, decided to play the field and be open to other dates. Yeah, like that would ever happen in my case! Recently we'd spent time talking about things and agreed that it was getting more and more difficult to suppress our urges. It was kind of funny, though. We'd talk about it after some pretty heavy stuff.

On Sunday, the day after the party, we were alone at Jen's and as things progressed, we were going farther than ever before. Our bodies touching brought a physical release I'd never experienced before with Jen. We'd been doing the pressing while kissing before, but this was new. Afterward and kind of embarrassed, we had a heart-to-heart about waiting longer, but, although unspoken, we both knew that 'longer' was only an attitude away. It was just physically impossible; we were telling each other that we were in love and had discussions about the degree of our love. Besides, as if it were justification, we both knew that Ella and Dan-el were having sex. And, if the internet statistics I saw were correct, we were over a year past the norm for our ages. For me, the desire was so powerful that it erased sensible reasons not to.

Later, at home, guilt-ridden I imagined if Dad and Granddad watched me play ball, I couldn't help but think they watched me as I lay on Jen's bed grinding away. I didn't dwell on the thought for very long, though. We both knew where it was going.

I was a sexual newbie and from our initial fumbling to where we were now, I supposed Jen didn't know much more than I did. That was what I wanted to believe, and we were having fun fumbling together as we called it. Intriguing, exciting, and stimulating described my feelings.

Guilty as charged your honor.

For Jen, sex was discussed more freely and matter-of-factly with her Mom. Being a nurse, Jen's mom had told her about STD's, shown her pictures of affected people, and discussed numbers and odds of contacting diseases if precautions weren't taken. All this explained before she knew Jess, Mrs. Steffen knew that STD's weren't the issue between her daughter and Jess. Her main issue was the fact that the burden of a pregnancy fell on the female. Jen, close to receiving offers of a full-ride scholarship to some prestigious universities, was fully aware that college basketball players weren't given maternity leaves. That's what made the most lasting impression on Jen.

Jen's weakness was also her ally—her mom. She could talk openly and would get support rather than admonition. Her mom shared her experiences, openly and frankly explaining that it was easy to preach abstinence, to lay shame, and extol puritanical stigmas on her daughter, but not very practical in real life. By simply saying. "I know, I was your age--yesterday" helped Jen tremendously.

Jen told me that her mom spoke of the urges and didn't preach abstinence, as much as to "be sure" about her decisions and methods. That's how I learned what I knew beyond the locker room, what Dad told me, and my one (or two?) excursion(s) looking at internet porn.

They decided to keep it the way it was. "Better to look forward with anticipation than backward with remorse," Jess said half-believably.

****

The week progressed and none of the teens heard anything about the 'plans.' They could only assume Mr. Martin and Detective Kinkade were going forward within their groups and they'd be told in due time. Dan-el maintained that the less they knew the better. Yet, it was Dan-el who was the main guy, the one most likely to suffer the consequences, and Jess could see the entire thing was working on his friend. Instances of distraction and periods of silence when his friend would stare into the distance were readily noticeable.

They were talking in his room one evening before turning out the lights and Dan-el said, "If I don't get psyched up and go into my fights with this lackadaisical attitude I have, I'll get beat. We're too even for me to just walk in and win like I were ordering a pizza."

Jess agreed. "That's true in every sport. It's why we play the game. If you knew who would win, why play?"

"Or bet on the outcomes," Dan-el added. Everything seemed to come back to that. He reached up and turned off the light, the twin beds on opposite wall of the room.

Jess kept the conversation going, his voice pensive, "Dan-el, you are absolutely my all-time hero. Okay, my super-hero." Jess had never said anything like this to anyone; he'd never met anyone like Dan-el.

I was glad we were in the dark. For some time now, I wanted Dan-el to know how much I appreciated him and now seemed like a good time.

"Man, from the time I met you, you showed me what courage was and how to look at things as positively as possible. I was so low when I walked into Biology class that first time after being stabbed that I didn't think my luck would ever change. You've led me to the right choices, you've never been condescending and you've been the best friend I could ever wish for. That's why I know you'll do the right thing for yourself and all of us this Saturday. I know you'll step into the ring prepared, win or lose."

I could sense Dan-el's appreciation and acceptance of my words as his quiet 'thank you' floated across the room. I knew he had tears from the thickness of his voice in echoing what I said.

"I'm glad you said that. The feeling's mutual."

"I'm glad I did too, bro."

****

Friday's game was against Jefferson's arch rival. The way their coach talked up each game, Jess thought everyone was their arch rival but this one more so than the others. Their conference included nine schools within metropolitan Trentsville and three suburban, independent schools that made a twelve-school total. The more intense rivalries were not so much for the teams themselves as for crowd incidents of the past that weren't always caused by students. Some kids came to the games for the sole purpose of causing trouble, but adults could get pretty chirpy over the officiating and comments could escalate into arguments and even fights. There was always a concern over security. Football was probably the worst, especially being at night and at the end of the week. Baseball was raucous in the sense that it was loud, but there was rarely any crazy stuff.

For the players, conference rules dictated a 'good sport' policy that could cost a player a suspension not for just that game, but for the season. For an act to be determined flagrant was entirely the official's call during the game and if an additional un-sportsman-like call was attached, a suspension followed. In baseball, if the pitcher hit two batters in an inning or three in a game, he was done for the day and the umpire had the prerogative to have him suspended if he or she thought it was intentional.

Jefferson's number one pitcher was a control artist that relied on spotting his pitches to accompany a good east-west curve. Both the number two guy and Jess threw a lot harder, and as the season was progressing, they were having more success than the pre-season number one. Long story short, Jefferson lost 7-2. Jess had two of the team's five hits.

We lost 7-2; no 'I' in team.

Friday night, Dan-el and Jess watched an old Jimmy Stewart movie with the companionship of Dan-el's mom and grandma. It was amusing that every time Jimmy Stewart repeatedly drawled "Well, well," to start a sentence, Dan-el would jump to his feet and shadow box for several seconds. During a conversation later that night, both were too stoked to sleep for what Saturday would bring. Dan-el had to be at the gym at 11:00, four hours ahead of his scheduled fight.

While talking about nothing of consequence around ten-thirty, Dan-el's phone rang and seeing "Unknown caller," curiosity got the better of him and he answered. Listening for a few seconds, he clicked off. "Those assholes!" he asserted loudly enough to bring a reprimanding "Dan-el" from outside his room.

"What was that all about?" Mrs. White asked as she came into the room from the living room.

Dan-el was livid. "My 'friends.' They just wanted to let me know that they're counting on me tomorrow."

"How did they get your phone number?"

Dan-el didn't know, of course, but the fact remained. Mrs. White was quite concerned and told Dan-el to turn his phone off for the rest of the night. "They could call you every 30 minutes and harass you all night."

Dan-el said, "Maybe one of us should call the police and see if we can get ahold of Detective Kinkade, too. We haven't heard anything all week and I think we need to know if everything is going as planned."

"Mr. Martin has kept us informed," Mrs. White said from the doorway, the hallway light behind her. Looking from Dan-el to Jess, she explained that the moms heard from Mr. Martin each day, but none of them thought it wise to get any of the teens more involved than necessary. "We all thought that the less you two and Jen knew, the less likely something could go wrong,"

Dan-el saw it differently. "That sounds like you people think we're going to screw something up; like you don't trust us."

Jess nodded agreement with Dan-el. They were the ones most at risk.

Dan-el was about ready to blow, and it reminded me of the time Dad told me about his job offer. I felt like I didn't count at first. Dan-el feeling like he'd been hung out to dry.

Dan-el started to say something, but sputtered when Mrs. White shushed him. "Before you get too worked up, Dan-el White, stop and think for a minute. What good would knowing have done? Detective Kinkade thought that all four of you needed to go on as usual. Nobody except you knew anything about this whole thing. It's not that we don't trust you, but you two have a role to play that doesn't require you to know what Mr. Martin is doing or what Detective Kinkade is arranging. And we moms want to know our children will be safe. So, don't get high and mighty to me like you've been forsaken." Mrs. White took off her glasses and pinched the bridge of her nose as she and her son glared at each other in the semi-darkness. Dan-el was the first to look away.

Jess chose to become invisible, not wanting to participate or be a part of this dispute.

Seconds later, Dan-el realized he over-reacted. "I'm sorry, Mom."

"You have to understand that Detective Kinkade and Mr. Martin have to work through channels to get things done. A detective must get permission and to put together a solid operational plan which is no small task. He can't just go to the commissioner or chief and tell them he's putting together a task force to bust a gambling ring. He has to convince his superiors that this is in the best interest of the citizens of Trentsville, not just you and our family. I know it sounds like an insult to you to have your veracity questioned, but you're the only person that's been approached. It's hearsay, dear, so from your standpoint, you should be honored that Detective Kinkade regards you so highly that he's acting on this. Rather than getting your socks in a bunch being ignored, appreciate all the work these men are doing in your behalf. Your job is to win your division and that's a pretty important role because if you don't, everything is circumstantial and a possible felony becomes a misdemeanor."

Mrs. White sighed, then continued; Dan-el had to know. "If you think deeply into this whole mess, it's pretty important that you win if you get to the finals. I know that sounds terrible, but it's true. Even if you fight to win and lose honestly and word gets out that the fight was rigged, you could be in big trouble. The least being banned from the Golden Gloves and carrying that stigma forward into your adult life. It might even run afoul of the law not to mention that the High Aces would own you."

Jess didn't know whether Dan-el had thought about what his mom said or not. Jess surely hadn't.

The similarity between Mom and Mrs. White was striking, I could imagine Mom explaining this with the same tone in her voice. Dan-el and I were fortunate to have mothers that dedicated themselves to their children. That Jon-el was in prison despite all of Mrs. White's efforts saddened me every time I thought of it. Her sense of loss must be great. She must have known I was thinking of her.

"And you, little mouse over there like you can't hear us. With your name on the Aces hit-list, you should be equally appreciative."

"It's nice to be included, I guess." Jess said, hoping that he didn't sound like a wise-ass.

"Okay, now let me continue. I mentioned how slowly the wheels of government move; you just can't go in and make things happen just because you're a detective or an army officer. So sometimes you have to find other ways to do things by going around the chain of command. Mr. Martin knows that and Detective Kinkade spent years on patrol learning how a bureaucracy works. As for me, I've learned through my associations and time in my position how to work the powers that be. You gentlemen with me, so far?"

"It's who you know," Dan-el said.

"And what you know," Jess said, paraphrasing the old saw to better fit the occasion.

"I don't think I'm compromising a confidence when I tell you Detective Kinkade received an approval, but with revisions and limitations. There'll be no stake-out because the High Aces are so entrenched, they'd know that something was up if their eyes and ears on the street start seeing a bunch of new faces hanging around where they usually hadn't been a few days ago. Put one and one together and that could add up to Dan-el and Jess. So, the police made arrangements to act, but solely on contingency depending on how my son performs. In short, they need provocation-a reason.

"And for Mr. Martin. He knew that his possibilities of getting the governor to call out the National Guard were nil, and he knew it last Saturday night, talking to us. Now before I go on, I want to tell you that this Mr. Martin is a remarkable individual because of his transcendental skills."

Dan-el started, "Wha…"

"By transcendental I mean that he has the capability to do things on two levels at the same time; for example, he was a school administrator that was trusted by students. As an officer in the Army, he accomplished combat missions given him because established a rapport with his men. Like we see in biographies, he seems like the type of leader whose men would follow him anywhere. I haven't known him very long, but I saw this trait in him Saturday night, and have listened to him several times throughout this week. And of course, I checked him out through some unofficial channels I was telling you about a minute ago."

Dan-el, shifting in his bed to face more directly toward his mother, asked," But Mr. Martin was fired from his school job last year. How was that an example of working with administrators and students synergistically?"

Syner…what? Like symbiotic in biology, fool.

Grandma, tired of straining to hear the conversation from her room, appeared beside her daughter. Jess thought she would offer to make everyone a little snack, but under these circumstances was quiet.

"As for Mr. Martin's being fired, suffice it to say that things may not have been as they appeared. He knew better than to do what he did, so to me, there was another reason behind it; an ulterior motive. I think there's a lot more to that story, especially considering how rotten everything was last year at Jefferson."

Jess was lost, and what he could see of his friend, so was Dan-el. Rather, he hopped off his bed, grabbed the basketball in the corner of his room, put his hands on the sides of it like it was a skull and recited, "Alas, poor Yorick, I knew ye well. Whether 'tis nobler to suffer the pangs and arrows of an outrageous fortune or to take arms against a sea of troubles… Sorry Mom, autonomic response to the word 'rotten.' Makes me think of our English Lit class. Methinks something's rotten in Denmark, and Jefferson High School."

Mrs. White had enjoyed the diversion, so Jess decided that he did, too.

"Okay, Prince Hamlet, let's leave Elizabethan England and get back to the present. Major, I think that's his rank, Martin, has appealed to some of the other soldiers in his battalion to help him on a personal basis; a non-military thing as one friend helps another. He didn't say in so many words, but to me and to your mom, Jess, this can only come about because of the type of influence he has with his men and women, something going beyond the typical officer-enlisted dichotomy. All said, Mr. Martin's 'army' consists of fellow guardsmen that he has simply asked for a favor."

"Mr. Martin has put together a team of vigilantes," Jess spontaneously chimed in. "His posse."

"And it's a crew of soldiers that are trained and pretty buff from the guys I see down at the Armory, Dan-el said.

"And kicked me around on the basketball court."

Mrs. White said, "You helped, Jess, by playing basketball with them. Several of those guys know you. And they've seen Dan-el down there for a couple of years, now. When Mr. Martin asked for some help, these men were more than willing. Another reason to not let you two in on all this, but you have been pretty safe this week thanks to Mr. Martin's guardsmen pals who've been 'kind' of watching. And that was the other reason to keep you out of it. If you'd known, you might not have acted in your usual way."

"And that's why it was easier to watch us if old Jess and I were together all the time."

Jess and Dan-el heard, "Some secrets are good to keep," as Mrs. White closed the bedroom door.

Saturday would tell it all.
They barely slept that night.

Jim Billman

Chapter 9

Jess remained with Dan-el until he went into the dressing rooms to prepare for the semi-finals. Jess, violating his driver's permit once again, drove out to pick up Jen from work. Ella was there, too, having stayed at Jen's overnight. The trio arrived well ahead of the time for Dan-el's fight and decided to go out for a walk along the Riverwalk, for Jess a bittersweet reminder of the time almost a year ago--their first date and the tragedy that followed.

Divisions in boxing are based on weight and Dan-el's first opponent was six feet three, taller than anyone he'd ever fought or sparred. Detective Kinkade and Dan-el knew his opponent was tall so the obvious plan was to work on body punches, which was what his opponent expected and was good at defending. Weight wasn't always an equalizer in the sport, taller fighters had an advantage because they had a longer reach and punched level at their opponent's head with more momentum. What a shorter fighter couldn't reach substantiated the advantage. Head punches were more spectacular to spectators and more explosive as knock-out punches, but the mandatory head gear alleviated that danger. In the Golden Gloves, a clean punch to the body scored the same as one to the head. Still, to casual observers, the advantage remained with the taller man if the difference was significant, sometimes comical.

The trouble for tall fighters was that shorter fighters didn't buy into the advantage because other factors counted: speed, footwork, conditioning, and heart to name a few. Whatever the attributes of one over the other, the bout is decided in the ring where Dan-el's 2 - 1 semifinal decision was decided. The finals would start at 7:00 that evening.

It was a difficult fight for Dan-el. He'd been surprised by his opponent's speed as he got jarred with a straight jab to his forehead, cleanly administered between Dan-el's paired vertical forearms ala Floyd Patterson's peak-a-boo in the first thirty seconds. A punch that, if Dan-el had been coming forward, would have done serious damage, far more than the point that was scored.

Opening blow aside, Dan-el's faster hands and feet prevailed. Using his more compact body with its lower center of gravity he dominated by bulling his way inside his foe's arms and taking away his leverage. He kept his foe backpedaling throughout and scored repeatedly.

During the entirety of the Golden Gloves, every fighter was thoroughly checked both mentally and physically. Broken wrists, stretched cartilage, scrapes, bruises and dilated pupils among the things watched. Concussions were first and foremost and trainers would report anything suspect to the attending physician, always present.

Dan-el would get checked, then rest and spend the interim time with Detective Kinkade and his assistant. The Trentsville PAL group Dan-el fought for had two other fighters who made it to the finals in their division, so it was a busy time for Detective Kinkade. Dan-el, however, was required to stay with his group and rest or even sleep until about an hour before his fight. "Relax" was the order given, as if it were possible.

Anxiousness best described Dan-el's support group; his entourage as he jokingly referred to them. With rain threatening, there wasn't much to do except hang around the Riverpark because going to a restaurant to while away time involved more effort than anyone wanted to expend and they wanted to be on hand if "needed"—for what, no one knew, So, unless it rained, they'd sit by the river and look at the people walking by and stare at the detritus brought downriver from last week's storm. Jess discovered delicious Creamsicles at the concessions stand and were a big hit while they lasted. "You gotta eat them like a sandwich, not lick on them."

Ella was a basket of nerves unable to sit. Jess and Jen played a kind of game pointing out people that looked like guardsmen, cops, gamblers or whatever came to mind.

"See that couple over there? The guy has to be one of them."

"Yeah, I 'd for sure put a stake-out on the park," Jen replied cynically. "Lots of betting going on."

Jen stopped the game when Jess made a condescending remark about a rather stout lady being a high jumper on the Central High track team.

****

Jess, Surviving Normal

The rain beginning, they returned to the arena with time to spare before Dan-el's bout.

The qualitative nature of judging boxing, whether amateur or professional, is deciding who won. Originally, in the early days of the sport when one of the fighters could no longer continue, the issue was settled without a judge. The "kill or be killed" attitude moderated through the years and boxing gradually evolved to become the "sweet science" as aficionados call it. This necessitated the addition of judges, time limits, protective equipment, and stricter rules that tempered the sport, but the object remained pretty much consistent—render your foe so he can no longer defend himself.

A middleweight, Dan-el would follow the light middleweight final and with only one ring being used, more seating was set up for a larger crowd. The air was electric with fan enthusiasm. With the fight preceding finished, Jess and Jen were watching the entrance for Dan-el and his opponent to appear when unnoticed, a man approached the judge's bench at ringside. The man, Mr. Martin, wearing a red baseball cap with "Staff" on it, spoke with the judges momentarily and motioned for the referee and his back-up to join the group.

While they were conferring, Jen happened to glance that way and see Mr. Martin leaning over with his hands on the judges' table. Not able to hear the discussion, it looked fairly animated. This was the first time any of them had seen Mr. Martin all day, and Jen alerted Jess and Ella to watch what was happening. Not being able to hear added to the drama. A few minutes later, one of the judges stood and joined the referees standing with Mr. Martin, who was holding his phone, apparently on speaker. As this was happening, Dan-el and his opponent had entered the ring and were going through their final warm-ups.

Golden Gloves were judged by two seated judges and the referee, each having one vote in deciding the winner. The judge standing with Mr. Martin and the referees was demonstratively expressing his agitation to whatever was being discussed as Mr. Martin put his phone in his pocket. The "whatever" resulted with Mr. Martin putting his hand above the elbow of the judge as inconspicuously as possible and escorting him from ringside. Although Jen and Jess watched the incident closely, the majority of the crowd hadn't paid much attention.

Meanwhile, the ref that was scheduled to be the back-up for the coming fight took the vacated place at the judges' table and the other entered the ring. All anyone watching could do was speculate, the most obvious one Jen voiced. "Do you suppose that judge was crooked?"

"How would anyone know? Jess returned. There wasn't time to discuss it any further as the fighters were being introduced and called to the center of the ring for their instructions.

Physically, the fighters were well-matched. Dan-el was younger by several years and less experienced, and the word was that his opponent was adept in the mixed martial arts. That had worried Dan-el in training to which Detective Kinkade answered sardonically, "All that stuff in the world doesn't block a good straight jab, and he's not supposed to kick you."

Boxing analysts historically look at the middleweight division in declaring the best pound-for-pound fighters in the world. This division in the Gloves was no exception with athleticism and cat-like speed on display. Like mirror images, Dan-el and his opponent stalked and then met in a flurry before backing off to start again, hits often difficult to distinguish from misses. Dan-el's ambidextrous style versus his foe's confusing left-handed-ness making it even more interesting. This was boxing at its best without the swagger. If there was a deciding blow in the fight, it was his opponent's follow-through elbow to Dan-el's chin after a missed uppercut—an illegal move. Whether intended or not, it was a penalty point in Dan-el's favor, a street fighter's move that may have influenced the ring referee toward Dan-el. The two judges split their decision and the referee declared Dan-el the winner--The Trentsville Regional Golden Gloves champion.

Surprisingly, three of the bettors cashing out from bookies located at sites outside the Armory were National Guardsmen, each accompanied by two officers from the tactical division of Trentsville's finest. Unsurprisingly, they hung around the now-skittish bookies so they could scrutinize people having bet on Dan-el to win. Not only was betting illegal on amateur events, but extortion became an issue when it became evident that the bets couldn't be covered—they didn't have enough money since there was no intent for the High Ace bookies to have to pay off on their "sure thing."

Having the option to sing or be stung, two of the three bookies opted to tell the police everything they wanted to know. All told, nineteen people, bettors, bookies, and High Aces were rounded up and taken "downtown." Charges ranged from illegal gambling to "outstandings" from past infractions for several of them. Interrogations were productive in naming names and a willingness to pass the guilt.

And this wasn't enough. Saturday night was the first of the chain of bombshell moves spearheaded by the Governor to "clean" the streets of Trentsville of gang influence. "Strike force Gangs" brought in the National Guard and lasted until it effectively shut down the High Aces and chaotically disarrayed their counterparts in Trentsville. Among all else, the concerted effort was a brilliant election-year opportunity for the incumbent governor to showcase his 'tough on crime' platform.

Skeptical during the first week of the sweep, Dan-el told Jen and Jess. "It'll be like buzzards on dead carrion. You can shoo them away, but as soon as you're gone, they're back."

"Right now, though, they're shooed away," Jen answered.

****

Dan-el's prophecy proved wrong. The gang crack-down was successful largely due to a combination of the political timing, a favorable financial hiccup in the state's coffers and a social movement dubbed "Enough is Enough." For once, effective leadership from the public and private sectors of the city bilaterally joined forces in a rare display of unity. The mayor made an impassioned appeal that proved immensely popular and donations from businesses, fraternal organizations, churches and concerned individuals poured in.

The Governor exercised his authority to use the National Guard and ordered units to conduct monthly exercises in Trentsville throughout the remainder of the summer. Under the premise of public assistance, there was no display of armed conveyances of weaponry and the Guardsmen carried their weapons in slings on their shoulders. A combat veteran's most dreaded order in effect: "Fire only if fired upon." Expected outcries of martial law were minimal for this was something the majority of the citizenry wanted. Convenience stores similar to the one where Mr. Jemison was killed had Guardsmen posted on the premises while other parts of the city had either mobile or boots units patrolling them.

As a person responsible for instigating the operation, Detective Kinkade received meritorious acclaim from both the city and his department for his involvement and was named the coordinator of the program. Further, local media attention was picked up by the networks, and amazingly, went national making the evening news. Detective Kinkade was a featured interviewee on two popular news shows, and Trentsville was poised to become the pilot for other cities with similar problems.

Dan-el, his face blurred and his voice altered electronically, appeared with Detective Kinkade on one of the programs. Mr. Martin remained quietly in the background working with guard units and briefing their commands on the operation. Displaying the typical officer's aplomb when being thanked for something, newly-promoted Major Martin replied, "Don't thank me, it's my job," always with an appreciative twinkle in his eye.

"Just think, Dan-el. All because one person refused to lose," Jess said.

Donations were used for more sophisticated local security systems: cameras were linked to centralized watching locations, metal detectors were installed, and public venues were staffed with experienced personnel. Other plans included an effort to expand the canine corps and provide pertinent training to privately-owned security guards. Combat veterans were voluntarily enlisted and formed watch groups.

Money was also used for recruiting and training police officers in order to increase their numbers in stressed areas and for satellite stations to give residents in places like Woods Park a truly representational presence. All this couldn't happen overnight and that very fact inadvertently kept the momentum for reform going; from becoming a mere fad. Planners and committees working with Detective Kinkade realized that this was their one chance to affect change.

The City Council hastily adopted, and voted 11-7 a bill limiting civilian ownership of certain weapons, to put age restrictions on purchasing guns, and to implement extensive background checks for gun purchases. Council members knowingly put their re-election hopes in jeopardy because any kind of threat to gun ownership was ever popular, and civil authority was questioned by the constitutionality of the events taking place. As Trentsville waited for adjudication, win or lose, a point had been made by those wanting reform—Enough being Enough. When the appeals eventually reached the state's Supreme Court, the new laws stood.

Predictably, the remaining High Aces and the other gangs initially scoffed at what was happening. Plans to fight back were made and there were incidents: torched buildings, rampant vandalism, harassed citizens, and two more random shootings. Five deaths occurred in a ten-week period over the summer. As others underwent training, rogue groups popped up and turned the tables on the gangs with "Guardian Angel" services in concert with the authorities--unofficially, of course. All said, the gangs were under siege.

Another part of the "Trentsville Project" was directed at the gang members, attacking them from the inside in an unprecedented move. First, Outreach Committees were formed within the Social Services offering group counselling for those coming forward voluntarily. Additionally, rather than jail terms, many of them were offered rehabilitation in the way of education, drug abatement, jobs, loans not unlike Pell Grants, and social programs specifically initiated for the Project. Again outraged, naysaying citizens were left incredulous when hearing of decreased jail sentences, amnesty, and expunged criminal records. It helped when this arm of the program was better understood: gang members had one chance to reform and it had to be earned through commitment and effort.

Even businesses and individuals wronged by gang activity became part of the focus groups. Exposing the psychology of gangs received media attention and helped those citizens removed from the gang environment to understand that the choice was often no choice. And public involvement was ongoing; it worked. It worked because the joint effort offered a way out for gang members where previously there was none. The tipping point being that the Project offered a chance for the little guys in the gangs, the serfs who cut ties and participated in restructuring their lives. The key component for success was placing people who cared, who understood the situation and believed in the intrinsic goodness of others smack in the face of gang members and creating a powerful stimulus for change.

And they aced it! The leopard could change his spots.

The kingpins of the gangs, the ones driving the Cadillacs and living the good life, rebelled against the programs and fought back the only way they could. But as the programs promised to be both enduring and eroding to the former way it was, gang leaders realized they couldn't fight a war without foot soldiers.

The Trentsville Project also reached out to the prisons, and Jon-el White became one of a hundred young men incarcerated for gang-related activity to participate in this new dynamic. Eligible for an early-out upon successful completion of re-education, he could be released in time for Christmas.

There were no hand-outs. Creating jobs to sustain the Program was the only way its success could endure. Naturally enough, benevolent foundations and donors expected results for their investments. Revitalization of buildings offered less expensive opportunities for manufacturing concerns to expand. Jess recalled that the window company his father worked for had considered an inner-city site at one time, and how this could have changed so much in his life had it been done earlier. Maybe they would reconsider for any future expansion. It was often less expensive to remodel than building when innovatively planned, especially in a safe, accessible environment.

Rebuilding infrastructure was another option. Trentsville was an older city by American standards with overhead electrical lines, rusting pipes, and deteriorating conveyances above and below ground. City workers often didn't know where water lines were until they broke. That substandard inner-city streets and sidewalks were badly neglected said a lot about how certain groups of citizens were treated. Owners of old buildings saw opportunity. Condemned, abandoned structures were sold for dimes on the dollar just to clear taxes. Existing fees were sometimes forgiven to offer entrepreneurs venture occasions. Red tape was cut for the greater good and TIF's were offered in certain areas. Planning committees envisioned beautification efforts, green spaces, and the creation of a throw-back business community as part of still another pilot program designed to instill pride in its residents. There was no end to the ideas or boundaries to this mostly non-partisan dream. Schools were in line for a trickle-down effect.

Yes, let us not forget the schools.

****

On a Wednesday afternoon in mid-August Mrs. Jemison received a phone call that she never would have thought possible. In the office where she worked, her screen showed a call originating from the Trentsville Police Department, Precinct Nine. Identifying himself as Lieutenant Greeley, he said that he had some classified information for Mrs. Rebecca Wilkerson Jemison, could she switch to Facetime and be willing to answer a few questions to further substantiate that she was indeed the person he wanted.

Immediately, she was skeptical of the methods used to get people's identity information. Sure, the alleged officer sounded like he was for real, but so many did these days. "You will have to verify your legitimacy, first. I'm going to hold my phone so you can't see me until I want you to."

On the other end of the line was a man dressed in street clothes. "You've probably never seen me. I'll hold up my badge and ID, first." He did. Next, "I'll walk around the squad room and show you other officers at their desks, our bulletin board and whatever else shows up. Some of the people will be in uniform. I'll let you watch until you're convinced. You can ask any of the people you see in this room anything you'd like."

Once Mrs. Jemison was satisfied, she moved into view on her phone. "Okay. This seems kind of ridiculous."

"Yes, Ma'am. My questions for you will come quickly and I'd appreciate it if you would answer them as rapidly and precisely while maintaining eye contact with your phone at all times."

Retinal scans? She was in this pretty far, now. "Wouldn't it have been easier just to meet someplace?" she asked.

He answered, "Yes, Ma'am. Would you prefer to do that? I was thinking this way to be more convenient."

"No, go ahead."

"Are you at a fairly private location? I saw other people in the background a few minutes ago."

She was mildly perturbed with the back and forth. "Mr....ah...Lieutenant, go ahead and tell me what you have that is such a secret."

He must have been convinced and proceeded without the back-and-forth. Mrs. Jemison saw Lieutenant Greeley hold up a file with Craig Jemison printed on its tab. "We know who killed your husband and we have him in custody."

With news she never expected to hear, she gasped as air rushed into her lungs that was followed with deep, convulsing sobs. Dropping her phone, it fell to the floor emitting an "Ouch! That hurt! Jess had installed an app to her phone a few days ago.

Needing time to compose herself, it was a few minutes later when Mrs. Jemison retrieved her phone. Lieutenant Greeley answered right away expecting to hear from her. With compassion in his voice and apologizing for the procedure his department demanded, he shared the information he was given.

"This all came about as a reciprocal of the Trentsville Project. Yesterday evening a young man came into the West Side Precinct wanting to talk to someone about our amnesty program. He thought he could confess to a crime and walk away a free man by saying, 'I killed a man.' The desk sergeant recognized him as being a member of the Calle Guerreros and had the man, really a boy, taken into custody. I was contacted to come meet him right away because we could hold him for only so long."

Asking if she was okay and should he continue, Mrs. Jemison assented, her voice barely perceptible.

"My office always thought your husband was the innocent victim of a CG drive-by. We knew they had weapons like the one that killed him, and our informants had heard things related to the shooting. But we only had hearsay without any names or just cause for a warrant. We couldn't say for sure it was CG originated although the business was in their area and we knew from the owner that they paid protection money to the CG's. When the store didn't pay up, they suffered the consequences."

"And my husband was taken in the prime of his life, I became a widow, and my children fatherless."

"Yes, ma'am. An irreparable tragedy. And the blame has to be shared. Yet you and your family are needlessly the ones left to suffer the consequences. I have seen this before and am sorry from the bottom of my heart and apologize for anything my department could have done but did not." Lieutenant Greeley was no longer sounding like a tough seen-it-all cop on robo-speak, but as a husband and father. "Despite efforts otherwise, the message emboldened on the right front fender of Trentsville's police vehicles, 'to protect and serve' is not inclusive. A perpetrator can only be apprehended after a crime has been committed in many instances. Recognizing his empathy, Mrs. Jemison was appreciative of the kindness in his words.

He continued. "In similar cases we sometimes get the attitude that it wasn't the shooter's fault that someone got in the way. I've watched lawyers present that as an argument in court. This CG told us he didn't intend to hit anyone and was contrite; several times breaking down. Said that learning your husband's name from TV made it worse. When we explained that the program doesn't except homicides and that, at best, he's facing manslaughter charges, he said he's haunted and been seeing a priest. He willingly signed the statement we gave him. We're still working on details such as cause and accomplices, but I'm convinced he was telling us the truth. He is fifteen years old."

Later explained to Jess and Julianne by their mom, Julianne didn't fully apprehend but seeing the tears on her Mom's face, started to cry. Jess, who had always thought he would be the one to solve the crime as well as the one to exact justice, stood stoically his jaw clenched and lips pressed together. Their reactions different, but their feelings echoing, what now? They didn't know what to expect next.

There would be a hearing with criminal proceedings to follow. Trial or not, if the young man were found guilty there would be a sentencing. When the Jemison's learned that it was their right to also press charges as part of a civil suit, Jess, Julianne, and Mom impassionedly discussed their options. They had several others including suing the owner of the quick-stop store and even the Trentsville Police Department. Rebecca Jemison would sue no one.

Jim Billman

Chapter 10

The school year loomed—Seniors!

A summer plagued with violent weather swings that saw extremely high temperatures slamming into the cooler more sedentary fronts from the melting arctic. "Thanks to global warming, this is only the beginning of violent weather swings," Jen nearly shouted during a downpour as she waited with Dan-el in-Jess's truck to make a dash into a meeting. The weather brought chaos on top of the other changes in the city. Baseball games were cancelled and rescheduled as double-headers, and Jess found himself busier than ever doing handyman chores picking up limbs, and repairing minor damage to houses. All this amid the news of Dad's killer left little leisure time with his friends—almost too busy to text.

I felt pangs of regret that I didn't spend more time thinking about Dad now that his case was solved. Just quiet time, not closure, but time to respect and appreciate his memory.

His star rose when Jess, like Jen in basketball, was named to the All-City League first team. Coming after the other athletic setbacks and decisions since coming to Trentsville, the distinction became a vindication of sorts that reached beyond baseball. It was no big surprise when the manager of the local American Legion team asked Jess along with two other Jefferson players to join his team for a short season occupying the first twenty days of August. "It's hectic, culminating in state and national tournaments that can last until Labor Day. You'd be the regular first baseman and get to work on the hill, too. There'll be some travelling and it's a good experience."

Because the high school team hadn't survived the Districts, Jess was elated to be able to play some more. The Tigers, as the team was called, enjoyed a tradition as being one of the better teams in the area and expectations were always high. Anything short of a state championship marked the abbreviated season as unsuccessful. Jess actually looked forward to the whirlwind schedule and traveling to other places outside Trentsville. He also liked the fact that there were few practice sessions unlike high school. Put on the uniform, show up and play a game.

I imagined this as the life of a professional ballplayer during the regular season. I loved it.

The team was good because it drew its players from a larger pool than some of the other Legion posts. One of three Trentsville teams, the best competition came from the other local teams, and there were always a couple "sleepers" that put together a competitive team. But, otherwise, a few games had the Tigers winning by lopsided margins, 17-3 14-0, more like football scores.

The coaching wasn't like it was at Jefferson. The sportsmanship factor wasn't stressed as much because some of the coaches seemed to want us to keep the pressure on our opponents that were already down by ten runs. There was no reason to take an extra base, to steal, to bunt just to advance a runner, or to show up another player in these cases. And it rubbed off on some of our players. We weren't popular, and I learned from some of the guys who'd played last year that all the Trentsville teams had the same reputation.

Some of the bus rides were long, and some of the ball fields were sub-standard with skinned infields sprinkled with pebbles that created bad hops on grounders. Some batter's boxes were almost holes. Jess spent a lot of the bus time thinking how Iowa-like these fields were where baseball was an after-thought sport.

I was always comparing then and now; where I'd be and what I'd be doing if I were still there. I wouldn't give up Jen and Dan-el for anything and I would give anything if Dad hadn't died. Go figure.

Jess had heard the saying "You play to the level of your competition," and tried to remain aware of it. He pushed himself to always play hard, but to respect both the game and his opponent. Most of the other players did the same because they knew how difficult baseball was; how easily things could change in an instant. A hitch in the swing, a kink in the wind-up, and worse of all, the yips when the ball wouldn't go where you threw. Further, a pulled muscle that was compensated for could bring about major change, a sprain or Charley horse could put you on the bench. You could easily do too little in baseball, but too much could hurt you, too.

Granddad told me more than once that the biggest thing that could mess up a player was to strain the gray stuff between his ears.

The Tigers won the State Tournament and without enough players after losing those with other obligations, opted out of the Nationals. Jess learned it was not the first time the Tigers folded this way. Being named to the all-tourney team was another feather in his cap. Along with the satisfaction the achievement brought, Jess learned a lot from playing Legion ball. He would never equate his athletic success with Jen's, who was being sought on the national level, or with Dan-el, who probably did have a shot at becoming the next black President. Jess, although not fully aware of it, turned a corner in his life that summer. His uncomplicated, innate compassion and sensitivity was now permanently etched into his personality, into his soul. The butterfly was about to emerge from its cocoon.

****

Mr. Martin had asked Jess, Dan-el and Jen to meet him in the conference room of the branch library on the Wednesday after Jess's last Legion game. "I'd like to make it 7:00. It'll take a while, but we'll be finished before the library closes at 9:00. You can bring your mom if you'd like, but it isn't necessary."

Nothing else. When they compared what Mr. Martin said, none of the three were given a hint. "I asked him what it was about," Jen said. "But he just said wait and see. I think you'll be surprised."

Dan-el agreed, "Me too. And I got the same cryptic kind of reply,"

"You're going, aren't you?" Jess had directed his question to both of them. "Mr. Martin must have something pretty important to say by asking us the way he did. Maybe it has something to do with the Project."

Dan-el was instrumental in the genesis of the gang takedown, but his name wasn't circulated in the media because he was a minor, kept out of the public eye for his and his family's (and friends) safety. As the Project materialized and grew into what it had become, he was referred to as 'the kid who did the right thing.'

They all had a laugh when Dan-el said he asked Mr. Martin what they should wear.

Per usual, Jess's Taxi Truck picked up Jen and then went down to Dan-el's. "If you get picked up, you're on your own trying to explain why this is a school function to the police," Mom always warned him. It wasn't the first time Jess stretched the limitations of his driving permit, and now seventeen, he could change that by simply going down to the DMV and getting a new driver's license. One of those things he just hadn't had time to do.

Making a dash from the parking lot to the library in the rain, they knew the Conference Room was on the second floor of the library. It hadn't really occurred to any of them that the invitation to meet in a larger room suggested the meeting to be more than a cozy little chat in a group of four. Nevertheless, they were surprised to see four rows of chairs and several people already seated. Mr. Martin looked up from the person he was talking with and greeted the three with an amicable welcome. "Glad to see you. Sit wherever and we'll start soon. Jess, I saw your picture in the paper. All-City. Congratulations. There's some water on the floor-be careful."

This wasn't going to be about the Project. I recognized some the others, and it was easy to tell that almost all of them were around my age.

Seven o'clock arrived and Mr. Martin told the assembly that he would wait another five minutes and then begin. Three more young people came and sat down, bringing the total to over twenty. There were seats unoccupied, but not many. "Reminds me of the Ambassador meetings," Jess whispered.

Mr. Martin again welcomed everyone. "Some of you will recognize me from my days at Jefferson High, and I've met the rest of you otherwise. The thing I've always hated in mixed crowds at meetings like this when I was a teacher was the monitor saying something like 'let's get to know each other.' Then we'd waste ten minutes to introduce ourselves to other people who could care less; who didn't come to the meeting to meet people. We won't do that tonight and I want to use that as an example for the future."

What's he talking about?

"When I was released from my position at Jefferson for what boiled down to thinking out of the box and trying to improve the situation without going through the proper channels, the door that closed led to another one opening. This is often the case as you may already know. I was fired on a Saturday morning and told to clean out my things as soon as I could. Monday morning, I made an appointment to meet with a man named Jon Isaacs at the Law Offices of Merritt, Merritt and Associates about helping me in a start-up venture. Mr. Issacs was a lawyer with the firm who often represented educators and a man I'd known from the Army. I talked to him about charter schools.

"By definition, a charter school can be either a public or a private school that meets State requirements for being a school. A public charter qualifies the school to receive taxpayer funding like other schools and a private charter has to come up with their own funding, like charging tuition. For licensure to become a charter school, applicants draw up a curriculum explaining how they will meet the State's criteria and how being a charter will serve their intended enrollees better than schools like Jefferson or Washington. Standards and testing procedures still have to be met and believe me when I say there's a lot of red tape involved. I'm giving you only the abbreviated version. Charter schools started in Minnesota and have grown since 1991. Some states don't recognize charter schools and some embrace them. California has over 4000 of them, for example.

"Any questions about charter schools so far? I always hated that too, when speakers begin by saying, feel free to ask a question at any time, but worse yet, when a teacher or speaker just says, any questions? Yes, Dan-el?"

Dan-el hadn't raised his hand or made any signal that he had a question, but he knew what Mr. Martin was wanting him to do. "Why are Cheerios round?"

Mr. Martin continued. "And there you have one of the reasons why I applied and received a charter: Specificity. A charter school can teach you as an individual, not as part of a group.

"Do any of you have a question about charter schools or anything pertaining to what I've said so far this evening?"

Okay, I get it.

"Why us? Why did you invite me?" came from a girl in the front row.

"That's another reason for a charter school: Selectivity. I would never discriminate, could never discriminate by mandate of my certification, but a charter school can have expectations that must be met."

Jess had wondered from the beginning of Mr. Martin's delivery about sports. He asked, "Do charter schools have sports like football?" Some others turned to look at him when he asked his question, which was kind of embarrassing because of the obviousness of the answer.

Mr. Martin answered, "That's a good question, Jess. Charter schools are typically small and if they can't support programs, number-wise or financially, like sports or the arts, so, they articulate with their public school that does offer the activity. In other words, a football player at a charter school can play as a representative of the public school where he lives, with exceptions that aren't worth discussing tonight. Just briefly, there's a difference between an academy and a charter school. We've all heard of great high school basketball players who leave their school and transfer to an academy known for honing basketball skills. High school military academies are pretty common, too."

There were no further questions at that time.

Mr. Martin continued. "The function of a charter school is to serve you. You and your parents, with charter personnel present for advisement, to discuss your educational goals and set the course for you to obtain them. Technology helps make this possible. Cyber-courses are readily available as you know, and many of them offer college credit. Granted, your needs may extend beyond our capability to deliver them so we'll go elsewhere to help you, to challenge you, and to serve you. You will be able to schedule such things as piano lessons during the day and get to practices on time.

"You hear of structure and function. Our school day will be in blocks, but not in blocks governed by a bell as much as into learning segments. Students in public schools often complain about boredom and waiting for the Pavlovian bell to signal what comes next. A bell to begin, to pass, to have lunch, to leave for the day…"

Someone offered a distinct, "Amen."

Mr. Martin smiled, "You agree. Good.

"Roughly, we plan to structure a typical day into two parts: learning for credit and learning beyond credit. Mentors are forever willing to share their expertise in virtually every field. Plus, there are few learning experiences that exceed an actual hands-on. In short, we will be structured, yes, but much more loosely than you are used to."

The girl who asked "why us" raised her hand and Mr. Martin nodded toward her. "Yes, Melinda."

"What about graduation so we can get into a college?"

"Not everyone knows this, but you don't need to graduate high school to go to college. It helps reviewing boards I'm sure but isn't an ironclad requirement. If you don't already have the credits, which most of you do as seniors-to-be, I would have each attendee take the test for the GED, the General Educational Development exam. You know what it is, the equivalency test for non-traditional high school graduation. My feelings are that each student in our charter school will pass that test on the first try, and if not on the first try, certainly the second. There's a technicality to that, however."

He looked at Jen. "Jennifer Steffen plays basketball at Jefferson and she plays the game at a very high level. If she takes the GED and passes it in September, she is technically a high school graduate and possibly ineligible to compete in a high school basketball game. Perhaps she'd even be barred from practicing with her team. You follow, I'm sure. It carries over to the state rules for every extra-curricular activity. That's a for instance, only. We'll be here for you to make sure nothing like that happens to preclude you.

"Anything else on the subject?"

Jess would still be able to play baseball for Jefferson because the rule allowed graduating seniors to play the following summer. So, was Mr. Martin inviting him to the charter school? Jess didn't feel that he was precocious (Dan-el's word) in anything academic. He didn't have any particular vocation in mind. Jen wanted to be an architectural engineer, and Dan-el talked a lot about political science. They knew what they wanted.

I'm just floating around. What would I do? How would I fit in? I'd like to be included if Jen and Dan-el are. Mr. Martin hasn't said when it would begin. And where would it be? I know they're people here that don't go to Jefferson by their shirts and stuff. Trentsville is awfully big. I could burn a tank of gas every week just getting to school.

As if Mr. Martin read Jess's thoughts, "Okay, I've talked about structure and function. What about the logistics that I'm sure you're concerned about? The when, where, and how.

"First, when? We will begin on September 15 with a skeletal enrollment of no more than seventy students. We will be publicly funded, but that money won't come as a bulk check before we prove to be delivering on our intent to operate within the parameters in serving our students-- you. The school will borrow on the collateral of governmental promise. We might operate in arrears for quite a while."

Jess looked at Dan-el. Whispering out of the corner of his mouth, Dan-el said, "Debt."

"Second, where? Our central office is at the old Taylor Elementary school off Morgan Boulevard, near the Springs Shopping Mall. It'll be easily accessible, but quite distant for some of you which brings me to the 'How' aspect of the *Odyssey of the Mind* – the name of our school.

"Essentially, you are home-schooling because the classroom part will come to you via interactive programming. You'll receive lectures from people eminent in their field of study. Professors and successful folks who've developed courses precisely for this purpose; not just for us but for the public. A good number of these courses are offered for college credit, and some of them are AP approved. At the end of each lesson, there is a Q and A session that you will access. Welcome to what education will become in the near future—cutting edge global education!

"Thanks to the Trenstville Project, you will receive your own computer and will be responsible for it and taking advantage of the programs and courses offered. There is no intent to inundate you or drown you in academics that you might not be ready for, but you will be challenged. You can expect to be frustrated at times, yet I'll bet that each of you has basked in the glow of intellectual accomplishment more than once. That's called empowerment.

"Satellite classrooms, weekly get-togethers, and the implementation of the second part of the program are all part of the program that will be explained later. Right now, I've given you plenty the think about. You'll be giving up a lot by leaving the

Jess, Surviving Normal

familiarity of your present school, especially if you're going to be a senior. It's a big decision.

"On a final note, I know your parents will have questions. They'll be contacted with your permission—how's that for a twist? I'm circulating the permission sheet, so after your name put a yes or no depending on your interest in Odyssey and also check to see that we have your correct email and home address. For now, you might share that we received our start-up funds from the Trentsville Project and your parents' out-of-pocket should not exceed what public school attendance costs. So...say yes and be prepared to embark on your personal odyssey.

****

"Shite, folks. That was a lot to absorb comin' at us outta the blue," Dan-el declared as they were walking to Jess's pickup.

"Who woulda thunk it." Jess said, coining a phrase that Granddad got from the time Dizzy Dean was broadcasting baseball in the early days of TV sports.

"It's still early. Let's stop and get a pizza. Okay?" Dan-el suggested. With thoughts buzzing around in each person's head, they needed some together time to discuss Mr. Martin's school.

"You did say yes, didn't you, Jess?" Jen asked while they waited for their pizza,

"Yeah. How else would you get to basketball practice?"

She came back, "Seriously, what're your thoughts about Odyssey?"

Jess shared what had occurred to him while Mr. Martin was speaking.

Dan-el spoke to Jess's lament. "So, you don't know what you want to be when you grow up? Why should you care, man? There's lots of time and that's what general ed is for. Seems that about all Jefferson teaches is what we don't want to be—not really, but you know what I'm sayin'."

Jess opened up. "We're going into our senior year. Most seniors can't wait to graduate and get out into the world. I'm kind of worried about that—I don't know how to say it. Where would I be since moving to Trentsville without you two? I'd have made friends, but not like you guys. I have a recurring dream where I'm all alone standing at an intersection with nowhere to go. You two know where to go... and with neither of you...well, you know."

"There you are, Jess. Listen to what you're saying. You're sensitive and thoughtful. You listen to people even when they don't have anything worthwhile to say. That's what attracted me to you as a boyfriend and made me fall in love with you. Jess, you have the ability to speak volumes without saying a word. You transcend, you are all that is good."

"I don't know if that's good," Jess replied.

"She's right, and I love you, too, dude. The world is your huckleberry. Sensitive and thoughtful: physician, teacher, social worker, philosopher, cleric, writer, researcher, to name a few. Add understanding, intelligent and compassionate to what Jen said. And why do you need to be just one thing? My mom says that she still doesn't know what she wants to be."

"My mom describes you as 'principled'," Jen said.

Jess didn't know what to think; all the accolades coming his way.

"Thanks, I wasn't looking for all this. I think my dream also tells me that I'll be without you two; that we may go separate ways after this year. I want it to last, and that's why I want to go to Odyssey if you do. I was worried one of you would and one of wouldn't…"

"Don't you think we felt that way, too?" Jen said and Dan-el nodded.

Jess, usually quiet about matters of faith, said, "In my prayers, I ask that no matter how far or how long we are apart that we will always be together in spirit.

The pizza came, piping hot with the delicious pizza smell.

Dan-el spoke metaphorically, "You ever notice a piece of pizza is like the three of us at Jefferson. Each piece touching the others at a vertex and all the good stuff in between."

Hearing that, Jen gave a little wink to Jess; their secret.

****

Jess was talking to Mom about Odyssey. She'd just returned from the parental meeting with Mr., Martin. "Mr. Martin has it all figured out. The school really isn't doing something that a regular one couldn't do."

Mom had a strange little smile that Jess imagined was happiness that he had elected to attend. "I would guess it has to do with flexibility. This school with enrollment no more than a hundred can give more of its time and effort to each student."

"He said something about getting money from the Trentsville Project. If every kid gets a computer with all the Apps, that'll be a lot right there. Then the building is an old school that probably wasn't cheap."

Mom again had a logical explanation. "The donations for the Project have been phenomenal and contributors can earmark where their gifts go. Mr. Martin explained to us that Odyssey got on board and wrote a business plan asking for help with start-up. You know as well as I that Mr. Martin was as important in this whole gang shut-down as anyone; he and Detective Kinkade. Mr. Martin stayed in the background, though."

"I think he's been very busy getting Odyssey started. As for the physical part, the Taylor Elementary was closed three years ago, mostly by shifting demographics—populations and location. There's really nothing wrong with the school according to Mr. Martin. And with no plans to re-open it, it became a liability that the School Board wanted to sell. There was a silent auction and Mr. Martin bought it for pennies on the dollar as he said."

"Yeah, I'd guess there was a lot of work. He made it sound so easy when he talked with us."

They were painting the upstairs bathroom. Jess was "cutting in" and Mom rolling. She'd chosen a light gray color, and it was covering the old paint pretty well. Painting was one of those "learn by doing" skills Jess had picked up with his neighborhood handyman service. You Tube helped a lot whenever a different task came along. There was information on just about every DIY undertaking possible. Of course, things didn't always proceed quite like they did on You Tube.

"I think he's put in some long hours. A charter school has been on his mind for a long time."

Did Mr. Martin say much about the, um, logistics at your meeting?" Jess asked.

"Oh yeah, he's set up rooms and meeting places for students to use in case their home situation isn't conducive to learning. He's concerned about students finding the home atmosphere too distractive. It's easy to pigeonhole school work when other things seem more luring. His solutions are simple; thought out but not over-thought. If you don't keep up, you'll be counseled and if it continues, you're dismissed. I don't think he'll put up with things like procrastination."

"I don't suppose he will."

Mom continued. "Each satellite room was set up as close to the students' home high school as he could find space. For Jefferson students, he's secured a dedicated room in the Second Baptist church that'll be accessible from 8:00 to 4:00 on weekends. Mike, Mr. Martin, hopes to have each room staffed and equipped with what you'll need. A lot of what you'll be doing will be on the honor system."

"All the bases covered, huh? I'm looking forward to it and I know Jen and Dan-el are, too. About the only thing we'll be missing by not going to Jefferson will be the milling around before school with the other kids. And the gossip!

"Darn! My brush touched the ceiling. Will you hand me that damp rag, Mom? Please?"

I was excited as the time to begin grew closer. Odyssey would start a week later than the Publics so it was a little strange when Julianne, looking nice in her new clothes came down the stairs. Normally, Mom took her to school and went on to work at the window factory, but today, she asked if I would drive Julianne to school. Mom had been a little different when we painted the bathroom, more talkative about general stuff. Yesterday, Labor Day, she said she might have some news to share, but couldn't talk about it, yet.

Jess had what he described as a ton of work to do in the neighborhood before next Monday. Also, he had to decide on what courses to take by Thursday and go over to the school to talk to someone about it. One downer at the Odyssey would be taking different courses than Jen or Dan-el. They planned to be together for at least one class, but Jen would gravitate toward architecture and engineering things. Dan-el mentioned just in conversation something about Roman Law. Because Jess liked sports so much, he thought Kinesiology would be nice. He still didn't know about anything else, but Mom said they'd help him decide.

Jess heard Mom telling Julianne to hurry as if she were late. Then, about a half hour before Jess would be leaving with Julianne, She and Mom came into the kitchen and sat down with Jess at the kitchen table. Jess was eating his cereal when Julianne said, "Mom has something to tell us."

Mom was dressed for work; her disposition visibly more vibrant than on a usual Monday morning. "I have an announcement. I resigned from the Window Company and have a new job."

Wham!

Julianne, now in the last year of elementary, was excited, "Where is it, Mommy?" Jess was silent, thinking about the last time they'd heard this kind of news. With thoughts of Dad, he immediately felt saddened.

But Mom was happy, bubbly about what she had to share. "You both know my feelings about the job here aren't like they were in Iowa. It's in the same department, but different. We knew so many people in Iowa, their families and last names were so familiar. Here, I just haven't felt comfortable. Plus, my work is more entry-level." The fact that Mrs. Jemison's transfer to Trentsville wasn't truly "across the board" had never occurred to Jess.

Mom sacrificed so Dad could advance. That's what made their decisions to move so difficult. And if Dad would've said no, he would've been frozen. Probably alive though.

"Where, Mom? Sounds exciting," Jess asked, taken up in her excitement.

"I will be working at your school. At the Odyssey of the Mind."

Julianne let out a "That's not fair," and then reconsidered wanting Mom to finish what she had to tell them.

"During the week before Dan-el's bouts when you were staying with him, Mr. Martin called and asked if I could meet him. He had some questions that he wanted to run by me. You remember Julianne, we went to the coffee shop and met him."

"I thought you were just talking about school," Julianne said. "I heard high school and didn't pay much attention. I was glad I took *Wonder* with me to read"

"You're right, we were discussing a different kind of high school. Mr. Martin announced that his charter plan had been approved, and told us, me, what would be involved and the things he needed to get done in a short time. I suppose he told me as much as he told you, Jess, at your first meeting. He spoke of the school and talked about the opportunities it held for you. I thought that was really his point, to sell me on your attending it.

"Charter schools grew from Montessori schools, borrowing on their concept of student discovery, of allowing students to freelance learning for lack of a better term. We must have talked for a half hour when Mr. Martin mentioned staffing. For some reason, out of nowhere I thought about myself—this is something I could do. I didn't even know what a person *would* do in a charter school."

Mom looked at the clock on the wall above the pantry door. "Julianne, you should be leaving in a few minutes. Anyway, Mr. Martin asked if I would consider being the administrator at Odyssey and gave me lists of the job description and responsibilities for me to look at while I was considering. And that's the short version. Oh, I start today!

"Okay kiddos, get along."

Mom would have the same hours as at the window company. She'd get Julianne to school and pick her up from After School when she was finished, about 4:30. Her drive to Odyssey would save her about ten to fifteen minutes each way compared to the window company. The window company wasn't exactly pleased with her resignation without proper notice, but there wasn't much they could do about it. Nevertheless, it was a burnt bridge and not a good thing for her to do career-wise.

Mom left a copy of the Administrator's contract with Jess. Essentially, she would be the person responsible for making sure things go smoothly—operations. Looking through it, Jess saw that she'd keep each student's Personal Progress Profile.

PPP. Made me think of Granddad's PPPPPP list.

There would also be a Learning Plan that would be kept current for each student by his or her advisor. She'd keep all this in a dossier for each student for quick referencing purposes. This reminded Jess of Mr. Martin's presentation about each student getting individual attention. Essentially, Mom would be the principal of Odyssey. She'd gather feedback from student partnerships as they articulated with the business and professional community. She would work with Mr. Martin to maintain and grow the partnerships, and establish and schedule meetings with the Odyssey's Advisory Board. All this, plus overseeing counseling and making sure the curriculum was being delivered in concert with the school's mission.

She will love this.

The list went on. From meeting state standards on achievement and testing to the responsibility for the school building being kept clean and in order.

Mom would get a custodian/maintenance person, and an office manager to help her.

****

What distinguished *Odyssey of the Mind* from the public schools in Trentsville was the opportunity for each student to work innovatively in an individualized program. Each student, with parental and staff guidance would write their own program. Students weren't given free rein to do entirely what they wanted to do, they still had to meet core requirements of the state, unless already done as high-achieving underclassmen. The morning classes would consist of the sequential fields of study: science, math language, the humanities and arts. Students could meet achievement levels by taking the standardized test-out exams in the various areas for each subject.

As Dan-el pointed out, "There's an 'A' after every 'Q'."

I got it. Q and A.

For example, the areas requiring separate tests in science were physics, earth, environmental, chemistry and biology. Not meeting the expectation meant the student would go back and re-prepare and work with the facilitator/teacher in the subject. The plus side of the morning was that a person worked at their own pace in the manner comfortable for their learning style. No one took five different core courses every day, but they would focus on areas where they needed to demonstrate proficiency. Mornings were vital for the core courses, and once met, students could take more advanced ones for college credit. This part of the day was on campus, marked with students at their work spaces, some of them wearing head phones participating interactively.

Not everyone was thrilled to learn Mr. Martin would have a twenty-minute physical training class right before the lunch break.

Hardcore! Hoo-ah!

The after-lunch sessions provided students with opportunities to advance their personal interests. Business, professional, and community articulation agreements were arranged for the participants to get involved. Mr. Martin's primary concentration was in this area. He interviewed people in the medical, legal, manufacturing, business and other fields to enlist them as volunteer participants. "Successful people rarely keep secrets," he told everyone. "They are happy to share their success with you."

The next step was to set up a program for each student to become fully involved in the job partnership he or she was interested. Mr. Martin made sure that the partners understood that Odyssey students were not there to just sit around watching but should be actively engaged as much as possible. "Make them work, but don't make them mere 'go-fers'."

Parents had to sign permission forms for articulating children. Students were prepped on times when they would be excluded from certain activities—patient-doctor conferences and legal consultations to list two of them.

By the time school began, Mr. Martin had talked to people ranging from ministers to public defenders, from contractors to accountants, and from curators to fashion designers in order to gather enough volunteers willing to work with the 68 students signed up to attend Odyssey. It was exhausting, but necessary if the school were to succeed. He had met with people across the spectrum as the school's emissary promoting its cause. Most people were very supportive. Throughout, he would be equally busy with drop-ins, ensuring the goals of each student's itinerary were being served, and each student was on task. He knew there would be situations where he would have to make adjustments; he had been an educator for too long not to.

Mrs. Jemison would be a key individual. Jess took some good-natured ribbing from the eight former Jefferson students that knew him. The fact that both Dan-el and Jen's mothers were signed on to be mentors as well as other parents of students didn't go unnoticed, either.

A big happy family.

At first, the details were devastating; transportation being a major one. How to get students to and from all the places they were going. Provisions for meeting mandates had to be met and justifying reports completed kept a pile of paper on Mom's desk. The building was in fair, not good shape, and it wouldn't maintain itself. Fortunately, Mr. Martin took care of the budget, and kept

Mrs. Jemison in the loop and a student that showed interest in becoming a school administrator helped tremendously.

Rarely was Dan-el surprised; his sensory receptors usually alert. Even when the High Aces contingent jumped him, he knew that he could have avoided the confrontation yet chose to enter their ambush, wanting a street confrontation. As he explained, he under-estimated them and over-estimated himself. Wearing his favorite bow tie, a pale blue shirt with a horse heads pattern, and three pens protected in its pocket, Dan-el walked into the opening assembly sharing the anxiety of this new adventure with Jen and Jess.

"There's three seats together. Let's take them," Jen said. "I want to be on the aisle just in case." Earlier she'd said she was a little queasy which brought a 'knowing why' look from Dan-el.

Thinking nothing about it, Dan-el went in the row and sat beside another student wearing a light-weight hoodie writing furiously. Dan-el. Not wanting to accidently bump the person in the tightly packed row, said, "Pardon me," as he sat.

A muffled "Clumsy cow," came back causing Dan-el to do a sort of reactive double-take. Immediately, the person turned to him and the trap was sprung. Ella! She was a student at Odyssey. Having attended different organizational meetings, she was able to keep it from Dan-el, and with Jen running interference, it worked.

Swallowed the whole thing. Hook, line, and sinker. Lmao!

Each of them had their afternoon assignments. Jess would spend his afternoons at a sports clinic, splitting time between the rehabilitation center and with a physician specializing in sports-related injuries. Mr. Martin found an architect eager to mentor Jen. She would learn the process for building a new hotel from driving forty-foot pilings to fulfilling the requirements of the specification book. Term familiarity and structural integrity were two areas of Jen's focus-to-be. "I'll be talking the talk and walking the walk," she explained to Jess. Dan-el would work much the same way as a grad student, even with minor teaching stints, with a Political Science professor at Trentsville University. Ella's interest was in Psychiatry and she was assigned a Psychiatric Nurse Practition as her mentor. Understandably, each of the four was a bit ne wondering what their experiences would bring.

Jim Billman

****

At home during their evening meal, the Jemison tradition continued; sharing the day's events. Julianne, two weeks into her school year was enjoying her "senior" status in elementary school. Her stories of the "little kids" weren't far removed from her own travails, and they enjoyed reflecting on those times—until Dad came up. Gradually though, they were getting more and more capable of speaking about Dad without remorse; the acceptance stage of losing someone precious.

One thing's for sure, I'll never have a negative thought about Dad again.

Jess was talking about his day. He liked the way Odyssey was structured, and was getting experience in the field. However, he was swimming in the terminology surrounding the field of human kinetics. "I'm fascinated with the detail and how deeply the doctors and therapists understand everything. It's applied physics, chemistry and biology all rolled together. Biomechanics and orthopedics are words I'd heard but never thought about. One therapist gave me all kinds of new ideas about my own workouts."

Mom, too, was through her first week since Odyssey had opened. Her assessment included words such as: frantic, berserk, "busybusybusy," over-wrought and "I love it."

Mom had another topic she wanted to discuss with her children that began with "I've been thinking."

Oh-oh. Hang on.

"Jess, you need to really get busy looking at colleges. Your SAT's were good, could have been better but your scores don't warrant taking them again just to gain a couple points. But you have to get started. You may have to write something to get into a school." She pushed her hair back off her forehead as in frustration. "I should have pushed you harder to get this done."

Jess knew all this. He had a stack of college brochures in ⁿ that he'd perused. Mom was right, he'd topped the elite ⸺ with his SAT, but not by much. He wasn't a Tier One ⁿ Ivy League school and didn't want to be, ⁿt scores to the schools that Jen mentioned.

She'd seen the brochures and recognized ıw was the time for her to broach the ation is obvious. You shouldn't follow

244

Jen. Knowing her, she doesn't want a puppy dog. You need to stretch the rubber band that holds you together, and if it breaks…well, it breaks. But if you don't test its strength, in most cases, you'll both regret it. Don't get me wrong, first loves sometimes are the only one two people need, and I'd love to see you and Jen together, someday.

For the first time in well over a year, Jess felt the dark mood descending. Fighting against it rather than lashing out, "I know, Mom."

I did know, too. That was the problem Jen and I had last year. Jen wants to be in the moment and I want to map everything out. It hurts to think about her being with another guy.

A thought suddenly came to Jess. One that would reoccur in times to come.

Is my affection for Jen one of love or possession?

Mom wasn't finished. "Jess, you and Julianne can talk to me whenever you have a problem. Just don't ignore that and get your questions answered by the wrong people. I'll do the same. I think I have. And please never think I'm being nosy."

Julianne was listening intently, 'Mee-maw told me that, too. She said that she was like a book of information and she didn't want to sit on a shelf never opened."

"Maybe, I'll enlist in the Army and pick up my degree along the way." Jess was testing the waters mainly to get a reaction.

"Well, that's not all bad. You could get into Special Services and play baseball."

Jess didn't know about that being an actual possibility, caught in his own trap. "If I did something like that, the money you've set aside for me to go to college could be used on paying off the house."

"Good thinking," She mused, aloud.

****

The Odyssey of the Mind was based on the tenet that teaching should be about facilitation and not remediation. This called for educators to be effective guides who lead their charges through inquisitive approaches along the right path; an enlightening one. Facilitators walk a tightrope. They neither work at the whim of the students nor do they serve as source books, rather, they direct their students and challenge them to gain the understanding that leads to knowledge—and more questions. A good facilitator, enabler, asks more questions than they answer. The premise being that students learn more when they are involved in their own learning process.

The teachers at Odyssey were mostly veteran educators, some of whom were burned-out from public education. They hadn't interviewed and accepted their positions for the money, because the money wasn't as good as the underpaid public schools offered. Many chose Odyssey because they felt federal and state mandates for the public schools had taken away the opportunity for a teacher to teach; to be innovative. Odyssey's target was to have one teacher/facilitator for no more than eleven students—a most favorable ratio.

Reasoning skills, both inductive and deductive were paramount. Analysis of information and handling data were high on the list. Facilitators integrated the various disciplines; for example, showing that music and natural science were cousins joined by the language of mathematics.

On her first day, Jen's mentor took her outside. Pointing he said, "Look at that brick and imagine how it came to be where it is. Not so much how it was made or came to the job site as how it is integral with everything else. What's below it, behind it and above it. How is it functional and aesthetically pleasing? Now imagine other parts of the building you don't see but are parts of the whole. The water in and out, the electrical configuration, the consideration for seasonal thermal variation, for extremes, for permanence, for accommodation. Consider all the parts coming together. And lastly think of putting them together in a coordinated and timely fashion. You are the maestro of an architectural orchestra."

Jen loved it.

Chapter 11

If Odyssey had a downside other than limiting the Hershey's time together, it was the loss of a traditional senior year. With the start of basketball practice, Jen noticed that she didn't know anything about many of the conversational topics that occupied the locker room, namely the gossip. She had no one to share her latest experiences with, and only partly knew of theirs. She felt conspicuous asking them to explain so she became a listener, putting the pieces together as best she could. Beyond her teammates asking "How are things at your school," there wasn't much to talk about. She couldn't say, "I pondered a brick, or I studied wiring schematics." The former Jefferson students at Odyssey tended to group during lunch and social times, but the atmosphere was lacking. Jess and Dan-el noticed it, too.

Effervescent as ever, Dan-el said, "Odyssey is too cliquish, we need to expand and mingle—make more friends."

Corny old Jess quipped back "Odd 'e say? E's the bloke that's odd, I say." Ella laughed and Jen rolled her eyes.

Although the articulation agreement allowed Odyssey students to be a part of their public school's activities, it wasn't the same. Mr. Martin, during a Friday morning assembly, mentioned this would be a problem that couldn't be avoided. Describing post-partum, he said, "As you've heard many times, a person can't go back in time. You've chosen to go through the high school portal early. I might sound callous, but this type of thing will happen more than once in your lives."

How well I know.

Mom started an early October mealtime conversation with her children. "You know, with our down payment and the way the real estate market is turning, we have a good amount of equity in our house." She had to explain to Julianne what equity meant. Jess knew that the source of their equity came from selling their house in Iowa and using some of Dad's insurance money to lessen the monthly mortgage payment. He also knew that Mom struggled to make ends meet month-to-month.

"Jess, you will be going to college, and Julianne, the time will fly and soon you'll be graduating, too. Even now, we have a lot of house for the three of us. And the upkeep—there's always something that comes up. I thank God that you're able to do so much to help, Jess."

Julianne needed no explanation. "Will we move, again? Back to Iowa? Mom…"

"No, we're not moving to Iowa, I love my new job and you are settled in. We live in Trentsville, now. I've been thinking of downsizing; selling this house and getting a smaller home. Like I said, the market's good right now and a real estate agent told me she has several buyers who would love to live in this part of town. It's quiet, with large lots and plenty of trees. And thanks to our handiwork, it's pretty much ready to move into.

Jess didn't want to contradict Mom. He knew there was more. She was correct by saying there is always something that needed fixing or replacing. More importantly, the three of them related the house to Dad and it made them sad; a sadness the house will always bring. If they move, Dad's memory could change to one of remembering the happy times more than the sad time. A different house would help them move on. Jess also realized the window company probably compounded it for Mom considering how easy it was to see that his mom was happier at Odyssey.

A move would be good for her. A lot of work for me.

"Will I have to change schools? Mom, I don't want to change schools, I have my friends."

"You'll be in a new school next year anyway, honey. And not all your friends will go to the same junior high anyway." Her words brought a little pout to Julianne's face.

The wheels were spinning. "Wait a minute. I didn't say I sold the house. I said I was thinking about it. No one needs to start packing." She smiled, "At the very least, I got your attention. Whatever, you will stay at your school until the end of the year."

There hadn't been any talk about Julianne enrolling at Odyssey for ninth grade, still two years away. Julianne was an excellent student according to her grades and teacher's reports. And there were no school incidents in her life lately. Mom, however, would harbor her feelings about the past occurrences.

Jess, Surviving Normal

Jess's bet was that Julianne would go to Odyssey if the school was able to go forward with its plans to expand to a four-year.

A few days later, Julianne mentioned that it might be fun to move to a new house. Jess kept his thoughts to himself feeling that he shouldn't interfere this time. He'd soon go to college in another place than Trentsville, then graduate, and be on his own—thoughts that intimidated him particularly because he knew most of his peers felt just the opposite. This would be the last home he'd have with Mom and Julianne. Thoughts circled around and came back to Dad. The scar on his heart would always be there.

Thinking about being on his own, living the life of an adult made it a hollow moment for what was ahead for him.

****

Jess and Dan-el attended Jen's games as often possible. The twins had improved considerably, and as she put it, "I come down and pass to one of the 'towers' and they shoot a duck. Not much to it."

Dan-el told her, "Girl, you're a master of simplification. The way you tell it, you could streamline your contribution to the team into six words: 'go to game, play, go home.' You're an interviewer's nightmare."

"You make it look easy, Jen. That's what you're supposed to do. You're over 45% from behind the arc," Jess complimented. He didn't say that Jen looked a bit more "mechanical" than last year.

Jen: "Coach calls it 'court cohesion,' her words for teamwork and cooperation during a game. We support each other and share more than the ball during a game. What worries me is we play the same way every game. I'm afraid when we play another really good team, we won't know how to react."

Basketball was still fun and her ball handling had improved from the past. One of the drills she did over the summer was a driveway exercise where she'd keep the ball alive while avoiding her brothers. She stayed within a boxed area within the width of the driveway and they were allowed to do anything to get the ball. It was rough and fun and explained the scratches and bruises on her legs.

"I'm not a sports prodigy; I work hard to succeed."

She'd narrowed her choices of colleges to three and was determined to declare before the holidays. One of them was a school Jess was interested in. but the 'puppy dog' reference gave him pause. Those two words made Jess think. Relationships were about feelings and reciprocating those feelings.

Jen isn't wanting to ditch me, but she wouldn't want me choosing a school just because she did. If we're to be together in the future, I need to earn my ticket in the present.

Other things were in Jess's thoughts, too. Lately at school, Jess found himself looking at other girls. During a Friday assembly, he and another girl looked at each other and their eyes locked for longer than a mere glance. She smiled ever so faintly in that second before Jess averted his eyes. Also, a trainer at the clinic, older than Jess, drew his glances more than some of the other employees. Jess didn't wear blinders; he noticed other girls checking him out, too.

Hormones at work.

There were other matters in play, too. In his own right, Jess had attracted attention on the baseball field. Mom knew of some interested colleges but wasn't aware of the recruiting process –that colleges would come to him. Knowing Jess's priorities put baseball ahead of the quality of education he might get, it could make getting into college easier which opened another avenue for their dialogue.

What is this quality of education, anyway?" Jess asked. "Isn't what I get from college up to me, what I get from it?" Mom knew Jess had a lot to learn not only about college but the way the world works.

"You may be right in some ways, but colleges are ranked much like their football programs. Whether it's totally valid or not is another matter; the very word 'quality' suggests something arbitrary; it's just the way it is. They take into account things like student satisfaction, community interaction, alumni success...all kinds of factors go into it. Even the faculty is assessed."

Jess knew this was true; he knew the prestige of an Ivy League school and the distinction diplomas from certain schools carried meant more than ones from other schools. He'd asked a question that carried a longer explanation than could be answered with a casual sentence. Mom saved him the pain of listening and let the subject drop.

Jess, Surviving Normal

One thing Mom was definitely against was Jess going to a junior college that boasted of its baseball success while also claiming a 'good educational experience' in the words of a telephone recruiter. As the conversational ball was passed back and forth, the one thing that Mom emphasized was that the final decision belonged to Jess.

She'll let me know what she thinks, though.

Dan-el was on his case, too. Jess thought unfairly at times. "Just because I don't know what I want to study or become in life doesn't mean anything. Aren't you the one always saying test the waters?"

"When I was fourteen."

"That's the point, Dan-el. When you were fourteen, you were reading Voltaire, Machiavelli and Locke while I was reading J. K. Rowling. You see math while I do math. You think on your feet; I think overnight."

Dan-el had no comeback. Jess was becoming a worthy adversary in some of their arguments.

Odyssey took a toll that way, inevitable as it was. As juniors, Jess was with his two friends throughout the school day and they shared the same experiences. Now, they had common times but their academic pursuits took them in different directions. Dan-el was still outgoing, Jen remained logistical in the classical sense, and Jess reflective. Fate had brought them together; with Ella, four intelligent young people not troubled by peer pressure, popular trends, or spontaneous whims. They'd been lured by the above and each of them struggled in their own way, in their own minds. Chance brought them together, time would insert its digressions, but there was an unspoken singularity that enabled them to avoid the perfidious pitfalls of youth—their mothers.

Fridays were spent at the school. Mornings consisted of group time, and afternoons were often assessment periods. Most students chose to test on Fridays despite having been told that this wasn't the best day for test-taking. "Just, an old teacher's tale," Dane-el remarked mainly for no other reason than to say something.

Friday sessions allowed students to discuss their week's activities in small homeroom-type sessions. Recognizing social issues this different type of school was bound to create, Mrs. Jemison assembled each group congenially with Jess, Jen, Dan-el and Ella prime examples of her gerrymandering. With the hindsight of experience, Mr. Martin anticipated the isolationist effect Odyssey would have by factoring socializing into the program. Throughout the year, there were dances and activities that lasted into the evening, some with student bands and others with student DJs. They had Fridays with TV-show parodies such as 'Odyssey's Got Talent' and 'The Voice.' Wheel of Misfortune with shaving cream and squirt guns was popular. Mr. Martin and Mom as Sonny and Cher doing "I got you, Babe" brought the house down on one occasion, much to Jess's chagrin.

Friday afternoons had subtle intentions, too. Proportionately Odyssey had a greater ratio of introverts and self-proclaimed nerds; students who excelled in the arts and academics to a degree that took them out of the mainstream. Mr. Martin recognized these students as needing to relax the strictures that set them apart: self-consciousness (Jess) and aloofness (too much parental pressure) were two examples. Some Odyssey students had never "just let themselves go" as Jen once told Jess. One student admitted to Mr. Martin that he could never do this type of stuff before unless he was drunk.

****

The Trentsville Project's make-over continued. City leaders, uncharacteristically for political factions, met at the middle and worked in concert. Improvements to items like infrastructure and public access; renovations to historical buildings and landmarks; and beautification to neighborhoods sparked interest for businesses and investment concerns. Getting involved was the trending thing to do. City leaders knew they were on the cusp and knew the importance of continuing it. Neighborhoods formerly forgotten were given political representation along with a governing presence from within. Funding was proportioned to quench proverbial fires and to prevent new ones from starting.

There were problems from the beginning for no group of diverse citizens ever think as one. People make comparisons, nit-pick, and have opinions from both sides of the fence. The wheels of government move too slowly to accommodate demanding citizens, and like old wounds, old misdeeds heal slowly and are remembered. The great human faults of stubbornness and selfishness persisted. Some claimed entitlement while others sought ways to cheat. New ideas and forward momentum didn't erase existing strife between neighbors, within families and inside souls. The underpinnings of change struggled amid the naysaying rumblings— it always did; it always would.

Decisions were made, but not necessarily etched in stone; some worked and some didn't. Trentsville's enlarged police department paired new recruits with senior officers while their sergeants kept them under close supervision. "Isn't that what we always have done?" the commissioner asked a talking head during an interview while detailing the department's already-in-place 'Hearts and Minds' psy-ops program relating to the interaction between the Police Department and the people. One more thing for the officers who conscientiously put their lives on the line every day only to get lambasted with the spectacularism the media places on the few unfortunate events in a nation of 300 million people and approximately eighteen thousand police departments employing over a million officers. There is good training, bad training, and training for training's sake in many professions. Yet, the perception of the public was prioritized in the Trenstville Project. One seasoned veteran said, "Now we gotta smile when we shoot back." "And make 'em feel good about us catching them committing a crime," another said.

A more popular, less controversial change was the expanded canine force that enabled the entire department to serve and protect their constituency better than before. Something about seeing an 85-pound German shepherd deterred trouble-makers. Additionally, schools inserted older, armed combat veterans to protect students from terroristic attacks reasoning that these men and women had experience under fire and respected the value of the lives they were protecting. Trentsville embraced the Second Amendment but modified what was acceptable within their city much the way the Federal Government outlawed machine-guns in 1934. The City Council recognized that most laws are compromises, but while satisfying few, they served the best interest and wishes of the majority.

If a downside existed to everything as far as Jess was concerned, Dan-el had less free time to 'hang out,' and Jen's basketball kept her exceedingly busy. Not that Jess languished in idleness feeling sorry for himself, he signed up for the Armory

League Basketball and was paired with a new group of guys. Thanks to being recognized from the past season, he felt comfortable although probably the youngest person playing. His association with recently-promoted Major Martin, who wouldn't be playing this year didn't hurt, either. Moreover, his issue with self-confidence had been over-ridden by attending Odyssey, and he felt better about doing things on his own.

Maybe this is good for me.

Odyssey proved helpful in other ways. In addition to finding an interest in sports medicine, Jess learned that prevention and maintenance were important factors not only for athletes, but in sustaining a healthy lifestyle. His mentors were friendly and personally helpful in sharing their knowledge. "Baseball is a sport that demand a lot of stop-and-go activity, and when you go, it's often with a maximum effort. Stretching is important not only before your activity but also during and after. Your body has to accommodate to what you're expecting it to do. Warm up and warm down. Develop a regimen to stretch your tendons. Start with light exercises and then work up. Pay attention to aches and pains; your body is telling you something."

Advice like this made Jess recall how the coaches at Jefferson had increased his capability to work deeper into games as a pitcher. There were also times as a fielder when Jess could only wave at a hard-hit grounder or line drive as it passed by. If he'd been "looser" as one trainer described in-game readiness, Jess could have been all over the ball.

Odyssey promoted independent learning and Jess found delving into the history of baseball very much to his liking. Comparing past and present players was a purely speculative activity, but the subject was captivating. With others at the clinic willing to discuss such matters, Jess enjoyed the commonness that love for sports offered.

The season of Pearl Harbor, 1941, was a great year for whites-only baseball. Joe DiMaggio got base hits in 56 consecutive games and Ted Williams hit .406 for the year. 1947 was the greatest of all when Jackie Robinson integrated Major League baseball, something that should have been done in 1869 with the first pro team, The Cincinnati Red Stockings.

As he often did in the afternoons after his time at the Clinic, Jess went to an athletic center where Jefferson baseball

Jess, Surviving Normal

players had a batting cage. Now fully accepted by the team, it was an enjoyable time to gather around the cage area and B.S. with some of the other guys and take a few hacks. One of the coaches was always there to supervise and, on this occasion, Jess was informed that he'd been chosen as one of the captains of the team for the upcoming season. A mostly-honorary position, it nevertheless made him feel good to be recognized.

There was more. Coach Grove, the assistant coach who was monitoring that day, motioned Jess over to where he stood watching the batters. After preemptory chatter, Coach indicated a man sitting on a bench behind the cages also watching. "Jess, there's an old friend of mine I'd like you to meet. We played ball together in college and we've remained friends over the years."

With introductions made, Jess was about to have his day made complete. The man, Pat Munford, was an assistant baseball coach at Southport State University, an NCAA D-1 school with an impressive baseball resume. This was Jess's fondest wish fulfilled; the dream he'd imagined since he first learned that grown men could play baseball. As a six-year-old Jess remembered asking Dad why he didn't play baseball as his job.

I gotta play it cool. This may be the first of other schools to come. Granddad talking about putting in the work to make something happen like in the old baseball movie, 'Build it and they will come.' My mind was all over the place in a matter of seconds.

The man facing him represented the reason he'd been slow to seek admission to college—he'd always hoped that, like Jen, colleges would come to him! Jess had to fight back the urge to tear up as he was overcome in anticipation.

There were a lot of colleges with baseball programs, and to have a school like this to be the first to talk to him was truly a testimony to his accomplishments on the field. The college in his home town had a baseball team, a good one that usually finished high in its conference, and Jess knew he could always attend classes there and live with Mee-maw. Mom also knew this and would be fine if he'd go to her alma mater which was probably part of the reason she hadn't hounded Jess.

Whatever the case, D1 baseball was the first step to being drafted; the equivalent to rookie league professional ball. Jess's mind was making a quantum leap.

After talking for a while about the school and its athletic programs, Munford started tossing some numbers around. "Schools like Southport are allowed eleven baseball scholarships. Well, 11.7 if that makes sense. Also, the number of high school players that go on to play in college is less than six percent. College baseball puts you in pretty elite company, and then a player in a program like SU's puts you in rarefied air."

Jess was attentive to Coach Munford but knew that he hadn't made the trip to Trentsville to share baseball data.

"In your case, Jess, as in the some of the others I'm looking at in this year's class, our scholarships allotment is full. We expect to be ranked pretty high this year."

So why did he make the trip? To tell me this?

"What we can do because of your SAT score, is offer you an athletic-academic grant. AA grants basically halve our athlete's costs for their first year and makes participants eligible for a baseball scholarship in the following years. Kind of difficult to grasp, but SSU seldom offers a full-ride to an incoming freshman." Munford smiled, "Grants also speak partially to the point seven."

So, this is his offer? I have to play a year and then maybe get a full-ride scholarship if I prove to be good enough?

Jess didn't take the time to recognize that it was this way on any team—you competed for a spot to play. It was that way for him in basketball.

"I know the availability of scholarships might sound a bit deflating, Jess, but I represent Southport Sate, one of the most respected baseball schools in the nation. Southport is in every conversation. To play for SSU says a lot. I can promise that if you play for us a scout will be watching. By the time our season is over a scout from every major league team will have attended one of our games. Few schools can make that boast"

Jess understood that Coach was too classy to name names of other colleges comparatively. Once, Dan-el had teased him after a game, "My man, you can take your skills to Big Bear Shitting in the Woods Mega College and play baseball. You're that good."

Coach Munford explained other aspects of the baseball team and the university with their remaining time. He told Jess that he'd requested videos from the season and voiced his confidence that Jess would be an asset to the program. The signing date would be in the early spring and they departed, the last words a familiar refrain, "Think it over, Jess. We're a great school with a great baseball program."

Mom would like that.

Other offers did come; twenty-some from various schools. Phone calls that ranged from simple "Could we talk?" to more specific things, "We are looking for a player to build our pitching staff around." Of them all, SSU was the school with the most prestigious program, by far.

Jess researched on his own and discovered how daunting the winnowing effect actually was. During most of the season each major league team can have twenty-five eligible players from a 40-man roster, making a total of 750 in the majors. Since its beginning, there have been approximately 17,000 major leaguers spread out since 1900 when the so-called "modern era" began.

Initially, 17,000 seemed like a lot. Jess looked up how many guys have made the Hall of Fame and saw that number to be less than 400 including players from the old Negro leagues who never had the chance to play in the Show. He did the math—slightly more than two per cent were good enough to be enshrined--one in fifty. He looked further and discovered that there are approximately 50,000 guys now playing college ball, and of that total, 1 in 200 get drafted into pro ball. There were other avenues than the draft, but that one in fifty number seemed to tell the story again: The odds were pretty small.

Jess found some other interesting things in his search, too. A player can go pro right out of high school if he's drafted and signs. Many scouts prefer the high school market because it gives their team more time to develop the draftee their way. "The Jerk" did that. Jess was surprised to see that if a player went to a four-year, he wasn't eligible to be drafted until after his junior year or he reached the age of 21. And he was even more surprised to read that a junior college player was like a high school graduate.

A baller at a four-year seems to be at a disadvantage.

When Jess presented all this to his mother, her reaction was predictable. "You gave me the numbers, Jess. Now factor the possibility of injury and how life often gets in the way into your equation and the answer is pretty obvious. Go to school to get a degree and play baseball if it doesn't interfere with that goal. From there, let the chips fall where they may."

Jess had plenty of "Yeah, buts, but there wasn't any sense in using them on Mom.

She'd change her mind if I showed her a contract with a 5-mil signing bonus.

That evening, now Jess's time to work out, he found a renewed source of energy.

****

Surprises continued for Jess on a chilly afternoon after a session at the Clinic. Leaving the elevator of the Med Plex's parking ramp to get his truck, he noticed a figure in the distance. Something about the way the person moved triggered a memory; Jess had seen him, should know who it was. Watching as he walked to his truck, the hoodie and jacket further obscured Jess from getting a good look.

It'll come to me. No big deal.

Not paying attention to where he was going, another person, a girl, rather suddenly materialized from between a row of cars, "Would you have a pair of jumper cables? My car won't start."

Although he wasn't certain, Jess knew that Dad kept jumper cables in a little storage space in the bed of the pick-up. Never having to use them, Jess replied, "I don't know. I'd have to look."

She nodded in the direction of the person Jess had been watching, "My car's over there."

Street-wise after two years in the city, Jess had doubts.

Why is she over here when her car's over there by that dude I can't remember? She looking for jumper cables on the floor? Smells fishy. I've seen this girl before, too. I remember the ring in her lip and wondering how she could eat.

"Um, I'll get my truck and look. I'll drive over and let you know."

The jumper cables were indeed in the little compartment on the side of the Jess's pick-up bed. He got in his truck, started it, and drove over to the where the girl was standing. No one else was on the entire floor of the parking garage, and the person Jess had been watching was nowhere to be seen. Rolling down the window to talk, "Sorry, I don't have any." He didn't wait for a response and drove away.

Congratulating himself for his awareness, Jess wouldn't have thought this way two years ago. He would have been all too eager to help a person in distress. He'd learned a lot and being altruistic was one of the things that changed.

This whole scene felt like a mugging about to happen. I'd get out of my truck and all of a sudden get hit with a pipe from behind. That guy didn't just disappear but was probably waiting to jump out and rack me. Joke coulda been on them though. My old truck shoulda told them I don't have enough money to make a mugging worthwhile.

Jess was 80-20 in his belief that he made the right decision.

Another thing, they could have found me to be a challenge they didn't count on. Bad call on her part 'cause I might've kicked some butt of my own. Savvy and belligerent—that's me.

Whether correct in his assessment or not, Jess wondered who he might talk to. Surely there were security personnel for the area; maybe a Head of Operations for the five-story complex that he could alert. He'd seen plenty of movies to know that parking ramps were often used as settings for crime. They were large and generally isolated except during rush hours. Jess knew that despite the renaissance movement taking place in Trentsville, there was still crime.

No matter what happens to make things better, there's always resistance. Some will find ways to criticize. Others will devise ways to cheat the system.

As he swept his pass card through the machine at the exit, for no particular reason his mind went back to last year in Humanities when they read John Stuart Mill's *On Liberty* and discussed Mill's contention that democracy was bound to fail when human diversity went unchecked. Of course, politics were the subject Dan-el could talk about forever and asked whether Mill was writing about racial diversity or ideological diversity. Whereas Jess had struggled mightily to find the meaning of the words or how they might apply to anything in his life, Dan-el's question was appropriate for the times.

Jen didn't like some of those books we had to read either.
His mind was wandering from one thing to another.

Coach Mercer talked about retrospective learning. When something doesn't make sense when we learn it, we should think about it later in a different context—without the pressure of a grade stressing us. We should try to apply it to a life situation. Coach said things that he didn't understand at the time sometimes came back to him later with perfect clarity. And here I am, using Mill's book to understand what just happened. Maybe stuff like this will help me hit the baseball harder. Weird I am. Sam I am. Weird I guess, Jess no less.

As he turned onto Roosevelt toward the batting cages, the revelation came to him. Completely out of the blue—Apex!

He doesn't really know who I am—wouldn't be looking anyway. That gives me an edge. Apex, a mugger now. He's found a good place to pull his crap because of the clinic. Why is a shitbag like him still loose? Who cares? This is my chance to jump him and clock the bastard. Got to figure a way to get the girl away. Also have to make sure he's a gang of one, now.

Jess's gut feeling and watching him move was enough convincing evidence that the person he saw was Apex. He began to create situations; 'what if' ideas for revenge with each one thwarted by Dan-el's caveat about going after a High Ace, especially this one.

I'm right, those two were in the ramp looking to mug someone. His girl screwed up picking on a guy like me—I sure don't look like a rich doctor. He's turned to petty stuff. She was probably looking for unlocked cars to see what she could steal, too. That's all they know.

Jess related the episode to Mom that evening but didn't mention anything about Apex. Mom showed concern, expressed empathy, but also recognized it not just for what it was to Jess, but for its implications to Odyssey. "I'll speak with Mr. Martin. He'll know the right person to contact. One incident like this, one accident related to the school could shut us down. And what if you'd been hurt?"

"Mom, I can handle myself."

I'm savvy and belligerent.

"That, too. No matter what you think, Jess, you've got to be careful. You were stabbed and remember what happened to Dan-el when he was attacked by those thugs. Don't go there."

I can handle it.

****

The crackdown on gangs like the High Aces that led to the Trentsville Project indeed brought change. Among them was the auxiliary program that dealt with gang members on a *quid pro quo* basis—give up the gang life and get a suspended or lighter sentence for your crimes. It all sounded easy enough, but in reality, giving it up promised to be an excruciating decision fraught with all sorts of possibilities. It wasn't for everyone, especially if the person had grown up distrusting cops. Gang members lived with a deeply entrenched mindset instilled by their environment that wasn't easily cast off. To wake up some morning and suddenly see the fallacy of their way of life was preposterous.

For those trying to bring about change, it was an equally steep and slippery slope. 'To divide and conquer' wasn't an option because it would be playing right into the way gangs operated. The only approach was to chip away, 'stay the course' and recognize that steps forward would bring steps backward in many cases. Yet, the Trentsville Project was making progress.

A prime example was Dan-el's brother. His get-out-of-jail-card meant accepting probation and house arrest, allowing him only the freedom to go to school or to a job. Jon-el hoped to eventually get a degree in social work like his mother and even thought of law school. There were hopes that felony crimes could be knocked down to misdemeanors in some cases and change a bleak future into one with promise.

For thugs like Apex, the leaders and officers in the gangs, it was even more complicated. They'd enjoyed the high life that the majority of their subordinates only aspired to. They were faced with a dilemma: If three-fourths of the gang entered the programs, the remaining one-fourth couldn't go around exacting retribution. Whether their legions left in mass exodus or in trickling numbers, it would be bad form—dangerous maybe. People like Apex recognized change was imminent regardless of the time it would take. The Project wasn't one of force, but rather, one of choice. Generals needed soldiers lest they become soldiers. Compounding it, Apex knew that his crimes weren't as easily pardonable having been the king rat.

Jess knew he was correct in his assumptions. The person he saw was Apex, and he had no idea he'd been recognized.

On Jess's part, he wasn't so much as considering Mom's advice. Not just Mom's but also the things Dan-el told him. Things like after years as a gang leader Apex was surely armed; if not a gun then certainly a knife. Furthermore, Apex was a survivor and as street-wise as they came. He obviously hadn't been free this long without this knowledge.

I'll watch for him in the ramp every afternoon after school. I'll put the little miniature bat in my backpack. And spray paint—I'll get a can and use it on him or his girlfriend. If I can get him like he got me, by surprise, he'll never know what hit him.

A sure-fire plan that was bound... to fail.

Merely by thinking, the adrenaline flowed through his body causing him to shiver.

What I'd like to do is see him in the open when I'm in my truck. I'll just run over him. I could say I didn't see him. Be a service to the community. Get a medal from the mayor.

In the days following, Jess would often find himself contriving new plans sometimes to the point of distraction. The trainer mentoring Jess noticed his student's change and asked if everything was okay. Jen sent him several 'Earth to Jess' messages.

Taking Jess aside one morning during the break, Dan-el confronted him. "Hey man, what's with you lately? You skitterin' around here like a man on a mission lookin' for his head. They put you in a trance over at the clinic? Maybe drop a weight on your head?" Dan-el's conversational prose was always different than his formal school one. Heading Jess from the hallway to a bench outside the lunchroom where there wasn't much traffic, he confronted his friend. "You actin' like you gotta be somewhere you ain't, like a fart in a skillet. Lemme see those hands, man." Dan-el reached out a took one of Jess-s hands and saw the back of it had red sore-like marks from Jess scratching on it. "What's this?"

"I itch. So what?"

"'Evah. You got a problem, Jess, tell me."

Almost instinctively, Jess started digging at his arm through his shirt sleeve. "You worryin' bout something the reason you're scratchin' like you got fleas. I'm not going away 'til you open up, man. Isn't that what you did to me?"

Reluctantly, Jess told his story.

Jess, Surviving Normal

Dan-el was analytical. "Let's break this down for what it's worth. You're healed up, Apex is reduced to stealin' outta cars and maybe muggin' somebody, all assumption by you bein' 99% sure that it really is Apex. But once that happens, he's gone from there, man. You know what I'm saying? He can't hang out in the same parking garage doing a mugging a day"

The way Dan-el was retelling the story made Jess feel that he was being put down. "You think I'm imagining this? This is my fight, got nothing to do with you."

Disregarding Jess's comment, Dan-el kept talking. That's a high-end parking lot and once the word gets out that it's haunted, they'll look at the video and be on him like stink on shit. And here you are lurking in wait much to the amusement of the guys watching CCTV monitors so you can jump out and throttle him with a little stick that'll probably break in half on the first swing. Hell, you'll make the six-o'clock news, Apex stickin' that bat up your ass for a new Guinness record. C'mon, Dude. Be real about it. You've already won your fight with Apex."

Jess started to argue but Dan-el wasn't finished. "All you got is a motive for revenge. Say you do what you plan, you won't feel any better. Hell, that's what this whole thing with the city's about—the Project. You're instrumental in that. You the star of that movie as much as me or Kinkade or Martin—anyone. Nothin's sweet about revenge."

Jess knew all this and he also knew that this was what the internal argument he was having with himself was about. The 'no one messes with me' versus Jack Armstrong, the all-American boy. (A radio series from 1933-1951 featuring a boy of integrity who surmounted uncommon adversity in every instance.) Yet he continued his glare toward Dan-el, considering shoving him aside and walking away.

"Tell you what, Jess. I'll leave early from the U for the next couple days and come to your clinic and we'll go on a stake-out. We'll watch to see if Apex shows up and take it from there. Then if you want to try to give him a beat-down, I'll keep his 'associates' away. When he pulls his gun, you better think fast—convince him it was just a joke."

Jess was yet to think about that possibility. In too deep, and far too stubborn to agree with Dan-el. "Okay. We gotta' get going to class.

It was a particularly cold winter by Trentsville standards. Arctic melt stirred up ocean currents and shifted the Prevailing Westerlies to create Arctic Clippers. Shivering against the cold wall enclosing the elevator shaft, Jess and Dan-el huddled away from the wind...when Apex and his companion stepped through the doorway.

Jess and Dan-el stood frozen, not knowing what to do, a rare occasion for Dan-el. Their reconnaissance mission now changed as they watched Apex, ever wary, look at them and assess the danger two kids, big kids, might have. They weren't standing like they were waiting to get on the elevator and they were too young to be employed at the clinic. They most likely would have an adult with them if they were patients. And they weren't cops, for sure. Pulling his hoodie over his head against the cold that whistled through the ramp, he recognized the darker, shorter kid—Jon-el's brother. "Yo."

Jess saw his opening. With a single step he would have a full frontal with Apex and could drive him back against the wall of the elevator that would cause a double hit, especially with Apex off balance from surprise. Jess would keep the pressure and stay inside Apex's arms so he couldn't reach any weapons he had. Also, with Apex having no room to maneuver Jess would work on the inside with a flurry of quick blows just as Dan-el would do in the ring. This was his chance. Perfect!

But he stood, transfixed, and watched as Apex and the girl walked past them.

Dan-el returned the greeting, but uncharacteristically was at a loss for anything further as they watched the man with "Schneider Medical Clinic" in bold golden letters on the back of his jacket turn and walk down the passageway. "He works here," Jess heard his friend say.

"Yeah."

****

Winter break came and the three friends plus one came face to face with the reality that they were about to enter their final semester of high school. For some of the students at Odyssey, Mr. Martin had looked into graduation requirements and reminded students what he said earlier: most of them could also receive diplomas from their former public schools...if they met a few criteria. Dan-el and Jen, for example, needed to show proficiency in writing and pass an algebra exam. In its first year, Odyssey was comprised mostly of seniors and the majority of them, with a bit of extra effort, thought it a good idea. "I'm going to do it," Jen proclaimed. "It'll save people wondering and questioning when they look at my resume."

It wasn't that simple for Jess, having transferred from Iowa as a mid-term sophomore. "I think they just want to jack me around," he told his friends. I missed over a month of classes when I was stabbed, and they have a problem with an attendance requirement. It's bull crap. Mom went to talk with the Dean of Students and the first thing he said to her was, 'I remember you.' You know, like here was payback for all the disturbance she caused by being a concerned mom. I would have to go to summer school just to have enough hours of attendance."

"Like community service. So many hours. to pay them back for their magnanimity." Dan-el offered.

"I'll take the GED test and if I pass, that's it for me. I have no sentimentality for good ol' Jefferson."

On weekends, the deli where Jen worked was a hang-out for the four friends. Jen worked Saturdays from six to eight in prep and then on the floor through the lunch hour. Most days, she was finished at one and joined the group. Her bosses, always agreeable, joked that they would hate to see her leave for college, her friends kept them in business.

Each in the middle of their pursuits, there was always something going on. Ella was a musician, a violinist, busy in her former school's orchestra and now preparing for a spring recital. Jen was busy with basketball. Jess was playing what he dubbed 'Army ball,' at the Armory and readying for the upcoming baseball season. Dan-el was forever busy in the gym; his club hosting and traveling to occasional tournaments. Not everyone made it each Saturday because of their activities.

Ella had the most difficulty, not always allowed to spend the week-end at Jen's. She was living half a lie to her parents; yes, she did stay at Jen's, but the root cause was to be with Dan-el. Further, the girls' mothers were sisters meaning they knew what was taking place, they'd discussed it thoroughly. Ella's father was the disproving one and wasn't privy to 'everything.'

On this particular day, it was Dan-el who was bursting to share his news. Sporting a Santa hat and obviously pleased with himself, he wouldn't share his news until they were all together.

"You're engaged," Jess posed.

"I would probably know that," Ella returned with her brilliant smile. She wasn't quite as tall as Jen, but they shared a lot of features that made people often mistake them for sisters.

Even before Jen had time to pull her chair in place at the corner table they preferred, Dan-el rapidly thumped the table and said, "Drum roll, please. Ladies and germ, I have received notification of acceptance to the United States Naval Academy in Annapolis, Maryland, for the summer semester."

Amid the congratulatory "Wows" and "Greats" Dan-el snapped off a crisp salute and sang a few bars of *Anchors Aweigh*. Some of the others in the deli looked up and smiled catching the drift that something good had happened for this handsome, charismatic young man. Others joined in as the news spread from table to table and the room erupted into applause for Dan-el. Two men stood as they clapped for Dan-el's achievement. Neither was the moment lost in another unspoken significance: two white girls with two young men of color joined by an ethnically-mixed clientele eating Italian sandwiches in an American restaurant.

Jess, Jen and Ella knew that Dan-el applied and he'd prioritized this as his number one choice. Needing some endorsement with political sway, his mom knew some people from her work, and Mr. Martin called on some of his educational and military associates to sway Trentsville's Congressional representative to nominate Dan-el. Even with endorsements, the acceptance rate was only eight percent, which made his accomplishment quite significant.

Between bites of his hoagie Dan-el shared some details. "I'll focus on Political Science as my major and because each Midshipman is encouraged to have an extra-curricular activity, I can do club boxing. I'm kind of behind 'cause I should've gone to the First Summer seminar last year, but they waived that for me, so I'll have a bunch of catching up to do."

Dan-el, exuberant, spoke of other things he wanted to do. "I hope to eventually join the SEAL program that's open to qualifying midshipmen. There's a five-year enlistment obligation upon graduation, and I'll be offered a Commission—an officer and a gentleman."

Ella interjected, "And the fact that you'll have to learn to speak when spoken to."

"That, too. I hope to graduate somewhere in the middle of my class, but definitely stick it out." John McCain was Dan-el's favorite political figure that he often mentioned in conversation. "I hope I don't get in as much trouble as Senator McCain did when he was a student."

****

Another topic for the quartet that assembled around the glass-topped table with curly-toed wrought-iron legs was Jess's encounter with Apex. Jess could only surmise that by some quirk of the Trentsville Project the leader of the High Aces avoided doing hard time. The High Aces were, for the most part, broken up and the best guess Dan-el could offer was that Apex cooperated fully with the authorities and was put on a work-release. "Probably spends his time at a facility as he works off his sentence," Dan-el explained. "The High Aces are history, but some of the other gangs are still around, layin' low for the time being."

Hearing of the encounter, the girls thought Jess did the right thing. Jen, recalled how she'd been knocked to the ground in the basketball game by Apex said, "Forget him, he's not worth it."

Ella, too, offered her opinion, "Jess, the event was karma and led you to where you are now. Apex made it possible. Not that you should go thank him for stabbing you or anything. But just let it go."

For Jess, the incident remained. He, of course, second-guessed himself over his inaction for avenging being stabbed. Morally, he'd done the correct thing; physically, he'd missed the best opportunity ever. Yet the opportunity still existed. Jess was still sure Apex hadn't recognized him— and never had despite Dan-el's comment otherwise. Jess could pick a time and place to his advantage and take Apex by surprise. In his mind, the fight would be but a single blow and Apex would crumble into unconsciousness. Imagining that he'd coldcock Apex with his souvenir bat then stand over him and let him know that HE messed with the wrong person.

No one messes with Jess Jemison without paying the price.

However, his incessant tennis match of back and forth thoughts wouldn't let him stop there. Grandad was at work. Jess had never hit anyone with a club, what if he killed Apex? What if the little bat snapped in half like Dan-el said and Apex wasn't even fazed by it and pulled out his knife? There were all kinds of contradictory haunts. The legal implications? What if everything worked and Apex, in turn, sought revenge, but this time on Julianne or Jen or Mom? What about the moral aspect of it—Jess would never be able to justify it.

The more I thought about it, the more it bothered me. I remembered Dad talking once at supper about compromise and a new thought grabbed me. I'll just confront him face-to-face. I'll let him know who I am and what he did to me. Like, I'll put the ball in his court and see what he does with it. But I'll be ready. If Dan-el is right, Apex has one foot in jail and can't get caught carrying a weapon. Yeah, if Apex wants to take it farther, that's up to him. At least, I'll let him know.

Still obsessed, Jess began to pay closer attention to those around him as he played out different scenarios in his mind. Still thinking of physical retribution, he noted places and, times that would be advantageous. The clinic where he spent his time was part of a four-story complex that included an emergency care facility, medical labs and doctor's offices, most of whom were specialists. A pharmacy took up part of the first-floor sharing space with a commons area and cafeteria. Situated on the end of an open shopping area that contained a large chain grocery, two banks, and numerous restaurants and specialty shops, the combination occupied an area equivalent to several city blocks complete with its green space. Apex, if his jacket saying Parkland Staff on it meant anything, worked with the facility's maintenance staff.

Because he'd seen Apex twice around the same time in the parking ramp, his routine was probably pretty regular. After all his thought, Jess simply decided just like before when he was with Dan-el to wait by the lower elevator shaft. This would also provide a measure of transparency if the encounter turned violent. It didn't concern Jess that the time of day hadn't coincided with much activity in the ramp—nothing like the morning and evening traffic glut. He'd also recalled the girl wore a white jacket that was visible under her overcoat, and he remembered that her hair was compacted by a hairnet.

Cafeteria.

Jess hadn't experienced any great amount of anxiousness when he and Dan-el waited for Apex a week ago. But now, by himself and plotting an action plan, it was totally different. Again, his emotions peaked.

He decided to drop by the cafeteria one afternoon to see if the girl did work there. Jess could feel the pulse in his head, his stomach queasy, and his vision clouding peripherally just by approaching the door to the cafeteria. Thinking himself not a stalker but as a spy on a special ops mission, he bought a chocolate milk and a stale muffin left from that morning, and sat at a small table in the mostly empty cafeteria. He did not see the girl.

Maybe she works at one of the restaurants. Never did really get a good look at her. Mission aborted!

Reverting to watching the elevator of the ramp, he found he could do that by sitting at a bus stop across the street. It offered a wind break and he would be semi-hidden in his quest to learn more about the man's routine.

They walk to the ground-floor elevator, and take it to the fourth floor where employees are directed to park. It takes five to seven minutes for their car to leave the ramp and turn north.

Choosing Wednesday to be the day because that was the day the ramp had the smallest number of cars in it. When he asked his mentor about why that was true, "golf" was the one-word reply. Then, shooting a chest pass of weighted basketball at Jess, "Docs like to take Wednesday afternoons off and they've done it that way for years, winter or summer. No doctors, no patients, fewer cars."

That Wednesday, Jess waited by the elevator on four. Looking down to the street, he watched Apex and the girl cross the street toward the parking ramp. The cold snap had broken, yet Jess felt himself shivering hearing the ascending elevator click and squeak. He'd put his little bat in the back pocket of his jeans like before, his jacket covered its protrusion.

Sliding a few steps to partially block the elevator door, "Hey, man got a minute?" his tongue thick. Hoping Apex wouldn't see his quaking.

"Yo, I figured you'd asks me sometime. Kinda' thought it'd be from behind."

"You know who I am?"

Apex gave something between a smirk and a smile. "Don't know your name, Brownie. Know who you is and you hang wit' Jon-el's little bruh."

Jess was at a loss for words and after standing open-mouthed for a couple seconds managed, "So you know…"

Apex was clearly in control. "That little stick I gave you heal up okay, did it?"

Jess noticed that as they spoke, the girl gradually moved away from Apex and took a position more to the side of Jess, keeping out of arm's reach, one of Dan-el's previously explained street tactics. He realized that there had been a role reversal. This wasn't going anything like he'd planned. Apex knew it, too.

"Know you went to the hospital an' the cops got involved. Nevah did figure it out but I was layin' low fo' awhile."

Apex took a step closer and Jess reflexively leaned back, the wall opposite the elevator blocking a retreat. Apex raised his hands, open-palms to shoulder height, he and Jess nearly the same height, Apex thicker, older. Man vs. boy flashed in Jess's head.

"Thas a long time ago. Shoulda let it go." And then, Jess couldn't believe what he heard. "Bothered me. Wanted to say sumptin but didn't wanna get pinned with an assault with a deadly weapon. Know what I mean? Then time passed. I remember dat time at Woods playin' basketball, too, but I hadda play it tough for my bro's, you followin?"

Jess didn't comment, but his eyes softened, his frown gone, his back now against stairway door. If it would open Jess would stumble backward.

Apex went on. "Anyways, ain't the way I am. Did stuff, bad stuff but me an' the Aces just makin' a livin' in the 'hood doin' the best we could. Oughta put that to music, huh? So, I'm sorry, man. I did make sure nothin' else gonna' happen to you."

Jess was incredulous that Apex would be saying this. No words came, thinking that if he said something, he'd break the spell.

Noticing that Jess was fairly cornered, Apex backed up and dropped his hands. "Easy, man, dint want to push you at first.

Believe me when I say I ain't got no fight left in me." He put his hands inside his jacket to show.

Recovering somewhat, Jess said, "But you were the leader of the High Aces and all the things they did." Jess didn't give Apex a list of the crimes such as murder, arson, theft. He was still wary and on guard.

"I was the baddest of the bad. That how you saw me?"

Jess gave a little 'I don't know for sure' shrug. "I'm not a judge."

Apex chuckled, "But you here to whack me ain't you?"

Jess's mind clearing and sensing opportunity; this was his chance with Apex directly in front of him. It was as if Apex was giving him what he wanted. Again, Jess deferred, choosing instead to ask why Apex wasn't in jail, a question that he immediately regretted.

"A long story. You know 'Tective Kinkade, right? He come to me outta the blue one time he saw me down by the Armory. Wasn't first time we talked. He show me respect each time and I understand where he comin' from. Ev'ry one think the High Aces deeper than they was, but we neva shoot nobody, no bitches fo sale. Sure, we sell weed, give protection, help ourselves to things like rides, but mostly we takin' care of ourselves. Crime is a two-way street. You nevah see me in no gold Cadillac 'less I was stealin' it back from the Man dat stole it hisself thinkin' he a honest biznessman. Yeah, we into illegal, but what choice we have, anyway?"

Still, Jess could hardly believe what was happening; what he was hearing. As they stood there talking. People working in the clinic and offices had completed their workday and started crossing the street coming to the elevator. The girl with Apex, quiet until now, suggested they move out of the way.

"What about betting?" Jess asked. "Weren't the High Aces behind threatening Dan-el White to throw a fight?"

"That's two questions. Yeah, we run a gamblin' operation, but people always want to bet on games so we take ova the area to keep it legit—away from crooks." Apex broke into a smile. "Sound ironic, know what I mean?"

Jess, smiled back, relaxing a bit more.

"The second question, is a need to know thing and I don't want to say nothin' bout it. Too complicated."

A hint of something bigger.

"Kinkade's a good cop. He knows the law and he know which way the wind blows."

There it is! Informant.

Jess came back with, "And also pretty simple."

Jess knew. Apex's roundabout answer had provided the insight for him to understand. He didn't want to push the issue, to make Apex spell it out. Some things were better to go unsaid. But Jess couldn't help letting Apex knew that he DID know what Apex was alluding to.

I like the word cooperation better than the word collusion.

Neither spoke for a moment. Apex looked skyward, his head back, then down catching Jess's eyes and returned to the original subject. "I had what they call anger issues and I'm workin' on it. Felt like I had to always be on top, winnin', showin' my boys who's boss. So, I 'pologize. Don't expect you to fo'give and fo'get, jus' know I'm sorry."

The tension gone; Jess noticed the contriteness in Apex believing what he heard. Here was a demigod of the gang world standing remorseful in a way that said, 'smack me if you want, I deserve it.' A product of his environment offering retribution the only way he knew.

Jess was witnessing a complexity of human nature in a moment of lucidity. Here was a warrior laying down his arms, relinquishing his physical superiority not so much as an example of good over evil because Jess's intent by the encounter was to exact revenge, 'an eye for an eye.' Rather, this was right over might--Jess becoming a mere spectator to a human metamorphosis. Real. Another definable moment furrowing into his being.

"You said you knew I was watching you before today. Why didn't you come to me?"

"Figured, I might spook you, and make you do somethin' I din't want to happen. Wanted to do it this way, but let you be in control. You know what I mean?"

He says that a lot.

Apparent that Apex was no simple gangland boss asking for his forgiveness. Jess realized Dan-el was right in describing the High Aces to him way back when. There was a military bearing that Apex exuded. He'd managed an organization that was on the other side of a righteous society because the righteous society had spurned him. Like Apex indicated, they broke the law, but maybe there was a bit of justification.

Jess thought of the Biblical story of, 'the good thief.'

"So, I'm doin' time in a half-way. Spent ninety in the County lock-up and now ten hours a week doin' civic restitution. Kinkade got me this job, payin' eleven an hour. I think if I stick, I can move up someday—maybe start my own biz'ness. Be totally respectable to the Man."

Looking at the girl Apex said, "This is Kat. She's been with me throughout. Helped me figure out a lot."

Kat smiled, sending a mental message to Jess that she really did have a dead battery when she'd approached Jess. That would also have been when Apex saw him.

****

Baseball practice typically got underway in late February, weather permitting. The old stadium provided some space under the bleachers for the pitchers to at least play catch if it was too inclement to practice outside. Otherwise, the team made whatever Mother Nature gave them work, more than a few times confining the team to the outfield grass in order to preserve the infield. The old groundskeepers frowned and complained throughout this time, but had a hard time concealing their passion for the game.

Jess experienced elbow tendinitis early and had to limit himself to soft-tossing and hitting. His mentor at the clinic advised a program for rehabbing and that rest was the best healer—exactly what a high school player didn't have. This was his last season and the games would begin with or without one their captains. By the time the spring tournament rolled around, Jess felt fine, but would be used as the designated hitter. Coach was overly cautious in Jess's opinion.

With her usual aplomb, Jen shared her news one morning before school. "I signed a letter of intent last evening at a prestigious engineering college, Voltmar-Hughes, a D-2 that offered a partial athletic scholarship supplemented by a student work grant in the Physical Plant of the college. I chose V-H, Veach we call it, for its reputation. The school generates its own power with a combination of solar-geothermal sources and is pioneering desalinization and reclamation of sea water into drinking water."

Pausing, she looked at Jess, then lowered her eyes to her hands resting on the table,

Here it comes. Sea water?

"It's in California."

A lump in Jess's throat forced an involuntary cough.

Dan-el recognized the awkwardness of the moment—a loose ball on the field that he had to pick up and run with it. "Reverse osmosis isn't it? The process of extracting salt from sea water? I'd think there'd be opportunity in the solute, the brine too"

Giving Jess time to absorb her news, Jen was all-too willing to answer the question. "Yes, the ocean water is forced through microscopic filters to separate the salt molecules from the lighter water molecules. The power to do this comes from the solar converters."

She was as excited as Jess had ever seen her. "Veach is a work-study school kinda like Odyssey as they work with energy conversion and development companies. They have a satellite campus in Japan."

It is what it is.

To his own amazement, Jess was accepting of the news. "Congratulations, Jen. You'll do the school proud."

Ella, already knowing, was in accord offering kudos to her cousin.

"There's a lot more stuff dissolved in sea water than just sodium chloride. Also, a lot of particulates that have to be separated, too," Jess contributed.

"Both good and bad. Some things can be separated mechanically and others with E and M—electricity and magnetism. And pure water needs additives like fluorides for human consumption, to make it healthy."

The only bell of the day rang signaling the beginning of school.

Jess sat at his work station, lost in thought. This would be the test of his relationship with Jen because he wasn't going to go to college where Jen was, probably couldn't get accepted. Surely there were other schools nearby, but he vowed he wouldn't follow her. As much as the thought hurt him, being apart would be the test that measured their mutual feelings, and if those feelings remained throughout, all the better. They'd spent a considerable amount of time talking about this very thing, and Jen had gone to great lengths to emphasize that IF they were to be separated by college, it wouldn't be by choice. "We need to do what's best for our careers and then we can love each other for the rest of our lives without second-guessing," she told Jess.

Jess, nonetheless, had to fight the 'property gene,' that somebody said must be linked to the single existent X chromosome in all males. Jen was his girlfriend. He had nightmares, and day-mares as Julianne called sad thoughts during the day, about getting dumped that sparked a hollow feeling whenever he thought about it. He struggled in trying to suppress selfish thoughts that put HIM first and THEM second. Funny that during his reverie he thought of the idiom, 'there's a lot of fish in the sea."

But not for me.

Basketball had a big role in Jen's decision. She liked playing and was blessed with the talent to excel in the sport. She picked it up quickly as a young girl, abiding the yelling of the youth coaches and working on the mechanics of shooting. When she was caught up in the drama of life, she found solace in shooting baskets—not idly, but doing drills and working on weaknesses. But it wasn't a passion. She couldn't name three professional women basketball players and idolized I.M. Pei and Zaha Hadid, as exemplary human beings for their architectural accomplishments. At this point, Jen needed basketball to help pay for college and when she discovered the curricular focus of Voltmar-Hughes, she knew this was the school for her.

She didn't want to be over two thousand miles away from home and all her close associations. She knew it would be a severe test but she prided herself at 'living in the day.' Jen loved the SEAL motto, 'The only easy day was yesterday.'

Jen's best friend and cousin, Ella, was an equally high achiever in her own right, and strangely, their differences circled around and connected them artistically. Whereas Jen approached basketball much the same way as a subject in school, it was a means to the end—a scholarship to study architectural engineering, Ella's forte was music. Music was truth, beauty and justice to her, 'unencumbered human expression,' as she described it.

Ella was a talented musician, one of few that are cognitively gifted with perfect pitch. Not a prodigy or wunderkind, she enjoyed performing, but recognized her limitations and had no aspirations to play in a band. Her life interest was music history. "Everyone knows that music brings people together and that different cultures have different musical tastes. I want to study primal music archeologically to find common bonds and missing links as well as reasons for divergence in musical preferences." She truly believed that music, as the universal language, could bring all people of the earth together.

However, Ella wasn't encouraged to pursue her dream. Her father was well-meaning but overruling without understanding what he was doing. He made the decisions for them. Mostly though, it was bothersome stuff that affected her brothers more than Ella until they made a kind of game of it. For Ella, he often finished her sentences when she was talking, decided who her friends should be, and what she should study. Set on applying to renowned schools such as Berklee and Julliard, she faced an uphill battle not unlike the one when she started dating Dan-el. That issue, thanks to her mom's support had slightly warmed him to the idea of Dan-el and Ella dating. She was convinced she would prevail on each front when she showed her dad acceptance letters.

Explaining, Ella said, "It's the method he uses. He always gives in when I sweat blood and prove that I really, really want something. Daddy knows that I used staying with you, Jen, as an excuse to see Dan-el. He told me when he signed my papers to attend Odyssey. He worries about money because one or more of us will be in college for the next seven years."

Jess sat and listened to his friends, a happy-sad feeling engulfing him. In their own way each must have the same feelings—going away to school and the excitement of meeting new people and forging a career choice. He'd turned down all the offers from other schools for the U of Trentsville deciding it to be his best option. It was a respectable four-year with lower tuition for in-state students. Once known as a teacher's college, it still had a strong education department. The coaches were certainly aware of Jess and had shown interest in his baseball ability saying they'd work with him to get financial help, if not a scholarship. There

were other compelling reasons: When Jen or Dan-el came home on break he'd be around, and he'd be able to help Mom.
Sounds like I'm a Mama's boy. So what, maybe I am.

****

Right before the annual trip to Mississippi for the baseball team, Mom brought up a heretofore unconsidered notion on the part of her children. "I want to ask you to think about something and let me know how you feel. Julianne was the one that glanced at her brother with 'the here we go again' roll of her eyes.

"So much has happened in the past few months. So much to change our lives and so much sadness," Mom started. "We'll never get over Dad's loss. It's an empty spot in our hearts that can't be mended. But life goes on." She was having a hard time, taking a breath after each sentence. "It's been a struggle for each of us in our own way."

Mom didn't know about my encounter with Apex.

"One positive thing for me has been my new job. I don't miss the plant and being away from it has helped me cope and to not be constantly reminded of Dad and that he was always nearby. No, I'll never forget…oh, you know. It's the same as when I talked about selling the house a few weeks ago." Her eyes filling with tears, Jess looked away, waiting.

And…

Mom wiped her eyes, and let out a little squeak as she took a breath. "I want to ask you what you think of Mr. Martin, Mike—he's asked me to go out to dinner. A date."

All their lives Julianne and Jess were asking Mom for things, and here she was in this turnaround asking them for permission to go out for dinner. Julianne immediately thought it was a good idea while Jess was thoughtful, wisely not reacting with something flippant. He felt a little jolt to his heart as his mind leaped forward to the implications. Mom was vulnerable; it would be easy to hurt her with some snide remark.

"Sure. Fine by me."

Actually, there was no other adult more influential in Jess's life than Mr. Martin—no one he respected and looked up to more. Dad, Granddad, Coach Mercer were in one way or another removed. Mr. Martin was already filling a fatherly role in loco parentis. Still…Dad.

"Can I help you pick out your clothes?" Julianne asked. "Are you going to a movie? Maybe dancing?"

"Mr. Martin suggested we leave from work and drive out to the air force base for a drink and meal at the Officer's Club. He said their food is excellent. I only said a date to see what you two would say."

Uh-huh.

"Do you suppose you could forage through the refrigerator for something to eat and get along without me?" I'm sure I'll be home by eight."

Jess couldn't help looking ahead to the possibility that Mom and Mr. Martin would someday get married. It seemed a possibility. What would he and Julianne call their stepdad if it were to happen: Dad, Mike, Mr. Martin? He decided not to ask.

There was always something for Jess to think about. So many things piling up that very well could have put the Jess of the past in a continual funk. Yes, some things already decided and others pending. More on the horizon sure to create even more— that's life. His friends had made their decisions on college; on their career pursuits and were elated. Mom thinking about downsizing and selling the house. What about Mr. Martin? Jess knew that he was truly fortunate to have the male family members and role models who left their influence on him. Better yet, he had listened to much of it and didn't fight or rebel against the wisdom given him. Only time would tell whether his relationship with Jen would endure, but it was up to him to make that time work in his favor, to accept love not as a conquest but as a harmonious sharing—a two-way street. He'd chosen his college responsibly although the jury was still out on what his pursuit would be career-wise. Like Dan-el implied, "Why do you have to know right now. Chill, dude!" Julianne was growing up so fast. His truck needed new tires. The upcoming baseball season would determine a lot. Baseball was more than a game to him; it was a place that he could go.

Much had been resolved in the past year—had worked out to his advantage. Resolving the threat to Dan-el the way it happened had also helped Jess find himself, however indirectly it came about. The Trentsville Project solved the mystery about Dad's murder, a small consolation capped with a humanitarian solution. The Project also brought about another strange twist with the confrontation with Apex providing Jess with a new understanding of life from another perspective. Apex had been the Number One Most Wanted on Jess's list. He spent almost two years harboring a hatred and lusting for revenge that, in a few minutes, dissolved into something else. His emotions were still mixed, but he felt a little sorry for Apex as a person who directed his intelligence and leadership abilities using the available options. If not to be admired, there was something to take away from the encounter, a lesson to be learned. Another defining moment?

His Dad's voice, clear, "You've had quite an ordeal, son," *Yes. I have.*

Jim Billman

Acknowledgements

My thanks go to many generous and talented people who've helped my writing adventure. I've come to know that it takes many contributions to make a book, not the least is the time it requires to indulge my writing obsession.

I write and give my work to my wife, Karen, who proofreads and assesses. I'll edit the perfunctory fourteen times and whatever else happens to get the book between its covers is entirely up to her. She worked far more getting *Jess, Surviving Normal* finalized than I did in arranging the words. We've been a team for fifty-two years and counting.

My daughters, busy with family and career, are always willing to help. Angie, a journalism major, whose editing offered a myriad of professional ideas from plot lines to cover pictures, and she always avails herself at a moment's notice. Lisa is my go-to reader and critic as well as my local sales agent who pitches my books to her many friends.

I thank my cohorts at the Owensboro Writers group who read my stuff and help solve my quandaries. Particularly to Debbie Schadler who is a magician with computer graphics and whose long-term influence and support along with Liz Camp means a lot.

And across the ocean, thanks to Peter Street for being a great supporter and leading by example in showing me what it takes to write from the heart.

To Suzanne Gochenouer whose encouragement, support and *Twelve Steps to Publication* ease the pathway to understanding the reality of writing.

Karen, Lisa, and Angie, you have been my life's blessing.

Debbie, Liz, Peter, and Suzanne, it has been my good fortune to sit in your presence and know you as friends.

Jim Billman

Printed in Great
Britain
by Amazon